The
Fall of
Mystery
Babylon

The Khazarian Conspiracy

Book IV in The OMEGA Watchers Series

Numbers 6:24-26

Jane E. Woodlee Hedrick

CATCH UP ON THIS SERIES:

The Omega Watchers: Book I
"As it was in the Days of Noah"

The Third Strand: Book II
"The End has Begun"

Daughter of Zebulon: Book III
"The End of days has begun...
The Chosen will be anointed & sealed."

— COPYRIGHT —

In Memory of:
Terry Conrad
Sandra (Sandee) Sheskin Brotman

— Foreword —

In my foreword to Daughter of Zebulon, Book 3 of The Omega Watchers, I stated that the future of The Omega Watchers series would be in the form of a series of novellas. This did not eventuate as Jane felt that world events were happening too fast, so the next instalment, the first of the novellas would instead need to be a full-length novel. And so here it is. However, now that Jane has finished this fourth novel, there is still more to reveal, so a fifth novel will be created, the grand finale! And I can say, this is going to be just that! Grand on all levels!

We live in a world today of increasing confusion, and deception of the truth. We are being told what is good for us, and what we need to do to ensure our safety while ignoring this at the expense of our freedom. What is the endgame of all this? Is it just physical slavery and entrapment? Is there a spiritual element to this? More and more people are questioning the reasons for what they are seeing and experiencing in their day-to-day lives and in the Media, and in our educational institutions, how they are to speak and behave, what is permissible and what is not. Destructive ideologies abound, disguised as enlightening humanity. However, if you do not follow the rules of these idealogies, there are penalties and restrictions imposed upon you.

Where is this leading? Well, it takes people like Jane whom we call Sentries, or Watchmen, as they identify, discern the signs of the times, interpret their meaning and show their Biblical connection. It is here that we get the spiritual background to the nefarious schemes of those manipulating all areas of our lives, bringing its final conclusion as instructed by the events in the Book of Revelation leading up to the final return of Jesus Christ. We are so close to all this happening, that we are seconds away from Midnight, when His Glorious Appearing will occur.

Who are these people? In this novel, they are called the Cabal, Mystery Babylon. Jane effectively shows the layers of their operations and their plans for humanity. Mystery Babylon has a Biblical explanation and Jane shows how this plays out in the novel. This is one function of those we have called Sentries, or Watchmen; through their discerning and interpreting of world events and their Biblical meaning and correlation, they educate, warn, enlighten and equip us in Eschatology and Apologetics.

What is the end result? We have a building up of our faith in Jesus Christ, we understand what His Word says to us about all areas of our lives, specifically towards the End of Days before Jesus' Return. We become prepared for future events and know what we need and must do to not become enslaved and ensnared leading to an eternity in Hell, but to live victorious in Jesus and live with Him for eternity. It is truly a battle for our soul and spirit.

All the novels in the TOW series, are not just a labour of love from Jane's point of view. She is passionate about her writing, and about being a novelist, but most of all she is following the Lord's directive and is doing this in all obedience to Him and out of love for Him.

Everything in The Omega Watchers series has been brought before the Lord and submitted to Him. The results are the product of His guidance. These are His novels.

Why does Jane write edgy, speculative Christian fiction? First of all, she writes under God's guidance and for His Glory. Secondly, It stems from being a long-time student of Bible studies, especially in the area of Bible prophecy. She has a passion for seeing Christians and those who do not know Him yet to be not just entertained but educated in eschatology, end-times deception, and the Gospel of Jesus Christ.

This platform of fiction reinforces one way we learn about the world. It has been proved that we learn best when we are entertained; when learning is based on fun. It is the power of story. Jesus used parables (another form of storytelling) to educate, edify and entertain his audience. This is what Jane achieves in her writing. The Omega Watchers series is more than just an incredibly entertaining, suspenseful, and compelling read. Your faith and relationship with God will be edified and encouraged. You will be educated in eschatology and how this relates to world events and fits in what Bible prophecy states. You will see the deception of Satan in enslaving humanity unless they come into the saving Grace of God. This will increase your spiritual discernment.

I pray that this new novel will lead Christians to allow God to do all these things as they read. I pray it waters and grows more of the seed of faith that was germinated upon their entry into His Kingdom. I pray for the unbeliever that this novel and indeed this series, will plant a seed of faith in some, water a planted seed in others and reap a harvest from those God has prepared to enter His Kingdom.

It is an honor to write about Jane and this series. I have been blessed, encouraged, challenged and more assertive in my faith from reading this series and being involved with her in these endeavours. Many others have as well.

So, Reader, before you engage in this journey into eschatology and edgy, speculative Christian fiction, pray for God to prepare your heart and mind to receive what God has in store for you through Jane's writing. She has created this series with you in mind.

Enjoy and be challenged, what you thought about life is not what it appears!

Peter Younghusband Avid reader, and reviewer of Christian fiction and Award-Winning blogger from Perspective by Peter. (https://christianfictionreviewguru.blogspot.com)

— Acknowledgements —

My deepest appreciation goes to my "village" who committed their time to reading, editing, and giving feedback as my manuscript developed. There are no words to express how valuable this assistance is in reaching the published version.

Peter Younghusband, Cornelia Stone, Nathan Brotman and Douglas Woodlee continued with me in this journey of writing Book IV, while Melissa Coetzee joined us for the first time - forming our team reviewing as the story developed, giving prompt feedback for any changes that needed to be made. Mere words cannot express my heartfelt gratitude for the time they devoted and the encouragement they gave.

In writing this novel, I greatly missed Terry Conrad who gave me reader reviews, chapter by chapter, as I was writing Daughter of Zebulon. She originally contacted me via email after reading my first novel asking questions about the prophetic content. Through numerous correspondence we spiritually connected and although I never met her in person, we shared a special bond. Between Books III and IV in my series, Terry lost her battle with cancer and is now in the arms of her Heavenly Father. Someday I will meet Terry face to face in our eternal home.

A special thank you to Graphic Designer, Vernida Campbell, for the book cover design and her many hours of layout creation to bring this novel to fruition. God has truly blessed her with amazing creative skills.

Once again, my husband and soulmate, Russell, was my greatest encourager. Through each novel he has continued to support and allow me the endless hours of seclusion necessary to research and develop the story. He is a blessing beyond measure.

I never want to fail to thank all of you, my readers, for the encouragement to continue writing and for taking your precious time to read my novels. I pray spiritual eyes are opened, prophetic truths are revealed, souls are added to God's Kingdom, and Yeshua (Jesus) the name above all names is exalted.

Soli Deo Gloria, TO GOD BE THE GLORY!

– Prologue –

Revelation 17:5-8: For her sins have reached to heaven, and God has remembered her iniquities. Render to her just as she rendered to you and repay her double according to her works; in the cup which she has mixed, mix double for her. In the measure that she glorified herself and lived luxuriously, in the same measure give her torment and sorrow; for she says in her heart, 'I sit as queen, and am no widow, and will not see sorrow.' Therefore, her plagues will come in one day—death and mourning and famine. And she will be utterly burned with fire, for strong is the Lord God who judges her.

Revelation Chapters 17 and 18 reveal Mystery Babylon, a satanic entity that has secretly ruled the world for millennia through sorcery and the day of God's judgment has arrived. Who this entity is has been debated by prophecy scholars since John authored the Book of Revelation. These two chapters are an interlude in John's prophetic vision which no one can identify precisely where it fits into the prophetic timeline of the end days. This novel seeks to identify who Mystery Babylon, the Mother of Harlots, is combining prophecy, history, and current events. It is by no means a definitive answer but is one to consider with prayerful discernment.

As with all novels in The Omega Watchers Series, I challenge my readers to research for yourself. Even though my characters and the story are fiction, the historical information is not. An internet search for each topic introduced will reveal their documented accuracy and give links for further research.

I have endeavored to connect history and current events to reveal the evil that has been perpetrated on our society for centuries, connecting those events with Bible prophecy. Although Bible scholars and students speculate on the meanings of prophetic scriptures, most prophecies cannot be completely understood until we see them come to fruition; and even then, many refuse to see. The greatest example: there are over 300 prophecies of The Messiah in the Old Testament which Jesus fulfilled verbatim, and most Jews still do not believe.

The world we live in today is unraveling the confusion of these ancient writings, foretelling the end of days for those "who have ears to hear." Satan has tried to keep his deceptions in darkness so we will not know the truth, but God's Word is shining the light on his lies - for all who will wake up to the world in which we live today.

The prayer of my heart continues to be that the truths in The Omega Watchers Series are a wake-up call to Believers and a call to salvation for those who are not.

Note to Readers: In this novel I have italicized Gabriella's dreams/visions for discernment of her transitions from reality to the spirit realm. As always, all Bible quotes are italicized.

— CHAPTER 1 —

Gabriella was captured by darkness. She could hear the humming and beeping of hospital medical equipment surrounding her and she felt an IV in her arm. She recognized Caleb's voice and intuitively knew she had crossed from the parallel dimension of untime, returning to the people she loved.

Her body could not move; however, her mind was strong, acutely aware of having been transported back to earth's dimension which was confined to time and space. She no longer resided in the supernatural spirit realm where prophetic visions of the future had unfolded. Replaying in her thoughts was the Prophet Elijah who had led her through the prophetic days ahead allowing her to see into the future. Gabriella could still feel the overwhelming love which radiated from Yeshua Jesus as he stood among the field of glorious singing flowers telling her she had work to do on earth for the Heavenly Kingdom. Now she had returned to complete her mission in the earthly realm, wherever The Lamb would lead.

Caleb's strong hand was wrapped around hers as he sat beside her bed praying for her to awaken from the coma which held her body captive. Gabriella tried to move her hand so he would know she could hear him, but she was physically unable to respond.

Her heart cried out from her comatose body, "Thank you, Father, for all you have shown me. Thank you for allowing the desire of my heart to return to my loved ones, but even greater is my spiritual desire to follow The Lamb through the end of days. Not my will but Your will be done in every day ahead."

Although she could not understand how her body had existed in two dimensions, one natural and one supernatural, she accepted the fact it was real. Her last memory of her supernatural existence was the horrible accident when she and Chris were being chased on the Haifa expressway in the middle of the night. The pursuing vehicle had caught up with them and the evil Morelli pointed and fired a gun at their speeding Jeep. She recalled the excruciating pain shooting through her head when she hit the window. She remembered nothing after that until she woke up in a hospital, returning to the realm of time.

Gabriella was trying to acclimate to her surroundings, questioning in her mind: "How long has it been since I blacked out? What day is this?" She recalled the series of fainting spells she experienced the previous weeks before the supernatural experiences began. Her last memory of the natural world was in her bedroom on the first day her research team had arrived at the mountain lodge. They had been taken to the secluded mountain lodge for protection after the attempted murder of Dr. Brotman.

Her thoughts replayed the scene: "I was so possessed with anger, and I shut everyone out, honestly believing they had all betrayed me, even Caleb. I had gone to my bedroom to isolate myself. I remember feeling dizzy, losing my balance and pain shooting through my head." Her mind searched for any other recollections, but none came. The next remembrance was waking up in an unfamiliar bunker with the police officer assigned to protect them. Everyone else had vanished.

Her memories then flashed back to the events unfolding in the lodge after everyone disappeared. She and Officer Chris Harris quickly bonded in friendship and were hiding in the bunker beneath with only the TV news for information of world events. There was no direct communication with anyone outside their place of safety.

Suddenly she remembered, "There was a flash drive that had everything recorded. Was that real?" She questioned. Her journey of memories ended with the seaside cottage where the two of them were in hiding just before the car crash which brought her back to the present time. The jumbled memories rolled through her in waves of turmoil as she tried to separate the supernatural realm from reality.

Words from the Holy Scriptures began to flow through her in waves of comfort. The promises she had read from her father's Bible while in the bunker with Chris had been embedded in her spirit, becoming her inner power to face any situation. Like a movie replaying, she relived the glorious transportation in the Spirit to her Cherokee people in North Carolina. The beautiful face of the little Indian girl born without a hand being miraculously healed was burned forever into her memory. "The miracles…they had to be real." Her soul could accept nothing less, remembering the holy atmosphere that infiltrated the mountain tribal village. "Where is the turquoise bracelet the beautiful child gave me?" She questioned, trying to feel for the bracelet on her arm where it was adorned when she and Chris were in the accident.

Once more Gabriella tried to force the slightest of a hand movement but to no avail. She longed to respond in some way to Caleb's hand around hers. Agony of soul possessed her in the desire to let him know she could feel his touch. A single tear of desperation escaped her eye.

She could hear Caleb's voice call out, "She's crying!" She felt his finger gently wipe the tear cascading down her face as he wrapped her in his arms. "Go get Dr. Nicholson," he pleaded. "Tell him to come…now!" She could hear hope in his voice as he held her head next to his chest. "I knew you were still with us, Gabi." His voice was pleading as he whispered in her ear, "Don't leave me, Gabby Girl." Tingles of warmth flowed through her body when Caleb called her by the nickname which he had given her in college.

Her attention was immediately drawn to the mixture of excited voices saturating the room. Footsteps could be heard, hurriedly leaving and quickly returning. A familiar voice told Caleb to lay her head back on the pillow. The hopeful doctor examined Gabriella as her loved ones waited, holding their breath. His expression reflected disappointment as he turned from her bed.

"This is not uncommon of a comatose patient after a brain aneurysm," he informed them with regret in his voice. "Often a patient's eyes may open, flutter, or even release tears while they're still in an unconscious state. It's called reflex without reflection, a brain stem reflex. There's still no way of knowing which direction this will go. I must be honest, when I first diagnosed Gabriella, medically I did not see any hope she would pull through. She's defied the odds so far." He obviously did not want to give them false hope, so he added, "It's a waiting game at this point, my friends." He started towards the door and turned back before exiting. "As long as there's life, there's hope. Keep praying."

The room was silent. Caleb returned to the chair beside Gabriella's bed and again took her hand. "I'm not leaving your side, Gabi," he whispered to her. He leaned over and kissed her forehead, gently pushing her long blonde hair away from her face. He watched her closely for any response. There was none.

Gabriella had heard every word spoken in the room. The doctor's voice was familiar, but she could not make a personal connection. She desperately wanted to give them a sign that she was still with them, but no movement was possible. She stopped even trying and listened closely to the voices now discussing what the doctor had said. No one in the room spoke as if she would not wake up from the coma. Faith was the prevailing spirit and hope was in their voice, no matter what the doctor said. With deep love she identified each one of them…Dr. Brotman, Sandee, Aaron, Faith, KJ and, of course, the love of her life Caleb.

"My father? Where is my father? He should be here," she reasoned. Reluctantly she questioned, "Was that a dream?" She longed to open her eyes and look full into their loving faces.

Fighting back despair from being a prisoner in her own body, she cried out from her inner spirit, "Elijah, can you hear me? Please, help me!" She longed for the prophet who had appeared to her numerous times with visions of the future and protecting her from the evil Arcturus. "Yeshua sent me back from His Heavenly Realm telling me I had work still to do on this earth. Please guide me again, Prophet. I don't know what to do."

She waited, expecting a vision of the bald man in sackcloth to appear once more. There was no response… not in the physical realm, not in the spiritual realm. Darkness was her only world.

She continued to pray, soon finding mental peace in the presence of the Holy Spirit. While praying in the spirit a dim light appeared in the distance. It began illuminating Gabriella's black existence as it grew brighter and brighter. Once more she tried to move her hand. Her body was still held captive, but her soul and spirit were being released. A form appeared amid the glorious light.

"The Lamb!" She exclaimed. "You promised you would lead me." Gabriella rose to her feet. She looked down to see her body still lying on the bed, motionless. She turned to focus fully upon The Lamb of God.

— CHAPTER 2 —

Gabriella did not look back as she exited the door of her hospital room. Eyes fixed on The Lamb leading her, she followed down the hospital corridor passing the nurse's station. No one looked at her. It was obvious she could not be seen. The Lamb stopped in front of a locked door marked with a no entry sign. Her eyes were drawn to the sign posted to the right side of the door which displayed "Psychiatric Unit". She looked back towards The Lamb for further guidance, but He was no longer there.

Instantly she was transported inside the locked unit. Gabriella did not question her mission. She knew just as The Lamb had led her to the remote village in the mountains of North Carolina, He had now led her to this hospital wing. Two women were looking through charts behind the nurse's station. One looked up as if she knew someone had approached, glanced from left to right and seeing nothing, refocused on her chart.

Walking down the hallway, she could feel the oppressive spirit building. A heaviness weighed upon her as she walked the corridor. Forces of evil permeated the atmosphere. "What is my purpose here, Father?" Gabriella prayed. "I am Your servant, guide me."

The cry of a child in agony pulled Gabriella into a private room. A beautiful eight-year-old girl lay in the bed rolling back and forth, moaning in despair. Her long dark hair was matted from the constant twisting and turning of her body. The child's hazel green eyes were open, staring into the distance but obviously not focusing on anything while her body convulsed. Her despairing mother sat beside her, clinging to her hand trying to offer comfort. However, the child did not respond.

Moments later the nurse who had glanced up when Gabriella entered the unit came with medication. The mother held the child while an injection was given in her bruised arm. Obviously, she had been given many injections in an effort to calm her. Again, the nurse glanced around the room as if she knew someone else was there.

The nurse did not speak out loud, but Gabriella could hear her thoughts.

"I must be imagining things today. Probably didn't get enough sleep last night."
Once more the nurse looked around the room and slightly shook her head at
what she thought was just her imaginations. She put her hand on the mother's
shoulder and in a loving, caring voice said, *"That should help soon. I wish I
could do more. I am praying for Lynna."*

The mother forced a slight smile of appreciation and refocused her tear-
filled eyes back on her beautiful daughter. The nurse took one last look around
the room before exiting and soon returned with a doctor. After reading the
child's chart and briefly looking into her eyes, he sat down in the chair next
to the mother. The child was calmer now and her mother could focus on the
doctor's words.

He was careful in phrasing his words. *"Lynna has a severe bipolar disorder.
This is a chronic mental illness that affects about three percent of children. It
is characterized by episodes of extreme manic highs followed by depressive
lows. Some cases are very severe, which is what Lynna is experiencing. Sadly,
medical science has not been able to determine what causes the condition."*
He took a deep breath, wishing he could offer more hope. *"Although research
has made some links to genetic, biological and/or environmental connections
there is no way of knowing for sure the source of your daughter's condition.
Medication is the only way to control it for now."*

"But she has no life," Lynna's mother cried. *"She is either uncontrollable
or a zombie from the drugs."*

Despair filled the doctor's face. *"I hope and pray every day for a medical
breakthrough, especially for our children. We cannot give up hope."* He patted
her mother on the back with compassion and left the room.

Gabriella stood watching the desperation of the situation. The spirit within
her moaned and groaned with utterances she did not understand. In a parallel
dimension time does not exist so she had no idea how long throughout the
night she was in intercessory prayer for this child.

As the Holy Spirit prayed through her the room was illuminated with a
glow of purity. The veil of spiritual darkness was pulled back and a demonic
being stood between the mother and child, staring directly into Gabriella's
eyes. *"What are you doing here,"* the evil voice filled with hatred shouted.
"You have no dominion in this place. This child belongs to me." The vile being
circled the bed in one move standing between Gabriella and Lynna. *"Go!"* He
demanded, believing he had authority over her.

Gabriella took a step forward, confronting the demonic being. She had no
fear as the power of the Most High overtook her. *"Reveal yourself, demon,"*

she spoke with boldness taking another step forward. "I come in the name of Yeshua, the Son of the Living God, and I command you to reveal youself."

When she spoke the demon's face distorted and eyes turned fiery red. "I am Mania, and she belongs to me." Evil eyes glaring, he screamed, "You! Leave now." With one quick move his ugly distorted form entered the child's body. Lynna convulsed and screamed out. From the child's lips came the words of the demon, "I own her."

The vision that unfolded became a revelation of the possession tormenting the child. Gabriella immediately discerned a history of sexual abuse that Lynna's mother knew nothing about. This child had been tormented since she was three years old. The abuser, a person trusted by the family, told Lynna he would kill both her and her mother if she ever told anyone. Any time this man was with the family he would whisper in her ear repeating the threat. Her fear and abuse became a doorway for this vile being to move from oppression to complete possession of the child's mind and ultimately control of her body. This was not a flesh and blood condition. This was a spiritual battle raging inside this helpless young girl. Medication could only sedate the body. It could not bring peace to her mind or deliver her from this demonic control.

Gabriella took another step forward and as she spoke The Word of the Living God a sword of flames appeared in her hand. "All power and authority have been given to me by my Father through the blood of His Son Yeshua. I command you to leave, you vile spirit. You have NO dominion here. Never return to this child, I command you and decree it to be so!"

The pure light which had illuminated the room engulfed the demonic being. A horrendous scream echoed over and over as the demon spirit was captured by the light, pulled from the child's body, and cast away into darkness. The overwhelming, unexplainable peace Gabriella had felt when she was face to face with Yeshua filled the room.

Lynna opened her eyes and looked directly into Gabriella's. "Can you see me, Lynna?"

"Yes, who are you?" The girl's questioning eyes stayed fixed on the vision before her.

Gabriella looked at Lynna's mother who had her face turned towards the window completely oblivious of their conversation. Hearing the cry of a mother's heart not spoken audibly, Gabriella knew her prayer had been answered. The mother was totally oblivious to the spirit realm battle that had taken place in the hospital room as she cried out: "Dear God, please touch my daughter. Bring her back to me and heal her. I want to believe, I truly do. Help my unbelief."

The Spirit of God within Gabriella was deeply moved by the mother's plea for her child. She turned her eyes to focus fully on Lynna's beautiful face. "Your Heavenly Father sent me to help you. You do not have to be afraid anymore." She stepped next to the child's bed and laid her hand on Lynna's head. "You need to tell your mother the truth. The man who hurt you and threatened you will never be able to harm you again. There is nothing to be afraid of. God has put a hedge of protection around you both. He has an incredibly special purpose for your life, Lynna. Seek God with your whole heart and He will guide you." She leaned over the bed and kissed the top of the child's head.

A smile spread across Lynna's face and tears of joy were running down her cheeks when her mother turned back to face her. "Lynna, what has happened to you?"

The transformation was immediate. In amazement, her mother screamed for the nurse who came running into the room. Gabriella with hands lifted in praise to the Heavenly Father watched the shocked nurse run for the doctor. When he entered the room, he immediately felt the atmosphere charged with an energy he could not explain. He fully examined Lynna with no explanation of what could have transpired.

The doctor took a deep breath and collapsed on the chair next to Lynna's bedside. He looked around the room feeling a presence he could not explain. He sat silently watching mother and daughter embrace, crying with tears of joy. All he could mutter was, "I have no explanation."

Lynna sat up on the side of the bed and for the first time in many months spoke with coherence. She looked again into the eyes of Gabriella for assurance. "Tell them, Lynna," she reassured her.

With the doctor and nurse listening she recounted to her mother the events that had taken place, giving the family member's name and details. "He threatened to kill us both, momma, if I told you." Lynna's voice faded away with her final words.

Her mother grabbed her and held her closely crying in both relief she had told her, and anger so deep she was ready to kill the man. The doctor and nurse struggled to not show their emotions. No matter how many times situations like this were revealed, they still were emotionally distraught.

The doctor cleared his voice, still amazed at this sudden transformation and how Lynna's confession of abuse released her body from the agonizing condition. This was medically impossible. He gently took the child's hand and *spoke with a soothing voice. "Can I ask, Lynna, what happened to you just now, and why all of a sudden you decided to tell your mother what happened?"*

Lynna was not sure they would believe her, but it did not matter. The only thing that mattered was the evil that had possessed her was gone. She simply stated, "God sent an angel to me."

The nurse gasped, realizing what she had felt had been supernatural. "I believe you, Lynna. I know when the angel came. I could feel the holy presence and I believe the angel is still here. Right?"

Lynna looked directly into Gabriella's eyes and nodded.

The doctor looked in the direction of Lynna's gaze but saw nothing. However, now he also understood the presence he had felt. In a revelatory moment, he accepted not all the psychiatric conditions were physical. "God, help me to understand more," he whispered.

Gabriella smiled. She knew she was not an angel; however, her visit was definitely supernatural. With her mission complete, she exited into the hallway returning to her own hospital room. She heard demonic screams as she passed certain rooms. In other rooms the patients were quiet, and she felt nothing evil.

The Holy Spirit spoke within as she moved through the corridor. "Some of these patients are fighting demonic spirits and some of them need physical healing. You will discern the difference, Daughter of Zebulon."

"I want to deliver them all. Can I?" She knew without the leading of The Lamb she could not go to them.

"No one has prayed for them. No one has taken authority over these powers of darkness. Prayer, fasting, and the spoken authority of My Word can change any situation when it is verbally declared and decreed in faith; however, these all must come together as one force for a demonic deliverance." The inner voice of God spoke into her spirit with revelation on satanic strongholds.

She was meditating on the revelatory words as she retraced her steps back to her room. She watched for any signs of being seen or her presence being felt as she passed through the hallways and by the nurse's station. She was totally invisible and undetected to those around her.

The door to her room was closed so she stopped before trying to enter. Police Officer Chris Harris was sitting outside the door monitoring anyone coming or going. He was dozing but quickly awakened as she stood beside him. Their eyes briefly connected and before she could say a word, she was back in her body feeling Caleb's hand still holding hers. She tried once more to respond to him but still no muscle would move.

She relived over and over the glorious expression of the precious child being delivered from the demonic oppression. It brought back memories of her supernatural transportation to her Cherokee people in North Carolina and the miracles of healing and provision.

Gabriella had been prepared for the journey through the end of days. She had experienced the wonder working power only the great I AM could manifest.

"I will not question you, Father. With you, time and space only restrict the body, not the spirit within. Your power has no limitations. My life is yours and I will follow The Lamb wherever He leads."

— CHAPTER 3 —

The sun was rising over Mt. Hermon. The brilliant rays cascaded down the majestic mountain heralding a beautiful fall day in Israel. The religious Jews throughout the nation were observing the High Holy Days, their holiest time of the year leading up to The Day of Atonement. However, after the unexpected attack by nations surrounding Israel on The Feast of Trumpets, the holy observance was vastly different this year. Citizens were filled with mourning, repentance, and determination to rebuild after the coalition of enemies destroyed a major part of Israeli cities including the Western Wall in Jerusalem.

Dr. Brotman and his team secluded themselves in the lodge bunker during the three-day war. Gabriella had remained in a coma the entire time with Dr. Nicholson administering the care she needed until it was safe to move her to the Haifa hospital where he was a resident physician. Once the Israeli enemies were defeated the doctor called an ambulance for transportation.

Against the advice of Officer Harris who was protecting the archaeological team, they all followed the ambulance to the hospital with the police officer protecting them. He posted himself outside Gabriella's hospital room suite and made sure everyone stayed inside her room to ensure their safety as the tests were performed.

Caleb would not leave her bedside. He sat constantly staring at her beautiful face praying for her eyes to open. Late into the night he had fallen asleep, his hand still holding Gabriella's. The last words he breathed before he went into a REM sleep were, "Heavenly Father, please heal the love of my life, return her to me." Even in a comatose state, she heard his prayer and echoed his soul wrenching request in her own spirit longing to do just that.

The hospital room was silent, but Gabriella's mind was speaking loud and clear as she prayed. "Please raise me up from this bed, Father. Return me to those that I love, and I vow to you my life is yours wherever you lead me."

Listening for any sound that would give her an indication of the time, the room was silent. The comfort of Caleb's hand wrapped around hers brought solace as all the events since she collapsed in her bedroom at the lodge replayed over and over in her mind. "Were they real, a dream, a vision...what?" She continually questioned the truth, knowing in her spirit whatever she had experienced had changed her life forever.

The sound of the door opening jolted Caleb from his sleep. He reluctantly released her hand and stood to his feet to stretch allowing the nurse adequate room to check Gabriella's vital signs. After changing the IV bag and making notes on her chart, she turned to leave the room stating, "Her vitals are all good. The doctor will be in shortly. He's making his rounds now."

"Thank you," Caleb replied. Gabriella could hear the exhaustion in his voice knowing he had not left her bedside and having no idea how long she had been in the hospital. The nurse's voice had also awakened the others in her room.

"Her vitals are good," Faith repeated the nurse.

"Thank God for that." The voices of KJ and Aaron quickly agreed.

Gabriella was doing a mental checklist of voices in the room. Memories flooded her of the many adventures they had all encountered as they worked on Dr. Brotman's Omega Watchers Project. She recalled they were finishing the project when the strange episodes of her passing out began. It all began with the evil Arcturus deceiving her into believing she was a chosen one by the Ascended Master. The journey to realizing the demonic Arcturus was a liar and deceiver; however, she thanked God it brought her to the truth. She *was* chosen, as Arcturus had told her, but chosen by the True Master of the Universe, not the counterfeit Lucifer who believes himself to be the Master. The astral coma which captured her became her gateway to spiritual truth.

It was the journey into the supernatural that prepared Gabriella for the journey through the end days. She could now return to her team as a daughter of the High King and knew the transformation would astound them all. She was not the same person that collapsed at the lodge, not even close.

She had distinguished the voices in her room: Professor Brotman, Sandee, Aaron, Faith, KJ, and of course Caleb. "But where's my dad?" She questioned, listening for the sound of his voice. "He was with me when I passed out at the lodge...or was he?" Mentally confused, she continued to question what was real during the events occurring when she crossed over into the alternate dimension of untime.

Interrupting her thoughts, Dr. Nicholson entered the room. He examined Gabriella while the team held their breath waiting for a diagnosis of hope. After several minutes he turned to face the group. "I wish I could say there has been improvement, but everything appears to be the same. The good news is her condition has not worsened and that gives me hope. I want to do another EEG today. The EEG done yesterday after you first arrived showed all the signs of an aneurysm"

He sat down on the edge of her bed and looked at the group of expectant faces. "I have been doing some research into what was mentioned when I examined her at the lodge. You told me about the stress she had been under and some of the very strange things that had been going on." He then looked directly at Dr. Brotman. "Professor, you asked me if I knew anything about astral comas. At the time, I had truly little information, but I've done some research and talked to some colleagues.

The doctor had the full attention of everyone in the room. "Apparently, astral comas are a very real phenomena connected to the spirit realm. On an EEG test brain activity can show similarly to that of an aneurysm making it difficult to diagnose, especially for doctors who are not familiar and/or do not believe health conditions could be connected to the supernatural. On Gabriella's EEG test there were some rare irregularities from just a normal aneurysm. This made me question if we were reading the results correctly as I recalled our conversation at the lodge. I've been praying over the results and asking Yahweh to guide my understanding. I do realize an astral coma is without a doubt a tactic of the demonic world to capture and hold the body, soul, and spirit. It is not a physical condition, it's spiritual. I have read testimonies of several people who have experienced these comas. The stories are remarkably similar in what they experienced. Some gave in to the evil side going deeper into the occult, some never awakened, while others had an experience with the true God resulting in a life changing experience."

He took a deep breath before continuing. "It appears the common denominator of those who return with a Holy God encounter had people praying for their healing both spiritually and physically." The doctor looked into the eyes of each team member. "I know you have all been doing exactly that."

Gabriella wanted to scream out, "Yes! Yes! That is exactly what has happened to me." Dr. Nicholson totally understood her supernatural journey.

Dr. Nicholson continued: "Keep praying. That is the best medicine we can give her right now."

The doctor had answered two questions for Gabriella. She had only been in the hospital for one day and what she had been experiencing since her collapse was not her imagination or tricks of the mind, it was very real. She tried to piece together the events just prior to being transported from the lodge where the coma began. She remembered the immense anger toward Caleb and the entire team, feeling they had betrayed her. Regret again flooded her being, as it did each time, she remembered her atrocious actions. She tried to get a grip on her current state of being and how much time had transpired since that moment. She remembered nothing from the time she collapsed until waking up in the lodge bunker. Everyone had disappeared except Officer Harris.

Then the truth hit her full force! She knew her loved ones were all still with her, so they had not been raptured from the face of the earth. Not yet. Everything from the point of awakening in the bunker after their disappearance and only Officer Harris left behind with her – everything took place in the spiritual dimension of untime. It then became crystal clear to Gabriella, "I have been given a revelation of things to come." That fact settled in her entire being solidifying a resolve for all situations she would face in the future.

She further understood that everything she had experienced for the past weeks was an answer to the prayers of her loved ones. While waiting for her to return to the earthly realm, her Heavenly Father was preparing her for her chosen calling before she could be released back to earthly time. Peace began to flow through Gabriela and truth dawned in her inner being as she understood her Heavenly Father must have a special call on Chris' life too, since he had been with her every step of the way.

Dr. Nicholson's voice refocused her on the conversation taking place. "Keep praying," he firmly commanded them. "There is deliverance and life changing power in prayer." Everyone nodded in agreement.

Dr. Brotman took charge of the conversation. "We all know that is true. Only a few days ago I was fighting for my own life after the car accident. Miraculously Yahweh healed and delivered me from death, and He will do the same for Gabi and we cannot doubt that. The Living Word of God tells us life and death are in the power of the tongue and we are to speak only life."

The atmosphere of the room changed as the group joined hands praying in one accord. Gabriella felt an energy flow through her body like electric shocks followed by the sense of warm water covering her from head to toe. That familiar feeling, experienced when the prophet Elijah poured oil over her head to anoint her as a chosen one, was experienced again.

"It *was* real," she whispered, not realizing her voice was now audible.

The circle of prayer warriors gasped and quickly surrounded the bed. Gabriella's eyes were open, and a glorious smile graced her face. Caleb gently took her in his arms cognitive of all the wires attached to her body. "You're awake, Gabi! Thank God, you're awake!"

"I thought I had lost you forever, Caleb." she responded in a weak voice.

"I told you I would never leave you, Gabby Girl."

"I know, but...," before she could finish Dr. Nicholson asked Caleb to step aside, giving him room to reexamine her.

Gabriella instantly recalled untime when she saw herself waking up and experiencing this exact scenario. Caleb's words were exactly what she had seen and heard in the spirit realm. Her loved ones surrounding her praying were also the same. Even Dr. Nicholson's examination of her was a repeated scene. "Was I shown in untime how I would return to the reality of time and space?" She questioned in her mind as the scene played out precisely as experienced in her alternate existence.

The voices in the room went silent to clearly hear the conversation as Dr. Nicholson reexamined. "Can you hear me, Gabriella?" he asked, while shining a light directly into her eyes.

"Yes," she softly replied.

"Are you in any pain?" The doctor continued to question her while retaking her vital signs.

"No," she answered. "None at all."

He asked her full name, date of birth, and what year it was to determine the clarity of her mind. Her voice was weak from days of being comatose, however her mind was coherent.

"Well," he stated in a matter-of-fact tone, "I still want to do some follow up tests, but she's awake and coherent. I believe she has returned to us." It was obvious he was trying to maintain a professional composure, but the amazement still showed through his countenance.

Gasps of relief resounded through the hospital room. Caleb again took Gabriella in his arms holding her as close as the medical equipment would allow. She treasured the moment of reconciliation; however, the scene was not complete. Her eyes darted around the room. The eyes of her friends followed to see what she was looking for.

"Where's Dad?" Her voice was emphatic indicating she expected him to be there.

In unity, everyone in the room gasped. Dr. Brotman's astonished eyes looked straight at Sandee who was as confused as everyone else.

— CHAPTER 4 —

"Where's my father?" Gabriella demanded to know. The room was silent. No one knew how to answer her. "Someone, *please* answer me! Where is my dad? Why isn't he here?" She struggled to sit up in the bed to face her friends.

"Easy, Gabi," Caleb soothed her. "I'll raise the head of your bed up so you can sit up." He was fumbling with the adjustment remote trying to buy some time for someone to come up with an answer. He looked at Dr. Brotman who raised his eyebrows in uncertainty. Sandee, who usually had an answer in every situation, sat motionless and silent.

Dr. Nicholson took charge of the situation. Caleb stepped aside and allowed the doctor to move close to Gabriella gently taking her hand. Hesitating, trying to find the right words, Dr. Nicholson said, "Don't you remember, my dear, remember the funeral for your father? Eyes darting towards Dr. Brotman and Sandee for approval, he continued: "It's been over twelve years now since he's been gone." He was closely watching her facial expressions and body language for any signs of emotional trauma that would cause a setback in her recovery.

"*No,*" she exclaimed. "That wasn't real. You all know it was *not* real. He just pretended to be dead to protect me from the men who killed my mother."

The astonished look on Dr. Brotman's face took Gabriella by total surprise. The faces of her friends reflected shock. Gabriella's eyes pleaded with Caleb. "Caleb, you won't lie to me. Tell me my father is still alive and revealed himself to you all when I collapsed. He was with me, praying for me. You were on one side of my bed, and he was on the other." The tears in Sandee's eyes rolled down her face as she struggled not to break out in an uncontrollable sob.

Caleb's eyes darted from Dr. Brotman to Sandee and finally to the doctor silently begging for help to know what to do. Pushing the doctor out of the way, Caleb took Gabriella in his arms. "You've been through a lot, Gabby Girl. That hit on the head when you fell was pretty hard, I think you're a little confused. You need to rest." He continued to embrace her, gently stroking her long blonde hair. "It's going to be okay, my love."

Surprising everyone, she pushed Caleb away. "I'm not confused. I heard you all talking in the bunker. I could hear my dad's voice. Where is he?" Gabriella's head fell back on the pillow in frustration and lack of strength to continue the verbal battle. She knew her demands were gleaning no answers. She began to question what she had seen, heard, and felt during her untime revelations. If her dad was not still alive, what else was not real? All that she saw in her parallel dimension, she was back to questioning again.

Dr. Nicholson tried his best to calm her. "Often when a person is comatose, they will hear things that are not real, especially things they desperately long for. Give it a little time for your thoughts to clearly focus, my dear. The mind can be very deceiving, especially after a head injury."

"I'm sorry, Caleb," she whispered, reaching for Caleb's hand. He tightly closed his hand around hers and she did not argue further. She was too weak and too unsure of reality to even try. The one thing she did not question was The Lamb. No one could make her doubt that reality; however, she did question the prior night's journey to the small child's room. Was she only dreaming she followed The Lamb?

Dr. Nicholson moved towards the door. "I must finish my rounds, but please make sure she eats and rests as much as possible. She needs to rebuild her strength, especially for what lies ahead." His voice emphasized the last words. "I will order another EEG. After the results, we will decide what the next step will be. In fact, all of you need to get some rest after all we've gone through the last few days."

When Dr. Nicholson opened the door to exit her room. After the doctor was gone, Officer Harris stepped inside closing the door behind him. He had heard most of their conversation through the hospital door and wanted to confirm to them there had been no suspicious encounters since they had arrived at the hospital. He looked at Gabriella with a warm smile, "It's good to see you awake." She looked into his eyes for any sign of personal recognition, but too quickly he looked towards the team. "I know you're all exhausted after spending almost 24 hours in this room. "I've talked to Detective Richards, and he is sending someone to relieve me so I can drive you back to the lodge. You know it's just not safe for you here, especially you, Professor. In fact, Detective Richards was pretty upset that I allowed any of you to come."

Dr. Brotman crossed the room and put his hand on the officer's shoulder. "Chris, you know, and we all know, you didn't really have a choice."

With a brief smile, Chris replied half-jokingly, "Tell that to Detective Richards. It might help save my hide." The officer focused back on Gabriella. "Do you need anything?" His eyes were kind and caring. She shook her head, looking deep into his blue eyes searching for a more personal connection. He abruptly turned around and headed back to the door to regain his post. She felt he was intentionally avoiding prolonged eye contact. "My relief officer should be here soon," he promised while exiting the room to give them privacy.

Everyone was silent not knowing how to address the elephant in the room...her questions about her father. Gabriella had closed her eyes battling the roller coaster emotions. Caleb's hand embracing hers was a comfort, but nothing could erase the pain of believing her father was still alive only to find out it was a comatose delusion. Sandee had managed to regain her self-control; however, her eyes kept questioning Dr. Brotman. All of the team were looking at each other with raised eyebrows but saying nothing.

Aaron broke the silence, bringing the group back to the task at hand. "Still much to do," he flatly stated, "and we are living in a whole new world now." His comment was followed by a group discussion on the Three-Day War and how not only Israel, but the entire world had changed.

"We only know what the news has told us," Dr. Brotman interjected. "Can we really believe all their details?"

A sarcastic laugh escaped Sandee's mouth. "Sure, we can." There was a chorus of groans from the younger members, knowing nothing about the mainstream news media could be trusted. "I know we've got a lot to discuss, but we have to wait until we get back to the lodge," Sandee continued, glancing to make sure Gabriella's eyes were still closed, then putting her finger over her mouth to indicate there could be listening devices in her room."

There was a knock on the hospital door and Officer Harris opened it to allow food service to bring in breakfast trays. Caleb gently nudged Gabriella. "Wake up, Gabi. You need to try to eat." He raised the head of her bed a little further and helped her sit up to reach the tray. "Looks good," he encouraged her while uncovering the plate and opening the juice bottle.

"Is there caramel coffee?" She slightly giggled desperately wanting a feeling of normality to return to her life.

Caleb laughed aloud so thankful the woman he loved had returned to him. "I wish, Gabby Girl. I promise you, as soon as we get back to the lodge you can have all the caramel coffee you want."

"I love that plan," she replied. "And can I ask all the questions I want and get real answers?"

Caleb's voice was deep with emotion knowing the truth, the whole truth and nothing but the truth had to be told. "Yes, my love, absolutely." Gabriella was content knowing he would not lie to her. She had doubted him before and almost destroyed their relationship. Never again.

Another knock on the door as a transport aide entered to take Gabriella for the EEG. He helped her from the bed and into the wheelchair. "This won't take long. She should be back within an hour," he stated dryly. He released the lock on the wheels and pushed her towards the hallway.

Officer Harris did not like allowing the team to be separated but had no control over the circumstances. Did he go with Gabriella or stay with Dr. Brotman and the team? Making a quick decision, he instructed Caleb. "Lock the door behind me and do not allow anyone in until Detective Richards gets here with my relief agent. He just texted and they're only a few minutes away. I'm going with Gabi." Caleb followed his instructions as Officer Harris quickly exited following the aide towards the elevator and past the nurse's station. His eyes were darting in every direction to detect any suspicious activity.

Shortly after, they arrived in the waiting room for the EEG. To Gabriella's amazement there sat Lynna and her mother, also waiting for the same test to clear the child for release from the hospital. Lynna was playing a game on her mother's phone while they waited, she did not look up. Her mother smiled as the aide parked Gabriella's wheelchair across the floor from where the child sat. Gabriella sat silent knowing this was her confirmation that following The Lamb to this child's room was real. The battle was real. The victory was real.

In her inner spirit she uttered: "Thank you, Father, for revealing the truth." In her moment of praise, she also questioned, "How do I react to this child and her mother now that I am in the realm of time? Do I allow anyone to know the miracle that occurred in the spiritual realm?"

The aide had left, and Chris sat down beside her jolting her thoughts back to the waiting room. It felt so natural for him to be close, protecting her as he had in her prophetic visions of the future. It was not the time or place to address anything personal with him; however, his presence had a calming effect and for the moment that was enough. She watched Lynna smiling and sometimes laughing out loud as her game progressed. Gabriella both marveled and inwardly praised God for the miraculous transformation.

She decided to attempt a dialogue with Lynna's mother. "It sounds like she's having a fun time with the game. She looks so happy." The mother's smile was glowing as she answered her. "Yes, she is, and you have no idea how happy I am just to see her normal again."

Gabriella pretended to have no idea what the mother meant. "What do you mean if I'm not being too personal? Your daughter looks perfectly normal to me, and she is so beautiful." Lynna continued with her game oblivious of the adult conversation.

Her mother took a deep breath. "It's too much to explain, but she's struggled with some major mental issues. Last night she was delivered, literally, from the agonizing pain she's experienced. This test is just a formality and then she can go home. My Lynna has been living in hell on earth for months and we've had no peace or joy in our life. I don't know if you believe in God," she took a deep breath before unashamedly proclaiming, "but we had a miracle in her hospital room last night. I don't even have the words to explain what happened."

Gabriella's heart was singing. This was the final confirmation she needed. "I believe every word," she affirmed. "Tell it everywhere you go and always give The Heavenly Father praise for what He did."

At that moment, a technician appeared at the exam door calling Lynna's name to come back. She jumped from her chair, started towards the door holding her mother's hand, and then abruptly stopped as she saw Gabriella. "You're my angel!" Lynna exclaimed.

The mother looked from her child's excited face to Gabriella's perplexed one. "I'm so sorry," her mother said. "I think she's still adjusting to everything that's happened." The mother and child followed the technician through the opened door. Before it closed silently behind them Lynna looked back one more time. Gabriella smiled and winked at her in affirmation.

Gabriella waited to see what response Officer Harris would have to the scene that had just played out. She did not say a word while staring straight ahead. His training as a police officer was to have no personal interaction with the person in his charge. However, he had already broken his own rules after spending three days secluded in the bunker with the team he was signed to protect. They all felt like family to him now and he felt a personal connection to Gabriella after listening to days of conversation about all the events surrounding her archaeological team. No one tried to hide anything from him during the days of the war. It was a time of complete openness, not knowing what the future would look like for any of them or even if they would have a future.

He shifted his position and turned to face Gabriella. "Now that was strange," he stated in a manner that was expecting an answer.

She looked straight ahead avoiding eye contact. "You don't believe in miracles, Officer Harris?" She questioned him with a tinge of sarcasm.

"Please call me Chris. The rest of your team does now. We've all gotten close these last few days. I realize you've been, how shall I say this, mentally unaware of what's happened since your episode at the lodge, but many things have changed. You'll see."

"If you only knew," she thought but did not speak those words aloud. "Okay, Chris," she spoke now in an audible voice, I ask you again, do you believe in miracles?"

"Had you asked me that a few days ago, I would have probably laughed out loud. Today, I see things very differently. The war and three days in that bunker with people I would have called religious fanatics prior to the war has me rethinking everything. Miracles though? I've got to simmer on that one."

"Did you not just hear what that little girl's mother said? Can you explain what happened short of it being a miracle?"

"In my police training we study lots of different mental issues and how they can onset and even reverse. I'm not sure I would call what she experienced a miracle, even though it sounds pretty incredible."

"It sounds like more than that to me," she stated emphatically.

"Excuse me for saying so, but the woman your research team described to me was not one to believe in all the religious stuff. In fact, they all believed you were what they called...lost. I don't really understand a lot of what they discussed but I did get a pretty good take on that opinion."

She continued to stare ahead avoiding any eye contact. It was obvious he had no knowledge of her spiritual journey where they were together learning and growing in understanding of The Word of God. She certainly could not tell him, and she did not want him asking questions she could not answer. So many dissected parts of her vision of the future were going to be difficult to address in the days ahead. She realized it sounded so absurd and questioned if anyone would believe any part of it.

She finally answered him. "They were right about that; I was as lost as lost could be. It's a long story. Let it suffice to say, I'm not the person I used to be."

Not knowing Gabriella prior to when they were taken to the lodge, he had no idea how to compare before and after. He only had the other's description of her which appeared to be vastly different from this woman who sat beside him.

"Tell me, Chris, what was it like in the bunker? I didn't even know the bunker existed until…," she hesitated to make sure she worded it without raising suspicion that she knew more than the natural events portrayed. "

He did not press her for further information but began to explain the amazing dwelling securely hidden beneath the lodge. "It was completely stocked with anything you could possibly need for an extended emergency. Not only food and a fresh water supply, but solar generators, medicines, ammunition, even a TV with satellite. That's how we knew what was happening outside our secluded existence. It was on 24/7 to keep us constantly updated on the war. It's an amazing place, no doubt about it."

"I don't suppose Michael Adelson was the main news commentator, was he?" She looked directly at Chris hoping that would spark a supernatural connection.

A strange expression crossed his face as he stared into her eyes. "Strange you ask that, Gabi. He was the main voice during the entire war. I don't think the man even left the news station during those 3 days; but how did you know that?" He thought for a few seconds then reasoned: "Of course, like the doctor just said, even in a comatose state of mind sometimes a person can still be hearing their surroundings."

That was not the response she had hoped for; however, some pieces were starting to fall into place.

The examination room door reopened, and Lynna and her mother came back out. "Gabriella Russell," the technician called her name. Chris jumped up from his seat to push the wheelchair into the next room. The technician gently pushed him aside and firmly announced, "I will take it from here. No one is allowed past this point."

The child's beautiful hazel eyes captured Gabriella's. "Goodbye, angel," Lynna whispered. One more wink from Gabriella bonded them in the spirit as she rolled past the child.

Chris tried to protest not being able to stay with her, but the technician would hear nothing he had to say. "I'm supposed to stay with her," Chris demanded as the door closed in his face leaving him alone in the waiting room. The registration clerk behind the closed glass window was the only other person he could see. There was nothing he could do but wait. He sat back down and texted Detective Richards to see if he had arrived. Confirming he and the new relief policeman had arrived gave him a sense of relief. He tried to relax but his officer's sixth sense kept warning him to stay alert. He got up and opened the door looking both ways down the hallway. Nothing looked out of the ordinary.

He went to the window and asked the clerk how long it would take. The young lady looked at her chart and smiled at the handsome police officer, "It shouldn't take too long. Do you want some coffee while you wait?"

"That would be wonderful," he answered. "Black, please." Exhausted from 24 hours of forcing himself to stay awake, some caffeine would be a welcomed help.

The clerk poured the coffee and reached it through the glass window smiling again. She attempted to make conversation while Chris waited. "The war caused a lot of damage not just to parts of our hospital but to the entire city. Luckily, this diagnostic section was not hit. We've needed it badly with all the war injuries."

In the middle of her conversation another technician came in and went to the window, ending the conversation. He had a medical mask on making it impossible to see his face. "I'm here to assist in the screening of Gabriella Russell. I was called by Dr. Nicholson to make sure the correct imagines are taken."

The clerk looked down at the orders and replied: "I have no notes on her orders there will be any assistant. I need to call Dr. Nicholson to update his instructions." She turned away from her desk to make the call. Chris felt something was not right and stood up to position himself for a confrontation, if necessary.

The clerk turned back to the technician. "I'm so sorry Dr. Nicholson is not available at the moment, and I can't let you back until he returns my call."

The masked technician hesitated. It was obvious to Chris the suspicious man was assessing his next move. As a police officer he had seen this situation too many times. The technician turned towards the door stating, "I will be back in a few minutes." Chris was not going to allow him to leave until Dr. Nicholson called back to verify who this man was and if he was supposed to have access to Gabriella. Just as Chris stepped in front of him to keep him from leaving, the door opened and a young woman with two small children walked in. Chris stepped back to allow them to enter. The technician took that opportunity to cut around Chris and exit the room.

Chris caught the door to follow the man. Simultaneously, the clerk's phone rang, and she motioned for him to come to the window. "Dr. Nicholson said he had not approved anyone to be with Gabriella other than the scheduled technician. He sounded very concerned."

Chris rushed into the hallway hoping to catch the suspect, but it was too late. He was nowhere in sight and Chris was not going to leave Gabriella unprotected in an effort to catch him. Quickly returning to the waiting room, he was joined by hospital security. "Dr. Nicholson sent us," they explained. "He said you might need help." Chris explained the situation but there was nothing that could be done at that point. The man was gone, and Chris could not give an accurate description since the man in question was wearing a medical mask.

"We will keep our eyes opened for any suspicious activity and if you need us, let us know." The two security agents left the room, leaving Chris to mentally analyze what had happened. One thing the incident validated: Gabriella, Dr. Brotman, and the entire team were in protective custody for a very good reason and that reason did not end with the unexpected war.

He went to the window instructing the clerk, "Please do not mention this to your patient. She's mentally fragile right now and doesn't need to be concerned about anything." The clerk quickly agreed the incident would be kept quiet.

Chris sat next to the door monitoring anyone coming and going until Gabriella was wheeled back out. He jumped up taking possession of the handles. I will take it from here," echoing the technician's comment when he would not allow the police office in the exam room.

"That isn't protocol," he stated firmly. "I can call for help."

Chris flashed his badge taking total control. Rolling her into the hallway he looked in both directions before starting down the corridor. His police officer instincts were on full alert.

Gabriella broke his concentration. "I want to go home." She hesitated, pondering, "Or do I still have a home?" She glanced back towards Chris. "Do you have any idea how much of Haifa was destroyed in the war, especially the old city area where my condo is?"

He really did not want to engage in conversation while trying to monitor everyone around him. He also did not want to be rude and not answer. "None of us are sure of anything right now. We only know what the news reported while we were secluded in the bunker and there were few details on what was destroyed. It was too dangerous for reporters to be out filming. The bombings ceased less than two days. I'm sure lots of details will start to flow now." Her face reflected both worry and exhaustion and he tried to change the subject when they reached the elevator door. "Let's get you back to your room where you'll be able to rest."

She nodded without a further attempt at conversation. When they arrived at the hospital room door another police officer sat on the chair Chris had occupied since they arrived the prior day. He got up to greet Chris with a firm handshake. "Good to see you," warmly commenting.

"Good to see you too, Micah. I didn't know who they would be sending to relieve me. Glad it's you. This is Gabriella Russell. Gabi, meet Micah Cohen, one of our finest officers."

"Please call me Gabi, everyone else does," she replied warmly as Chris pushed her through the door. Caleb immediately took the wheelchair handles guiding her back to the bed. He lifted her in his strong arms holding her close.

Wrapping her arms around his neck she whispered in his ear, "I'm so sorry, sorry for doubting you…sorry for everything, Caleb." Again, she was immediately reminded this was a playback of the very words she had spoken to him while in untime. She felt she was watching a movie rerun.

"It's all in the past now, Gabby Girl. We've got our future ahead. You need to rest now." Caleb reluctantly laid her on the bed and pulled the blanket over her. He pushed the bedside chair as close to her as possible before sitting back down and taking her hand in his.

Her full focus being on Caleb, she was unaware Detective Richards had been in the room when she arrived. Chris had motioned for him to step outside into the hallway where they could talk privately. Filling him in on the exam room encounter, Richards knew the situation was still very dire.

Detective Richards began to make immediate plans. "Whoever is behind the attempt on Dr. Brotman's life knows Gabriella is here and probably knows the others are too. The question is how do they know? Have they been watching the lodge entrance and followed the ambulance here?" He paced back and forth in deep thought before stating, "We must get them safely out right away but taking them back to the lodge is too risky. Apparently, that location has been compromised."

Chris smiled, "I have an idea."

— CHAPTER 5 —

Officer Chris Harris directed Detective Richards to a private waiting room. Making sure the room was secure, the two men sat down facing each other. Richards was very curious what idea his officer would have to secure the team's safety.

"Okay, Chris, let's hear it," the detective said expectantly. "I'm open to any possibilities."

Chris leaned in towards the detective ready to give a quick review of the prior day's events. "When you left me at the lodge to protect Dr. Brotman and his team, none of us had any idea how quickly things would change and the complexity of it all," Chris smiled continuing, "and you definitely had no idea how complex the lodge itself was." Chris watched his boss's face fill with confusion.

"An explanation would be appreciated," he replied. "The sooner the better, time's a ticking, you know."

Chris knew his boss well and the faster he got to the point the better. "After you left the lodge, there was a major episode with Gabi. I still don't know what all happened, but she went into a, well, sort of coma." Chris hesitated, trying to decide what to explain now and what could wait. "Lots more details to fill you in later, but they called Dr. Nicholson knowing they couldn't leave the lodge. I stayed outside while he examined her."

"So, she was in a coma from the day we took them to the lodge?" Detective Richards clarified. "All during the three-day war?"

Nodding to confirm, Chris continued, "It was just after the doctor arrived that the fighter jets flew over the Golan Heights from Syria. There was no doubt in my mind about what was about to happen. I was uncertain what to do, having no idea the layout of the lodge grounds and where the safest place would be to take them. I tried to call you and it wouldn't go through. That's when we were all instructed to get whatever personal items we had brought to the lodge and gather in the kitchen. Caleb was told to carry Gabi down from her bedroom to meet us."

The detective leaned towards his officer fully intrigued. "Go on."

"We were guided to a secret underground bunker, actually it was a massive underground home and totally supplied with anything several people would need to survive for years."

"What!" He could not hide his amazement as he motioned for Chris to give further information.

"Yep, I've seen a lot of hiding places in my life but nothing like this." Chris let that settle in his boss's mind before he continued. "It's the perfect place for the team to go back to. Whoever is behind Dr. Brotman's attempted murder and trying now to get to Gabi, well they obviously know they were in seclusion at the lodge. Would they expect them to go back to the same location now that we know that they know? And even if they did come to the lodge just to make absolutely sure they hadn't returned, they would never find them in the bunker. They could look all over Israel and not find them, in fact, all over the world." Chris felt like he was rushing through his idea leaving out many pertinent details, but time was not on their side.

Detective Richards scratched his head muttering how amazing the bunker must be and verifying he could go along with Chris' plan. "There's only one problem, how do we secretly get them back to the lodge? These people are definitely professionals and they're going to be watching every move."

A shadow of doubt showed in Chris' eyes. "That's the kicker, Boss, I haven't figured that part out yet." Musing more to himself than answering the detective, he said emphatically: "There has to be a way."

Detective Richards got up and motioned for Chris to follow him. "We best figure it out soon, because they can't stay here." He abruptly stopped and turned back to face Chris. "You never said who revealed the hidden bunker."

Chris' response was a mixture of grave concern and bridled excitement. "That's a whole other story, Richards, and it can't be discussed here."

The detective did not press his officer for more information trusting Chris knew what he was doing. The two men exited the waiting area and quickly returned to Gabriella's hospital room. Dr. Nicholson was at Gabriella's bedside with the test results.

"I put a rush on the results hoping to get Gabi out of here quickly and get you all somewhere safe." The doctor glanced at Chris confirming he was fully aware of the suspicious encounter. "The test didn't show anything that concerned me, not even the earlier signs of an aneurysm." He looked at Dr. Brotman smiling, "I've seen two miracles in less than a week."

Gabriella had no doubt everything would be perfect. She knew all she had been through was spiritual, not physical, and she had been delivered. She was aware her loved ones surrounding her had no idea the transformation that had taken place while she was in what they thought was a coma. There was so much to tell them, but this was not the place or time.

The doctor's report caused a burst of praise from the team that had prayed all through the night for Gabriella to be healed. Caleb dropped Gabriella's hand and took her fully into his arms, thanking God for hearing his prayers. Detective Richards allowed them a few moments before interrupting.

"This is all wonderful and I know there's much to celebrate, but we must make plans to get you to a safe place until we find who tried to murder Dr. Brotman. After that you'll be able to really celebrate." He could tell by the expressions on the faces there was something he had not been told. Looking at Chris with raised eyebrows, everyone in the room focused their eyes on Chris to see how he would respond.

The officer put his finger over his mouth showing he did not want to take any chances of being overheard by undetected electronic ears. Dr. Nicholson motioned for Detective Richards and Chris to follow him to his office. Dr. Brotman trusted them to work out whatever was necessary and motioned the team to just be silent. The three men exited the room.

"What's that all about?" KJ asked, being the first to break the silence.

Dr. Brotman wrote on a notepad and passed it to the team to read. "Do not discuss anything about where we were hiding or who was with us." Each person nodded in compliance as the note passed to each team member one by one. They realized they could take no chances. The atmosphere of praise had settled into a foreboding of what was ahead and where they would be taken.

Gabriella decided this was the time to begin sharing her spiritual journey, but only a little at a time. There was too much which she was still personally trying to resolve in her own mind before she could explain to anyone else.

Only her team was left in the room, the people she desperately wanted to apologize to and tell of her transformation. It was difficult to know where to begin. "Roll the head of the bed up please, Caleb, I need to talk to all of you."

Faith laughed out loud. "Talk? You? Gabi is back guys, and hasn't changed a bit," she replied with a loving voice moving to sit on the bed next to her best friend. "Caleb doesn't call you Gabby Girl for nothing." The jesting ushered in an air of relief. Everyone relaxed and focused on Gabriella. "You talk, girl," Faith jokingly demanded, taking her best friend's hand.

"First of all, I have changed drastically. I'm definitely not the same person that collapsed in my bedroom a few days ago. That woman is gone forever."

"I hope not," Caleb responded without hesitation, kissing her hand. "I love that woman."

Holding Caleb's hand for support, she continued: "Well, Caleb, I hope you love *this* woman even more," she replied pulling his hand to her lips for a quick kiss. She smiled at him and turned again to look into the eyes of her beloved friends. "I am so sorry that I was hateful and doubted all of you. You were all right and I was so wrong. You all knew I was being deceived by an evil entity and tried to tell me, warn me, and I would not listen. I was so deceived it resulted in anger, horrible outbursts of mean words, and total doubt of everyone I truly loved." Tears of regret cascaded down her face. "Please, please forgive me." Her eyes were pleading as she brushed the tears from her face.

The entire team was fighting back tears, tears of relief and joy. Sandee was the first to gently push Faith from the bedside and reach out to hug Gabriella. "I knew you'd come back to us, Gabi. We've prayed so hard for you." Sandee gave her a big hug and then moved over for Dr. Brotman to sit down beside her.

Caleb released her hand to Dr. Brotman who took both of her hands into his and looked deep into her eyes. "Now tell me, Gabi, just what happened while you were, well..." he stuttered, trying to find the correct words to explain her supernatural experience. "I believe before this last collapse you called it untime. So do you feel well enough to talk about it?"

Immediately she knew she could not share all the prophetic visions, not yet; however, she could share her salvation experience. "What I mean by saying that I'm not the person I used to be and without going into all the details right now, I have accepted Yeshua as my Savior. I literally came face to face with Him and I will never be the same person I was."

The hospital room became a chorus of praises and rejoicing for answered prayer. Caleb took Gabriella in his arms and held her as close as humanly possible. "I knew it! I knew my prayers would be answered." He released her far enough to look fully in her face. "Even your countenance has changed, Gabi" he marveled.

"So much has changed, my friends, so much. You probably won't even believe it all." She knew what had to be clarified first. "You all know I was deceived by an evil spirit into believing I was chosen by an Ascended Master of the universe and I followed that deception into a demonic realm of astral travel." She took a deep breath struggling with her explanation. "I know this sounds unbelievable, but I actually had beautiful experiences...at first." She hesitated, looking into their faces that were filled with acceptance of what she was sharing.

"Go on, Gabi," Dr. Brotman encouraged her. "We believe you."

"I could hear your prayers even when I was in that spiritual realm. I could even hear the prayers of my dad, even though," again she hesitated, "well, you know." She noticed Sandee shot a quick glance of confusion at Dr. Brotman.

Caleb quickly interjected, "We were praying, Gabi. Night and day we were praying."

"I know, Caleb. It was those prayers that pulled me away from the evil presence. I even saw a familiar spirit that claimed to be my mother calling me to come to her, but it was your prayers that revealed it was all a deception. I was at the edge of a gulf between the lying entities and myself. They were calling me to cross over into the eternal, celestial realm of peace and harmony with the universe. Your prayers created a holy protection as I was pulled into a tunnel of light away from the abyss, gravitating back to my human body. I was saturated with tranquility and peace."

She briefly relived what she had seen as she returned to the dimension of time, but knew that was to be shared later. "I could distinctly hear each of your voices praying as my soul reunited with my body." She took a deep breath as tears welled in her eyes, recalling the voice of her father praying the loudest. Apparently, that was a desire from her soul, and she would treasure that moment privately. She concluded with, "I desperately wanted to tell you, give you some kind of sign that your prayers saved me but not a single muscle in my body would move. Your intercession pulled me from the demonic deception of the astral realm into the Holy Presence of the One True God. I will never be deceived by evil again. There was no way to let you know I had been freed, then I lost consciousness of everything until..."

Gabriella laid her head back on the pillow, totally exhausted. Her voice was growing weak, and she obviously needed rest.

"There's plenty of time to talk," Caleb instructed her. "Just rest now, Gabby Girl. I'm not leaving your side."

She wanted to stay awake and savor the moment of spiritual unity. This was the first time the entire team was all in one accord spiritually and everyone present sensed the holy presence she spoke of saturating the atmosphere. Physical exhaustion overtook Gabriella and she drifted into a deep sleep...the first restful, dream-free sleep she had experienced in weeks. Caleb leaned his head back on his chair to also rest, still holding her hand. The physical touch was his lifeline of confirmation that she was not leaving him again.

Dr. Brotman motioned for the others to gather around him away from Gabriella's bed. He spoke softly aware there could be listening devices in the room: "While Detective Richards is deciding where we go from here, we have to make some decisions also." The team leaned in closer waiting for his directions. "The Omega Watchers Project is not over with your archeological discovery. That was our confirmation that we have an even greater work to do as we're reaching the end of days." He gazed out the hospital window assessing the limited time ahead and then reiterated, "Yes, much, much to do. The dynamics of the entire project has changed now with...you know." He put his finger over his lips, just as the officer had done, silently saying the details must be kept secret. They all nodded their heads in confirmation.

Dr. Brotman's team was making their plans while Detective Richards, Officer Harris and Dr. Nicholson were privately secluded in the doctor's office, also making plans for the safety of the team. Several possibilities had been discussed on how to secretly get the team out of the hospital with no options appearing to be workable to keep the team from being totally undetected by whoever was tracking them.

Detective Richards stated the obvious: "They know Gabi is in this hospital and probably know the entire team is with her, the perfect setup to get to them all at once. However, they surely know they cannot overplay their hand in a hospital with high security. I know how the minds of these nefarious people work. They'll wait until we take the team out and follow us, waiting for just the right opportunity, just like they did when they ran Dr. Brotman's car off the mountain road, making it look like an accident. They thought he would die in the car crash, and no one would ever know the truth."

Dr. Nicholson leaned back in his chair and smiled. "They had no idea...," then abruptly stopped.

"No idea of what?" the detective asked.

Officer Harris shook his head at the doctor, signaling not to continue, and then took control of the conversation. "Back to our current situation, how do we smuggle seven people out of that hospital room undetected?"

Dr. Nicholson was silently praying for wisdom and direction when the answer dawned on him. "Of course," he exclaimed. "I know exactly how."

The other two men leaned in closer waiting in expectation. "First of all, we can't get seven people out all at once, but one at a time is very doable."

Detective Richards reminded the doctor, "I'm sure Gabi's room is being surveilled. Even one at a time, they will still see them leave."

The doctor smiled believing he had just the right plan. "Hear me out. Elisha Hospital has teams of student doctors that will go into the patient rooms with the head doctors for training purposes. We can smuggle into Gabi's room some student medical jackets using housekeeping. We add a medical mask to cover their faces and one by one Dr. Brotman's team leaves with a group of students. These students are so attentive to the lead doctor, they wouldn't even know someone else had joined them."

"That's brilliant," the detective exclaimed, reasoning in his mind how that just could be the answer when Chris interrupted his thoughts.

"But how do they separate from the students and where do they go? You realize, Dr. Nicholson, you can't be an obvious part of this plan. They already know you're deeply connected and that puts you in danger too."

The doctor nodded he understood the danger. "I've been Dr. Brotman's physician and," he hesitated, not sure what or how much to say. "Well, since the beginning of their project. I knew the day would come when the truth would be revealed, and it would become dangerous for all of us. My wife and I discussed it at length, and we agreed it was worth the risk."

"Okay, apparently you know a lot more about this than I do, but for now we must get them all out of here and to a safe place. Then you and I have a long conversation ahead of us, doctor. I must know absolutely everything if I'm going to find out who's behind Dr. Brotman's assassination attempt. Back to the plan though, what would the next step be after they leave with the students?"

Dr. Nicholson went into complete detail of how his plan could work: "When the group of students finish their rounds they disperse to return to their individual classes or assignments. I will give each of Dr. Brotman's team members instructions on exactly where to go to meet up with me secretly. Then I can escort them to a safe place until we can get all the team out. Since it will take a couple of days of doctor rounds, I will keep Gabi as a hospital patient. I know she won't like that, but it will give her more time to regain her strength for traveling."

Chris knew there was still the possibility they would be detected leaving the hospital grounds. "I know we can get another vehicle to leave the hospital, but there's no absolute guarantee we wouldn't be detected and followed. These people have obviously done this many times before." He shook his head in perplexity. "I just don't see a way to get off the hospital premises that is guaranteed secret."

"I do," Dr. Nicholson smiled. "Have you heard of Rambam?"

The detective quickly responded, "I have but what does that have to do with this situation?"

"Then you know Rambam Medical Center has a massive underground hospital designed specifically to be used during times of war. Right?" The doctor was affirming the two men were following his chain of thought before continuing. "Rambam serves as the tertiary referral center for twelve district hospitals including this hospital."

"And...?" The detective wanted him to move faster with his information. "Again, what does that have to do with getting out of this hospital without being seen?"

The doctor leaned forward almost in a whisper he answered, "There are underground tunnels that go from all twelve district hospitals to Rambam. The tunnels can only be accessed by authorized personnel. Most people don't even know these tunnels exist and even if they do would not be able to access them." The doctor did reluctantly admit, "Nothing is one hundred percent guaranteed without detection, but I do believe this could be our best option." They all quickly agreed.

After sorting out a few more details, the detective and officer returned to Gabriella's hospital room leaving Dr. Nicholson in his office. They wanted to separate him as much as possible from the plans that were about to be initiated.

Walking down the hallway, the detective spoke out loud hoping to be heard by anyone surveilling them. "I just don't see any way out of here that would be safe."

Officer Harris knew exactly what he was doing. "Yep, I agree. This is a tough one, Boss. It could take a while to get that entire team out."

Gabriella awakened when they entered her room. Detective Richards brought the team into a huddle around her bed reminding them to speak softly to not be overheard. "We need to decide the order in which each of you will leave, one by one. Dr. Nicholson will be orchestrating all the details and, of course, you will be the last Gabriella.

KJ whispered, "I need to go first, then Aaron. That way we will be there when the ladies arrive to make sure they're protected." He looked at Faith to signal his great concern for her. She blushed as the team agreed KJ would be first in line, then Aaron.

"This will take a couple of days to get you all out of here, and that gives Gabi more time to get her strength back." Chris informed them, keeping his voice low. "Dr. Nicholson is working on all the fine details."

"I'm not leaving without Gabi," Caleb said firmly.

"We figured as much," Chris answered. "We've got a plan for that, too."

A knock at the door and Officer Cohen waited for Detective Richards to allow him to open it. "Housekeeping is here." He pushed the door open wide to allow the cart to be rolled in piled high with fresh towels, linens and toiletries.

"Dr. Nicholson told me to just leave the cart and get it later," she informed them. "If you need anything else ring the assistance bell." The officer held the door open for her as she exited.

Chris began to look through the pile of linens and wrapped in each bath towel was a student medical jacket, a stethoscope, a medical mask, and a fake name badge. "The doctor sure didn't waste any time," he said, giving instructions on how the plan would be started. "KJ, I'm putting yours in the bathroom now. When the first group of students make their rounds, slip in there and get ready. Be very quiet coming back out and joining the students. They will be focused on Gabi and the doctor training them, and Dr. Nicholson assured us the group will never question your joining them. When the group disperses, Dr. Nicholson will be waiting for you for further instructions."

Another knock at the door and lunch was brought in. The team ate in silence, each pondering what the days ahead would bring. Despite their joy of Gabriella's miraculous salvation, they each struggled with their individual future uncertainty. The hardest part was not being able to contact their families to know if they had survived the war and let their families know of their survival.

They were living a nightmare with no end in sight.

— CHAPTER 6 —

Officer Cohen opened Gabriella's hospital room door allowing a team of students to enter with their instructor. All were wearing the same medical coat, stethoscope, badge, and facial mask that had been provided for their escape. The large private room was now extremely crowded, so Dr. Brotman motioned for his team to move back as far as possible out of their way. KJ was undetected as he slipped into the bathroom where his disguise awaited. In short order, he quietly reopened the door and stepped to the rear of the students who were fully attentive to their instructor. When the instructor completed his comments, he motioned for the students to exit the room. KJ subtly turned his back to the group, moving slowly so the other students could surround him as they moved into the hallway awaiting further instructions. He avoided any eye contact with Officer Cohen.

As the group was led down the corridor, their instructor was making some additional comments holding the attention of the students. KJ could see both an elevator and stairway sign at the end of the hall. Caleb was relieved when the doctor pushed the door to the stairway open, giving him the opportunity to step to the back of the others. The sound of pounding feet on the stairway echoed so loud any attempt at conversation would have been drowned out. Several flights down the doctor stopped and waved his badge unlocking a secure door. They entered a large area that was obviously restricted to doctors and resident students only. Immediately, KJ saw Dr. Nicholson.

The instructing doctor dismissed the class and as they dispersed KJ followed Dr. Nicholson at a distance down a long hallway to another elevator marked authorized personnel only. The doctor looked both ways to make sure no one was watching. Holding his badge to the security scanner to prove authorization of use, the door opened. Dr. Nicholson motioned for KJ to follow him in. Once the door closed behind them KJ felt a sense of relief.

Dr. Nicholson patted him on the shoulder. "I believe our plan worked, KJ. I pray it works for all the team without anyone getting suspicious." The doctor again held his badge in front of a scanner on the elevator panel.

"Down we go," he stated. "Now to get you to a safe place to wait for the rest of the team."

"Do I even ask where we're going?" KJ knew they were moving downward beneath the hospital.

"You'll see soon," he smiled assuredly.

The quick smooth movement of the elevator ended with a soft landing and the door opening to a huge underground parking lot. A transit bus was waiting. KJ looked at Dr. Nicholson in both amazement and confusion.

"Only highly authorized personnel have access to this parking lot and the tunnels." The doctor informed him as KJ marveled at the massive underground structure where ambulances, private vehicles, and the small transit buses were parked. "These tunnels were built mainly for times of war for both quick and safe transit of patients and doctors among the twelve major Haifa hospitals."

"Absolutely amazing," KJ muttered. "I've heard of tunnels like these but to be in one. Wow!"

"Let's get going," the doctor said moving toward the vehicle. "We can't waste any time."

The bus driver opened the door for the two men to board. No one said a word during the underground trip from Elisha Hospital to Rambam Medical Center. KJ stared at the concrete walls as the vehicle sped through, wondering how long it would be before the rest of the team would be coming this same way. Within minutes they exited the tunnel into another underground parking lot even bigger than the one they just left. The vehicle came to a stop and the doors opened in front of the secured entrance. Again, the doctor authorized their permission to enter.

"This is the exit to the underground parking lot at Rambam Medical Center, the main hub for all the connecting tunnels to the other hospitals," he announced unpretentiously. "Follow me, KJ."

Instead of getting on an elevator up to the street level, the doctor led KJ down a hallway and into an area much like a college dormitory. There were private sleeping rooms, a fully stocked kitchen, and a large area with couches, work area with a computer, and a big screen TV. "This is where the resident doctors stay when they are required to remain at the hospital. Again, it was built mainly for safety during war, but is commonly used even in peace times."

KJ followed the doctor to one of the private sleeping rooms. "This will be your room until we can get the team all moved here and ready for transport out. I'm going to make sure student resident rounds are often until we get all your team out safely; hopefully within the next couple of days. I have you registered as a temporary doctor assisting me during the aftermath of the war. No one will suspect a thing. Just keep to yourself and have little or no interaction with any other personnel. Just go by the name on your badge, Dr. Jameson." He smiled briefly before continuing, "The rooms are provided with toiletries and clean hospital attire, food is in the kitchen, you should have everything you need while you're waiting."

"I think I've got it." KJ answered. "When the others get here you won't need to go through the instructions again. That can be my job and to make sure they're all safe." KJ was thinking specifically of Faith.

"That's my plan," Dr. Nicholson confirmed. "I've got to get back. I'm going to try to get at least one more out before rounds end this evening."

"We've decided in what order for the team to leave. Aaron will be next, then Faith. Sandee and Dr. Brotman wanted to come last." KJ added, "Detective Richards said they had a special plan for getting Gabriella and Caleb out together."

"I'm working on those details," he assured. "Pray hard the plan works." The doctor gave KJ a fatherly hug and left him in his secluded world.

Watching Dr. Nicholson leave, KJ chuckled to himself. "Well, here I am in an underground bunker hiding again." However, he did not like being separated from the others with no way of knowing if they were safe. For his peace of mind and to encourage himself in the Lord, he quoted out loud from Psalms 91, a scripture his mother had taught him from the time he was a small child: *"Because he loves me, says the Lord, I will rescue him; I will protect him, for he acknowledges my name. He will call on me, and I will answer him; I will be with him in trouble."*

Peace flowed through KJ as the words echoed in his small room. He continued the afternoon in prayer for the safety of the team and guidance for the days ahead.

Several hours later, Aaron joined him relaying his experience which had been exactly as KJ's. "Nobody suspected a thing," Aaron proudly announced. "I blended right in with the student doctors until I met up with Dr. Nicholson."

KJ filled him in on what to expect, repeating the words of the doctor. "Now we just wait for the others, stay to ourselves, and pray. It's probably too late today for anyone else to come." There were no other doctors in the lounge, so the two men took their opportunity to watch the news for the latest updates before they needed to seclude themselves in their rooms.

"Well, wouldn't you know there's Adelson still giving the news," KJ jested. "You would think since the bombing has stopped the man would get some rest."

Aaron motioned for KJ to be silent and turned the TV up. "Listen, KJ!"

Adelson's face was very grave as he read from the teleprompter. "There is breaking news. There has been an assassination attempt of our Prime Minister. We have no further information as of now about his condition but will keep you posted as updates come in." The reporter took a deep breath and apparently spoke his own thoughts, not on the teleprompter. "This is not good news for our nation, especially in the aftermath of the war." Adelson paused again and murmured to himself more than his audience, "Who do we trust?" He motioned for the camera to cut and go to a commercial.

"Hmmm, that was odd," Aaron commented. "I'm not surprised at the assassination attempt, but Adelson's response was strange. Just wonder what he meant by who do we trust? Apparently, he knows something that he's not allowed to say."

KJ pondered for a moment then replied, "The end of days will be a time of deception like no man has ever known. As Professor has told us, don't trust anyone. Verify everything, especially when it comes from the TV news sources, but when even the news media doesn't know who to trust, well that does open Pandora's Box, so to speak."

After a commercial break, the newsroom came back into focus; however, Adelson had been replaced with another reporter with no explanation. The replacement totally changed the direction of the news focusing on the aftermath of the war. Since the bombing had stopped, camera crews had been out filming and reporting from various locations that had been hit.

"The damage is not nearly as bad as was expected," he reported. "Our military was able to intercept most of the incoming missiles. Sadly though, the Western Wall in Jerusalem was destroyed, and the Orthodox Jews are in an uproar to rebuild their temple without delay." He hesitated, adding, "Our Prime Minister had vowed he would assist them in any way."

"Do you get the sense something is amiss here, KJ?" Aaron questioned. "Seems to me there might just be a connection."

KJ rubbed the top of his bald head in contemplation. "Sure, would love to get on the web and do some research. I've got thoughts on the attempt on Professor's life, and the dark web might help me make some connections."

He glanced at the desk in the corner of the lounge where a computer was used by the doctors. "Can't use that one though. I'm sure every internet link is recorded, can't take the chance of leaving a trail behind us." He got up and stretched. "I'm going to take a shower and get some rest. I sure couldn't last night in that hospital room. You need some shut eye, too, my friend." He patted Aaron's shoulder as he walked by. "Could be a long day tomorrow."

Aaron nodded in agreement, getting up to follow KJ to their rooms. "I just hope I *can* rest. My mind seems to be in a tailspin that never stops."

During the night the two men would awaken each time they heard doctors coming and going. They knew that was a normal activity; however, they were constantly on mental alert. Towards morning everything grew quiet, and they were finally able to sleep. The voice of Dr. Nicholson and Faith awakened them. KJ glanced at his watch. It was already 9:00 am. He and Aaron exited their rooms at the same time, excited Faith had arrived safely.

She laughed at the two of them as they came bounding out of their rooms running to give her a big hug. She clung a few moments longer to KJ. Reluctantly she released him when Dr. Nicholson spoke.

"I know it would be easier to have someone else bring the team over, but I simply do not trust anyone to keep this private. I'm not taking any chances." He turned to leave stating, "Sandee and Professor will be next. This will be more challenging because of their age; they're not going to blend in with young students like you did." He was murmuring something under his breath when he exited.

"I didn't have any problems at all getting out with the students," Faith announced. "I hated to leave Gabi, but she's sleeping most of the time. The doctor said she needed the rest and I'm thankful to be with you guys. She shot a quick smile directly at KJ. Even Aaron, who was slow to notice any overtures of romance, noticed something was going on; however, he kept his thoughts to himself.

KJ gave Faith the quick rundown of their rooms and the situation at hand while they were waiting for the others to join them. There were doctors coming and going throughout the morning so the three of them sat close together, guarding their words, and not interacting with anyone else.

Early afternoon Dr. Nicholson reappeared with Sandee who ran to each team member with a big hug. "Oh my, honey bunnies, I've been so worried about you." That was her pet word for the young team who felt like children she never had. "Everyone okay?" They affirmed to her all was well.

They knew Sandee's expressions well and could see the concern in her face. "Now we must pray Professor gets out undetected. Instead of the student rounds, I came out with a surgical team that not only had face masks, but their heads covered with hairnets. Dr. Nicholson set that up as an added disguise. This thick black, curly hair of mine, plus my age could have been a dead giveaway without the extra cover and I would never pass as a young student." She paused thinking of the professor still waiting for a way of escape. "I will be so thankful when we're all away from here to a safe place, wherever that is."

"You and me both," Dr. Nicholson stated dryly as he turned to leave once again. The next two trips out of that hospital room are going to be much more challenging.

On his way through the tunnel between hospitals, the doctor was praying for precise details on how to get Dr. Brotman, Gabriella and Caleb to safety. The professor was still rebuilding his strength after the car accident and was not strong enough for a long walk, especially with several flights of stairs. Neither was Gabriella and he was convinced Caleb would not leave without her. "Help me, Father," he silently prayed as he entered the elevator to ascend to the doctor's private floor in Elisha Hospital. On this floor he felt safe. No unauthorized personnel were allowed, and he personally knew every person who would have access. However, he knew he had a job to do outside of his safe zone and Gabriella's room was his next stop.

Exiting the elevator onto the patient's floor, he could sense being watched although he had no evidence. He knew any areas of the hospital open to the public could be easily surveilled. He also was certain Gabriella's private room was safe as there had been no opportunity for anyone except hospital personnel to access her room in the brief time since her admission; but how did he get the three remaining in her room from that safe place to the other?

So many thoughts were churning in the doctor's mind as he approached Gabriella's room. He resisted the temptation to look around to locate any signs of surveillance, that would be too obvious he suspected they were being watched. Officer Cohen was stationed at her door monitoring everyone coming and going. He got up and opened the door for the doctor to enter and quickly closed it back, keeping the occupants of the room in seclusion.

Gabriella was awake and having a late lunch. Caleb was firmly planted by her side in the recliner. Dr. Brotman was resting on the couch and while Officer Harris was at the table making notes. All seemed well but the doctor had a strange foreboding.

"What is it, Doctor?" Chris asked noticing his odd expression.

"Nothing, I guess," he replied. "I'm not used to all this Sherlock Holmes stuff and it's a bit unnerving, especially since the biggest risks are still facing us. We've got a plan for Gabi and Caleb, but Dr. Brotman is my grave concern. He's still weak and the main target in all this. As long as he remains in this room, he should be safe, but as soon as he exits there are no guarantees unless we have divine inspiration on how to accomplish it. The others are safe, I have no doubt about that.

Caleb set straight up in the recliner. "What plan for me and Gabi?" He demanded. "When will we know where the rest of the team has gone?"

"In good time, Caleb," Dr. Nicholson replied firmly. "We've got to focus on both of you now. You and Gabi need to be ready to leave first thing in the morning, and we all need to be praying about how to get Professor out too." All the eyes in the room were drawn to Dr. Brotman sleeping on the couch, oblivious to their conversation.

The doctor turned towards the door. "I've got other patients to attend to and won't be back tonight nor in the morning. Lots of details to take care of. Just follow Chris' instructions in the morning. He knows the plan."

The doctor opened the door to leave and immediately felt that same foreboding, like an inner radar picking up dangerous signals. He went to the nurse's desk and tried to concentrate on his patient's charts. Finally, he asked a resident doctor to cover his final rounds of the day and quickly returned to the restricted area of safety.

He called his wife who had returned to their home after they left the bunker at the mountain lodge. "Honey, I'm going to stay at the hospital until Gabi is released. Are you okay?"

"I'm fine, dear. You do what you need to do and let her know I'm praying for her." Her sweet voice still made his heart melt after forty years of marriage.

"I will let her know. Keep all the doors locked and the security system on. I don't like you being alone."

"I'll be fine, you just take care of the professor's team. That's most important right now." She ended the call with, "And take care of yourself. I love you."

"Love you more," he responded feeling so blessed to have such a precious soulmate. Leaning his head on the back of his office chair he closed his eyes in prayer. "Please, Father, there must be a way out for my friend. I'm the only one in this group that knows this hospital well enough to find a way of escape." He was praying for a divine revelation when there was a knock on the door.

"Housekeeping," the male voice announced.

"Come on in, Joshua," the doctor replied.

Joshua had been with the hospital for as long as Dr. Nicholson could remember, and he was loyal and trustworthy. No doctor was ever concerned about him overhearing or repeating anything he might be privy to. He was now in his sixties and soon to retire. His back was slightly curved from all the years of bending over as he mopped floors and cleaned the offices. The black pants and white shirt hospital uniform were stained but clean. The mask he wore, protecting him from inhaling cleaning chemicals, covered most of his wrinkled face. A ball cap with the hospital emblem he wore with immense pride showing he was a part of the Elisha Hospital Employee Team. A very humble man he was, willing to give one hundred percent to his job, and appreciated by the hospital staff.

"I'm going to miss you when you leave us, Joshua. You're going to be impossible to replace."

"I'll miss the people, but not the work," he chuckled. "You especially, Dr. Nicholson. You've been a good friend to me. If there's anything I can ever do for you, all you have to do is ask."

The doctor sat straight up in his chair. "That's it!" He exclaimed to Joshua as the plan unfolded in his mind.

Joshua stopped working, startled at the tone of the doctor's voice. "What?"

"Come sit down beside me so I can explain. I do need your help." As the plan unfolded, Joshua's eyes widened in surprise, but he kept nodding his head affirming he understood and was willing to help.

"I can't thank you enough, Joshua." Dr. Nicholson's voice was filled with relief. "And don't worry about cleaning my office today. It can wait. Take the rest of the day off and be ready in the morning."

A big smile crossed the worker's face. "I'll be there."

Dr. Nicholson felt a heavy weight lifted from his shoulders. He was convinced a solution had been reached. He dared not make another visit to Gabriella's room to inform Officer Harris. Too many could raise suspicions. He sure was not going to use a phone that could be tapped into, so he decided to wait until time for execution. Tomorrow could not come soon enough.

— CHAPTER 7 —

Throughout the night, Gabriella tossed and turned, her mind replaying her visions of the future. She had no fear for herself, but she knew most of the citizens of the world had no idea what they were facing. Knowing the end of days would be a time of tribulation like the earth had never experienced and there was nothing that could stop what was coming, weighed heavy in her spirit. If the Word of God declared it, it would be so. The writing of John the Revelator came flooding through her mind: "*Woe for the earth and for the sea: because the devil is gone down unto you, having great wrath, knowing that he hath but a short time.*"

Her restlessness, plus concerns for their secret escape from the hospital in just a few short hours, kept Caleb from sleeping. He leaned across the hospital bed and took her in his arms, whispering, "Are you alright? Do you need anything?" He did not want to awaken Dr. Brotman or Officer Harris. Everyone would need their strength for the day ahead.

She wrapped her arms around his neck and clung to him. "I'm physically fine, Caleb, just so many thoughts churning in my head."

Releasing her, he sat down on the side of her bed. "Anything you want to talk about?" He took both of her hands in his, encouraging her to share her concerns. The dim light in the room made it difficult to read her expressions, but he knew well the tone of her voice.

She hesitated to share her supernatural journey. It was so extreme, she doubted anyone would believe it, even her precious Caleb. "There's so much that I don't even know where to begin. I'm still trying to process it all myself: what was real, what were visions, even my current reality." She held tight to his hand praying she would not black out again and awaken in a world without him.

He narrowed his eyebrows in confusion. "I'm here, Gabi. You're alive and well, that is all real." He dropped her hands and caressed her face, leaning over to kiss her he stated emphatically, "And I love you with all my heart. Never doubt that is real."

He could see a glimmer of tears in her eyes as she responded. "I know, Caleb. I truly do know, but…"

"There is no 'but' to it," he interrupted her in a caressing voice.

"No, that's not what I mean," she quickly replied, struggling to find the right words. "I just, well… how can I explain?" It was obvious to Caleb she was questioning herself, not him.

"You spit it out, Gabby Girl, you've never been at a loss for words." Caleb's effort to lighten the mood was unsuccessful.

"Okay," she finally replied, "here it is. I saw many visions of the future while I was in the spirit realm; and at times, I could see all of you in this natural realm which is bound by time and space. I could even see myself lying in bed unable to respond in any way. Even though you couldn't see me in my supernatural existence, I could hear your conversations and feel your sorrow believing if I died, I would be lost forever. I felt the pain of your agony transcending from time to untime." She tried to read his face through the dim lighting. "Do you think I'm crazy, my love?"

"Of course not, Gabi," he assured her. "There's a lot to sort out but we'll do it together. We've got our whole future ahead of us." Caleb expected a smile, but instead a great sorrow crossed her face which he could detect despite the faint lighting.

"The problem is," she hesitated not wanting to voice what the whole team knew to be true, "our future will be short, and full of tribulations. I've seen it." She stopped short of saying she saw herself as a Chosen One from the Tribe of Zebulon. She did not tell him that she had not seen any of her team with her during her visions."

Caleb knew she was right; they were running out of time. In fact, that was the entire premise of Dr. Brotman's Omega Watchers Project. However, a man in love longed for a future to enjoy marriage, family, and a full life. Reluctantly, he admitted, "I know, Gabi, but let's enjoy every moment we can for as long as we can." He lay next to her in the hospital bed, holding her in the security of his arms as they fell asleep.

"There's one more thing," she whispered. "When I had glimpses back into the natural realm, I also saw my father. He was alive and sitting by my bedside."

Caleb did not know how to respond so he pretended to be sound asleep.

The morning light was shining through the hospital window. Officer

Cohen opened the door to allow a nurse access to the room. Caleb got up to make room for her to check Gabriella's vital signs.

"Everything looks good," the nurse commented. "Your doctor has noted on your chart there's going to be one more EEG before he releases you. Someone will be here in about an hour to transport you. In the meantime, I'll send someone to help you shower and get dressed before you go. Looks like you could go home this afternoon," the nurse said as she unhooked the IV and blood pressure monitor.

Gabriella did not comment on home. She was not even sure if she still had one after the war. "A shower sounds wonderful." Sitting up on the side of her bed, she questioned, "but do I have clean clothes here?"

Caleb opened the small closet door revealing Gabriella's roll bag. "Faith brought it when we came to the hospital." He noted the startled look on her face. "Everything you packed to bring to the lodge is still in the bag. It's not even been opened," he assured her.

How did she explain that it was the same bag that traveled with her as she and Chris escaped from the bunker, hid at the seaside cottage, and she hastily packed when they had to flee from the cottage knowing they had been located. This same bag was in the Jeep when they hit the light pole and her world went black. The next thing she remembered after the crash was waking up in this hospital room back in the dimension of time...and here is that same roll bag.

She was trying to settle in her mind how to deal with the intertwining of the natural and supernatural realms. She could not explain the mental perplexity to herself, much less Caleb. She simply stated, "I'm fine, I should have known Faith would take care of details. She's the best."

The discussion had to end when the nurse's aide came in to assist Gabriella into the shower. Caleb put the bag inside the bathroom and closed the door. As the aide unzipped the bag Gabriella held her breath not knowing what to expect. Would the contents be thrown in as they were when they were escaping the cottage? Or would it be neatly packed as it was when they arrived at the lodge? To her amazement everything was exactly as it was when she packed at her condo for departure into protective custody. Everything except the turquoise bracelet given to her by the Cherokee Indian child. It rested on top of all the other contents in full view.

Gabriella collapsed on the shower seat. Her head grew dizzy with confusion. The aide struggled to keep her from falling off the chair.

"I'm going to ring for help," the aide said in a panic.

"No, no," Gabriella assured her, holding her head in her hands. "I just need a minute. I've been in bed for days and my legs are weak, but I'll be okay." Gabriella was praying under her breath for strength as the aide remained uncertain what to do. "Really, I'll be fine. Would you get my blue jeans and the blue shirt out for me, and that zip bag with toiletries?"

"Sure," the young girl replied, carefully pulling the items from the bag. She placed the turquoise bracelet back on the top in its original location before re-zipping the bag. She neatly placed the contents Gabriella requested on the counter and prepared her for her shower. The flow of the warm water across the top of her head and down her body brought back memories of the oil the Prophet Elijah poured upon her, anointing her as a Chosen One. Everything she experienced in the spiritual realm was deeply embedded in her spirit, every detail of her supernatural journey; however, there were so many questions playing over and over in her mind.

Gabriella felt refreshed and ready for whatever lay ahead despite the two entwining existences. She had just finished getting ready when Officer Cohen allowed entry for the same orderly who came the prior day to transport her again to the diagnostic floor. She knew this trip was more than a screening. Without complaining, she sat down in the wheelchair ready to go. Caleb and Chris both followed behind as she was pushed down the hallway to the employee elevator. As soon as they reached the door to the EEG waiting room, Caleb took control of the wheelchair, releasing the orderly from his duties. The young man hesitated but relinquished control promptly turning to leave without a word.

Entering the empty waiting room, the desk clerk immediately motioned for Office Harris to come to the window. After a brief conversation she opened the door to the examination room and allowed the officer to come back, leaving Gabriella and Caleb alone waiting for instructions.

Simultaneously, in Gabriella's hospital room Officer Cohen was allowing the housekeeping employee to enter her room for daily cleaning. Only Dr. Brotman, the main target to be assassinated, remained in the room, ready and waiting to escape. The plan was in motion on both fronts.

Officer Harris remained in the screening room when the clerk opened the door motioning for Gabriella and Caleb to join them. Caleb pushed the wheelchair through the wide door and paused, waiting for further directions. The machines were off, and no technician was in the screening room. The clerk told them to follow her. Caleb helped Gabriella out of the wheelchair following the clerk though a rear door, where hospital lab coats and face masks were waiting for the three of them.

"Quickly, put these on and follow me," she instructed. The three did as directed and then followed the clerk down a private hallway. "This hall is used only by authorized personnel. It allows the doctors and technicians to come and go to the various testing areas privately. No one can enter or leave without a code."

The three following her knew she was reassuring them they were safe. At the end of the corridor was an elevator requiring a code for entry. The clerk instantly sent a text message.

They all noticed her flushed cheeks, making it obvious she was aware there could be danger associated with helping them. "I'm waiting for the code to open the elevator," she informed the trio. "Press L2 when you get on. The door will open automatically when you get to that level." Her phone signaled a text, and she quickly entered the code. Waiting for the elevator to ascend to their floor, she stated further, "I knew when that man came in yesterday saying Dr. Nicholson sent him, something was very wrong. I just had a gut feeling about it. The doctor gave me instructions on what to do today to get you to safety. I don't have any idea who you're running from, but godspeed." The door opened and the three stepped inside. "I'm praying for you," she said breathlessly, turning to rush back to her office.

Office Harris pushed L2 on the control panel and the door quietly closed. The elevator began descending into an unknown location. Not even the officer was sure what to expect when the door reopened. Coming to a smooth landing, the elevator door slid open, and they were face to face with Dr. Nicholson.

"Follow me, walk normally, and don't say a word," he instructed them. They passed numerous private offices with doctor's names as they looked straight ahead following the doctor. Without being told, they were aware this area was for only authorized personnel. They understood now why the lab coats and masks were provided by the clerk. No one paid any attention to them as they neared another elevator where a housekeeping employee stood with his cleaning cart. Dr. Nicholson waved his badge across the electronic reader and the highly secured elevator door opened. He motioned for the trio to follow him in. Officer Harris, Gabriella and Caleb were so focused on the doctor and his lead that they did not notice the housekeeper also stepping into the elevator. The door closed leaving them all secluded in total privacy.

Dr. Nicholson sighed a long breath of relief. "Well now you're all out and ready to join the others," he said in a voice of accomplishment.

"But what about Professor?" Gabriella demanded.

Meanwhile back in Gabriella's room where they had left Dr. Brotman, Officer Cohen left his post and went down the hall for a restroom break, intentionally leaving the room unprotected. When the restroom door closed behind him the same pseudo technician that had followed Gabriella to the prior day's EEG test stepped from behind the nurse's station and silently entered Gabriella's hospital room. He knew from monitoring her room, Dr. Brotman would still be in the room and he was their main objective. The intruder immediately locked the door from the inside of the room before turning, shocked to find only Joshua, the janitor, sitting on the couch reading a magazine.

"What? No!" In anger the intruder rushed back out of the room and down the hallway in the direction the janitor had gone.

Officer Cohen watched the infuriated man running down the corridor in desperation. The officer knew he would not find Dr. Brotman, he was already in a safe place. He would have laughed aloud had the situation not been so grave; however, he did savor the moment of seeing the enemy in chaos.

He pushed the door open to Gabriella's room and gently slapped the elderly man on the back. "Good job, Joshua, we can both leave now. Our current assignments are over. Thank you for your help and I'll walk you to your car, just to make sure all is well." The officer retrieved Gabriella's roll bag from the bathroom, then looked around the room to affirm no other personal items were left behind. "Let's go." Officer Cohen opened the hospital door one final time.

As the two men were exiting the hospital simultaneously the rest of the team was exiting in the underground elevator.

Gabriella again demanded to know where the professor was. The bent frame of the housekeeper straightened, and he took off the mask and hat. "I'm right here with you, Gabi," he revealed giving her a big hug.

Officer Harris was in shock, having no idea Dr. Nicholson had planned this. "The idea only came to me late yesterday, and one of the hospital employees who I trust completely was willing to help. He went to Gabi's room at the time of normal cleaning time this morning, had an extra housekeeping uniform for Dr. Brotman to wear, then Dr. Brotman left with the cleaning cart, leaving Joshua in the room. I informed Detective Richards late last night what the plan was, and he relayed it to Officer Cohen after the professor left the room in disguise. He had to know the plan, but Detective Richards wanted to make sure Professor was out before informing him. Just one more level of security, he said. Sorry, Chris, we couldn't take the chance of getting that plan to you before the fact. Detective Richards thought it would be too risky."

Officer Harris ran his hand through his thick black hair and nodded his head. "He's right. Now to continue to follow the rest of the plan until we get all this team to safety."

"Can we ask what the plan is?" Caleb questioned.

"Richards is still working on some of the fine details, but you'll know soon, very soon." The officer answered.

Dr. Nicholson put the elevator in motion going down to the underground garage, and then on to join those waiting at Rambam Medical Center. Before they boarded the transit bus for departure, Office Harris warned them to stay quiet until they were in a restricted area to talk. "Remember, trust no one."

— CHAPTER 8 —

The underground transit bus stopped in front of the doctor's entrance where KJ, Aaron, Faith, and Sandee anxiously waited for the final members of their team to arrive.

Dr. Nicholson, Dr. Brotman, Gabriella, Caleb and Office Harris stepped off the bus and stood in silence until it departed.

Making sure no one was within hearing range, Dr. Nicholson broke the silence. "Make sure you act normal when we go in. Any outbursts of emotions and big hugs would draw immediate attention and that's the last thing we need," he warned them. "Follow me." The doctor opened the door with the wave of his badge for all to enter.

The part of the team that awaited them at Rambam was having lunch when they arrived. The lounge was empty except for their team, which was a great relief to Dr. Nicholson; but he still cautioned them to act normally knowing there were security cameras everywhere. Even though there were no big displays of emotion, an air of relief saturated the atmosphere. The team gathered closely around a table as doctors often did when they needed to discuss a patient's case. Nothing appeared abnormal.

Dr. Nicholson gave his final instructions: "Detective Richards has arranged for your transport out of here. A Suburban should already be parked in the doctor's underground parking lot. The lot is highly secure and accessed only with a code that is changed daily. It's parked in slot D-7, unlocked, and the key is in the glove box. Chris, you will be taking control from here. You know the rest of the plan."

Chris affirmed, "Yes, I do." The team looked at each other all wondering what that plan was, but no one dared to ask. "And you be very careful, Doctor. Whoever is watching this team could be watching you, too. Like it or not, you've associated yourself with all of us, even though we tried to make it appear to be only professional."

The doctor realized the risk he had taken; however, he would not allow his friends to see his concern. "Don't worry about me, just get yourselves to safety asap. Keep your masks on until you get in the vehicle. It will look perfectly normal since the Israeli government is requiring all citizens wear masks outside until further notice; it's because of the post war residue of chemicals in the air." He wanted to give them all a big hug, but instead reached out with a warm handshake and pointed them in the direction of the doctor's parking area. "Follow those arrows and slot D-7 is just around the circle on the right. Remember security cameras are recording everything."

The team silently followed the officer across the subterranean parking lot to the D-7 slot where a black Suburban awaited. The doors were unlocked and keys in the glove box, just as the doctor said they would be. The officer opened the door and helped Dr. Brotman into the front passenger seat. It was obvious the whole ordeal had taken a toll on him. The others took the back seats and buckled in.

The team was ready for the final phase of the plan. They knew their safety lay in the hands of this police officer and Almighty God, whatever that plan was.

"I'm familiar with the tunnels in this hospital," Officer Harris assured them, backing out of the parking spot. "Part of our police training is to know the geographical layout of Haifa both on the surface and beneath." He circled around the parking lot passing several exits marking the underground passageways to the other hospitals and medical centers in Haifa.

When he came to the exit for Assuta Hospital, he entered the tunnel speeding up to travel the twenty-two miles of distance. "Assuta exits the closest to our destination." Office Harris announced. "Whoever has been surveilling us would have no way of knowing which hospital we're going to, even if they suspected we were escaping through these tunnels, which I seriously doubt; plus, they would need an army of people to watch every exit of all twelve hospitals and track all the vehicles. This Suburban is a police force issued decoy vehicle. If tracked by license number, they would only find dead ends. Thanks to Dr. Nicholson, we have a near perfect plan." He took a breath and finished his thought, "You know nothing is absolute, but this is as close as it gets."

"And what is that destination you're taking us to, Chris?" Dr. Brotman asked.

"I can tell you now," he answered. "I informed Richards about the lodge bunker which of course he had no idea existed; and neither would the people behind the professor's assassination attempt. Whoever wants Professor out of the picture, so to speak, would never expect us to return to the very place we came from. That would break the first rule of protective custody."

His voice was assuring despite the team's concerns. "It's the perfect location plus we need to get back to..." Office Harris stopped when Dr. Brotman shot his a warning look to not say too much.

"We're going back to the lodge?" Gabriella could not believe what she was hearing.

"Yes and no. We are going back to the lodge bunker. We all know it's supplied with everything we need for an extended stay until this case is solved. Hopefully, it won't be that long, but if it is it will be the safest place to hide."

The team all began to chatter at once with questions, comments, and concerns about returning to the lodge. Caleb expressed the biggest concern: "What if they're still surveilling the lodge entrance. They would be suspicious of any vehicles entering or leaving, wouldn't they?"

"Yes, I'm sure they would, but don't worry I've got this under control." The officer's voice was definitive. "It may not be easy especially for you, Professor, but I'm positive it will work. You'll understand once we get there."

The team chattered as they traveled through the tunnel between the two hospitals, speculating on what their futures might hold, when they could contact their families and how difficult staying underground was going to be for an unknown length of time. When they reached the subterranean parking lot of Assuta Hospital, they followed the exit to Hwy. 4. Driving up the ramp to daylight, Office Harris maneuvered through the heavy afternoon traffic onto the expressway, heading back to the Golan Heights.

Gabriella watched the familiar landscape of this same journey made only a few days prior, recalling how angry she was and her uncontrollable emotional outbursts. "What a difference a few days can make," she whispered to Caleb sitting next to her knowing exactly what she meant.

He squeezed her hand and smiled from ear to ear. "In spite of everything we may be facing, I am one happy man, my love," leaning over to kiss her cheek. Gabriella laid her head on his shoulder savoring the moment of tranquility. She knew there would not be many more.

Faith was sitting next to Gabriella and commented on their gestures of affection. "It's been a rough road getting here, but after all these years, we're all happy you two are finally together." She glanced at KJ sitting in the middle row of seats hoping they might have a future together also and giving him a subtle hint with her next comment: "Gabi, if you hadn't been so committed to work instead of living life, you two would have been together long ago." Faith gently pushed against Gabriella's shoulder. "And you know it's the truth."

"I do know," she responded to her best friend. "I only wish we could turn back time." She took a deep breath and exhaled slowly regretting all the years of bitterness and refusing to open her heart to love and be loved. "So many things I would change if I could."

Caleb quickly interjected, "Well, we know that's not possible, but we can certainly make the best of the time we have ahead of us." He put his arm around Gabriella's shoulders and pulled her closer.

"Do you think it's possible to see back in time, even if we can't go there?" She was remembering her mother and father's conversations while she was in untime. She saw them in her father's office and heard them talking about their fears of being surveilled and how they had been deceived by a United States government agency. Gabriella fought back the tears recalling the vision of her mother's murder.

The scholarly Aaron answered her question. "There's a lot of research being done in relativistic travel, and I've been closely following. I recently read an article on how space can be bent, and if it can be then spacetime can be bent also causing overlaps of time both in the past and the future. Simply put, space is the three-dimensional body in which all things in the universe move. Spacetime, however, is the combined concepts of space and time into a four-dimensional continuum."

"That's simple?" Faith answered, raising her eyebrows. "I'm totally lost."

Aaron replied in a monotone voice, "Well, more simply put, yes, it is possible."

A gamut of comments and discussions exploded in the vehicle from Gabriella's one question. She decided it was not the time to share the things she had seen both past, present, and future. It appeared there would be plenty of time for conversation while they are kept in hiding.

While the discussions on time travel continued, Gabriella gazed at the beautiful vineyards as they traveled the familiar road through Hula Valley. It was harvesting time and normally the roads and tourist attractions would be overrun. The war had stopped all normality in Israel. She wondered if anything in life would ever be normal again.

Soon they reached the foothills of the Golan Heights and started the ascent up to the mountain lodge. Fall flowers were in full bloom and the colors were brilliant. Autumn in the Israeli mountains was breathtaking. At least something felt normal.

Dr. Brotman questioned Officer Harris again as they were now only a few miles from the lodge entrance: "Chris, when do we know the plan on how to get back to the lodge undetected?"

"You're about to find out, Professor," he replied pulling to the side of the road. He waited for a few minutes just to make sure no one was following them. There were no other vehicles in sight when he pulled back out and immediately turned onto a dirt road that was more of a hunter's path than a road at all.

Gabriella caught her breath when she realized where they were. Did she tell them, or should she wait to make sure it was the same mountain path she and Chris had traveled on in her father's jeep?

She leaned over and whispered in Caleb's ear so the others would not hear. "I know this road. I'll explain later."

He turned to face her in confusion. How could she know this mountain path? Every time they came to the lodge for a retreat they were always together and never had they traveled on a trail such as this, but he did not comment. Her eyes were telling him to wait for further information and wait he will.

The vehicle was in four-wheel drive as it climbed the step trail over rocks and small branches that had fallen from the trees. The rushing creeks and the mountain scenery calmed their soul. The group savored the natural beauty knowing it could be a while before they were out of seclusion.

"Will we miss all the beautiful fall colors?" Sandee questioned. "How long...?" She did not finish her sentence, but everyone was asking themselves the exact same question.

"Detective Richards is hard on the case," Officer Harris assured them. "He did tell me he had some new leads that actually developed because of the war, but little time to go into the details, and there's still a lot of leads for him to run down. He's brought Micah Cohen in to help him since I'm spending all my time with you. He's careful about who he trusts."

KJ and Aaron looked at each other both remembering Reporter Adelson saying off script who can we trust. Then Dr. Nicholson firmly admonishing them all to trust no one. They raised their eyebrows questioning, but said nothing.

The vehicle jarred back and forth over the rough terrain continuing to ascend upward. "Even the deer would have a problem navigating this path," KJ commented trying to lighten their mood.

Gabriella recognized the path and knew for sure now it was the same one she and Chris had traveled in her father's jeep. Before she thought she commented, "Not much further now."

"What? How would you know that?" Sandee said out loud what they were all thinking.

Still not ready to go into the private details of her supernatural journey, she deflected. "There's Mt. Hermon. The same view we have from the lodge so we can't be too far away." Caleb still had his arm around her shoulders and pulled her closer to him affirming he understood there was much more to the story.

Within minutes, their vehicle pulled up to a flat location and stopped. There was nothing but trees, a running stream, and one small concrete block garage, literally in the middle of nowhere, intentionally camouflaged in a grove of trees.

"Here we are," the officer announced, parking the vehicle under a grove of trees out of aerial view.

"Here we are?" Faith repeated him, disheartened. "Where are we? The lodge is nowhere in sight."

Gabriella was attempting to mentally sort her two worlds. Chris in untime would have known this location well and the mountain trail that brought them here. However, how would Officer Harris in the real world know?

Dr. Brotman looked around summing up their location. "Brilliant idea," he muttered as the team exited the vehicle.

"Someone *please* tell me where we are and what the plan is." Faith demanded. The normally meek Faith was showing a side seldom seen by the team. "Please!"

KJ went to her side and put his arm around her shoulders. "It's going to be fine, Faith. We've got to trust what Chris is doing." She leaned her head on his shoulder and sighed. "I'm sorry. It's just been a tough, very tough, few weeks. So much uncertainty about everything."

"I know," he answered, in a soothing voice. At that moment of touching, there was a bond that solidified between the two of them.

"We've got a long walk ahead of us. Do you think you can make it, Professor?" Officer Harris questioned.

"I'll be fine, Chris, there's plenty of time to rest once we get back to the bunker."

"And just how do we do that?" Faith asked in a softer tone still pushing for an answer to all the mystery. "Do we sneak up some other mountain trail to get back to the lodge?"

Gabriella laughed out loud at her friend, knowing exactly what the plan was from this point. The team watched the officer go to the concrete block building, put in a code on the lock and pull the garage door up. Gabriella gasped seeing her father's jeep parked in the garage, the same Jeep she and Chris had escaped in when they went to the seaside cottage; the same Jeep they wrecked in trying to escape from that cottage ending in their horrible accident. Now here it was parked in perfect condition.

"Are you okay," Caleb asked, seeing the expression of shock on her face.

"More to tell you later, just not now," she replied in a raspy voice.

Officer Harris went inside the building and quickly returned with flashlights for each person. "Follow me," he instructed.

No one had taken personal items with them to the hospital so there was nothing to carry as they walked closely behind the officer. Gabriella suddenly realized her roll bag was left in the bathroom at her hospital room. Her personal contents did not matter, but the turquoise bracelet was her tangible proof of her supernatural existence, and she desperately wanted it. She had promised the Indian girl she would keep and treasure it forever and now it was gone. She accepted the bracelet was gone, but the memory of the beautiful child's miraculous healing would be forever branded in her heart.

She also remembered the flash drive downloaded with all the evil plans for a one world order and questioned if it was even real. She tried to push all the questions from her mind and focus on getting back to the bunker where she could attempt to mentally sort things out. Being still weak in body and knowing this would be a thirty-minute walk, she prayed for supernatural strength.

After the officer had parked the SUV under a thicket of myrtle trees to hide it from aerial view, the team followed the officer down a path to a camouflaged cave opening. Any mountain hikers along the trails would most likely not realize it was there. However, if they did discover it and ventured in, Gabriella knew what they would find, a dead-end cavern.

Turning on their lights as they entered, their journey through another underground tunnel to safety began. When they were walking past the rock where Gabriella had fallen and hit her head while she and Chris were escaping the bunker, she asked if they could stop and rest for a minute.

"I'm sure Professor could use a rest too," she commented. She wanted a bit of time to reflect on the intertwining of reality and the supernatural world which took place in this exact location when she moved from untime to time and back again.

She recalled everything going black and then waking up in the bunker surrounded by her loved ones, including her father. It was a brief encounter filled with love and rejoicing before her world went black again and she awakened back in the cave alone. She remembered the sounds of gunshots from within the bunker and the fear, not knowing if Chris had made it out alive. The flash drive with all the surveillance videos downloaded of the evil men who took up residence in the lodge was securely held in her hand. It was at this place, in this cave, and at that time the Prophet Elijah appeared to her anointing her as a Chosen One. Rather she was in her natural body or in the spirit she did not know, nor did it matter, the moment was glorious as she was sealed as a Daughter of Zebulon.

For a brief time, she returned to that supernatural realm and everyone around her faded away. Again, the wall of the cave illuminated as it had previously with what appeared to be a giant movie screen replaying what she had seen in untime.

She saw the future with UN President Sotoreo and the Black Pope making plans for The New World Order and preparing for the Antichrist to take his position.

She saw the recent past with all the events that had transpired, from the time she had collapsed on the bedroom floor soon after arriving at the lodge. She saw Caleb carrying her to the bunker when the war began; her lifeless body lying in her bunker bed with Caleb on one side and her father on the other. She saw everything and heard every conversation, but her body was incapable of responding to them.

The vision on the cave wall faded away as her natural realm came back into focus, she realized the Spirit of God was confirming to her all that she had seen past, present, and future.

The team was chattering, oblivious to the fact Gabriella had briefly transcended time and space again. Acclimating back to the dimension of time, she held her hand out for Caleb to help her up from the rock she was seated on.

"Would you give me a hand here, KJ," Dr. Brotman asked attempting to get up also.

KJ immediately reached out for the professor's hands gently, pulling him to his feet. "Are you ok, Professor?"

"I'm good," he assured him. "Let's get this journey over."

The team continued through the cave. It was a very natural experience for Gabriella, Caleb, Faith, and Aaron. Exploring caves was their life's work; however, for the others, it was not a comfortable journey, and they were anxious for it to end. The half-hour walk brought them to what appeared to be a dead end. Only two people in the group knew what to expect. Chris had been given detailed instructions in the natural realm and Gabriella knew what lay beyond the wall, having experienced it in untime. She wondered, how often time and untime overlap like this?

She focused on the present and addressed the immediate situation: "Don't keep them in suspense, Chris," Gabriella commented. "Open the wall."

The entire team looked at her in amazement.

"What do you mean?" KJ questioned.

Chris stuttered in confusion, "But...but, how do you know, Gabi?"

"Just open the door, Chris." She spoke in a tone which reflected an intimacy indicating a close relationship. The group looked at each other not understanding any of it and Caleb stepped closer to Gabriella in a movement fringed with jealousy. Chris looked stunned.

"As I told you all at the hospital, there's so much to explain," she stated, gently pushing the officer towards the side of the wall where the lever was located to open the fake stone passageway.

He reached behind the wall and pulled the lever and the team marveled as the door slid open allowing access to the underground seclusion. One by one, they stepped into the bunker storage room. Once everyone was inside, the officer pulled another lever on the inside. They watched as an entire shelving unit moved back into place totally concealing the exit.

"I've been in this room a dozen times in the last few days," Faith stated in a mesmerized voice. I had no idea."

"That's the whole point," Dr. Brotman replied to her. "This bunker was built with the entire intention of safety even if safety meant safely escaping."

"And who built this lodge and bunker?" Gabriella questioned desperately desiring what she saw in the natural realm from her supernatural view was real.

They all turned when someone entered the stockroom from the kitchen. "I did, Princess."

"Dad! It's true, it's really true!" Gabriella was crying with joy as she ran to her father's arms. He wrapped his arms around her never wanting to let his daughter go again. They clung to each other for several minutes with tears of joy flowing openly.

Gabe reluctantly let her go to explain: "When they took you in the ambulance, I couldn't go with you. It was taking too big of a chance for all of your safety, so I stayed here in seclusion as I've done most of the last twelve years. I have prayed so hard every minute since you all left the bunker. Finally, around noon today, I felt peace."

"That's when we all knew we were safe," Dr. Brotman interjected. "And how we escaped, well that's another story for later." His face portrayed his concern for the safety of Dr. Nicholson.

Gabe did not want to release his daughter after over a decade of being separated. "This has been the hardest twelve years of my life, Princess. I had to pretend to be dead so you could live a normal life." His voice was quivering with emotion. "I made them all promise not to tell you the truth, I wanted to savor the moment you found out with us together."

The entire team was in tears watching this reunion unfold before them as her father continued. "So much to explain to you but for now I just want to hold you and let you know how much I love you. This was all for you, Gabi. I didn't care what happened to me, but I knew you wouldn't be safe as long as certain people thought I was alive. You would have been their target to get to me. This lodge, this bunker, it was all built for you. It gave your team a place to rest and relax, but it gave me a time to have you near, even though you never knew." Her father was struggling to explain. With a quivering voice, he continued: "This bunker was designed for the possibility of a time such as this."

"Dad, I know. I know so much more than you realize, and there's so much I need to tell you." She glanced back at the group confirming, "to tell all of you."

"Honey bunny, let's get you and Professor comfortable. You both need some rest." Sandee had a way of taking control in a truly kind manner. She was always looking out for the welfare of everyone else and knew this was extremely straining, especially for Dr. Brotman.

Gabe wrapped his arm around Gabriella's shoulders holding her close, leading her through the kitchen and into the great room. The room was exactly as she had seen while in untime. She was aware the entire team thought she had no idea of the layout or anything the bunker consisted of. She giggled thinking, "I know more details about this place than they do."

Her father squeezed her tighter when she giggled, thinking it was from the joy of being reunited, and she did not want to dampen that thought. For the moment she was completely filled with joy being together again. However, her mood began to somber, knowing she had to tell him the revelations of truth shown to her in untime. He was completely unaware that his enemies now knew he was alive and well.

Gathering in the great room, Gabriella sat in the middle of the couch with her father on one side and Caleb on the other. Her mind kept questioning if this was real? Would she stay this time or black out and wake up again in another time and another place? She took the hand of her father on her left and Caleb on her right and held tightly. "I can't leave again," she kept repeating in her mind. "Please, Heavenly Father, my heart's desire is to be with the people I love." She looked around the room and treasured the moment encircled by her friends, being wide awake to enjoy their newfound unity of mind and purpose. "Nevertheless, not my will but yours be done," she silently prayed.

Sandee demanded the professor sit in one of the recliners and put his feet up to rest. "You've pushed yourself too hard, Professor. You're still recuperating, you know."

Dr. Brotman grunted, "I'm fine. Don't make such a fuss." However, it was obvious he was exhausted and appreciated her concern.

Sandee got a blanket from the closet and covered him. "Don't argue with me," she teasingly demanded. "We're going to need your sharp mind and you're no good to any of us if you're too tired to concentrate." She patted his shoulder and headed for the kitchen area. "I'm going to make us supper. I know you kids; hungry all the time." As she was cooking, she sang in a beautiful soft voice the old hymn, Amazing Grace. A tranquility began to fill the air as everyone sat and silence and listened.

As she continued to sing the entire room joined her in one voice, "I once was lost, but now I'm found, was blind but now I see." A supernatural peace saturated each team member and for a brief time, it seemed all was well with the world.

Little did they know Dr. Nicholson was not at peace, not at all.

— Chapter 9 —

D r. Nicholson boarded the mini transit bus transporting him back to Elisha Hospital. The events of the previous days played over and over in his mind. He and Dr. Brotman had been friends for many years; however, he had no idea Dr. Brotman's project was of such immense importance, and he certainly did not realize the danger involved, not until Gabriella's collapse. The information revealed during the three days spent in the bunker had changed his world. He was thankful his wife was with him during these revelations. Just the thought of her loving face brought a smile to his face, and he was anxious to get home to her.

The transit pulled up to the underground hospital entrance. The doctor thanked the driver as he exited. A dread overwhelmed him as he ascended back to his office floor. Although he knew this area was secure, he had no idea what awaited him on the public floors. He walked the glistening clean floors to his private office thinking of Joshua and how hard he worked for decades to keep a clean, sanitary environment for the staff, never expecting any recognition for his job. He wanted to do something special for him, especially with Joshua's willingness to help with the team's escape. Ideas of what to do were circling in his mind as he approached his office door. Several doctors were standing nearby in deep discussion. Obviously, something was wrong with the tone of their voice. One of them noticed Dr. Nicholson, and motioned for him to join them.

"What's going on?" He questioned as he joined their discussion.

"We've just got some very disturbing news about Joshua." One of the doctors took the lead in the conversation. "He's in ICU."

Dr. Nicholson's heart raced suspecting it was related to the escape. "What happened?" he exclaimed.

"No one knows. He's in a coma so he can't give any details. A hospital employee leaving work saw him in his car with his head slumped against the steering wheel. His door was wide open. When she approached the vehicle, he was unresponsive. Heart attack, stroke? We have no idea yet, but a team of doctors will be running tests."

"If you need me, I will do anything I possibly can to help," Dr. Nicholson stated in a distressed voice and left the group for the seclusion of his office. He closed the door behind him as he entered and went straight to his knees and prayer. "Dear Lord, is this my fault? Is this because he helped the professor escape?" Waves of agony rolled over him as he prayed for Joshua's healing. "This is a good man, Father, touch him with your healing power." He continued with intercessory prayer until his cell phone interrupted with his wife calling.

"Hi, my love," Dr. Nicholson answered struggling to sound normal.

"What's wrong?" she immediately demanded. "I know that tone. I can read you like a book, and you know I can."

He knew there was no reason to try to hide his emotions and simply stated, "I will explain everything when I get home. I've been here for two days straight and headed home soon. I need to check on a patient first, then out of here."

Exiting his office, he locked his door. Apprehension began to build as he approached the elevator that would take him from his secured zone. Under his breath, he repeated Bible scriptures of protection and peace. He held his badge in front of the security scanner to gain access to the elevator which would take him from the doctor's restricted area to the third floor ICU unit.

"Good afternoon," he addressed the nurse as he entered. He accessed Joshua's medical chart quickly scanning for any information that could be a clue to what had happened.

"If you're here to see Joshua Abrams, doctor," he's been taken to EEG for a brain scan. The vascular neurologist suspects a stroke."

"Thank you," Dr. Nicholson muttered, "I'll be back to check on him later." He returned to the personnel elevator and pushed the floor number that would take him to the private corridor leading to EEG Diagnostics. The hallway was empty except for the wheelchair which he supposed was the one Gabriella had used before entering the elevator to escape just a few hours prior. As he approached the clerk's office that familiar feeling of foreboding overwhelmed him. Leah, who had helped the team with the escape from the EEG lab was sitting with her back turned from him as he entered. When she turned to face him, fear was written all over her face.

"What is it, Leah? What's wrong?" The doctor tried to disguise his grave concern.

She made sure the privacy window was tightly closed so she would not be overhead. In a whisper she replied, "That man, the one that said you sent him when Gabriella Russell was having her EEG done, he came back a few minutes ago looking for her again. I would recognize that odd voice anywhere. I told him she wasn't here. If you could've seen the look on his face, doctor...well, let's just say he was terribly angry and if looks could kill, I would be dead right now." Her words were saturated with fear as she continued: "As soon as he came in, I rang for security, but he left before they arrived. There were several people in the waiting room, and I think that's the reason he didn't make a big scene, but I have the feeling this is not over, not by a long shot."

Dr. Nicholson realized he had put yet another person in danger, while trying to help the team escape from danger. "Dear Lord, what have I done?" he silently questioned. He watched the beautiful young face looking into his eyes, searching for comfort. The doctor made a quick decision. "Tell your supervisor you need to take the rest of the day off and call for security to escort you to your car. I'll approve both."

"I don't have a car," she answered with apprehension growing. "I take the public transit."

Dr. Nicholson stated without reservation. "Then I will drive you home but go ahead and call security to escort both of us."

"What have I got myself into?" She exclaimed, realizing just how serious the situation was.

The doctor tried to calm her by attempting to assure her this was just a precautionary measure. "I don't want this thug harassing you. Go ahead and take care of what you need to so you can leave. I'm going to step into the lab and check on the patient that's being screened."

Leah turned back to her desk to follow the doctor's orders. Dr. Nicholson was aware the EEG technician was not qualified to professionally read the screenings, but he had done them so often he would recognize obvious signs of a stroke.

"What's your opinion?" he asked as he was finishing the test.

"I see no signs of a stroke, Dr. Nicholson. Nothing abnormal at all is shown in brain activity."

"Well, that's good news," the doctor responded. He went over to Joshua laying comatose on the lab exam table. He leaned over and whispered in his ear, "If you can hear me, Joshua, squeeze my hand or move your fingers."

Dr. Nicholson felt Joshua's fingers move slightly. "I'm going to ask you some questions and just move your fingers to answer yes."

The doctor glanced at the technician who was busy working and paying no attention to him. "Did someone do this to you?" Joshua forced his fingers, saying yes.

The fears of the doctor had been confirmed. "A couple more questions. Do you know the person?" Joshua's hand did not move. Dr. Nicholson was trying to quickly evaluate what could be done to put him in this state of being without any obvious bodily harm.

Joshua had not been given any details on why he was to help Dr. Brotman escape or where he would be going, so he could not possibly have divulged any information. However, wanting information may have been the motive of the person who did this, not knowing that fact.

"Did they try to get information from you?" Joshua immediately moved his hand to respond yes. "Did they give you a shot?" Joshua's fingers did not move. "Did they force you to take a pill?" There was an immediate response indicating yes. Now it all made sense to Dr. Nicholson, perfect sense. "Thank you, Joshua, may God bless and keep you." Tears filled the eyes of the doctor with his last words, "Goodbye, my friend." Under his breath so Joshua could not hear, he whispered, "Rest in Peace. I know you'll keep the streets of gold shining until I join you."

The doctor trying to bring his emotions into check went immediately to Leah's desk and borrowed her computer to do a search for specific drugs. Shortly he muttered to himself, "That's it!". He had found exactly what he was looking for. He added to Joshua's chart an order for blood work immediately, specifically looking for sodium amytal and to report the results directly to him asap.

"Are you ready to go, Leah?" He was anxious to get away from the hospital and get her to safety. Joshua knew nothing so nothing was all he could tell. On the other hand, Leah knew too much and that created a whole new conundrum.

"Security and my replacement will be here any minute and I'm ready to go." She answered.

"I'll be right back," he replied, exiting back out into the private hallway where he could make a call to Detective Richards without being overheard.

With one ring, the detective answered, "Richards here."

Quickly Dr. Nicholson informed him of what happened to Joshua and the encounter Leah had. "I'm driving her home to make sure she gets there safely."

A quick response from the detective derailed Dr. Nicholson's plans. "That won't work, not at all. It's highly likely your car is being surveilled too, given all the other things happening. Give me a minute to work out some details. Sit tight and I'll get right back." The phone disconnected and Dr. Nicholson could do nothing but wait for instructions. He paced back and forth in the hallway praying for protection over his wife, alone at home, and anxious to get to her. He kept questioning who these evil people were. He knew why, it was all connected to the professor's project and the information Gabriella's father had had for decades. But who? And what is so important they are willing to take out anyone associated with them?

His thoughts were interrupted when Detective Richards called back. "Here's the plan, doctor, write the details down."

The doctor quickly got his small pad and pencil out of his pocket and began to make notes as instructed.

"Any questions?" the detective questioned.

"Got it," the doctor answered. "One more thing, detective, I'm fairly sure I know what happened to Joshua. He was forced to take a pill that I know for sure, and it was probably sodium amytal or something close."

"Truth serum?" The detective questioned.

"Exactly, and I'm sure they found out he really did not know anything other than letting the professor pretend to be him. When given too much of the drug, the person administering this drug would have time to ask Joshua questions and Joshua is forced by the amytal to give only truthful answers. There's a window of time for interrogation before he goes into a deep sleep. Just a few grams more than a normal dose will..." the doctor paused taking a deep breath before finishing his analysis, "will result in a deadly overdose."

Dr. Nicholson was struggling to keep his personal feelings at bay as he continued explaining what the next step would be. "I've put orders in for the lab to do blood work and report back to me, but it all makes sense." He took a belabored breath before continuing, "There's nothing that can be done for him. I will have to live with the guilt of this until my dying day. Lord, help me." He could no longer cover the agony in his soul which echoed in his words.

The detective tried to encourage him. "I understand, believe me I do, but now we must focus on getting you and the clerk out safely. Follow those instructions to the letter. If your car doesn't leave the doctor's parking lot at the hospital, hopefully, these guys will think you are still somewhere on the hospital grounds. The clerk has no idea what's going on, but you on the other hand, Doctor, you know every detail of Dr. Brotman, and his team's escape and we sure don't want any truth serum going in you. It's a good thing you don't know the details of where they've been taken to."

Dr. Nicholson started to interrupt the detective, "But..."

Detective Richards instead interrupted him to make sure the doctor said no more. "Follow my instructions to the detail. Got it?"

"Yes, got it," the doctor replied, surprised at the sudden change of the detective's tone of voice. The phone immediately disconnected.

He rejoined Leah and informed her there had been a change in plans. Security had arrived and the doctor thanked them, but they would not be needed. He motioned for Leah to follow him into the back storage room.

"Get one of the technician's jackets and put a surgical mask on."

Leah did as he said, following him into the private hallway where she had led the team to safety earlier that day and eerily, she was using the same escape. Dr. Nicholson did not need a code, he simply held his badge in front of the infrared scanner and the elevator doors opened. Reentering the secured area for doctors, he instructed her to stay right by his side and not say a word. He looked down the corridor and it was clear except for a man who had taken Joshua's place in cleaning. He had never seen the man before and his inner radar was picking up something was not right.

"Just walk normally," he directed her. They passed his office and went straight to the elevator that would transport them to the underground parking lot. "Lord, please give us one last safe trip through this underground tunnel," he prayed aloud. He used his security pass to access the elevator once more, not knowing it would be the final time. He motioned for Leah to go first as he watched the janitor out of the corner of his eye. The doors closed, he sighed with relief.

Leah looked at him questioningly but afraid to ask what he meant by one more safe trip. She had no idea what had happened to the people she aided in leaving the EEG exam room after she escorted them to the restricted elevator. Once the elevator doors closed, her part was done. She could clearly see now how they escaped, but fearful of why or who they were escaping from.

The doctor checked the time while they waited for the transit to arrive. "We're good on time. We're supposed to meet someone in an hour."

"Can I ask where we're going?" She was anxiously questioning. "I'm still going home...aren't I?" With each passing moment that hope was fading.

"We'll find out shortly. I wish I knew all the details. I was only given the information of exactly where to be and when."

Leah was way out of her comfort zone and growing more fearful with every passing minute. "I wish I'd never gotten involved in this. I don't know why all this secret stuff, I just know it feels extremely dangerous and I don't like it, at all."

The transit pulled up as she was expressing her inward fears. Dr. Nicholson put his hand on her shoulder assuring her everything would be fine. "No talking while we're riding over."

"Over to where," she insisted on knowing.

"First to Rambam Hospital which is the central location for all the hospital underground connections. There we will take another transit bus to Carmel Hospital. Then we find out where we go from that point."

Leah just shook her head in total confusion. "Why did I ever agree to this?" she kept repeating.

Dr. Nicholson answered: "Believe me, none of us wanted this; but we are living in exceedingly grim times, Leah. Everything has changed with the war and I'm just beginning to realize the scope of it. I have the eerie feeling that life would never be like it was before."

They both sat quietly as they sped along the concrete tunnel to Rambam Hospital. Arriving at their destination, he got out and helped Leah step down. Glancing at his watch, he informed her, "We have a few minutes before we head to Carmel Hospital." He sat down on a nearby bench and motioned for her to join him.

"I'm too restless to sit," she said matter-of-fact. Pacing back and forth, she kept repeating, "How did I get myself into this mess?" She noticed Dr. Nicholson nervously watched the parking lot which caused her fears to grow even more.

"Thank the Lord," he muttered as the transit for Carmel Hospital pulled to the curb. "Let's go, Leah." They both boarded and said nothing during the ride through yet another tunnel. The doctor's apprehension continued to increase even though he struggled to stay calm. He was reviewing the instructions given to him by Detective Richards when they came to a stop. Immediately he noticed the signs directing to the various areas of the underground parking lot.

"Next item of business is to find D-17 in the physician's designated area." Leah stayed close to Dr. Nicholson as they walked across the lot towards the number in the instructions. "In D-17 there will be someone waiting for us in a white Toyota."

They could see the vehicle several parking spots ahead just as planned when another white Toyota came speeding down the ramp towards them. The doctor grabbed Leah and pulled her to safety between two parked vehicles. The Toyota stopped right in front of them with the driver's window open. "Get in now, hurry!" Micah Cohen commanded them. Dr. Nicholson did not hesitate. Pushing Leah towards the car, they both jumped in the back seat as the police officer was driving away.

"Buckle up, this could get rough," the officer commanded as he sped towards the exit from the subterranean tunnels. "Hold on!" he shouted. "We're not stopping for identification." Their vehicle went speeding by the infrared reader setting off alarms and locking down the exit completely. They exited just before the barricades came down.

Dr. Nicholson and Leah held on for dear life in the back seat. Leah was choking on the screams that were trying to escape her mouth; the doctor was feverishly praying. Officer Cohen meticulously maneuvered the vehicle in and out of the traffic not saying a word until they reached Hwy. 23 where he felt they were safely away from their followers. His passengers in the back seat simultaneously exhaled in relief.

Keeping his eyes on the road, the officer finally spoke. "Detective Richards was right again. That man has a brilliant detective's mind."

"What do you mean, right?" Dr. Nicholson asked, finally able to breathe normally again.

"He suspected your phone was tapped, doctor. That would mean every detail he gave you step by step was also being recorded by the enemy. It was a set-up by Richards so they knew exactly when you would arrive and where you would go but Richards was planning for you to get out before he closed in on these guys. The plan was to pick you up when you first arrived at Carmel Hospital, before you even started walking towards D-17; but a brief hold-up in traffic made a couple of minutes difference in getting here, which made all the difference in the plan. Richards put this plan together so quickly timing was a major issue, and the moving parts were a nightmare. Thank God I got to you before you got to D-17." Officer Cohen laughed and proudly announced, "Richards knew these evil people couldn't get out of the tunnel once the alarms went off. He had security ready to arrest whoever was in that white Toyota parked in D-17."

"And a little sodium amytal would be just the right prescription for them," Dr. Nicholson added thinking of Joshua, and wondering if he had passed yet. "I'll explain that later."

Leah just continued to shake her head in disbelief, regretting the day she went to work at Elisha Hospital. She was about to ask, again, where they were taking her when Dr. Nicholson blurted out.

"My wife! If they've tapped my phone, they know she is home alone. I must get to her, now." His voice was pleading with the officer.

"Richards has your house being watched for any suspicious activity until he can safely get your wife out," he assured the doctor. "He's working on a plan now."

Dr. Nicholson leaned back and sighed in relief while Leah moaned in distress. "This is like a James Bond movie," she cried. "Only this is real and sorry to say, Officer, you are no James Bond." She leaned her head back on the seat and cried, "I'm living a nightmare I can't wake up from."

The officer tried to console her. "You are in no danger now. However, you will be in protective custody until we solve the case, it's the only way we can guarantee you're protected. Richards has already had a background check on you and found you live alone after a divorce and have no family in Israel. So, no one will expect you to come home."

"That sounds really sad when it's spoken out loud," she stated in a melancholy voice. "It's true though." Dr. Nicholson had no children and was old enough to be her father. He felt an immediate protective spirit towards her and took her hand in his to comfort her. You'll be with me and my precious wife, Ruth, when she can join us. Nothing to be afraid of, Leah." She attempted a smile, but apprehension still covered her face.

"And I've been told to stay with you both until further assignment," the officer said, hoping both felt safer.

The sun was starting to set over the Mediterranean Sea when they finally pulled into a driveway on the coast. Officer Cohen stopped at the gated entrance and entered a code allowing the security gates to open. They drove through the entrance down a graveled drive. Coming into view was a quaint seaside cottage. The scenery was tranquil, but the moods of the new occupants were nothing close to the peaceful setting.

Officer Cohen unlocked the front door for Dr. Nicholson and Leah to enter. He went back to the Toyota and pulled a roll bag from the back. "This belongs to Gabriella; it was left at the hospital, so I took it with me when I left. I thought this might be the best place for safe keeping until we can get it back to her. Let's go on in and get you settled."

Inside, he retrieved a metal box. "Before you settle in, put your cell phones in here where they can't be tracked. No electronics allowed, at all."

"What?" Leah cried, "I'm cut off from everyone and everything normal in my life. I might as well be dead." Then she hushed, realizing she very well could be, had they not rescued her from the hospital.

"It will be an adjustment, but everything we need is supplied here. Hopefully, the case will be solved soon, and you can return to your lives. Richards' office will be taking care of notifying the hospital that you are taking some time off for health reasons, Dr. Nicholson. Same for Leah."

"This is your new home," the office announced. "At least for now."

— Chapter 10 —

It had been an extremely long day for all concerned, especially for Detective Richards who was dealing with many fluid parts attempting to get everyone to safety. It was early evening when Office Cohen called him, both men using analog phones which could not be tapped, tracked, or hacked. He simply stated, "Mission accomplished."

Sighing in relief, Detective Richards stated, "You know the plan, Micah. I'm working on the best way to safely retrieve Mrs. Nicholson. Assure the doctor we will do our best to protect her."

"Yes, sir," the officer replied ending the conversation.

"Now I can get down to business," the detective said to his empty office.

Only one man was in the white Toyota parked in D-17 and he had been taken into custody. Next stop for Detective Richards was a face-to-face questioning. Entering the Haifa City Jail, the detective walked directly to the interrogation room where the man waited. He was surprised at how young and clean-cut the man was. From his appearance he would never have been suspected as one with ill intentions; but that naturally would have been part of their deception; and his background check was squeaky clean but that could have been faked as well.

The detective sat down across the wooden table from the suspect and stared into his eyes before beginning. He was an expert at reading both body language and eye movements. He turned on his voice recorder before beginning. "Tell me your name, please."

"David Berg," he promptly answered, "and I have no idea why I'm even here. I was just doing my job." The young man's voice was sincere, and his body language indicated he really did not know.

"And what is your job?" He questioned further.

"I'm a contract labor driver for Uber," he answered with a quivering voice.

"What were you doing in the D-17 parking lot at Carmel Hospital? That's a private parking lot reserved for doctors only. How does an Uber driver get access to that?"

His voice was steady as he began to explain: "I was contacted by the company I work for asking if I could do an immediate pick-up for a doctor and his companion. If I could go right then, I would be paid a big bonus. They told me I would be contacted after pick-up as to where to take them. They gave me a code to get into the parking lot and told me where to park. I followed the directions given to me. I was waiting for the two people to arrive when a white Toyota, almost identical to mine, came flying through, stopped briefly, and then sped through the parking lot exit setting off all kinds of alarms. The next thing I knew, I was being arrested. For what? Parking in the doctor's parking lot?"

Detective Richards felt totally deflated. It was obvious this young man was telling the truth and they would have nothing to hold him on, and with no helpful information at all from him. "Man's best laid plans often fail," he thought to himself before continuing his questioning. "So, you know nothing whatsoever about the person who hired you for the pick-up?"

"Maybe my dispatch would know, but I've told you everything I know, and that's the total truth." Not one body movement indicated he was lying, and Detective Richards knew them all.

"What's the number for the company you work for? I need to verify this information and if it all checks out, you'll be free to go."

Within an hour David Berg was being processed for release. Detective Richards would have one of his younger detectives question the Uber company to try to get more information on who contracted with them wanting specifically a white Toyota; however, he already suspected it would be a dead end. People at this level of crime knew well how to cover their tracks and this looked more and more like being a high-level organized crime syndicate.

During the walk back to the police station he was wondering what to do next. He now had two of his best officers assigned to protective custody and the list was growing short of those who could be fully trusted. Some strange circumstances had developed because of the war which he intended to investigate He had never fully trusted the Israeli Mossad when he was forced to work on cases with them and recent events had thrown up some serious red flags that just might be connected to Dr. Brotman.

Arriving at his office he opened his computer, researching to try to connect some dots. He desperately wanted to bring closure for all concerned in this case, himself included. The deeper he delved the stranger the connections were getting. It was the most difficult one he had ever been assigned and Dr. Brotman's project and that mysterious black box of Gabriella's were the two main keys to solving it; and, apparently, the two of them were the two main targets to take out. He felt relief they both, along with the entire team, were now safely hidden.

It was going to be a long night for Detective Richards; as well as Dr. Nicholson who was fearful for his wife; and Mrs. Nicholson who was in a panic not knowing where her husband was. Only the team at the lodge had any measure of temporary peace.

Dr. Brotman and his team had spent the entire evening celebrating Gabriella's awakening and the reunion with her father. She had so much to tell her loved ones and yet was not sure what to tell or what they would believe, so she had given no details of her untime experiences. She wanted to treasure the moment of reconciliation. Her priority was time with her father after twelve years of separation. For hours they reminisced about their years together as she was growing up, losing her mother, the constant fear of being followed, and his decision to fake his death.

"I wrote my journal mainly for you, Gabi. I wanted a detailed record explaining what I had discovered both for my own records and for you to understand when you were old enough - what I did and why. I kept it in the black leather box always hidden from any possible intruder. As you know now, Dr. Brotman was secretly involved in my research for many of your growing up years. He has been my salvation in more ways than one. I don't know where my life or yours would have ended had the professor not led me out of the extraterrestrial deception." He looked into her crystal blue eyes and stated matter of fact. "We both would have been dead by now; the CIA would have made sure of it."

Gabe pulled his daughter close to him with tears in his eyes. "My decisions almost destroyed your life, and I am truly sorry for all the agony you've gone through, Princess. My heart has been breaking every day since the day you thought I died." He cleared his throat to finish. "I do believe it saved your life and for that reason I have no regrets. The CIA wanted my research so badly they would, and still will, do anything to get it. Also, I have no doubt the Mossad is working with them."

Caleb was still clinging to her right hand. "I'm so thankful you did protect her, Gabe," he said raising her hands to his lips. "I can't imagine my life without her."

Gabriella had spent many weeks in emotional turmoil and thought she had herself now in control, but this was just too much. She leaned her head on her father's shoulder and allowed the tears to flow one more time; however, these were tears releasing years of agony, tears of joy to replace the sorrow.

She knew it was time to share a portion of her untime visions. "Dad, I can't explain all that happened while I was in the supernatural realm, but I saw you alive. I saw and heard it all, including whoever these evil people are, they now know you're alive."

Her father did not know how to respond. He wanted to be sensitive to her condition. "Gabi, that's impossible. It's been over twelve years and there is not a sign of anyone following me. I officially died; you know. That's the reason I didn't go to the hospital with you, I couldn't take any chances."

"You're right, dad, they really believed that until you visited me dressed as a Hasidic Jew at the coffee shop near my condo."

Total disbelief covered his face. "What? How do you know? He stammered. "I've used that disguise since I arrived in Israel and my true identity has never been suspected."

"Not until they recorded our conversation at the coffee shop. They were following me knowing I had been given your research and ultimately it led them to you. They did a voice analysis and discovered you are still alive." Her eyes were begging him to believe her. "Dad, I believe it's true and, if so, they also know you own this lodge. The one thing they do not know about is this bunker beneath it."

The entire team sat in silence. If this was all true, then she in fact saw things and knew things that could not be explained other than a supernatural experience.

Dr. Brotman rejoined them after resting. He could tell by the atmosphere of the room something was wrong.

"We may have a big problem, Professor." Gabe clued him in on what his daughter had shared. "I don't understand how it could be, but *if* what Gabi saw while she was in a coma is true, the dynamics of everything has changed."

She wanted to shout out loud that she knew it was true, but doubts still shadowed her mind. She needed more proof for herself and for her team.

Sandee had prepared dinner and the group gathered around the large wooden table continuing to discuss the possibilities of what Gabriella had seen and how the truth of Gabe being alive would affect their project.

Although there was much to be joyous about with Gabe being alive and Gabriella now being spiritually in one accord with the team, still the ominous future awaited. Gabriella was convinced she had seen future events and knew she would eventually share everything. Just finding the right time and the right way so they would not think she was delusional after waking up from what her loved ones still believed was a coma. They had accepted her spiritual conversion through the Blood of the Lamb, but would they accept her supernatural visions of the future, especially her anointing as a Chosen One?

Naturally, Dr. Brotman wanted to discuss the impact this possible revelation could have on his Omega Watchers Project. "Gabi, we had many discussions during the three days of the war which you are not aware of. We need to bring you up to speed so we can move forward. We may be stuck in this bunker for a while, and we will make the best of the time. Yahweh didn't raise the two of us from our death beds to waste time."

"Yes, Professor," she agreed. "There is definitely much to do...and time is short."

KJ, the technological genius, interjected into the conversation: "Now that the internet is accessible again, I have some possibilities to research, but my computer is upstairs. That's the one thing this bunker is missing." He looked at Gabriella and explained, "During the war there was no internet anyway, so it really didn't matter. We did have television reception, but that was it for any information."

"Do you really think with all the details I put into this survival bunker that I wouldn't have a computer?" Gabe questioned KJ. "I have an area off my personal bedroom none of you have seen yet, except Chris. I thought our resident police officer needed to know." He smiled at his meager attempt at humor.

Before she could stop the words from escaping her mouth, Gabriella blurted out, "The security room."

Both her father and the officer looked at her shocked. "You know about the security room, Gabi? How could you?" Officer Harris questioned, in total perplexity.

"This is what I've been trying to tell you all. "While my body appeared to be in a coma, my spirit was not. I've told you that I saw things: I saw the past, and the present and things that are still to come." She thought before she said anymore. "I was in the security room with you, Chris. We saw the lodge filled with evil men planning the New World Order." She knew everyone in the sound of her voice thought she had totally lost her mind. "I'm going to prove I saw it." Gabriella went into every detail of the room in a perfect description. The faces of her father and the officer went from disbelief to total amazement. The rest of the team sat silent, not sure what to think. They did not even know a security room existed.

"And if you don't believe me," she added, "a couple more details just for final proof. "The password is Princess5, and the IP address cannot be traced back to this location. Right, dad?"

Gabe looked at Officer Harris stating, "I didn't even tell you the password, Chris. This blows my mind." Her father sat silent trying to come up with a reasonable explanation.

Gabriella knew her father's scientific mind would try to analyze all possibilities and she simply stated, "There is only one way to see this, dad. It's supernatural."

After the initial shock, the questions began to pour out. "What did she see in the future? How would it affect their project?"

She shared with them some of the events she saw play out just to test the waters on how they would react. She did not say anything about the deep friendship she and the Officer Chris Harris had developed. She knew full well how Caleb would react to that bit of information. She had too many unanswered questions about her untime still to sort out before too many details were shared.

Aaron interjected his opinion, "Isn't it possible, Gabi, that you heard our conversations about prophecy while in a coma and it became part of some futuristic dream?" He saw the others did not care for his comment and attempted to explain further: "I'm just saying, let's look at all possibilities here. A lot of what you're telling us we discussed in your hearing distance. Even some of it was on the news. Maybe it all wrapped together in your mind and played out as if you were actually living it. Don't get me wrong, I'm not judging here, but we all want to understand what really happened. I'm sure you do, too, right?"

"No one wants that more than I do, Aaron, believe me; but how do you explain the security room and the password?" She questioned in a somber voice.

"I guess time will tell," Aaron reasonably replied.

"Exactly," Caleb jumped to her defense. "If things Gabi saw start actually happening then we all will know." He reached for her hand and pulled her closer. "I'm right beside you whatever the future holds."

Dr. Brotman echoed Caleb's words. "We all are, Gabi. We are living the end days and we will see things never seen before." He quoted from the book of Acts: "*And it shall come to pass in the last days, saith God, I will pour out My Spirit upon all flesh; and your sons and your daughters shall prophesy, and your young men shall see visions, and your old men shall dream dreams.*"

"No doubt we are in the final days of time as we know it," Gabe confirmed. "It could very well be that Gabi is fulfilling ancient prophecies. I've prayed for many years she would know the truth of the Word of God, and now she is living it. I've always believed she was chosen for a very special purpose."

"If you only knew, Dad," she thought but did not say verbally.

It was after midnight when Sandee suggested the team all get some rest. "Tomorrow you'll be refreshed and ready to get back to discussing the project. Professor is chomping at the bit." She patted his shoulder in affection.

"Yes, I am," he admitted, pushing himself from his chair.

"Gabi, you're rooming with me," Faith informed her, "and I've got extra clothes and toiletries you can borrow since your bag was left at the hospital."

"Thank you." She answered her, deciding not to mention the turquoise bracelet again. She would treasure the memory and that would never be lost. "I'm going to stay up for a while." She glanced at Caleb indicating they needed some private time.

"I can take a subtle hint, my daughter, even though it was not so subtle," he laughed. "You two kids have a lot of time to make up for." As he was leaving for his bedroom he motioned for KJ. "You want to take a quick look at the security room? That's where my computer is. You can get started researching first thing in the morning."

KJ followed him through his bedroom door and shortly the entire bunker heard an explosive "Wow!"

The whole team went running to see what had impressed KJ so greatly. Lots of chatter filled the room and they felt a sense of relief they were not totally cut off from the world around them.

In short order, Gabe ushered them back towards their bedrooms, finally leaving Caleb and Gabriella to be alone for the first time since before her collapse.

"Before you say anything, Gabi, I have something to say." Caleb reached into his pocket and retrieved his grandmother's antique ring. The ring he had placed on Gabriella's finger when he asked her to marry him. The same ring she threw at him when she was so angry, thinking he had deceived her. Oh, how she regretted her horrible actions.

"Let's try this again," he softly spoke, getting down in front of her chair on one knee? "You know I love you beyond what human words can express. I'm asking again, will you marry me?"

She nodded her head with tears of joy streaming down her face as he placed the finger once again upon her finger. "Oh, Caleb, I love you so much," she declared throwing her arms around his neck. "Yes, yes and double yes." He took her fully into his arms and neither was thinking of what tomorrow would bring. This moment was all that mattered.

— CHAPTER 11 —

The sun was rising over majestic Mt. Hermon as the birds sang in nature's harmony. The rays cascaded down the mountains illuminating the glistening fall foliage kissed with the morning dew. Tranquil streams of water flowing down the hills among the picturesque array of autumn flowers gave the illusion that all was well with the world. However, nature was not reflecting the danger of Dr. Brotman's team being held in underground protective custody.

KJ was already in the security room hard at work on the computer. There were too many dots not connecting and he was determined to find some answers. It was now apparent to everyone that the assassination attempted on Dr. Brotman was done by professionals, internationally connected.

Gabe joined KJ pulling a chair next to the security monitors which surveilled both inside and outside of the lodge. A quick glance showed nothing of concern. With a sigh of relief, he turned to KJ. "Can I interrupt you for a minute?"

KJ turned to face Gabe with full attention. "Sure, what's up?"

"There are things I know and things I suspect. I need help figuring out if the two are connected. You're the computer genius and I'm praying you can help me find some answers."

"There's only one way to find out," KJ answered turning back to his computer. "Where do we start?"

"First, I need to explain where my thought process is going. You've just recently become part of the professor's team and what I'm analyzing goes back for decades. Professor and Sandee are the only two other people alive who know all the details." An expression of regret crossed Gabe's face as he continued. "It boils down to this: because of me everyone involved in this project, or even slightly associated with it, is in danger. It's the result of me knowing too much."

"Too much about what?" KJ questioned. "I do know some of it. Gabi shared portions of what she was reading in your journal about the extra-terrestrial research you were doing, and you had a meeting with the CIA in Washington D.C. which turned out to be the wrong thing to do. Right? My details other than that are pretty sketchy."

"I made the big mistake of trusting the CIA. I thought they would appreciate my research and want to investigate it further. I had taken it as far as I could with the resources available to me. I had no idea how the Pandora's box I opened and all the multitude of revelations it would spill out. I've since realized none of the three letter agencies can be trusted, including both the CIA and the FBI; any agency foreign or domestic connected to the US Government, cannot be trusted. I'm not talking about the little guys who are employees just doing what they're told, I'm referring to the hierarchy who are all in cahoots together, worldwide. Discovering this corruption, plus my research, put me on their Ten Most Wanted list. The only way I could protect Gabi was to fake my death." Regret still reflected in his eyes, remembering all the pain he caused her. "That plan worked well for over twelve years. Gabi believes they now know I'm alive; and if they do know, it will explain why after all these years everyone involved now must be in protective custody."

KJ had suspicions of his own, but no one had ever put it as matter of fact as Gabe had just done. "I don't doubt any of it," he agreed. "But I also don't understand any of it. I need more details."

"I know you do and that's what we both need." Gabe agreed. "I've attempted over the years to piece it all together, but I always hit a wall. No doubt, they create those walls, so they won't be exposed."

"Everyone refers to this enemy as they. Do you know who *they* are?"

"That's what I need your help with, KJ. Professor and I both agree on some extraordinarily strong possibilities, but we have no proof...yet," he answered emphasizing the last word. "And if we're right, well, I'll stop there for now. Our suspicions need to be discussed with the entire team at the same time. We're all in this together."

Gabe pushed himself from his chair and patted KJ on the shoulder. "Let's go get some of that coffee I smell. I'm sure Professor will be ready to get into the crux of all this very soon."

Sandee was knocking on bedroom doors as she announced: "Breakfast in 30 minutes."

Slowly the bedrooms emptied, and the team gathered around the table. Gabriella sat down next to Caleb and leaned over to give him a quick kiss announcing, "Good morning, my husband to be." She held up her hand displaying her engagement ring.

"Yeah," Faith exclaimed, pushing her chair back and circling the table to give her best friend a big hug. "This time don't mess it up," she teased her friend.

"No way," Gabriella answered. "Believe me, I have seen the light, literally."

Congratulations were echoing around the table. Gabe was smiling ear to ear finally seeing his daughter experiencing complete joy, spiritually and physically. His prayers had been answered; however, he wondered how joyful their future could be knowing they were living the end of days. He would not voice those concerns. Instead, he would plan for the future for as long as there continued to be one.

"Maybe I will actually get to walk my daughter down the aisle to give her hand in marriage, and to a man I highly approve of."

Caleb answered him with a smile and a sincere, "Thank you, sir."

Gabriella's heart was running over with love for both men. There were no words to describe the emotions she felt having her father and her soul mate by her side. "I know we can't make plans right now for the wedding, but being with Caleb and knowing that day is coming is all I need. We've got to get out of the bunker before life can resume."

The celebratory mood began to shift as they focused on their current situation. Office Harris now felt like a friend more than a protector after being secluded with them in the bunker during the war. He was privy to all conversations and often participated in them.

It was obvious the officer had something important to say so the team hushed, allowing him to speak. "Before you all get started with your project, I wanted to update you on a couple of things. You all know there is no cell phone reception here in the bunker so the only way I can talk to Detective Richards is to go back out the tunnel the way we came in. So, I made a trip out before you all were up this morning."

Faith immediately interrupted him. "When we came to the lodge last week, we had to leave our phones in Gabi's condominium in Haifa because they might be tracked. What if they track yours, Chris?"

He held his phone up for them to see. 'This is a KalOS flip phone, it's an analog phone which is impossible to tap or trace. All police officers use these so we can communicate freely." He sensed their relief and continued: "Richards told me after we safely escaped the hospital, he had to get Dr.

Nicholson and the clerk in the EEG department out also. Apparently, what we suspected was in fact the case. They were surveilling all of us and knew as soon as we left Gabi's hospital room. Any person these guys thought might know anything about our escape became a target. That became evident when..." he hesitated to tell them the rest.

"When what?" Dr. Brotman pushed him to continue.

He took a long deep breath and slowly exhaled and paced back and forth before continuing. Gabriella felt a sharp twinge in her stomach, remembering Chris dealing with his frustrations exactly this way when she saw visions of him in the future. She knew him so well that the challenge of covering that deep friendship was growing. She struggled to keep a normal countenance as he continued to relay Detective Richards information.

"When they tried to get information from the janitor that helped you escape, Professor." Chris answered, not wanting to give them the full details. He tried to move on with information when Dr. Brotman stopped him.

"Is he okay?" Dr. Brotman pushed for an answer. "Did Doc and that clerk get out?"

"Richards said Dr. Nicholson and the clerk are safe in protective custody, unfortunately the janitor was in a coma when the doctor last saw him." Chris decided not to tell them Richards had checked with the hospital late last night and Joshua had passed away.

Dr. Brotman shook his head with disbelief. "This is my fault. He was helping me and didn't even know why. He did it as a favor for Doc, that was all he knew." The professor very seldom showed extreme emotions; however, there were tears forming in his eyes and he did not even attempt to hold them back. "God forgive me."

Sandee walked over and put her arm on his shoulder in comfort. "No one is to blame, Professor. "Right, Chris?"

"Absolutely right. When you're dealing with this level of evil, they stop at nothing to get what they want." He admitted.

"How about Mrs. Nicholson?" Dr. Brotman asked, trying to control his quivering voice. "She must be a target too, since she was here with us during the war."

"Richards has an officer surveilling their home until he can get her safely out. He's been working night and day on making sure everyone is safe so he can get back down to business on the case." Chris knew the severity of her situation, but no one needed to worry more than they already were.

"He told me to check in with him every day for updates and assured me he had some good leads to follow up on."

"Can he have someone check on my family and make sure they're okay?" Faith asked. "I know they're worried sick about me." Aaron and KJ chimed in wanting to know about their families.

"He's already thought about that, too. He said he needs to determine who he can trust to delegate to. Right now, he trusts no one."

KJ and Aaron looked at each other, knowing this was yet another confirmation that the trust factor, or lack of, was dominating everything.

"He will let me know asap." Chris again kept information from the team knowing their families most likely were being monitored in the event they tried to make contact or return home. More worry was something Dr. Brotman's team did not need.

Gabriella saw both discouragement and fear in Faith's face and felt guilt overwhelm her, realizing she personally had everyone she loved safely with her in the bunker, even her father after years of separation. Everyone else secluded safely in this subterranean hiding place had loved ones outside in harm's way. Guilt was joined with great apprehension and grave concern for the families of her friends. It was only common sense that Detective Richards could not have enough police officers to protect everyone connected to this group.

She interjected into the conversation: "We must continually pray Psalms 91 over your families for protection. There may not be enough police officers, but our Heavenly Father has a multitude of guardian angels, and they are waiting to be dispatched."

The entire team focused on Gabriella and was amazed at the transformation from a woman who had been greatly deceived by an evil spirit to this woman proclaiming the Word of God. When she collapsed just prior to the war, she was angry at everyone for not believing she had supernatural powers given to her by an Ascended Master of the universe. When she awoke, she had been totally transformed following the true God of the universe. No one was doubting something miraculous took place during the time she appeared to be comatose.

Dr. Brotman agreed with her. "Yes, we have the powers of heaven which can be released by praying for those we love," He looked directly at Gabriella. "We have proof prayer changes things sitting here among us."

Gabe wrapped his daughter in his arms and kissed her cheek. "Sometimes it takes years to see our prayers answered, but we keep praying and believing. The psalmist David wrote that God sees every tear we cry and stores them in a bottle. Let's pray now."

The team made a circle praying for their loved ones, for each other and for wisdom in the coming days ahead. The sweet presence of the Ruach ha-Kodesh filled the atmosphere confirming their prayers had been heard.

Chris felt the atmosphere change in the room. "This is all very new to me, but I know it's real. I just don't understand."

"You will," Gabriella stated as if she knew something no one else knew.

He looked directly at her. "You sound so sure."

"I am sure, Chris." She was aware Jews did not believe in the Messiah Yeshua and accepting him as Savior went against everything Chris had been taught; however, she had already seen the future and knew he would accept Yeshua as his Lord and Savior. "Why not make that decision right now to follow The Lamb of God who died for your sins?"

Tears welled up in his eyes. "I wasn't going to tell anyone this, but I had a dream last night. In my dream Gabi was praying with me. It was just a dream, but I felt this same presence. I prayed that if Yeshua is the Messiah, I wanted to live my life for him."

Dr. Brotman put his arms around Chris's shoulders and tenderly spoke. "I don't believe that was just a dream, my friend. Is that the true prayer of your heart?"

"Yes," Chris whispered. "I don't know if my parents would ever approve," Chris reluctantly admitted. "I've always been taught the coming of the Messiah was a future event."

"I believe you will be very surprised," Gabriella stated confidently. Again, she decided not to reveal all she had seen in the future. "Perhaps your parents have already seen the truth and have been praying for you." She knew it to be true but left it as a puzzle for him to piece together.

"Let's pray, Chris. Are you ready to become a child of God?" Dr. Brotman led him in the sinner's prayer and another child was born into the eternal kingdom. Everyone secluded in this lodge hideaway was all in one accord.

That spiritual unity would be their guiding force in the truths about to be revealed, truths so shocking it would alter their entire project.

— CHAPTER 12 —

The mood was somber as Dr. Brotman's team gathered around him to discuss The Omega Watchers Project. There had been many changes since they first arrived at the lodge and now even the project itself was about to take on an entirely new dimension.

For the first time, they were all in one accord spiritually. Also, for the first time, Gabe Russell was with them, instead of monitoring from a distance. Gabriella no longer needed the black box with her father's journal to know the truth, he was sitting close beside her ready to answer questions and reveal even deeper truths discovered since he faked his death and the journal entries ended.

Gabriella snuggled between Caleb and her father on the couch as they focused on the professor. She wanted both men to be as close as possible. The constant nagging thought remained that at any moment she would find herself in an alternate existence separated from them again. She turned towards her father and gave him a kiss and a big hug.

"I love you, Dad," she whispered. "Don't you dare leave me again."

Her father briefly held her in his arms emotionally replying, "Never again, Princess, never again."

Dr. Brotman allowed them a bit of time by shuffling his papers in preparation for discussion. Momentarily, he began by opening in prayer asking for wisdom and direction. "Father, we know we have entered the end days and the ancient prophecies are coming to fruition all around us. Let us be like the sons of Issachar who discerned the times and had great wisdom to know what to do. We are your vessels, Lord, ready to be filled with knowledge and understanding of the days in which we live. Amen." All the voices in the room echoed, "Amen."

He opened by addressing the archaeological team, "It's only been a few weeks since you returned from Saudi Arabia and yet it seems a lifetime ago, so much has happened."

Gabriella jested, "You got that right, Professor," looking from Caleb to her dad.

"True, but that's not exactly what I meant," he smiled. "You know, Gabi, your father had no intention of letting you know he was still alive; he knew it still wasn't safe for you...or for any of us in this room. When you collapsed, he made the immediate decision to be with you, no matter what the consequences might be. I do believe it was the timing of Yahweh. The return of Gabe from the dead is going to be a major asset to our project as we go forward. Right, Gabe?"

He nodded in agreement, "There was nothing that could have stopped me from being with my daughter when I thought I might lose her forever." The very thought sent a rush of agony through his soul. "I am praising The Lord she is okay and restored to us is a woman of God." His tone changed as he addressed the issues at hand. "However, now we have a tangled web to unravel, and the strands have already started separating. KJ is going to help me research to see how all these strands are connected."

Dr. Brotman agreed there was a lot of work still to do. "I thought we were reaching the end of our project with the cave discovery; but, in fact, it has instead opened what I see now as the missing element in all my research."

Gabriella was the first to comment, "The return of the Nephilim is not the crux of the research any longer?"

The professor reached to the side table by his recliner and retrieved his pipe. The team waited as he lit the cherry tobacco soon filling the room with the familiar fragrance. This was his sign a profoundly serious discussion was about to ensue. "Yes and no, Gabi. The Nephilim is a big piece to the prophetic puzzle, and one I have dedicated many years of my life to researching, but it's not a puzzle unto itself. It's part of a much bigger picture."

"I'm really confused, Professor," Aaron interjected.

"I understand," Dr. Brotman replied patiently. "What we have all discovered together sets the stage for placing the fallen angels into the total picture of the end of days." He looked at Chris and explained: "I understand this is all new to you. We'll fill in the blanks as we go along so, hopefully, you can grasp the importance of what we're doing."

"When you say end of days, what do you mean? The apocalypse?" Chris questioned.

"Again, my answer would be yes and no. The apocalypse refers to the final destruction of the earth as we know it, a specific event. What I am referring to are the events that led up to the apocalypse. The signs are laid out for us all through the Bible as the ancient prophets wrote, but specifically in the final book as given to John the Revelator almost two thousand years ago. He saw in a vision the final years before the return of Yeshua, our Messiah to rule and reign on earth, the worst years humanity would ever experience. Yeshua said that unless those days be shortened no man would survive, that's how bad it will get."

Gabriella's mind immediately went to the visions given to her, knowing they were confirmation of the ancient prophecies being fulfilled in her lifetime. Her thoughts were brought back to the current conversation when Chris questioned further.

"And this return of the Nephilim you guys talk about is one of those signs?"

"Definitely yes," Dr. Brotman stated emphatically. "Aaron can fill you in later. He's both a biblical scholar who truly is discerning the times, as well as a great archaeologist."

Aaron felt compelled to give an explanation: "Actually, it is how the two intertwine that created my passion. Living in Israel I had the opportunity to dig truths both out of the Bible and the biblical ground it is written about." He patted Chris' shoulder in a gesture of friendship. "We'll have that conversation about our research later. You'll be up to speed in no time."

"Yes, you will," Gabriella stated with strong conviction, based on her visions of the future.

Chris was beginning to suspect Gabriella had a spiritual dimension which he did not yet understand. He was keeping his police officer radar on full alert for everything she shared with the group not wanting to miss anything that could be even the slightest clue to breaking the police case.

"Let's recap where we are," Dr. Brotman continued. "All the ancient prophecies are aligning in this generation. Yeshua told us in Matthew 24 and Luke 21 what to look for right before he returned. Those physical signs are happening everyday so that's no mystery. When we get into the Book of Revelation, we find metaphors and mysteries which are much more difficult to interpret. We all know there are so many opinions of that final book in the Bible that it can make one's mind so overloaded, many just don't even try to understand. I believe that is the very reason Revelation begins with the promise a special blessing is upon everyone that reads it, a promise not given anywhere else in the Bible."

The professor relit his pipe and took another puff once gain filling the air with the fragrant aroma before continuing his recap: "The greatest mystery in the final book of the Bible is even called a mystery." He picked up his Bible and turned to Revelation 17:5 and read, "A*nd on her forehead a name was written: MYSTERY, BABYLON THE GREAT, THE MOTHER OF HARLOTS AND OF THE ABOMINATIONS OF THE EARTH.*" He took another puff and emphasized, "It's translated in all caps for a reason, it is a mystery to be solved."

He hesitated, watching the anticipation in the faces of his team. "Our next assignment, Team, and this is the biggest challenge we have had thus far - to solve the identity of Mystery Babylon." The faces of anticipation morphed into confusion. The team was expecting an answer to the mystery. "I know none of this makes any sense but believe me it will. All that has happened since you returned from Saudi Arabia is starting to paint a picture for me of just who Mystery Babylon could be." Then he added, "I truly believe the Nephilim is a big part of identifying the Harlot." He sat back in his recliner, took another puff from his pipe, and waited for the questions to flow, knowing they would.

The buts, whys and hows flooded the conversation until Dr. Brotman held up his hand signaling enough. "Step by step we go, and you all will have a major part in unraveling this conundrum. First, Gabe has a list of things for KJ to research. Gabi, you and Caleb can help with that too. Four people is all we can squeeze into the security room. Faith and Aaron, your research is going to be in the ancient scriptures. I have plenty of notes, books, and references for you to get started," he paused desperately wishing he had the books from his office library at Haifa University. Knowing that was not possible, at least for now, he continued his team organization. "Chris, if you want to join Faith and Aaron, it will be an effective way for you to learn about our project from the biblical perspective. I will be assisting your biblical research while Gabe oversees the internet searches."

"Sure thing," Chris quickly agreed.

"Sandee, of course, will be cooking and taking care of all of us during our unwanted stay here as well as participating in the project updates." Dr. Brotman warmly smiled, "She's been with me since day one and knows as much about it as any of us."

"And with that," Sandee announced, "I'm going into the stock room to plan meals and organize supplies we will need for the next few days." She looked directly at Chris, "Do you think I need to prepare for longer?"

"I wish I could answer that," he sadly replied. "Plan for a few days and then we can reassess."

"Sure thing," she replied on her way through the kitchen area and disappearing into the stock room.

Gabriella was thankful she would be working with Caleb and her father. Every moment together was precious, and she cherished each one. There were only two chairs in the security room, so Caleb brought two extra placing them as close to the computer monitors as possible. Once settled Gabe opened the desk drawer and pulled out composition books and pencils for each team member to make notes. In her father's notebook, Gabriella noticed many notes had already been made. She remembered how he organized and researched and, obviously, his methods had not changed during their years of separation.

"KJ, I've got a list here of names and organizations I want to research, and we can discuss them as you find information. We'll work our way down the list one at a time trying to connect the dots." Gabe laid the list in front of KJ and while he waited, monitored the security cameras. Except for the occasional rabbit scurrying by there were no other movements outside the lodge. For now, all was well.

It was very familiar to Gabriella as her father monitored the rooms in the upstairs lodge. She and Chris had monitored those rooms for hours in her supernatural experience. For a moment she closed her eyes and recalled the things she saw in her vision of the future. The lodge was filled with evil men planning world dominance. She saw their faces, heard their names, and was privy to their plans. Forcing her eyes to open she tried to concentrate on the present, the here and now; and wondered if those future events would soon become reality.

KJ interrupted her thoughts. "I have a few links ready. Khazaria? Right, Gabe?" He questioned, wondering where this was all leading.

"Right," he assured. "I just recently heard about this, actually after your last cave exploration, and my gut keeps telling me to dig deeper. What have you got there, KJ?"

"I've brought up several different articles on Khazaria. Let's take a look." KJ skimmed through the history and gave them an overview. "The word khazar means to wander, and there was a barbaric tribe who wandered through several nations over many centuries before finally settling in eastern Turkey bordering Russia. In the 7th Century they declared it their own nation and broke off from Turkey. It's the same area as modern-day Ukraine." KJ read further in the article. "Now this is interesting. What was known as the Silk Road went directly through Khazaria and that seems to be the reason they took that area. It was the main route for merchants coming both from the east and the west to bring their goods by caravan. The Khazarians were extremely evil. They would steal all the travelers' money, and the goods they were transporting to sell. If the merchants tried to defend themselves, the Khazarians simply murdered them. As a result, the rulers of Khazaria became extremely rich." Reading further, KJ hesitated. "I hate reading this part." He hesitated again before reading further. "Any children that were in the caravans would be tortured and sacrificed to the god of the Khazarians." KJ turned and looked at the other three in the room. "This makes me sick."

Gabe nodded his head as if the information was confirming what he already knew. "Child sacrifice has been going on since Lucifer became the god of this world. It's his counterfeit of the blood sacrifices God commanded of Israel in the Torah. Lucifer counterfeits everything Yahweh does, so if The Most High was to receive blood sacrifices, Lucifer demands the same of his followers. Why do you think God prohibited the worship of Baal and Molech? It was child sacrifice to Lucifer," he answered his own question. "Even though it's not directly mentioned in the New Testament it is mentioned many times in the Old, and it has not ceased to this day. In fact," he dropped his head and tears formed in his eyes as he struggled to form the right words. "There is so much more to this information, but not now."

"Abortion being one of the ways," Gabriella stated with a voice full of sorrow, thinking she knew what he was about to say, not realizing it was going to be much darker and much more horrendous than she ever could imagine.

"True," her father responded, regaining his composure. "Those are sacrifices we all can see. As horrible as abortion is, child sacrifice goes much deeper and much darker than that; and the Bible warns us that in the end days, this evil will again be done openly as it was in the days of the ancient prophets." He decided to go no deeper, not yet.

"What happened to Khazaria, KJ? Does the article say?" Gabriella asked. "I've never heard of that nation or those people in all my history studies."

He searched through several articles. "I believe a lot of the information has been intentionally suppressed and what is available appears to be conflicting information; but from a couple of these articles the Khazarians became so barbaric with no travelers being safe on the Silk Road that Russia and Turkey, who bordered them to the east and west, joined together to invade their country and put a stop to the evil. Apparently that was sometime around the tenth century. The King of Khazaria and his oligarchs took their immense wealth and fled to western Europe subtly integrating as wandering Jews, taking on new identities and assuming Jewish names."

"That's all really interesting," Caleb commented, "but I don't see how it fits with anything we've been doing."

"There still a lot of digging to do," Gabe answered him. "But I believe you will soon see, at least I hope we're moving in the right direction."

"Where do I go from here?" KJ queried. "That was just a quick overview."

"Two main things we need. Where did the Khazarians originate from and what happened to them after they integrated into the Jews of Europe." Gabe answered, getting up from his chair. and motioning for Gabriella and Caleb to join him. "Let's give KJ some time to research. Another cup of coffee sounds good to me."

KJ immediately turned to the computer and began searching various links and making notes as he investigated. Caleb wrapped his arm around Gabriella's shoulders pulling her close as they exited the security room.

Gabriella noticed her father's black leather box sitting on the floor close to his bedside. "Dad, I've got a lot of questions about that box," she said walking past it. "There's so much I didn't understand about the extraterrestrial investigations."

"And so much I want to explain. It's another piece to this massive prophetic puzzle and all these pieces are about to become one big picture. I truly believe that." Her father's voice reflected no doubt whatsoever. "Everything we've gone through was preparing us for this time, Gabi, for such a time as this."

She took his hand in hers treasuring the moment. "I know, dad. I know so much more than you could possibly imagine. Let's find time to talk privately." She turned to Caleb and clarified, "Caleb included, of course. He must know everything." She took both of their hands and led them back to the couch to join the others who were hard at work.

"Making any headway?" Dr. Brotman asked them as the trio settled on the couch.

"Getting some foundation laid, Professor," Gabe answered. "KJ is researching some more details and then we will share with the rest of you. How about you?"

"We've been searching the scriptures for every reference to Babylon. We know it was the first worldwide kingdom when Israel went into their captivity, but Babylon is used many times not as the nation but referring to evil governments or societies."

Aaron entered the conversation with further explanation: "We also know Babylon originates from the word babel. Babel is when God confused the languages and scattered the people all over the earth because they were trying to build a tower to the heavens. The details are written in Genesis 11 of Nimrod and the tower. Everything in Torah is there for a reason, both literally and prophetically." Aaron looked at Dr. Brotman signaling for him to resume with his information.

"The Tower of Babel was not just a tower built of man-made bricks, they were trying to create a portal, a portal for demonic spirits in the supernatural realm to reenter the earth. Remember, Genesis 6 says the Nephilim were both before the flood and after and they needed a supernatural gateway created for their return." He paused for a moment and ended with, "The Babylonian Kingdom was not only the first and most powerful earthly kingdom, but I also believe it will be the last worldwide kingdom just before the Antichrist takes the throne as the world leader. If I'm correct, that means it exists now." Dr. Brotman leaned back in his chair with a look of certainty in his analysis.

"This *is* a mystery, one that makes no sense whatsoever to me," Gabriella admitted.

Dr. Brotman understood her confusion. He felt the very same way when he first began to question the possibilities. "Like I said, Gabi, it is a big piece of the overall picture that will soon become crystal clear. Let me correct that, I believe it is the main piece and every other prophetic piece of the puzzle is connected to Mystery Babylon. The connections throughout the scriptures from Genesis to Revelation are like a silver thread tying all the prophecies together to this main event. Yahweh said he would do nothing unless he first tells the prophets. So, the writings of the prophets are our end of days outline. We just have to build it out based on discerning the times."

KJ rejoined them with some notes in hand. "I've got that information you want, Gabe."

Gabe quickly filled the others in on their Khazarian research which none of them, except for the professor, understood why these ancient people mattered, not until KJ read his notes: "The Khazarian's ancestry is traced back through many nations. They would temporarily settle and then be forced to leave because they were so evil. They were so evil they were referred to as the serpent people, some believing they possessed serpent DNA. From my research, the tribe of people that eventually became known as Khazarians originated in ancient Babylon during the time of Nimrod." The room was completely silent as pieces began to fit together.

"Serpent DNA? Hybrids? Isn't that what the Nephilim were?" Chris questioned quickly catching on.

"Now we are getting somewhere," Gabe's excitement was escalating. "Did you find out what happened after they fled west through Europe, disguising themselves as Jews?"

KJ's countenance emitted both excitement and a grave concern. "That's the part you won't believe."

— Chapter 13 —

KJ had everyone's full attention. "There is still a lot of research to do into the Khazarian roots and timelines; but, in my researching I found the Khazarian king, and his inner circle of oligarchs kept practicing ancient Babylonian black-magic, also known as Secret Satanism, as they integrated into the European Society. Their worship and sacrifices to Satan empowered them with the knowledge and ability to acquire great wealth, and ultimately to overthrow kingdoms, taking control of their governments and their wealth." KJ referred to his notes on what to share next. "There are just too many details to give right now. I need to tie more of the information together and that could take a while. It appears history was intentionally buried deep regarding Khazaria in an effort to bury their tracks."

"The darker the evil, the more Satan keeps it secret," Dr. Brotman replied. "But, just as Yahweh said, He would do nothing unless He first tells his prophets, Satan also *must* follow that rule. His demonic plans must be first revealed." He thought for a minute, then said, "We now have another research project to add to our list: how has this been accomplished with humanity not realizing what was happening?"

Gabe's anticipation was beyond control. He could not wait any longer. "Who, KJ? Who are these Khazarian people today?"

KJ's face still reflected his unbelief of what he had found. "These are the very people society has accepted for centuries as powerful world and financial leaders without any idea they are Luciferian, names you will immediately recognize with the Rothschild and Rockefeller families being at the top of the list. There is a list of thirteen connected families, and they do not marry outside of these bloodlines so to keep the purity of their ancient Babylonian blood. These families still conduct their black magic rituals and sacrifices to keep control of the nations. The term we are all familiar with is the Deep State; and the Deep State Cabal is deeply hidden and connected all around the world."

KJ hesitated to see if there were any questions. "Go on," Dr. Brotman instructed. "I want to know everything you've found."

"Okay," KJ answered, going to the next point on his notes. "There are the major pillars that control the world: religion, finance, government, education, business, medicine, media, and entertainment. These thirteen families have systematically taken control of all of them."

"How?" Faith questioned in bewilderment, expressing the question the entire team wanted to know.

KJ continued his explanation: "I found this quote from 1815 spoken by Nathaniel Rothschild: I care not what puppet is placed upon the throne of England to rule the Empire on which the sun never sets. The man who controls the British money supply controls the British Empire, and I control the British money supply."

Gabe interjected, "Henry Kissinger made a similar statement in the 1970s when he stated: he who controls the money controls the world."

"Exactly," KJ continued. "and from what I have read, these thirteen families own over ninety percent of the wealth of the world. With their money they have taken control of these pillars of society which ultimately control all individual lives and families; and their end game purpose is a one world government giving Lucifer total control of the earth. They've accomplished all this through Luciferian black magic and without most of humanity even realizing what was happening."

"And according to II Corinthians 4:4, Satan is the god of this world. No doubt these Khazarians are his demonic oligarchs," Gabe added.

Dr. Brotman sit straight up in his recliner. "This makes so much sense," he exclaimed. "These people have taken on a Jewish identity without even a drop of Jewish DNA in their blood." John wrote in the Book of Revelation 3:9: *behold, I will make them of the synagogue of Satan, which say they are Jews, and are not, but do lie.*"

In unison, a gasp of shock filled the room. Each person was trying to process how these world-renowned and highly respected families had deceived the nations, becoming the fulfillment of Bible prophecy.

Dr. Brotman picked up his Bible quickly turning the pages. "We know Mystery Babylon is Lucifer's spiritual kingdom on this earth. There are many descriptions of her in the Bible, listen to this one in Revelation 18:23: *Your merchants were the great men of the earth. By your sorceries all the nations were deceived.*" He laid his Bible in his lap and interpreted the prophecy for his team. "Who are the most important people on the earth today, the ones who are in control of the merchants, the ones who control through deception? It is obviously this thirteen family Deep State Luciferian Cabal. How did Mystery Babylon in the Book of Revelation get control of the nations? Through magic spells and sorceries, they have *deceived* all the nations. That's exactly what this evil cabal has done with their Babylonian black magic."

Aaron smiled from ear to ear. "Professor, do you really think Mystery Babylon are the Khazarian Jews?"

"I believe it's very possible," he exclaimed. "The Deep State Cabal, controlled by the Khazarian Jew families, could very well be the center piece of the prophetic puzzle which all other pieces will build around. Team, there is still much research to be done and pieces to find, to complete this picture; but we are definitely on the right track."

Dr. Brotman leaned back in his recliner and re-lit his pipe, processing the revelatory information. "The last book in the Bible tells us what will be revealed in the end of days so we will know the truth and not be deceived. Lucifer's millennia of lies and deceptions are now being exposed which is added verification of where we are on the prophetic timeline."

KJ further solidified the professor's analysis: "I've barely scratched the surface of the details, there are so many more to verify; but I have discovered proof that since the birth of America, this satanic cabal has been behind the scenes taking control of her government and financial system to add to their centuries of controlling the European nations...and their ultimate plan to control the world."

Chris was trying to quickly assimilate the information. "You are saying this rich cabal is controlling entire nations behind the scenes, am I understanding right?"

"Absolutely," KJ answered. "For example, in 1913 the Federal Reserve was established in America. The Federal Reserve is neither a federal organization nor are they reserving money for the United States. It is owned and controlled by these thirteen families as a private entity, giving them total dominion over America's finances. There're too many details to go in to, but the overview is US citizens pay their taxes to the Internal Revenue Service, which is also not a government agency but another private entity owned by guess who?" He paused and then verified, "Yep, the same thirteen families. The IRS was established as a private corporation for the purpose of being a collection contractor for the government. The taxes are collected by the IRS then deposited into the Federal Reserve. The Federal Reserve loans it back to America with interest, which, according to the US Constitution is illegal; and yet it's continued for well over a century."

"I have always believed they were government agencies," Faith admitted, totally amazed.

"Most Americans don't even know the truth. Because it says federal, they just assume," KJ continued to explain. "This system of usury began in 1798 when Nathan Rothschild, head of the Rothschild Dynasty at that time, established the first fiat banking system. They continued their banking system throughout Europe and eventually into the English-speaking countries, creating the Central Bank, which now controls the international banking system."

"This is blowing my mind," Chris admitted. "I've never heard any of this before."

KJ responded, "They planned it that way, Chris. It was a Luciferian long game, and each cabal generation kept the strategy going. Satan's ultimate purpose of ruling this world keeps inching closer and closer to his total dominion. It's like boiling a frog. The heat increases so gradually that the frog doesn't realize what's happening until it's too late. These Luciferians first disguised themselves as English Aristocrats, deceived the people into trusting they were using their wealth for the good of the common man, and they exploded their wealth with an illegal banking system."

"I'm missing something here," Chris questioned again. "If people were willing to use their banking system, why was it illegal?"

"Good question," KJ answered. "Fiat is a type of currency that's not backed by any commodity like gold or silver. A government can allow it to be used as legal tender, but it is still just paper. With nothing required for backing, the cabal can print all the paper money they want converting it into their personal wealth through bank loans, credit cards, anything you pay interest on, and all the establishments that loan money are owned and controlled by these thirteen families. With their black magic and riches, they have hijacked all the other pillars of society just like Professor read from Revelation. I'll be digging deep and reporting back on the details, but I already have a glimpse at how deep this evil goes. So deep and dark they are often referred to as the Khazarian Mafia."

"Now that is a name I have heard before," Chris' voice was filled with excitement. "This is starting to make sense."

KJ knew the detective wheels were turning in Chris' mind. "There is so much more, and we can spend some time together in the security room going down internet rabbit holes, if you want to."

"Sure do," Chris quickly replied. "I have some specific things now to look for."

Gabriella's thoughts immediately went to the men that she and Chris had watched on the security cameras making plans for a One World Government. She believed her visions were clues to both what she was hearing now and to the prophetic days ahead. She wanted to blurt out everything she had seen in her vision of the future but decided to take a totally different approach.

"KJ, in your research did you come across any information of The Vatican being connected to this Luciferian cabal?" Gabriella was going to pace herself to ask questions, one at a time.

KJ looked surprised. He glanced down at his notes and replied: "That's at the top of my list to do more digging on. One of the many rabbit holes I just mentioned to Chris, but why would you even suspect that, Gabi?"

"It's one of the many things I saw in my visions. You might also want to research the Black Pope." She decided that was as far as she would recommend at this point.

"Who or what is the Black Pope," Faith questioned. "Never heard that term." She looked at Dr. Brotman expecting an answer.

Dr. Brotman replied, "As you know, Jewish history, languages and ancient writings of the prophets have always been my area of study so my information on The Vatican is limited. I am aware the Catholic Church owns a lot of land in Israel including the Church of the Holy Sepulcher, traditionally believed to be the place of our Messiah's death and burial. There was an agreement made between the Israeli Government and the Holy See back in the 1990s regarding land, taxes, etc., but I don't know the details. I do know, The Vatican has deep roots here in Israel and they have never recognized her as a sovereign nation."

"As KJ says, I believe this rabbit hole goes really deep." Gabriella replied. "Let's let KJ do the research and then we'll see if it verifies what I've seen in the future."

KJ was making a note. "If its anywhere on the internet or the dark web, I will find it." He looked towards the kitchen where Sandee was both preparing lunch and listening intently to their conversation. "Right after lunch," he added smiling.

Sandee motioned for the group to gather around the table. Aaron blessed the food and discussion of the Khazarian Jews dominated the conversation.

Chris was trying his best to keep up with the information flow, which was overwhelming. He was starting to question if this evil cabal was in any way connected to the assassination attempt on Dr. Brotman's life. He needed to verify his thought processes. "Am I understanding this correctly," he questioned. "Are you saying this cabal ancestry goes all the way back to the Tower of Babel and they control entire nations, even today?"

KJ answered, "From my research, yes. It all ties together."

"It goes back even farther than the Tower of Babel, Chris," Dr. Brotman continued, "all the way to the beginning in the Garden of Eden. The first written prophecy of our Messiah and the spiritual war that would rage throughout all of time, the war we are specifically in right now, is in Genesis 3:15: *I will put enmity between you and the woman, and between your seed and her seed; he shall bruise your head, and you shalt bruise his heel.*"

Dr. Brotman allowed a moment for Chris to process the scripture before continuing: "There is a literal seed of Satan. This is not metaphoric. It ties into the Watchers in the Book of Enoch, the Nephilim, and amazingly takes us full circle in our project, but then everything in the Bible is circular, not linear. As King Solomon wrote, *what is shall be again.*"

Chris shook his head in confusion, "How in the world do you make all these connections, Professor? My mind is in a continuous battle trying to understand."

"Years of study," Dr. Brotman answered. "You're getting the bottom line to decades of research on many diverse levels. It will take some time to make sense."

"It will be sooner than later," Gabriella thought, but this time she did not speak aloud.

Chris pushed his chair back from the table. "I'm ready to start if you are, KJ?"

"You bet," KJ responded, pushing his chair from the table.

Dr. Brotman addressed the rest of the team: "Aaron, Faith and I have new leads now for our biblical search of Mystery Babylon. I think maybe Gabe, Gabi and Caleb need some time to themselves. They have twelve years of separation to reconcile, and some time alone will do them good."

Gabriella longed for daylight and fresh air. She suggested, "Let's go to the end of the tunnel. I need nature around me to clear my head. The walk will be good for me, too. I need the exercise." She looked at her father and he could read her mind knowing a long explanation of the past would be expected.

— Chapter 14 —

Shortly, the trio was exiting through the pantry into the tunnel with flashlights in hand. As they made their journey through the dark cavern Gabriella began her questions: "Dad, how did you get the idea of this bunker and this secret tunnel to the outside? It really is amazing."

In a voice filled with emotion he answered: "There are so many details to share, Princess. Years of separation to explain and make up for; and I promise I won't leave out a single detail as I did in my journal and letters to you. I wanted you to have all my research, but I knew the grave risk it would be. As you know, most of my research and my journal were in safe keeping for over a decade, until Professor and I thought we were reaching the end of the project and the time had come for you to know the truth."

"All those painful years I thought you were dead, now I understand why you did it, all to protect me." Gabriella was struggling to keep her emotions in check.

"Yes, Gabi, it started out being all about you. Then it became about the protection of the entire team as they all got deeply involved in what started out as my personal project. I was also concerned that with all my efforts I wouldn't be able to keep my research hidden forever. Even the people you trust most can sometimes turn on you. So, for an extra layer of secrecy, there were some things I did not include in the box you received. Only Sandee and Professor know, you might say, the rest of the story."

"I didn't get a chance to read all of what *was* in the box. I intended to read it while we were to be held in protective custody, but...," she paused, remembering the events of that first day at the lodge which changed her life forever.

"I know, Gabi. I can explain everything to you now, you don't have to read it, and I can fill in the blanks not included in the box," her father added as they neared the end of the tunnel and glimmers of daylight appeared before them. "Let's get comfortable outside. We have all afternoon to spend alone together." He patted Caleb on the shoulder. "Alone time with my daughter and soon to be son."

At the exit to the cavern, fresh air was filtering in, giving birth to the hope they could soon be free from their bunker existence. Stepping out of the darkness, the early fall sunshine basked them in warmth. Gabe led them to a grassy area by the creek where they could enjoy the sounds of nature as they shared the depths of their hearts. Gabriella sat in the middle of the two men she loved thanking her Heavenly Father for the time she had with them not knowing how long it would last.

The sound of the water cascading along the mountain streams was a balm to her soul. She closed her eyes and took a deep breath of the mountain air. She did not share that she had been in this same place in her vision, the place where she and Chris camped out when they had to flee from the bunker. It was the night before they escaped from the bunker to briefly hide at the seaside cottage.

Questions as to why all the details of her visions were so vivid kept swirling in her mind. "I know there is a reason, Father, and I trust The Lamb will lead me," she whispered beneath her breath, then forced herself to refocus attention on the present.

"You didn't answer my question about how all this came to fruition, Dad."

Gabe took his daughter's hand and began to explain: "Professor helped me plan details of what would occur after I faked my death. We both knew I had to get out of the United States and assume a new identity. I could not force myself to leave you behind. You had just graduated high school and were looking at various universities to continue your education. It was at that time the circumstances were perfect for me to die of a supposed heart attack. Shortly after my pseudo death is when you received the grant offer to attend Haifa University and it was an offer too good to refuse. Professor and I planned it all in advance. After you arrived at the university, Dr. Brotman would invite you onto his research team, which was a very prestigious position. He knew you were highly capable of the work he needed done, but also a way of keeping continual personal contact and watching over you, reporting back to me. I had hoped he would become a father figure in my place until we could be reunited, which he did. I had to keep my watch over you at a distance. You never noticed that man disguised as a Hasidic Jew that often would be at the same coffee shop you frequented or on campus when you were having classes, and many other places throughout the years, but I was there."

She leaned against her father, and he put his arm around her shoulder continuing his explanation. "I told you that when you were young your mother and I had explored caves at Mt. Hermon. It was at the cabin we rented during that exploration that you were conceived after many years of our hoping for a child. So, even before I moved to Israel, I bought that cabin. I had invested all your mother's life insurance money into new tech companies that were just start-ups at that time and those stock dividends exploded like crazy making me a very wealthy man. You already know that my attorney, Jim Tomaw, held all the money you would need in a trust fund taking care of your expenses until you graduated from Haifa University thereafter he turned the trust fund over to you."

Gabriella's mind immediately went to the vision she had of the Smokey Mountains where The Lamb had led her to Attorney Tomaw and his wife in Cherokee, North Carolina. She had seen what the future held for them, and it was not pleasant. This was another vision she would hold in her heart and say nothing about for now, it was too sad. She simply nodded her head in agreement.

"That cabin is now the guesthouse behind the lodge. Right, Dad?"

Gabe was no longer surprised at the things his daughter already knew. He was convinced most of it she had heard in conversations taking place around her while she was comatose, and the information was embedded in her memory; however, there were some things she knew that were in-explainable.

"Right, Princess. As soon as I moved into the cabin, I began construction on the lodge. The main purpose being a place for the professor's team to both have a retreat and a private place to discuss the project. Of course, my main objective was to have you near me. With the security cameras I could see and hear you, even though I couldn't touch you; and how I longed to hold you in my arms."

Leaning her head on his shoulder, she whispered, "You can now, Dad."

He turned and gave his daughter a full bear hug before he continued: "During the time of watching you, I came to love the entire team from a distance. It was obvious to me in everything Caleb did and said that he loved you deeply. He didn't even try to hide it, and yet you never noticed. Sometimes I wanted to jump through that camera and shake you to wake up. You were letting work consume your life. No one knows better than I do that life offers no promises of tomorrow."

Gabriella knew he was referring to her mother who was murdered. It was her personal reminder to cherish every moment with Caleb not knowing how many more they would have.

"I was so devoted to the project I was missing out on life and love," she admitted. "I know I've said it over and over, Caleb, but I am truly sorry."

He took her hand and held it up softly kissing her palm. "We have each other now, that's all that matters." Her father released her into Caleb's arms. No words were spoken for several minutes.

Gabe allowed them time before continuing. "I had always planned to put a bunker under the lodge for several reasons mainly for temporary protection for the entire team, if needed. One never knows when Israel would be attacked, and bunker living becomes a necessity. However, the plan kept developing as the building project continued. I kept thinking of possible scenarios needing long term protection and kept adding more provisions to be included. When the construction crew was digging out for the bunker, they stopped the work to inform me they had dug into a cavern. I knew it was divine intervention when I explored through the cavern tunnel and found where it exited. It was the perfect avenue of escape from the lodge if the need ever arose. It also allowed me a way to go and come from the lodge without ever being detected if suspicion arose that I was still alive, and efforts made to find me." He paused and laughed out loud, "I never dreamed we would be escaping *into* the tunnel."

Gabriella giggled and squeezed his hand. "God knows what we have need of even before we ask."

Both Gabe and Caleb were still adjusting to her quoting from the Bible when she had never had an interest in even reading it, but they both were extremely thankful for this amazing transformation.

"I planned for every possible scenario I could think of. That garage over there," Gabe pointed towards the small structure camouflaged beneath a grove of trees, "I built that myself. I didn't want anyone to know about the secret tunnel so over time, and I had plenty of it, I completed my project. It took a few years but I'm so glad I did. That garage holds secrets yet to be revealed," he ended with a mysterious tone.

Gabriella started to question what he meant when she was interrupted. "We're all glad you did," Caleb reached around Gabriella hand slapped Gabe's back. "Without the bunker and this way of escape, both in and out, I don't know where we would be." He took a deep breath at the thought, "Maybe dead." He had stayed mostly silent, allowing father and daughter time to share; however, he needed Gabe to know how appreciative he was.

"I'm so thankful for all you've done for us, and beyond thankful we are all still alive and Gabi has her father back."

"I'm just thankful Yahweh made provisions and gave me strength to complete the projects. All glory goes to Him, not me." Gabe never failed to thank his Heavenly Father for guidance through the years of his separation from his daughter.

Gabriella was reflecting on her childhood when her father was not a believer, wondering how different their lives would have been had he believed in Yeshua then. She accepted, nothing can change the past, but she was determined to make the best of every day of her future.

As the afternoon progressed, father and daughter shared memories while they laughed and cried together. Caleb relived the walk down memory lane with them. He understood better now why she was so easily captured by the deception of Arcturus. He also understood why she struggled to trust people, resulting in her extreme emotional displays when she felt betrayed. It was all due to the pent-up anger and hurt that had been festering and building since her mother was murdered when she was only five years old.

Caleb watched Gabriella's beautiful face filled with a joy he had never seen before. He loved the woman who had rejected him throughout the years, but now he loved this transformed woman even more deeply. Now he knew her painful secrets she would previously share with no one. Some of which she had never admitted even to herself, until this moment.

"Dad, let's talk about your journal. All the time I was growing up, you believed in extraterrestrial existence. I well remember all the caves we explored with the ancient drawings which appeared to be like nothing on this earth. When your beliefs changed, why didn't you tell me then? That's the hardest thing to accept in everything I read in your journal."

"I understand, Gabi, I really do. I wanted to explain everything, but I was fully aware of the danger if you knew too much. You were just a teenager and to put you in further danger than you were already in, well, I just couldn't do it. Maybe it was the wrong decision, but I was not willing to take the chance. That's the reason I journaled most everything, so at the right time you would know; and in knowing, understand why it had to be this way."

Her heart agonized, realizing how difficult this had been for her father. "As they say, better late than never. Are you going to tell me now or do I have to wait longer?"

"It's not as simple as a one conversation explanation but we can definitely begin. You read in my journal about how I met Professor and when I realized Ufology was, in fact, a demonic deception?"

She nodded her head affirming and he continued: "After I accepted Yeshua as my Savior and began to research from a Biblical perspective praying for guidance, all the UFO details that never seemed to fit right before, became crystal clear. I do believe people had close encounters, but they were, in reality, encountering demons masquerading as extraterrestrials. I also believe that MK Ultra was used to make people believe they had extraterrestrial encounters and shared them as proof of alien existence."

"MK Ultra?" Caleb questioned.

"MK Ultra for decades was a top-secret CIA project that began in 1953. They would conduct clandestine experiments on unwitting U.S. citizens. They would choose people who had no family connections so the changes they experienced would not be questioned. Drugs were used for mind control and new identities created for that individual. The subject genuinely believed everything they were told during a form of hypnosis. Many times, extraterrestrial encounters would be planted in their consciousness, and it became reality to them, convinced the delusion was real. There was a death bed confession in 1990 of an ex-CIA agent describing how they chose their candidates, erased their memory, and through hypnosis could make them believe and do anything they told them, even brutally torturing, and killing without any remorse whatsoever. Details of this horrendous program became public in 1975 during a U.S. congressional investigation into the widespread CIA activities. Supposedly, the program ceased."

"Supposedly?" Gabriella questioned.

"I'm convinced it never ended," her father explained. "I'm convinced MK Ultra is still used by the CIA and the Israeli Mossad, which are both part of the international corruption. I didn't realize until today with KJ's discoveries that it's all under the control of the Luciferian Khazarian Cabal, every bit of it. With that fact, it all makes more sense. There are so many secret programs that have been exposed, for instance the Blue-Beam Project."

"I've heard of that one," Caleb said. "Not sure what it really is though."

"The mainstream media will tell you it's a conspiracy theory; but let's make one thing perfectly clear, if the MSM says it, believe the opposite. The CIA has been giving them their talking points for decades and they report what they are told to report. True journalism is not seen on TV. That said, the Blue-Beam Project is very real. It's a NASA and United Nations program also connected to making society believe in extraterrestrial existence.

With all the so-called proof they have created of extraterrestrial life, and convincing people UFOs are real, their ultimate goal is to use that deception to create the New World Order. Their plan is to create a simulation, or better said, a hologram that will appear in the sky of the Second Coming of Yeshua. The world will be deceived in believing it is true, because they will see it with their own eyes."

Gabriella was astounded. "Dad, are you serious? Is that what you couldn't tell me?"

"It's a major part of it," he admitted. "But much more still to explain. The main point here is people may not believe what they hear, but they do believe what they see. With modern technology you can make anything appear to be real."

Gabriella decided to share one of her visions. "While I was in the supernatural world, I saw a future event that included something like this. The Virgin Mary appeared over the Vatican for everyone to see. She also spoke to the multitude of people gathered in St. Peter's Square with words of hope after the world had been shaken by a major war. The Pope was declaring her as co-redemptive with Christ. Everyone fell on their knees and worshipped her. The news media filmed it as it happened and the apparition was broadcast around the world. Everyone believed it was real."

There was no doubt in her father's mind she had seen into the future. "That's exactly the way Satan's minions have planned the appearance of the Antichrist." Then he quoted from Matthew 24:24: *"If it were possible, the very elect would be deceived."*

"I know the United Nations is corrupt, but are you saying NASA is too?" Caleb pushed for more clarification.

Gabe nodded further explaining, "The hierarchy is as corrupt as it comes, just like every other government agency; however, the people employed do their job most having no idea what is really going on. I've got further thoughts on NASA, but I'll hold those for now."

"Back to the original topic, extraterrestrials can be both man created and demons masquerading as beings from some galaxy far, far away. Movies, especially, are being used to program our minds to possibilities, so we are not shocked when the deception is played out in real time."

"They don't just masquerade as beings from some far away galaxy, Dad, my personal encounter was with a demonic spirit pretending to be an Ascended Master and luring me into the New Age lies. I didn't realize it then, but I needed something spiritual in my life, something more than just believing we live and die and that's the end, and that was what I was offered by Arcturus."

"And Satan knows that, Princess. He deceives us according to what we need in life, making it all look so good until we are held captive. I've wondered if I had told you the complete truth when you were young, if you would have been spared from that deception."

Gabriella could hear the remorse in her father's voice and assured him, "It's that demonic experience that opened my spiritual eyes not only to who the One True God is but also to see into the supernatural realm. Satan will never deceive me again. God's Word promises us the elect will not be deceived and I am standing on that promise."

Her father took her hand in his. "Those words make a father's heart sing with joy, especially knowing that great deception is soon to appear. I don't know how it will all play out, but there is no doubt it's not far away."

Caleb interjected, "It sounds to me like rather it's extraterrestrials, Ascended Masters, or even holograms in the sky...the end goal is still the New World Order under Satan's control."

"No truer words could be spoken," Gabe confirmed.

The sun was starting to set, and the air grew cool. "We better start back," Gabe directed. "Knowing Sandee, she will be complaining we're not there for supper." The three all smiled. They knew her well.

"We still have so much to discuss," Gabriella longed to continue their time of being alone.

"There's always tomorrow, Princess," he replied.

"I hope so," was her reply beneath her breath.

Just as they were nearing the cavern entrance Chris met them coming out. "I've got to call Detective Richards. I'll catch you up when I get back in the bunker."

It was obvious he wanted privacy, so they did not linger. Flashlights in hand they returned through the dark tunnel. Each one of the three was lost in their reflective thoughts. Gabriella reached for Caleb's hand and pulled him close as they passed the wall where the Prophet Elijah appeared and anointed her as a Chosen One. Although there was nothing visual, she sensed the Presence of the Ruach Ha Kodesh and smelled the familiar aroma of Elijah's anointing oil.

"Do you smell that, Caleb?"

"I do, what is it?" He replied, moving his flashlight around the cavern searching for the source.

Gabe stopped in his tracks. "What is that sweet smell? I've traveled through a lot of caves and never encountered that aroma before."

Gabriella stepped by her father's side pulling Caleb with her. "This is one of the places Elijah appeared to me. He called me a Chosen One. That aroma is the same as the oil he poured over my head anointing me as a daughter of Zebulon." She reached up to touch the top of her head where Elijah had poured the oil and suddenly gasped. She pulled Caleb's hand to the top of her head.

"What is that?" he questioned in confusion.

She rubbed the top of her head with her finger and held it under his nose. "That is the anointing oil Elijah poured over my head, the oil of YehoVah."

Gabe reached up and touched the top of her head. "That wasn't there when we were outside," he stated emphatically. "I would have smelled it then." His mind grasped for some other explanation, but there was none.

"Dad, what I saw in the supernatural world is beginning to manifest in the natural world. There could be no other explanation. We are in the Presence of the Lord. Let's pray now for answers - who we are hiding from, and they be revealed." Gabriella took the hands of both men and led them in prayer decreeing the light of truth shine in the darkness to reveal these evil men. The aroma of the oil lingered in the atmosphere as they worshiped their Heavenly Father.

They heard footsteps approaching and Chris' flashlight was shining on them. "I thought you would already be back in the bunker," he said as he joined them. "What's that smell?" He immediately sensed the Holy Presence and stood silently in reverence.

"It's a very long story, Chris," Gabriella answered. "One I think you will be extremely interested in."

Caleb put his arm around Gabriella and pulled her close. He did not like the apparent bond developing between her and this police officer. Gabriella was oblivious to his jealousy. Her only intent was to understand why Chris was a major part of her visions, she knew it was for a reason.

"Well, I've got some information for you all too," Chris informed them. "KJ and I will explain it to everyone over dinner. Sandee is waiting for you all to get back before we eat."

A few more minutes and they were back in the bunker settling around the wooden table already filled with food. "I've been waiting on you," she pretended to be aggravated but they knew her too well to fall for it. She patted Gabriella on the head as she sat down. "I know this has been a wonderful day for you, honey bunny." Then she paused and asked, "Do you know you have oil in your hair?" She leaned over to inspect further, "And it smells wonderful."

Gabriella, Gabe, and Caleb all smiled. "Yes, we know," they said in unison." Over dinner Gabriella explained as the rest of the team sat in amazement. Gabe told them about the prayer they prayed in the cavern where the fragrance of the oil permeated the atmosphere.

KJ and Chris were soaking in every word Gabe said. The more they heard the more anxious they were to tell the team what they had discovered that very well may be the answer to their prayers.

KJ motioned for Chris to be the one to share the information. Chris had not had a moment of privacy to tell KJ about his concerning conversation with Detective Richards, which added icing to their proverbial research cake. "Well, I have good news and bad news. What do you want first?"

— CHAPTER 15 —

Chris had the team's full attention as Dr. Brotman voiced their thoughts: "Good news first, it helps soften the blow of the bad."

"Good news is Detective Richards has some strong leads that could help break this case. When I informed him about what KJ had found regarding the Khazarian Mafia, he's now convinced his information and ours are somehow intertwined. It does make sense, you know, and we're both going to dig a lot deeper and compare notes." His expression changed to one of consternation as he continued: "If we had a good lead on who is doing the leg work for the hierarchy it would give us a desperately needed vantage point."

Gabriella cleared her throat and all eyes immediately turned to her. "I think I know not only one person but two, maybe more. I saw them several times in my visions." She explained. She was not sure how much information to give at this point and decided on just the basics. "I only have their last names, Moretti and Russo. Moretti is tall with thick black hair and a bit heavy. Russo is bald, average height, coughs a lot, and is a chain smoker. Also, he wore a very distinctive ring that had a triangle on it. They work for Ugo Strozza."

"Strozza, the International Intelligence Agency Director?" Chris questioned, amazed at the details Gabriella shared.

"Yes, exactly," she quickly replied. "If my visions are true, all the intelligence agencies from every country, like America's CIA and Israel's Mossad, they are all connected under this global agency, which is ultimately controlled by the United Nations' President, Sotoreo."

Chris was making a list of names and organizations to research. "I'll get right on this. We've got lots to track down. If your information is correct, Gabi, it could be a game changer."

"That's something I want to know for sure, too, Chris," she admitted. No one uttered a word; however, they were all very anxious to know how accurate Gabriella's information was.

They were all dreading the next part of the conversation. "What's the bad news, Chris?" Dr. Brotman questioned.

All eyes turned back to Chris who obviously was distressed. He took a deep breath, before he spoke. "Mrs. Nicholson is missing."

Faith jumped from her chair in fear. "What do you mean, missing?" She exclaimed.

Chris tried to conceal the concern in his voice as he gave more details: "Richards had a surveillance officer watching her house. The last activity he saw was a pizza delivery car with two men in the front seats. He thought it odd but dismissed it as someone in training."

The atmosphere of the room was suddenly charged with trepidation as Chris continued: "Officer Cohen had allowed Dr. Nicholson to call his wife with his police phone that could not be traced. Naturally, the doctor just wanted to assure her that he was okay and make sure she was also. He made several attempts to call, and it went straight to voice mail. So, Richards wanted an in-person check done. He had his officer surveilling the house to check on her. He went to the back door of her home, following the same driveway the delivery car took. The door was standing wide open. When he got inside it was obvious a struggle had taken place with the kitchen chairs overturned and...," he hesitated, obvious to everyone he did not want to share all the details.

"Tell us everything," Gabe instructed. "We have to know what we're dealing with."

"Okay," Chris agreed, taking a deep breath. "There was fresh blood on the edge of the table and on the floor. She probably fell and hit her head trying to escape."

"No!" Sandee exclaimed. "That sweet woman, this should not be. She's like family to us after spending the war days in this bunker together." Tears were rolling down Sandee's cheeks as she struggled to regain her composure.

Chris waited for the team to process what he had already shared before he went further. "The blood trail led outside and stopped, probably where they put her in their vehicle. The surveillance officer didn't notice the blood when he first went in the house because he was focused on the open door and concerned an intruder might still be inside." He hesitated once more. "All indications are she was kidnapped by the two men."

Dr. Brotman stated emphatically: "Doc has one of the best security systems available in his home. Surely, they caught these guys on the cameras."

Chris shook his head no. "That was the first thing checked. According to the time recorded, the security system had been deactivated just prior to the incident. Richards already has a specialist working on how that happened, but as of now there are no leads. These are not just common criminals we are dealing with; these guys are professionals." It was written all over Chris' face that there was more he needed to say.

"And...?" Dr. Brotman insisted he continue, bracing himself for the worst.

"If Mrs. Nicholson survived the kidnapping, they will no doubt be interrogating her, maybe even with truth serum." Chris had to say no more.

"Oh my, God help us!" Faith exclaimed in fear. "She knows everything about this bunker and the secret entrance."

The atmosphere of trepidation quickly morphed into one of immediate danger. Each of the team members was struggling to mentally adjust to what this could mean.

Gabe tried to bring a measure of comfort to the overall situation. "Mrs. Nicholson does not know everything," he assured them. "She doesn't know about the security room that monitors everything and everyone on the grounds. She also doesn't know about the secret door in the pantry that exits to the tunnel escape; all she knows is one way in and one way out. Plus, no one knows that I have a few security tricks up my sleeve," he added with a forced smile.

Gabriella knew exactly what he was referring to but said nothing. In her visions Chris had used that security tactic as a last resort when they escaped from the bunker invasion.

Gabe's words offered a measure of relief to the team, but grave concerns persisted. "Where would we go if we do have to escape...again?" Faith questioned with a quivering voice.

"I'm sure Richards is already considering that possibility and making plans." Chris assured them all. "We must stay alert and be ready to leave at a moment's notice, if necessary. We may be prematurely jumping to conclusions, however it's best to stay on guard. That means monitoring the lodge and grounds 24/7 from the security room."

"That won't be necessary," Gabe informed him. "There's a built-in alarm system that when activated sets off an alarm in the bunker. If anyone trespasses anywhere on my property, I will know immediately. Also, the cameras will record every movement."

"You've really thought of everything," Chris responded with incredulity.

"I've tried," he admitted. "Through the years as more technology became available, I kept expanding it. I guess I knew in my spirit this day would come eventually." He looked at his beautiful daughter and his soul was filled with thankfulness for being able to protect her, at least for the time being. "I'm so glad I did."

KJ pushed himself from his chair announcing, "If there's nothing else that I need to know right now, I'm going back to work there is much to research and time is not on our side. Chris, you coming?"

"I'm right behind you. Just one more thing, I'll be checking back with Richards in the morning. He thinks he'll have more information about Mrs. Nicholson; and he said to tell KJ, Aaron, and Faith he should have updates on the welfare of their families. It's too risky to let you all try to contact them. We've got enough people in danger right now, without adding to the list."

Mixed emotions were battling in the minds of the team: fear for Mrs. Nicholson, fear for their families; fear for themselves, and yet hope they may have some leads now that could end this nightmare.

"There's much to pray about," Sandee stated, assuring them Yahweh was still in control. "As soon as I clean up from dinner, I'm going to my room to spend some time with my Heavenly Father who has all the answers we need."

"I'll help clean up," Faith offered getting up from the table.

"Me, too," Gabriella arose to join the ladies, leaning over to kiss Caleb's cheek before she left the table to help. "I'm sure Professor has plenty to talk about. He's never lacking for words," she smiled picking up dirty plates from the table.

"Definitely, never lacking for words, but sometimes lacking in wisdom," Dr. Brotman stated with personal conviction. However, the team knew that was not true.

Gabe, Aaron and Caleb pulled chairs in a circle around Dr. Brotman. The ladies in the kitchen area remained silent allowing them also to hear the professor's commentary. He settled in his recliner and opened his Bible back to Revelation 17 also placing a page marker to Isaiah 47.

"In light of the Khazarian information, these prophecies may require an expanded interpretation. Before we begin, let me explain that many modern-day scholars view the New Testament as a whole, and Revelation in particular, as a corpus of writings put together by Christians apart from any Jewish influence. My concern with that theology is all the New Testament was written by Jews."

Dr. Brotman wanted to verify they were following his train of thought. "Wouldn't it make sense that the men who wrote the New Testament, who were Jews, would write from the foundation of their knowledge of the Old Testament? If we do not understand their vantage point, we could be misinterpreting the most important aspects of Mystery Babylon."

Aaron interjected, "I agree totally, Professor. In my studies I see the New Testament authors confirming everything that was prophesied about Yeshua in the Tanach. The Book of John starts by saying Yeshua was The Word made flesh, meaning He was the Torah, The Word of God, living in human form. The New Testament writers knew the ancient prophecies which proved to them Yeshua was the promised Messiah. Jews need a sign, and the Old Testament prophets gave the signs to look for to know when The Anointed One had come."

"Well said, Aaron, and that's my point exactly," Dr. Brotman agreed. "We cannot read John the Revelator's writings with accurate understanding without building it upon the biblical ancient prophecies. Before we get into discussion on Mystery Babylon, we need to understand the chronological order of Revelation. Chapters 17 and 18 specifically have always been questioned as to their placement in John's writings; and I believe that is another part of the mystery, no one knows just where it fits into the end of day's events. Between the judgment scenes concluding with the wrath of God in Revelation 16 and the victory of the Lamb in Revelation 19, one finds an interlude devoted to the Harlot of Babylon and her ultimate destruction. No one can say definitively when that interlude occurs on the prophetic timeline."

Gabriella finished clearing the table and joined the group discussion with pen and paper in hand to make notes. "Do you have any personal thoughts on the interlude timing, Professor?" Gabriella questioned, knowing nothing in the Bible was happenstance.

"We will fit that piece of the puzzle a little later. I will say, I believe the Harlot interlude in Revelation exists as a reminder of the past—God has redeemed His people and punished their captors in the past, and He is going to finally bring an end to Israel's persecution. Although times and circumstances may change, God remains the same. When you read Chapter 16 and have a prophetic view of the day of God's wrath, the following two chapters are a reminder that the satanic spirit of Babylon was prevalent throughout the Bible; and not only does it still exist today, but the pure evil has infiltrated every aspect of society. Revelation 16 tells us her final destruction is already planned once and for all. Dr. Brotman paused momentarily and lit his pipe, allowing time for the information to be processed. "Since the Old Testament prophecies are not directly quoted in Revelation, it becomes necessary to study the inferences throughout John's prophecies."

"What particular prophecies do you believe parallel?" Gabriella questioned, ready to make notes. "I'm referring to the foundation prophecies you mentioned."

Without hesitation, he replied, "Numerous Old Testament references support the Revelation text; however, Isaiah 47 doesn't just support it but stands behind the Chapters 17 and 18 interlude as a whole." He took one last puff from his pipe and laid it on the side table before continuing.

"The Whore of Babylon's image, name, arrogance, power, riches, and fate are consistent in both texts. The parallels are too significant to be ignored. The interpretation challenge goes back to what we just discussed, metaphoric or literal? Coming from the perspective of John's writings two thousand years ago, when Israel was being horribly persecuted under the Romans, most eschatological scholars believe Mystery Babylon is Rome or even more precise, The Vatican. This is without using references to Isaiah's prophecies which were written when Israel was under the Babylonian captivity."

Gabriella was convinced The Vatican and especially The Pope would play a big role in Mystery Babylon. Her prophetic vision confirmed that fact. She would wait until KJ had more information before sharing those details.

Dr. Brotman turned the pages to Isaiah 47. "As of now, just a quick overview. The Whore of Babylon believed she was like God, and nothing could destroy her. She believed her sorceries and magic spells gave her the power of earthly control."

"KJ said that very thing about the Khazarian Jews. Their black magic gave them vast riches with which they control the earth," Gabriella observed.

He nodded his head in agreement. "That is what solidified for me the connection of these scriptures. But, before we delve into Revelation Chapters 17 and 18, I want to read the 19th verse in Chapter 16: *The great city was divided into three parts, and the cities of the nations fell. And great Babylon was remembered before God, to give her the cup of the wine of the fierceness of His wrath.*"

He laid his Bible back on his lap while he commented on the verse: "As I said, the end of Chapter 16 refers to the wrath of God which will destroy wicked Mystery Babylon once and for all. The term *the great city* fetches differing opinions on the location. It also brings into question whether it is a geographical location or a mystical metaphor. Scholars are on both sides of the fence regarding this interpretation. Those who do believe it is a literal city vary in their opinions as to which earthly city. Some say Jerusalem, others Rome, and yet others believe it is New York City; however, they all pretty much agree there will be a Capitol of Mystery Babylon during the end days."

"What do you believe?" Gabriella asked.

"Personally, I agree with a literal city but will explain that later also. The next part, the *cities of the nations*, I believe refers to the unified political forces, the Kings of the Earth. As stated in the prior Revelation texts, these Kings all fall simultaneously when God pours out His wrath."

"The great city will divide into three parts," Caleb repeated. "What does that mean?"

"I admit, that has always been confusing to me. You would automatically think it means the great city will be split into three parts, but I'm not so sure. No matter how I've tried to fit that literal translation into prophecy, it never fits right. However, the overall picture is becoming much clearer and if we have accurately identified Mystery Babylon the three parts should be revealed also. To know for sure that we're on the right prophetic path, we need to analyze in depth both Revelation 17 and 18, along with the Old Testament texts, and see if all the paths lead to the Khazarian Jews."

Dr. Brotman placed a bookmark in his Bible and laid it to the side. "We've made good progress, but it's getting late. We will continue tomorrow."

"You definitely need some rest," Sandee stated, concerned about his welfare.

"Okay, mother hen, and I do agree, this time." The prior days had been exhausting for all the team, but especially the professor. The car accident, protective custody, concerns for Gabriella, and now the uncertainty of the bunker security and if they would have to flee again was weighing heavy upon his shoulders. He felt responsible for everyone on his team. "A good night's sleep and I will be ready to face another day," he remarked as he departed to his bedroom.

Gabriella leaned her head on her father's shoulder still in wonder that he was still alive. Events were swirling in their lives so fast, she barely had time to acclimate to each one individually. Plus, there was the constant agonizing thought it could end at any moment. She had transitioned between time and untime so often the last few days that she still found it difficult to believe this was real and would last.

Gabe put his arm around his daughter, sensing her emotions. "Whatever the future may hold, Princess, we are together now. I'm here for you and so is Caleb."

Caleb took her hand in his and without words affirmed he would never leave her.

"I know, dad. It's just overwhelming. I have you back in my life and it is wonderful beyond words, and being engaged to Caleb makes me desperately long for a future; but the uncertainty of everything else going on overshadows the joy."

"You know better than most that there's no promise of tomorrow for anyone, Gabi. So, we make the best of every day. Let's enjoy every moment together, solve end time mysteries, and work for Yahweh while there is still time." He squeezed her tight, released her to Caleb, and pushed himself from the couch. "Speaking of solving mysteries, I'm going to check on KJ and Chris."

Gabriella jumped up pulling Caleb with her. "Let's go, too. I'm anxious to know what he's found."

Although Caleb longed for time alone with Gabriella, he knew their project and their safety had to take precedence. He muttered to himself, "There's always tomorrow." At least he hoped so.

KJ and Chris were discussing their discoveries as the trio joined them. "Squeeze on in," KJ said, "I've got some things to run by you before I do more research."

Gabriella sat down beside them with Gabe and Caleb standing behind. "Let's hear it," she instructed.

KJ picked up his notes and turned to face the others. "I've researched The Vatican and the Khazarian Jew connection which has started a whole new rabbit hole...the Papal Bloodlines which is a totally separate entity from the Khazarian Jews. These two rabbit holes keep leading to the same place, the Jesuit Order."

"Papal Bloodlines?" Gabriella raised her eyebrows questioning.

"That's new to me," Gabe chimed in.

KJ read from his notes for accuracy: "There are thirteen Papal Bloodlines who were secretly behind the creation of the Jesuit Order. Some of these bloodlines date back to the height of the Roman Empire and the founding of The Catholic Church. These ancient dynasties have controlled Kings and Queens from behind the scenes since the beginning of The Catholic Church. They would create wars, financing both sides, and determine who would win, placing on the throne of kingdoms whomever they determined to rule; and in essence the Papal Bloodlines were the ultimate rulers both of Kings and The Catholic Church."

KJ made a side comment: "And that's exactly what we see in governments today. World leaders and politicians are puppets, controlled by Luciferians behind the scenes using sorceries, money and blackmail as their means."

Caleb entered the conversation. "Has there ever been a legitimate government that was for the people?"

With a sorrowful voice, KJ answered, "Some started that way, but eventually were infiltrated by the Luciferians who would gain control. My country, America, is one of them." A mixture of anger and sadness could be detected in his voice. "But we won't go into that right now. Back to the current rabbit holes."

KJ refocused on his notes. "As the Khazarians through the centuries integrated more and more into western culture as wealthy European Jews, they pretended to convert to Catholicism and joined the Jesuits. They became the bankers for the Papal Bloodlines. By the 17th century, with combining their massive wealth with that of the papal bloodlines, they were solidifying world control of both religion and finance and became known as the Black Nobility."

"And money controls everything," Gabe added. "So said Nathaniel Rothschild."

"Exactly," KJ agreed as he continued: "The Rothschild Family is the main one publicly known at the top of the Jesuit Pyramid but secretly behind them are the Papal Bloodlines and they wanted to remain secret." He slightly laughed as he added, "But nothing can remain secret now with modern technology."

"*For nothing is secret that will not be revealed, nor anything hidden that will not be known and come to light.*" Gabe quoted from Luke 8:17. Mystery Babylon was a mystery to be revealed. Apparently, the Jesuit Order is a big part of this mystery and that would explain the religious harlot in Revelation 17."

KJ agreed looking up from his notes. "The Jesuit Order is literally a satanic division of the Catholic Church, and this secret society has infiltrated Catholicism to the highest level."

"This keeps getting deeper and deeper," Gabe commented in astonishment.

"Oh, you've not seen anything yet," Chris chimed in. "Go on, KJ."

KJ referred back to his notes. "Researching their connection brought me to information on The Crown. I didn't know there are actually two Crowns in England; one being the Queen or King, who is largely ceremonial and the other is the English Parliament who gives royalty their marching orders. Now the interesting thing is, the Parliament Crown, is controlled behind the scenes by the Bank of England which is owned by the House of Rothschild."

"Really?" Gabriella gasped. "So, these Jews, who are really not Jews at all, control the nation the sun never sets on; and in unison with the Papal Bloodlines control The Vatican. Unbelievable!"

"Oh, there's still more," KJ continued. "The Crown owns the 677-acre, independent sovereign state known as The City of London, or simply called The City. The City is not a part of England nor is Vatican City part of Rome. They are both independent of any ruling nation and owned by The Crowns, who are controlled by..."

"The Khazarian Jews," Gabriella finished his sentence.

"Yep," he affirmed. "It's estimated the House of Rothschild is worth over $700 trillion dollars of known assets, that's over ninety percent of the world's wealth. Today, this satanic cabal holds the bonded indebtedness of the world."

"Satan is the god of this world and this cabal, through their Luciferian Black Magic and riches, control the world." Gabe added. "And this perfectly describes Mystery Babylon."

Gabriella tried to listen to the chatter that ensued among the men but kept thinking about the visions she had of the lodge meetings. They were all fitting perfectly into what KJ was finding. She understood now The Black Pope and UN leader she had seen represented the Black Nobility, the control of both religion and nations in the final days of time. She surmised that Strozza represented the international lies and deceptions perpetrated upon the nations. She had only seen snippets, but now the picture was coming into full focus that her vision represented Mystery Babylon and these evil ones would try to destroy anyone who is a threat to their kingdom. She understood why they wanted to eliminate Dr. Brotman's entire team.

"What about the Black Pope? Anything on him?" She questioned KJ.

KJ flipped through his notes. "An internet search immediately brings up The Black Pope and most people would stop at Wikipedia's information which is nothing of real concern, it just says he is the Father General of the Jesuit Order and holds the highest known position of the Jesuits. Of course, he is a puppet controlled by the evil Black Nobility. Now when you dig deeper it gets very interesting."

He paused to emphasize his next question, "There are actually three popes. Have you ever heard of The Grey Pope?"

"Three popes?" Gabriella exclaimed.

"Yep, three popes," KJ reemphasized. "The Grey Pope is the secret pope who is the real head of The Vatican also controlled also by the Black Nobility."

"Help me understand all this," Caleb stated with confusion. "Are you saying the Black Nobility, controlled by the Khazarian Jews, dominate the entire world from behind the scenes?"

KJ nodded his head in agreement. "All the information points to them using religion, finance, property, health, weather, the media, mind control, literally everything to wield their power over the masses; plus, they control all other secret satanic societies - all through the Jesuit Order, headed by The Grey Pope, ruled by the Khazarians."

"The pillars of society that Professor was referring to," Gabriella confirmed.

"It definitely appears that way, secret societies working in unison." KJ agreed.

"Makes more sense all of the time why John the Revelator called it a mystery." Caleb interjected, still a bit confused by all the details pouring out.

Gabe was analyzing the information as it fell into the prophetic perspective. "This is becoming a perfect description of Mystery Babylon. Dr. Brotman is going to be ecstatic to get this information." Then he wrapped his arms around his daughter. "You knew exactly where to start looking for the answers, Gabi. You've convinced me your visions were real."

She kissed her father's cheek and stated emphatically, "This is only the beginning."

— CHAPTER 16 —

The team had gone to bed except for Gabriella and Caleb. Settling on the soft blue couch Caleb took her in his arms holding her close.

"I need some time with my soon to be wife," he whispered in her ear.

She snuggled closer to him treasuring the moment, knowing these private intimate times would be few and far between in the foreseeable future. "Caleb, even when I was in the spirit world, I still had glimpses of reality, especially you, and longed to be back in your arms. My love is so strong, I could not let go even during my supernatural existence. During that time, I wasn't sure what was real and what was supernatural, but I never questioned my love for you."

He decided to ask the question weighing heavily on his mind. "What about you and Chris? You said he was with you in your vision. Why him? Why not me?" Caleb's jealousy was obvious, and she knew she had to squelch it before it became a real problem.

"I really don't know. I believe it was because in my vision the rapture had taken place and all my loved ones had disappeared, leaving only me and Chris who were not believers. Maybe that was part of the meaning, Caleb. What I felt and experienced is what so many will go through when it really does occur. At what point in the end of days' timeline the rapture takes place, I don't know; but it will happen and it gives me both empathy and a strong resolve to reach the lost with the truth."

"I guess," he soberly commented, his jealousy still obviously dominating his emotions.

Gabriella pulled away and looked Caleb directly in his eyes. "Do not worry, my love. There has never been and will never be anyone else for me but you. Don't let the enemy use my visions to cause conflict among us. That's his tactic, you know. If he can't control us, he will try to divide us. We must trust each other. Unity is a mighty weapon."

She briefly paused, remembering Chris constantly protecting her in her vision. "I believe in the days ahead you will find Chris to be very important in our protection. God uses people to carry out his missions on earth. That was his mission in my vision, and I believe it will play out in real time."

She could see his demeanor changing and he began to relax. "I know, Gabi. It's just the thought of losing you again is more than I can bear." He took her back in his arms and they both sat silently regretting all the years that had been lost, which made the present moment more precious.

Exhausted, Gabriella fell asleep in Caleb's arms. He gazed at her beautiful face with her curly blonde hair cascading down the sides. It was one of those moments when love saturated every fiber of his being. "Please Father, let her become my wife before we leave this earth. You promised us the desires of our heart." He reluctantly released her and got up from the couch. Covering her with a blanket, he kissed the top of her head. "Sweet dreams, my love," he whispered as he closed his bedroom door behind him.

The next sound Gabriella was aware of was Sandee's soprano voice softly singing as she made coffee. Gabriella stretched and listened to her song of worship. The atmosphere of the bunker was transformed into one of peace as she sang praises. "*Worthy is The Lamb, Worthy is The Lamb to receive honor, and receive glory, worthy is the Lamb.*"

Gabriella's mind immediately went to The Lamb who led her through the mountains of North Carolina to the tribal village where miracles took place; and to the little girl who was delivered from a demonic stronghold. She quietly reaffirmed her vow to her Heavenly Father she would go wherever The Lamb led her and began to sing with Sandee, "*Worthy is The Lamb.*"

The team emerged from their bedrooms and joined in the melodious worship. Dr. Brotman exited his bedroom with his arms raised in praise harmonizing with his baritone voice, "*Worthy is the Lamb, worthy is the Lamb, you are worthy to receive glory and honor, worthy is the Lamb.*"

Chris sat silently basking in the glorious Presence. Any lingering doubts regarding the validity of what this team spiritually believed completely faded away. He raised his hands joining worship with the others, now feeling he was truly part of this team, not just their protector. The Presence of the Holy Spirit gave each of them the strength needed to face the uncertainty ahead.

The serenity continued in the atmosphere while Sandee prepared breakfast and KJ filled the rest of the team in on all he had discovered.

Dr. Brotman kept shaking his head in amazement. "It appears to me these evil families are at the core of the mystery in John's writings. He would have known the Luciferian Babylonian practices of sorcery had existed all through the Old Testament and was contemporary to the time he wrote the Book of Revelation. I think he would have assumed any student of the Old Testament would recognize who Mystery Babylon was. I reiterate, you cannot understand the New Testament, and specifically Revelation, without the Old Testament foundation. However, my question now is how could these Babylonian Luciferian secret societies that have evolved since John's writings exist for centuries and people today be totally unaware of their control?"

KJ knew this question would come. "They gained control discreetly through governmental changes with the information hidden from the masses. They were able to exist without detection until the explosion of knowledge that came with the internet. They tried to erase their history to maintain their secrecy, but they cannot stay hidden any longer from anyone who is seeking the truth. Sadly, many people are ignorant and choose to stay that way. They continue with the status quo not realizing their entire lives have been manipulated by Luciferians."

"The masses are about to have a rude awakening when Mystery Babylon falls," Dr. Brotman stated emphatically. "The foundation of The Omega Watchers Project was to discover the end of days' timeline based on the return of the Nephilim. I truly believed we were living in the final generation of time and their demonic return would be a major timeline clue. Now I question if these demonic hybrids have been on this earth all along, some in the form of man deceiving the nations generation after generation; and will continue to deceive until the day of God's wrath. Yahweh created man to worship Him and be His body on this earth through the blood of Messiah. Lucifer created a hybrid counterfeit to worship him and be his body on this earth controlling through blood sacrifice sorceries."

KJ repeated what he had shared prior, "Historical writings called the Khazarians, who migrated originally from the region of Babylon, serpent people. That could mean evil people or perhaps indicating they were actually the seed of Satan. What you're saying, Professor, makes perfect sense."

The team was silent as Dr. Brotman mentally processed all the new information.

Chris had listened silently to every word with his officer intuition in full mode. It made sense to him now as to who most likely was trying to take this team out. The Khazarian Mafia had become the obvious answer. They thought Gabe was dead and all that he had discovered was silenced. Then they found out Dr. Brotman had Gabe's research and tried to take him out. Now they know Gabe faked his death and is very much alive and that puts anyone connected to him in imminent danger. What Chris did not know was the why. What did Gabe discover decades prior that demanded he be silenced? He had written in his journal about the microchip discovery; however, there had to be more, something still hidden that the world controllers had to keep secret to maintain their dominance. The professor interrupted Chris' thoughts.

"KJ, you said both The City of London and Vatican City are sovereign and privately owned by the Black Nobility. Right? There is no governmental control over these areas?"

"Yes," he affirmed wondering where the professor's thought process was going.

"I keep going back to Revelation 16:19, the mystery of the great city which broke into three parts and then all three cities were destroyed simultaneously on the day of God's wrath." Dr. Brotman queried further. "You said The City of London is simply called The City?"

"Correct," KJ answered still in confusion.

A revelatory smile crossed Dr. Brotman's face. "I'm just thinking out loud here, but what if *The City*, The City of London, is one and the same as the great city in Revelation 16 that broke into three parts?" His eyebrows narrowed in perplexity as he continued his chain of thought. "But that's only two cities when you include Vatican City. There would have to be one more city with world dominance to fulfill that prophecy. The Black Nobility, aka Mystery Babylon, controls London which would represent Financial Control and The Vatican, religious control; but what would the third city be?"

Gabe interjected with a possible answer. "I have a thought on that, Professor."

All eyes were fixed on Gabe as he revealed a fact from American history which was intentionally no longer taught in schools. "During mine and Gabi's explorations in America, we dug deep into history. I became aware that most Americans are totally unaware of many historical truths, and related to our conversation now what happened after the Civil War. America was bankrupt and President Lincoln was struggling for answers for survival. Even back then the Government was filled with corruption, and The Crown took that opportunity to take control through politicians who could be controlled."

Gabi nodded in agreement with what her father was saying. "I remember, Dad. We had gone to Gettysburg where the Civil War ended, and we began to dig into the historical years following the war. Go on, tell them."

"In 1871 a seditious act was performed by the United States Government. A coup was initiated to rewrite the constitution and transferred the Republic of the United States of America into the new Corporation of The United States of America financed by loans from The Crown." Gabe hesitated. "I hope that's not confusing, but this is the part that applies to what you're asking, Professor."

Dr. Brotman leaned forward intent on every word as Gabe continued: "When America became a corporation, and owing money now to The Crown, it placed all its citizens as property of the new United States Corporation, assets would be a better word. The new government corporation was centered in Washington D.C. which made the city a Foreign Entity on American soil of sovereign states. In other words, Washington D.C. is private ground, not part of the U.S."

Dr. Brotman smiled from ear to ear. "You are telling me The District of Columbia is a city to itself, just like The Crown and The Vatican?"

Gabe nodded and added, "Controlled by the Khazarians."

"You can't be serious," Dr. Brotman exclaimed, anticipating Gabe's next comments.

"Absolutely true," Gabe affirmed. "The loan from The Crown actually came from The Vatican, brokered via the Rothschild's Bank of London. The new corporation transferred all the assets of our government into the new Global Estate Trust, which is controlled by the lenders who are the real rulers of our nation. The City of London, Vatican City and The District of Columbia, all three of these international city-states are independent of their respective countries."

Gabriella added to her father's information. "The Bank of London made sure massive amounts of money went into building the military of America creating the strongest military force on the face of the earth, which would be essential for world dominance. Why do you think England and America have supported each other in every war since the new corporation when they were always mortal enemies before?" She paused to let her father continue.

"The bottom line is America is ultimately controlled by The Crown, House of Rothschild, who now we know are Khazarians. They own the government and the citizens through the Act of 1871 controlling all our taxes through the Federal Reserve, the IRS, and others of their privately owned agencies which Americans thought were part of the government and were not. They only act on behalf of We the People."

"I did not know this," KJ remarked in amazement. "And I am an American...born, raised, and educated there. I was never taught this."

"Was President Lincoln part of this corruption?" Dr. Brotman asked knowing historically he was one of America's greatest leaders.

"No, he would not support the corporation decision made by a corrupt Congress and intended to veto it. He knew it would destroy the original constitution the founding fathers had created. Conveniently, he was assassinated." Gabe answered, adding, "That's the final answer for these evil people. Whoever gets in their way and can't be controlled, kill them."

Silence permeated the room as the team realized they were all uncontrollable targets of this evil cabal.

Dr. Brotman broke the atmosphere of trepidation by refocusing his team, analyzing Gabe's new information. "Even more so now, I believe the city in Revelation 16 represents a literal city which is the capital of Mystery Babylon. *She will be broken into three parts* could mean there will be two more locations of world powers: in addition to The Crown City of London controlling the earth through her riches, the other two could be Vatican City as the harlot of false religion and the City of Washington D.C. as her military dominion which causes her to believe she cannot be destroyed. In Isaiah 47:7 and repeated in Revelation 18:7, the whore of Babylon says she is forever and cannot fall. That is a mirror image of the arrogance of Lucifer himself."

"Oh, but down she *will* go," Gabriella paraphrased the scriptures.

Aaron had sat quietly soaking in the conversation and decided to add his understanding to the commentary, "And in Revelation 18, John writes it won't just be in one day, but in one hour. The whole world will be in a panic and mourning when they see the financial kingdom of this earth collapse instantly. Literally, all commerce will stop."

In an unfamiliar tone of voice, Gabe recited the very end of the 18th chapter: "*for by her sorceries were all nations deceived, and in her was found the blood of prophets, and of saints, and of all that were slain upon the earth.*"

Gabriella looked deep into the eyes of her father. She knew that tone of voice well and there was something more, something sagacious he was not saying. She discerned it was connected to what he did not dare write in his journal.

— Chapter 17 —

Chris was making notes in preparation for talking to Detective Richards. "I'm heading out to the end of the tunnel," he informed the team. "Hope to have some good news when I come back."

Gabriella looked at Caleb, "Let's go with him. I need the exercise and the morning sunshine." Caleb was more than willing, hoping to linger outside for some alone time with her after Chris came back to the bunker.

"Be careful, honey bunny," Sandee advised with concern. "Don't overdo with all you've been through."

Gabriella gave Sandee a quick hug on her way through the kitchen. "I'll be fine, don't worry." And quickly the three were gone.

The trio was quiet, carefully shining their flashlights through the dark tunnel. Passing the wall of anointing, Gabriella felt a rush of warm air, convincing her once again her visions were of divine origin. She moved her light from side to side hoping for a glimpse of the prophet, but nothing was abnormal. She turned the flashlight off when streams of sunlight were visible filtering into the entrance of the cave, lighting their path into the glorious fall day.

Chris exited first and then suddenly halted, motioning for Caleb and Gabriella to remain inside the cave. He quickly stepped back inside just enough to not be detected from an aerial view. He gazed over the trees for several minutes then pointed his phone towards the sky. Caleb and Gabriella stepped closer to him also gazing at the sky to know Chris' concern.

"What's wrong?" Gabriella questioned.

"I'm not sure," he answered, while he checked his phone. "Look at this, Caleb. What do you think?"

Caleb took the phone and held it closer for a better view. "A bird?" He enlarged it a little more and then stated, "Or it could be a drone."

"That's what I'm thinking, too," Chris agreed. "It looks like a large crow, but the movement isn't natural. When we get back to the security room, I'll scan the picture into the computer for analysis. Don't say anything to the others until I know more."

"If it is a drone, do you think they're looking for us?" Gabriella could feel a spiritual warning stirring inside her. "Something tells me this is not good."

"Let's not get overly concerned," Caleb spoke in a soothing voice as he put his arm around her shoulders in a gesture of protection. "It's probably just a bird, right Chris?"

Chris neither agreed nor disagreed with Caleb. His silence spoke loud affirming without words what they feared. He decided to only share the pertinent information: "I worked undercover with the Mossad a few times and as a side note, I can assure you that I do not trust them; however, I hoped to obtain some inside contacts just in case I needed them in the future. I found out the Mossad uses a military intelligence operation called Maverick; bird drones used for undetected aerial surveillance. They look like crows, and to the common eye no one would ever suspect these were cameras searching the ground and not just birds soaring through the sky." He silently watched the bird for a few more minutes, then added, "I just pray that the SUV and Gabe's garage are camouflaged enough by the trees."

"You're pretty sure it's a drone," Gabriella stated emphatically.

He ignored her comment, stepping back into the mouth of the cave where he could not be detected by the drone. Checking his phone, he commented: "Good, I still have signal to call Richards. I need to let him know."

Gabriella snuggled closer to Caleb needing the comfort of his embrace. The vision she had in the supernatural realm came flooding into her mind: she and Chris had been discovered in the bunker and had to flee quickly to another location to hide. The vision morphed back into reality as she listened to Chris updating Detective Richards on both the drone and the information regarding the Khazarian Mafia.

For several minutes the phone discussion ensued between the two men. Chris ended with, "Any information on Aaron, KJ and Faith's families?" He smiled a couple of times as he listened to the detective's answers. "Okay, I'll let them know. One more thing," Chris referred to his notes for accuracy. "Do you know anything about two men named Russo and Moretti, possibly works for Strozza with international intelligence?" He glanced at Gabriella with raised eyebrows to make sure he had the names right. She nodded, confirming his information.

Chris was silent as he listened to Richards' response. He glanced at

Gabriella and Caleb a couple of times but made no comments for several minutes. His expressions were impossible to read.

"Okay, will do," Chris commented ending the conversation. "I will fill you in as we go back to the bunker, but I've got to wait until a picture comes through. Richards is texting it to me now. There's no news on Mrs. Nicholson yet, but they have a good lead. This picture could be it."

"Picture of what?" Gabriella asked about the time his text notification signaled.

He opened the text and before showing it to Gabriella explained: "One of the Nicholson's neighbors had security cameras that picked up the pizza delivery car when it pulled out of the doctor's driveway. It had a surprisingly good video of the two men in the front seat. Richards sent me a picture for you to look at, Gabi." He slightly enlarged the picture and handed her the phone.

One glance and her legs went limp. Caleb caught her before she collapsed. "That's them," she exclaimed. "That's Russo and Moretti!"

Caleb held her shaking body in his arms trying to soothe her.

"They're killers, Chris, you know they are. They tried to kill us, remember?" Gabriella quickly realized she had said too much.

Chris' face filled with confusion. "What are you talking about?"

She quickly struggled for an alternate answer, "You know, at the hospital. We all had to escape secretly. I'm sure these men were involved in murdering the janitor."

Chris quickly discerned the personal nature of her original comment and intuitively knew the later explanation was a cover. Even though he was confused by her comment, he pressed no further. He was acutely aware of Caleb's jealousy and did not want to add any fuel to the fire. "I need to text your confirmation to Richards. This will be a strong lead for him." After sending the text, he further commented: "You need to understand, Gabi, that Richards considers what you know as psychic information. He's worked with psychics in the past and some have been incredible."

Gabriella was not surprised, but quickly made sure Chris knew the difference. "Psychics get their information through Satan's dark sorcery. My visions came from the light of Yahweh's Holy Spirit."

Chris was beginning to understand the two forces battling in the spirit world. A mysterious world in which formerly he did not even believe. "Got it," he assured her. "Now we need to get back and analyze these bird pictures.

Let's not say anything about either of these pictures right now, the drone or the men in the car. I want to avoid any panic. At least I have good news about KJ, Aaron and Faith's families. Richards said they are all alive and well. He got a message to them assuring their children were okay and would be in touch after their project was complete. Naturally, he couldn't let them know any more than that."

Gabriella sighed in relief for a bit of good news, knowing anything positive going forward would be few and far between.

Caleb desperately had hoped for a little time alone with Gabriella, however he accepted that was impossible. The circumstances demanded they return to the bunker and prepare for any possible scenario.

As they neared the transcendental cave wall a stream of light could be seen. "Who's there?" Chris called out with his words echoing through the tunnel.

"It's just me," the voice of Gabriella's father echoed in return.

The three walked faster to get to Gabe. They found him sitting on the same rock where Gabriella had her vision of the Prophet Elijah. "Dad, what are you doing in here alone? Are you okay?" Gabriella questioned with a troubled voice.

"I'm fine, Princess," he assured her. "I just needed some private time to think and pray. Sometimes I need some space. I guess I've lived alone too many years." He motioned for Gabriella to sit beside him.

Chris knew that was his clue to leave. "I've got some serious work to get done. I'll fill you in later, Gabe. I'm going on back." With a slight wave of the hand, he disappeared into the darkness.

Gabriella joined her father on the rock while Caleb sat down on the cave floor next to her. "What is it, Dad? After all the years of separation, I still can read you like a book. It's what you could not write in your journal, right?"

"Yes, Gabi. It's so horrible, so secretly hidden by the Luciferians, that I hoped you would live your entire life without knowing." He paused, praying for the right words and yet knowing there was no way to soften the horrendous truth he was about to reveal. He set his light down on the cave floor next to Caleb illuminating the area enough to watch their faces as he poured out his heart. "When I first discovered these demonic activities, I spent days without being able to sleep, my mind tormented with what I had seen."

Gabriella tried to make it easier on her father. "Dad, I'm a big girl now.

You don't have to protect me anymore; you can tell me anything." She took his hand in hers squeezing in support.

His voice was moaning as he continued: "Both of you, in fact the entire team, must understand the demonic realm, the depth of depravity that controls this earth. Last night as the professor read from the Book of Revelation I had an epiphany, I finally understood how the ancient prophecies connect both to what I am about to share with you and to the horrible evil that exists today as part of Mystery Babylon."

Gabriella looked at Caleb with questioning eyes. Caleb shook his head that he had no idea where the conversation was going.

Gabe's eyes filled with tears as he struggled for the right words. "This is so difficult to even say out loud, so evil; however, putting all the pieces together, it becomes unquestionable and has to be voiced. The Old Testament scriptures numerous times refer to Baal and Molech child sacrifice; and then KJ found information that the Khazarians throughout their generations had continued the Babylonian child sacrifice worship. We have to be realistic, since the Khazarian power and riches came from the blood of child sacrifice, continued through the centuries through the blood of child sacrifice and has brought them to world domination in this end of days, then the blood of the children continues even as we speak; and I'm not just referring to abortion. Lucifer demands the sacrifices continue to him for these satanist to maintain power." He had to pause and take a deep breath to maintain enough self-control to continue.

Gabriella leaned against her father for emotional support. "We know all this, Dad. I guess I just never wanted to think about it. I realize ignoring the facts doesn't make the horrible truth disappear and child abuse makes me physically ill. I can't imagine how people can do these things, not for any reason."

"Only a person who is consumed with evil would," her father answered. "It doesn't stop with just the Khazarian Cabal, they enlist their foot soldiers from all of mankind, anyone that will bow down to the satanic altar of riches, fame, beauty, power...all the attributes of Lucifer himself. He wanted to be as God and when he was cast down to earth, he has counterfeited everything the One True God is and does."

Gabriella knew there was still more to be revealed. "What are you not telling me, Dad?"

The light on the cave floor illuminated her father's face enough to show his expression change to one of pure mourning. The peace that previously prevailed at Gabriella's anointing wall was replaced with extreme heaviness of spirit. A sorrowful atmosphere saturated the cave tunnel waiting for the decades of silence to finally be broken.

"Gabi, you are aware now from all the information contained in the box I left you that my study of Ufology led me to Dr. Brotman and the truth regarding extraterrestrial activity. I used to believe this earth had been visited for millenniums by aliens outside our realm, that even possibly our planet's humanity began with extraterrestrials migrating from another galaxy to ours. I know I digress because I explained all that in my research journal you read but stay with me, this all ties together.

"Yes, I read all of that, it was when you met Professor it all changed," she affirmed. "Your journal refreshed wonderful memories of our explorations. They were the best times of my life. When you were no longer with me, my life was so empty," Gabriella paused and looked at Caleb still sitting in the same position on the cave floor, "until I met my team, especially my Caleb." She reached out and touched his face. Turning back to her father, she asked, "What changed and when? I never detected anything different when we went exploring."

"That was my intention, Princess. It was when Professor revealed to me the ancient writings, both biblical and historical, explaining who the Nephilim are; that's when I understood the demonic nature of what I had been pursuing my entire life. It also led me to evil truths that are hard to even speak of." Again, he hesitated, still searching for words to reveal those truths but cover the horrendous details. "You were a teenager, Gabi, when our explorations took on a new dimension. We kept our home base in North Carolina but spent more time exploring in other countries. I made these trips appear to be our normal educational times, like we had always had, perusing the tunnels of the underworld, searching for artifacts and clues from ancient civilizations; but it had become a totally different mission for me. When we would find cave wall drawings depicting scenes that appeared to be visitations from extraterrestrial beings, I would no longer look through the lens of Ufology. I now saw them from a demonic Nephilim history being forever recorded in the form of art."

"I had no idea," she exclaimed. "Now that you've told me this, I do remember you would often have me focusing on and taking pictures of particular wall drawings while you would others. That was so I wouldn't see specific things and ask questions, wasn't it?"

"Exactly," he confirmed. "The graphic nature was more than I wanted you to focus on. Many were too graphic for a young mind to process."

Remembering the detailed depictions, he added, "I also believe the drawings were instructions for future generations to know exactly how to continue their satanic rituals."

His daughter understood why he had averted her attention. "You can never unsee what you've seen," she mused. "I want to know the whole truth and nothing but the truth, don't hold anything back."

Gabe rose from his rock seat and stood near the light sitting on the floor deciding where to begin. The illumination in the dark cave gave an ominous glow as he recounted where his mission began. "I began to research what had already been discovered in ancient cave art. I looked at pictures in science and archeological journals, piecing different elements of the drawings together; and it started to paint a picture of thousands of years of not only child sacrifice but horrible torture in ways unimaginable. The sacrifices were all done as worship to the gods of man, the Nephilim, which are ultimately Luciferian controlled."

Caleb had remained quiet mentally processing all Gabe was saying. Himself, having explored for over 20 years, began to see exactly what he was referring to. "I've seen the type of cave art you're talking about and considered them ancient paganism which died away long ago."

Gabe gently corrected Caleb: "With Lucifer nothing dies away. He keeps building towards his world dominion by seducing generation after generation, ever expanding his satanic worldwide control."

Caleb questioned further: "If this was still going on during the days Yeshua walked on this earth why aren't there references in the New Testament, especially by Him?"

Gabe quickly answered: "I believe there were. We read the Bible with a western society mentality. The people of Yeshua's days understood very differently from our modern day interpretations what Jesus and the New Testament writers meant. They based their understanding on their contemporary culture which would have been a reference to the evil that was taking place. We often quote from Matthew 24 where Yeshua Jesus said when the Son of Man comes it will be like Noah's day; and some of us, very few but some, understand that was referring to the destruction of the Nephilim and their ultimate return in the end days. Correct?"

Gabriella and Caleb simultaneously answered, "Yes," not sure what was coming next.

"But what do we understand about the part that says in the end of days it will be the same as described in Verse 8, *For as in the days before the flood, they were eating and drinking, marrying and giving in marriage, until the day that Noah entered the ark?"* Gabe answered for them, "Commentaries will mainly describe this as a generation just going about their daily lives, having a good time and not serving God or concerned about spiritual things."

"That isn't what it means?" Caleb asked, obviously confused.

"I definitely do not believe so," he replied. "What was the context for his answer in this verse? It was Noah's day. What was happening during Noah's day? The ancient biblical and extra-biblical writings tell us exactly what was happening; and the people of Yeshua's day would know what he was referring to. The Nephilim were eating of living flesh and drinking of living blood --of animals and humans-- and the marrying and giving in marriage of fallen angels and their offspring to the daughters of men. The unholy offspring of giants spawned by the miscegenation between spiritual bodies and mortal flesh and their subsequent atrocious actions is what Yeshua is referring to, not the simple and innocent acts of eating, drinking and getting married."

A dawn of understanding swept through Gabriella's mind. "Of course," she exclaimed. "Why have I not seen this? That makes perfect sense!"

In the dimly lit cave, she could see her father nod in agreement. "When you compare Yeshua's prophecy with Genesis 6 you can see this more clearly, and the disciples knew exactly what he meant. Enoch 7 also describes Noah's day: *the daughters of man became pregnant, and they bare great giants, whose height was three thousand ells: Who consumed all the acquisitions of men. And when men could no longer sustain them, the giants turned against them and devoured mankind. And they began to sin against birds, and beasts, and reptiles, and fish, and to devour one another's flesh, and drink the blood."*

"The Levitical Law says absolutely to not drink blood," Gabriella added. "So, naturally that is exactly what Lucifer would demand."

"The Levitical Law came centuries later and that is true, but immediately after the waters receded from the earth Noah was told directly from Yahweh in Genesis 9 to not drink the blood of man or animals."

"That gives a whole new meaning to the vampire cult," Caleb observed. "I always thought there was nothing to vampires, but sure makes you wonder."

"Vampires are very real, not in the sense movies portray them, but it is another sect of the whole in Satanic worship. Luciferianism goes so deep and so worldwide that I've never found the end."

Gabriella thought through all her father had shared and knew there was still more. "Go on, Dad." Even though much had been revealed she braced herself knowing it was about to get worse.

He sat back down beside her sharing the progression of events to the fateful day that changed his life. "The cave art told the story of child torture, sacrifice and drinking the blood of the children. I went to the ancient writings and found many links, one being in the Book of Jasher, Chapter 28. It was during the plagues of Egypt that God inflicted on Pharaoh excruciating leprosy from the top of his head to the soles of his feet. His sorcerers told him if the blood of tortured innocent babies was applied to his wounds he would be healed. He sent his sorcerers to the land of Goshen to take innocent babies from the arms of the Hebrew mothers and prepare their blood for his healing. Jasher wrote 365 babies were drained of their blood, but in God's anger he worsened the curse on Pharaoh."

"How can a loving God allow innocent children to be tortured?" Gabriella moaned. "I just don't understand."

"I have asked that question a million times, my daughter, and I wish I had an answer for you. The only answer I do have is the Bible makes it clear that Lucifer is the god of this world, and he rules through men's actions. Man chooses to do these horrible things for power and riches on earth and man has free will. I was like Caleb, I wanted to believe it was a pagan ritual that eventually stopped, but my rude awakening came when I read a book in 1995, Bloodlines of the Illuminati, which explained the Illuminati are generational satanic bloodlines which have gained world power as Lucifer's elitist. From that book the rabbit trail led me to other books and the mountain of information built beyond belief as to the practices of these evil humans, if you can even call them humans. I didn't realize until two nights ago when KJ discovered the Khazarian connection that the Bloodlines of the Illuminati and the Khazarians are one and the same. That was a missing piece of the puzzle for me identifying who Mystery Babylon could be."

Gabe stood back up and paced back and forth with the cave light reflecting on his mournful face. "This is the worst, the part I have held secret for many years, always praying for the children but seeing absolutely nothing I could personally do to help them."

Gabriella tried to brace herself emotionally for what was coming, but nothing could have prepared her for the horrible truth. She had never heard this agony of voice coming from her father, not even when her mother was murdered.

"First, the backstory. You remember Mr. Donaldson, the funeral director that helped me fake my death?" he questioned her.

"Sure, he was so very kind to me during that time." She wondered what Mr. Donaldson could possibly have to do with where her father's information was leading.

"I lived with the fact every day that what happened to your mother could happen to me at any time. As cautious as I was, I had to face reality, so I went to the funeral home to make prearrangements in the event I died suddenly. I didn't want that burden on you, Gabi."

"I know you always wanted to protect me," she acknowledged, clinging to Caleb's hand for emotional support. "What happened then?"

"I had met him a few times. Cherokee NC is a small town, and everybody knew everybody, but I didn't know the funeral director on a personal level. We immediately had a personal connection. Very soon I realized it was a God appointed meeting and this man could be trusted. I started sharing with him our UFO cave explorations, even circumstances of the death of your mother and why. When I told him about the cave art, the satanic child torture and sacrifices betrayed in the drawings, his countenance completely changed; it was obvious I had touched on a subject that made him extremely nervous. I expected him to change the subject, but instead the journey to these truths I am about to share began."

Caleb tightened his hand around Gabriella's silently confirming his support. The atmosphere was charged with ominosity.

"I need to tell you the details of the back story so you can understand how this all played out. Mr. Donaldson, his given name was Bob, had recently made his annual trip to the mortician convention in San Diego, California. He had friends he would meet up with at these conventions for social time. A particular friend asked to speak with him privately outside the convention area. They planned a time to meet at a city park nearby. When he met his friend, another man joined them. Bob was literally blindsided by the conversation which pursued. The unknown man identified himself only as Jim, a journalist seeking truth. He began to share with Bob things he had learned in his quest asking Bob about certain child death situations he may have encountered, especially pertaining to babies. Bob was shocked at the information shared and questioned the validity. He also assured Jim he had not personally seen anything like what he had described. The journalist left after assuring Bob there were some very strange child deaths occurring and asked if he had any information in the future to please contact him. He gave him his business card and left." Gabe hesitated to decide which information to give next.

"So, what happened then?" Caleb asked anxiously.

"Bob's mortician friend related an experience he had with a baby's corpse previously. The remains were brought to him by local police. The baby girl had been tortured in unspeakable ways; her blood completely drained while she was still alive, and she had been left in the woods for wild animals to consume her body. Whoever did this horrendous thing, never expected hunters to find the body first. The baby's remains were brought to Bob's friend for an autopsy and proper disposal.

"One of the hunters informed the journalist of what they had found which led Jim to the mortuary where the baby's remains were taken. When Jim explained to Bob's friend his research for an article to expose the truth regarding the child atrocities, Bob's friend agreed to secretly connect him with morticians at the convention to see if any other similar situations had occurred." Gabe took a breath and added, "I know that's a long trip around the barn, so to speak, but necessary to understand the foundation of where it goes from here."

Gabriella's eyes had filled with tears as a visual of this horrible scene played in her mind. Caleb got up from the cave floor and sat beside her on the rock, holding her in his arms as Gabe continued: "When I was telling Bob about the cave depictions of child sacrifice, he immediately made the connections. That's what solidified our relationship and a mutual resolve to explore wherever the demonic rabbit hole took us. Bob still had Jim's business card and immediately called him. Via the phone call, he introduced me telling the journalist I would be the contact point. With his work and family demands, Bob didn't have the time I had to devote to our new mission, but I kept him updated every step of the way."

A revelation came to Gabriella. "Was that when you unexpectedly announced we were going to California to explore? I remember being so excited to see an area we had never visited before."

"Yes, it was, Princess. I made sure it looked like a normal exploration and not a predetermined meeting with the journalist."

"But when, how do you meet with him? We were together the entire time?" Gabriella asked, confused.

"If you remember, the first day we arrived you were exhausted from the trip and the time difference had your sleeping routine off schedule. I left a note by your bed that I had gone out to get us breakfast and would be back shortly. That's when I met Jim at a nearby coffee shop. Again, there was an instant discernment this man could be trusted. Thank God his Holy Spirit within us can guide as we pursue truth. I shared with Jim my knowledge from ancient writings and cave art and my suspicions the practices had never ceased. He confirmed I was correct with his knowledge of current child abuse, sex trafficking, torture, sacrifice, and..." He stopped trying to control his emotions, not knowing if he could tell his innocent daughter the satanic details.

Gabe sat down on the floor next to the cave light and looked Gabriella in the eyes. He felt their bond of love as father and daughter would give her the strength to accept and emotionally process the lies that have controlled humanity for generations.

"In all the years of exploring caves and tunnels as my occupation and for the love of the adventure, I never dreamed of what the belly of the earth was hiding. I had heard the term DUMBS, Deep Underground Military Bases; and I thought they had formerly been used by only the military and most now vacated. Well, that was far from the truth. Over centuries these underground cities and tunnels had been built and used by members of the Luciferian Illuminati, which we now know are the Khazarian Cabal, or commonly referred to as the Deep State, it's all the same demonic entity. DUMBS were disguised as military bases. Jim showed me pictures provided to him by a person planted inside the Luciferian Cabal to expose their atrocities."

The vivid pictures replayed in Gabe's mind like a PowerPoint slide show. "There were pictures of kids in cages, like animals, being held for sex trafficking. Pictures of children being used as research for harrowing experiments being done beyond our normal human imagination. I could not sleep for days knowing children were tortured like that. Those pictures still haunt me, and I pray every day of my life for the children." Tears had filled Gabe's eyes as he struggled to continue.

Caleb was also fighting the emotional turmoil within him while Gabriella could not control the sobbing.

Gabe tried to ease the shock with a bit of history before he told the most evil element of child sacrifice. "This may seem out of place but it all ties together. Have you ever wondered how superstars in entertainment suddenly appear on the world scene and become an overnight sensation?"

"Many times," Caleb answered. "Also, I've wondered about politicians, sports stars, news reporters, and the lists go on. How is it you've never heard of them and suddenly they are at the top of their industries?"

"From what Jim discovered, almost all of these people have made a deal with the devil. They were sucked into the satanic cult little by little until there was no turning back. They sell their soul for fame and fortune and the demonic Cabal controls them from that point. Their full initiation into the Illuminati is for them to personally sacrifice a child using the Illuminati rituals after which the magical ritual of spirit-cooking is performed. Yes, they then get what they asked for, all that the god of this world offers, but there is now no redemption for their soul. It is the unpardonable sin. They have no guilt, no remorse and can commit any vile deed without any hesitation."

Gabriella did not want to know but knew it was necessary, "What is spirit cooking, Dad?"

He again hesitated but knew the total truth must be told; however, he decided some of the most horrendous details he would leave out. "It is an ancient witchcraft ritual of sacrificing a child, eating body parts and drinking the blood, all of which were prohibited in the Torah, one of the reasons being the satanic powers and control that can satanically be induced. Once the sacrificial initiation process is completed, it's necessary for the inductees to continue certain rituals to maintain your 'blessings' from Lucifer."

"I think I'm going to be sick," Gabriella moaned. "I just can't wrap my mind around all of this. Are you absolutely sure this is all true?" she questioned her father.

"Jim had pictures of it all, plus he had documentation from many other sources. In fact, he gave me a flash drive with a copy of all the proof. There is even proof of Royalty, Presidents and world elites being involved. That's why they wanted to make sure the information never surfaced. Jim wanted me to have the information, just in case something unexpected happened to him. I knew exactly what he meant."

"Flash drive?" Gabriella exclaimed. "With all the proof on it? Could that be what my vision meant?" She knew they would not understand and quickly added, "I will explain later, but wasn't that dangerous to have the proof in your possession that could prove all of this? We were already living on the run for the microchip you have."

"That was the reason I was willing, Gabi. I knew the dangers and had learned how to dodge their pursuit; my only fear was for you. Last night it all came together for me when Professor was reading Revelation 18. My discerning spirit told me these evils were a big part of what John was referring to: *And in her was found the blood of prophets, and of saints, and of all that were slain upon the earth.* I believe the last part refers to the innocent children slain for the demonic pleasures of Mystery Babylon who has existed from the days of Nimrod."

Gabriella remembered questioning the strange look on her father's face when that particular verse was read. Now it made sense, it was all making sense in the most horrible of details.

"I've seen movies with some of this stuff in them and would wonder what kind of twisted mind could come up with such and call it entertainment," Caleb commented.

"That's another important point to add." Gabe explained. "The entertainment world is one of the many ways Luciferians tell what they are going to do in advance. Amos 3:7 *says that Yahweh does nothing unless he first reveals it to the prophets.* Well, Lucifer is held to the same standard. So, he uses all forms of media and entertainment to reveal without revealing, if you know what I mean. In movies, animation, video games, music and such; it's referred to as predictive programming. The mind becomes so desensitized that when truth is revealed, it is easier to accept."

"If I have time to watch any more movies, I will be doing so from a whole new perspective," Caleb remarked with animosity.

Gabe stood back up ready to reveal the final secret Jim had revealed which the Luciferians had concealed from humanity. "Have you questioned how Hollywood actors, entertainers, royalty, global and political elites manage to stay energetic and youthful looking?"

"Of course, I have," Gabriella muttered, sensing it was all connected.

"The final thing Jim told me was the worst of all. For these elitists to maintain their youthful lives, there is a particular blood of innocent children they must drink on a continuous basis." He desperately dreaded revealing this last truth. "There is a ritual where they torture a child until there is an extreme surge of adrenaline in the blood. When the oxidation of the adrenaline reaches its maximum, the blood is immediately drained, while the child is alive, and preserved for ingestion. The chemical compound created from the blood reverses aging, maintains health and energizes the body. It is known as Adrenochrome."

"Oh, my God, how in the world?" Gabriella moaned in agony of soul.

He regretted adding the final comment; however, he had to bring it to completion. "The adrenaline induced blood must be continually ingested to maintain the effects, which demands the need for a continual supply of babies and small children to satisfy these world elitists, Mystery Babylon; and they will take out anyone who could expose them."

Gabriella dropped her head in her hands and cried out loud. Caleb remained silent, but his body shook with the agony of these revelations. Gabe's heart was broken for them both, having experienced the same emotions when this was revealed to him. He sat down next to Gabriella and took her in his comforting arms. Gradually the sobbing subsided, and she gained her composure.

Finally, she broke the silence with a question. "Do you still have contact with Jim?"

She could feel his body tense. "Sadly, what Jim feared might happen, did happen; both Jim and the man who smuggled out the pictures were mysteriously found dead. They knew too much. Both were truly martyrs for the cause of the children."

It suddenly dawned on Gabriella the real reason her father faked his death. "And after your meeting with Jim you knew too much also and had the proof. You were literally treading on Mystery Babylon's secret territory."

He nodded his head in agreement. "My first instinct was to find any means I could to reveal the truth and try to save the children. Then I knew I had to save my own child first. I knew no one of any power I could take the information to, the media nor government, could be trusted. I found that out years prior. All I would be doing was create a new reason to take me out and come after you, Gabi. Ultimately, nothing for the children would be accomplished.

"When I returned to the hotel that fateful day, you were still sleeping, totally unaware of how our lives had changed. We spent a few days sight-seeing and exploring while I was deciding what I had to do to protect you. When we got back to Cherokee, I immediately went to see Bob and he had already talked to Jim. When I arrived at his office, one look told me something was very wrong. He informed me he had been visited by some men who identified themselves as CIA asking questions related to Jim. They had been following Jim when he met Bob in the park in San Diego and wanted to know the content of their conversation. It was obvious they were surveilling Jim, which meant they probably had seen me with him too. When we moved to Cherokee, North Carolina, I had finally felt for the first time since your mother's murder that we were safe and off their radar. The meeting with Jim changed everything and I knew big decisions had to be made immediately."

"That's when you and Mr. Donaldson began the plan to fake your death." His daughter could see the total picture now.

"Yes, and planning began with Professor to move you to Israel where I would be going; and now you know the rest of the story and why I could not take the chance of writing this in my journal. I could in no way affirm that

I knew about these secret chambers in the belly of the earth where hellish atrocities were taking place with innocent babies and children. Only Bob knew the truth and I knew he would take the secrets to his grave...literally. It was not long after he helped me fake my death that he mysteriously died also."

She was aware the funeral director had passed but had no idea it was connected to her father. "So, the Cabal assumed Jim's information would have been added to your microchip research and included in the box that contained your journals. They now had a double reason to find it and were waiting in the wings in case it ever resurfaced. When Sandee gave it to me after the Saudi Arabia exploration, the battle began. It's amazing I had been surveilled my entire time in Israel and had no idea." She stated in amazement.

"Mystery Babylon will stop at nothing to destroy anyone in her way," Gabe added somberly.

"Dad, you said you were leaving out some of the more horrific details. I don't think I could mentally endure anymore right now anyway. I need time to process all this. I didn't see anything like this about the children in my visions. I did see myself ministering to children as the Holy Spirit healed and delivered them."

"God was preparing you for the greater mission, my daughter. When Mystery Babylon is destroyed there will be children coming from the belly of the earth who will need both healing and demonic deliverance. Yahweh is raising up a righteous army for the end of days. I always knew you were chosen, and it is for such a time as this."

— Chapter 18 —

Gabriella, Gabe, and Caleb were silent, each captured by their mental turmoil. Gabe was questioning if revealing these horrible realities had been the right decision. Gabriella fought back the tears as her mind was replaying her father's revelations. Caleb was grief stricken for the children, still in shock that after all of his years of exploring he was totally unaware of these secret underground cities where demonic atrocities were occurring.

When they returned to the bunker, Gabe paused before entering. "Professor and Sandee do know all the things I've told you. They are the only ones who know the whole truth. I'll find the appropriate time to share this with the rest of the team."

"One last question before we go back inside, Dad. Where is the flash drive now?"

Gabe unbuttoned the top of his shirt pulling it open. Gabriella shined her flashlight on his upper chest revealing the necklace she had made for him when she was a child. "I remember the day I gave that to you. You promised you would always wear it." She could see that next to the heart necklace she had created was an unfamiliar locket. "What's that?" she asked, confused.

"All the information the journalist gave me is literally next to my heart. I removed the microchip from the flash drive and it's in this locket hidden with the first microchip, it's all the information the evil cabal wants destroyed: proof of their satanic child rituals and proof of the third strand of DNA to create human hybrids. The proof was always with me, and I never had to fear the microchips may have been found. When they thought I was dead, they hoped the information would never be released. They watched you all those years, Gabi, just to make sure my research didn't resurface."

"But they know now you're alive," Gabriella moaned.

Gabe tried to comfort his daughter, "Perhaps it's Yahweh's timing, time all truth be known. I do believe we are in the end days and time for all this evil to be revealed. Nothing can stop what's coming."

Gabriella clung to her father again thanking God he was with her for whatever time they had left. Gabe treasured every moment acutely aware it could end at any moment. Caleb watched them in the dim cave lighting while fighting his personal anguish of soul. His whole being longed to have Gabriella as his wife; however, with each passing day it looked less likely it would ever be.

The bunker was quiet when they reentered. Sandee was in the kitchen preparing lunch. Chris and KJ were working hard in the security room while Aaron and Faith were researching and making notes.

Sandee looked up from the stove and immediately knew the dreaded conversation had finally taken place. "Professor is in his bedroom resting and praying. This has been an extremely emotional time for him. He feels responsible for everything, you know."

"I'm the one that's responsible," Gabe quickly clarified. "I pulled him into my plan and none of this is his fault."

"He believes The Omega Watchers Project pulled you in, Gabe, and had it not been for his project none of the rest would have occurred." Sandee quickly replied.

Gabriella took control of the debate: "This is no one's fault, and Yahweh is not surprised by any of it. He brought us all together. He allowed you, Dad, to find out the truth for a reason and brought you and Professor together for such a time as this. We are all part of God's plan, and we must follow where The Lamb of God leads us. We should be excited that He has chosen us, and not be questioning."

Gabe took his daughter in his arms. "Such wisdom from one who didn't believe any of it just a short time ago."

"That's the truth," Faith added joyfully. "All my years of persistence finally paid off, right Gabi?"

Smiling at her dear friend, Gabriella agreed. "And you'll be surprised at how much I do know, how much I've seen that is coming in the near future." She was ready to share some of her visions but before she began Chris called from the security room for them to join him.

"I've got some questions, Gabi. I need you for a few minutes."

"Coming," she replied, pulling Caleb with her. Gabe followed close behind. Immediately on entering she saw the faces of Russo and Moretti on the computer screen. "That's them," she informed Chris, "no question about it."

"KJ's been following the internet trail on these guys, and they are exactly who you said, Gabi. They work indirectly for Strozza the Director of the International Intelligence Agency; and Strozza is trusted by all individual government agencies. Very few common citizens even know an international agency exists." Chris paused and looked straight into Gabriella's eyes searching for deeper truths. "But you knew, Gabi."

She knew he was waiting for an explanation. Searching for the right explanation, she decided to use the words of the Prophet Amos, "*Surely the Lord GOD does nothing, Unless He reveals His secret to His servants the prophets.*"

The confusion on Chris' face required further clarification from Gabriella. "Yahweh is unveiling through His servants the evil that's exploding in the earth. He promised in the last days all that is hidden would be revealed. Acts 2:17 says: *And it shall come to pass in the last days, says God, That I will pour out of My Spirit on all flesh; Your sons and your daughters shall prophesy, Your young men shall see visions, Your old men shall dream dreams.* I can't explain why I've been chosen, but the things I've told you are the things that Almighty God has shown me through dreams and visions, and they will happen. Russo and Moretti, these thugs are just low hanging fruit from the ones who are planning the One World Luciferian Government."

Gabe put his arm around his daughter encouraging her to continue. "Maybe it's time you tell us all you've seen, Princess. It's obvious God took what the enemy meant for destruction and turned it to His perfect plan. While you were in a coma, alternate dimension, whatever it was, there is no doubt in my mind you were filled with the Holy Spirit and seeing the future."

She nodded in agreement. She knew the time had come. "Let's get everyone together. I think it's time that *all* secrets are revealed," she added, looking into her father's eyes.

"No more secrets," he confirmed, dreading to repeat to the team all he had shared with his daughter and Caleb.

They exited the security room with Caleb murmuring under his breath, "I hope the rest of the team is ready for this, I sure wasn't." He pulled Gabriella to the back of the others and briefly held her in his arms, assuring her of his support. "You can do this, Gabi."

"With you and Dad by my side, I know I can," she replied, praying for the strength needed to hear her father's secrets of the past again, plus sharing all she had seen in the future.

Dr. Brotman had already emerged from his bedroom and been informed by Sandee that Gabe had finally broken his silence. He settled in his black leather recliner while the others gathered around him on the couches and pulled side chairs to form a circle.

Chris started first, informing the group regarding the bird sighting and his verification it was a drone and not a crow. "It could mean nothing," he tried to soothe their apprehensions. "It could have been hunters scouting the area, but we must be cautious and prepared for any possible scenarios, just in case."

"How about sweet Mrs. Nicholson," Faith inquired. "Any word on her."

Chris explained the video footage of her kidnapping and the two men Gabriella identified. "Sadly, Detective Richards has not located the doctor's wife. That leaves us very uncertain as to what her captors may know about this lodge. Another reason to stay on alert."

Gabriella had been mentally filtering through her visions, deciding how to explain each one. She started with the war. "I dreamed you had all disappeared, raptured, and Chris and I were the only ones left in the bunker. It was the Psalms 83 War; the coalition attack of Israel's surrounding nations and Israel's stunning victory was nothing short of miraculous. All the nations that attacked became the territory of Israel giving her all the land that was promised to Abraham. Jews from all over the world began to move to these new territories exploding the Israeli population. DNA tests began to identify the ten lost tribes of Israel resulting in millions more making Aliyah. As a result of Israel's expanded borders and unexpected military dominance, every nation turned against her. That's where the story begins."

Gabriella spent hours walking her team through the visions that followed, remembering vividly every detail, and ending her recount questioning, "I really don't know how much of what I saw is allegorical or will be literal. I saw men I did not know: Sotoreo, Strozza and the Black Pope in the lodge above us. Now I find out they are real people in the actual roles I saw them. These men spent days in the lodge planning their world control and I heard it all. Maybe it was God's way of identifying the Luciferian Mystery Babylon to me, maybe? I just don't understand it all, but one thing for sure, the evil that emanated from those men cannot be described in human words." She added one last thought as she looked at Chris. "I don't know why you were with me throughout the entire vision, Chris; but if I could venture a prophetic guess, Yahweh has chosen you also for this time and His purpose." She looked around the room and concluded, "Every one of us have been hand-picked by our Heavenly Father for this time in human history, a time like has never been before and will never be again."

The room was silent for several minutes. Chris was speechless that he had been ever present in Gabriella's prognostication of the future; however, since part of her vision had already become reality then he was not going to question the rest of what she had seen. He was determined to follow every lead she could offer."

Dr. Brotman was mentally struggling with the pre and post comatose Gabriella. Never in his over seventy years of living had he seen such a dramatic change in anyone. He could only describe it as miraculous, just like their divine healings, which all together laid the foundation for him to believe everything else she shared. He broke the contemplative atmosphere with solemn commitment. "Here we are, Lord, use all of us according to Your divine purpose."

"Amen," the team said in unison.

Sandee quietly went to the kitchen and began dinner preparations. She knew what was coming next and escaped so she would not hear it all again. She silently prayed for Gabe as he recounted the real reason of why he had faked his death. Within a few minutes she could hear sobs and then exclamations of unbelief. She knew without hearing Gabe's words what was being revealed during those moments. Escaping to the pantry and closing the door behind her, Sandee cried out in anguish for God to save the children. She interceded in prayer while Gabe struggled to get through the horrendous truth one more time. When she re-entered the kitchen, the room was silent with a heaviness of spirit.

All the facts now revealed solidified the team's resolve to complete both Dr. Brotman's and Gabe's missions, which had merged into one: UFOs, the return of the Nephilim, the third strand of DNA creating a controlled hybrid human being, and Mystery Babylon - they were all connected into Lucifer's plan to rule the earth.

Dr. Brotman leaned forward in his recliner solemnly instructing his team: "We know the time is short, very short. It's obvious Satan knows our mission and is doing all he can to destroy us; however, we're protected by The Most High and nothing can harm us until our mission is complete. Yes, we must be vigilant, but we cannot fear. I do believe each one of us has spent our lives preparing for such a time as this, the greatest time in all humanity...the final battle of good and evil."

"What's the next step?" Gabriella asked, ready to act. "I can't just sit here and wait to be found. I need to be proactive; we all do."

The team were all in agreement and suggestions began on how to proceed. Gabe shocked them all with his next question: "Chris, do you believe

Detective Richards can be trusted with the journalist's information on the microchip?"

Even Dr. Brotman was in total amazement. "You are willing to take that chance, Gabe?"

"If we're running out of time, there is no better time. Perhaps even Detective Richards has been brought to us for such a time as this. Any better ideas?" Gabe asked, looking from person to person.

Gabriella remembered her vision of the cottage conversation which she and Chris had with the detective. Now she understood the Holy Spirit was showing her in advance to trust him. In her preview of the future, the detective was very open both to salvation through Yeshua and willing to go undercover, risking his life, to expose the evil captured on the flash drive. She knew he could be trusted but she allowed Chris, who had worked with him for years, to deliver the confirmation before she shared hers.

"Without a doubt, Gabe, he can be totally trusted; and I believe he would use every means available to him to expose this kind of evil even to his dying breath."

Gabriella added, "I can confirm with my visions, Chris is absolutely right. Dad, this could be your answer to pray regarding who you could trust with the microchip information, both microchips. It's playing out just like I saw in my vision."

"The next question is how do we get the microchip to him?" Gabe looked at Chris hopeful he had ideas.

Chris looked at his watch before answering. "I'm supposed to call Richards soon for an evening update. Should I tell him and see what he thinks? I could fill him in on details, but he will need the pictures for absolute proof. That means a meeting some time, somewhere."

"I'm sure he's being watched very closely," Dr. Brotman interjected. "That's taking a very big chance."

"I *know* they are watching him," Gabriella confirmed. "That's another thing I saw, and his police phone at the station is tapped too."

Chris replied, "That's the reason he uses the non-hackable phone, just in case. He trusts very few people, even some within our own police force. This will be tricky trying to arrange a meeting."

"Yahweh always has an answer," Sandee interjected while motioning them to the dinner table. "Now let's eat. We all think better on a full stomach."

In the middle of dinner, a strange alarm went off. Gabe jumped to his feet and ran to the security room. "There's someone on the property," he announced as he exited. The entire team was right behind him even though they knew they would not all fit in the small area. KJ joined him in monitoring every area of the lodge grounds.

"I don't see anything outside, do you, KJ?" Gabe inquired in a breathless voice.

"Nothing," he answered, continuing to move from one camera view to another, completely surrounding the lodge. "The sun's gone down and it's harder to detect movement."

Gabe changed the monitors to the interior view of the lodge. The team was all holding their breath in anticipation. "Nothing here either," he commented monitoring room by room. "The live view shows nothing inside or out so let's go to history, KJ, and see if it shows anything." Gabe made the video recording adjustments and focused on the grounds directly around the lodge.

"There," KJ exclaimed. Gabe froze the screen which displayed two men in dark attire in the grove of trees to the left of the lodge just past the creek. "I'm going to zoom in for a closer view."

Gabriella squeezed by Chris to get a full view of the monitor just as KJ zoomed in on the men's faces. "Well, wouldn't you know." Her voice was a mix of certainty and concern. "Good ole' Russo and Moretti."

Faith could not see the screen but wanted clarification. "The men that kidnapped Mrs. Nicholson?"

"One and the same," Gabriella confirmed. "But where did they go, Dad, if they're not on the live monitors? Could they have deactivated a camera like they did at the doctor's house?"

"These are satellite-controlled cameras and cannot be hacked or deactivated, nothing like the internet or phone line systems. In a normal situation I would just turn on the flood lights and intruders would be revealed, but that would be a dead giveaway someone is here. We will just have to wait. If they're still on the grounds the alarm will go off as soon as they move again. They may have already left since all the lights are out in the lodge and no cars are in the driveway. They could've just been checking for any signs of activity."

"Too close for comfort," Faith mumbled. "Just the fact they're this close is very eerie, even if they don't know we're here." She signed deeply and added, "These walls are starting to close in on me.

Sandee put an arm of comfort around her. "I know, honey bunny. We all are feeling a bit claustrophobic. Hopefully soon we will have some answers."

KJ felt her frustration. "How about we go out the tunnel when Chris goes, is that okay with you, Chris? At least Faith can get a bit of fresh air."

"Perfect," Chris assured him. "I prefer some company on these trips out."

Faith blushed slightly trying to cover her excitement for some time with KJ. Sandee smiled and leaned over to whisper in the professor's ear, "Some things never change no matter what the world conditions."

Dr. Brotman nodded and winked. They both had detected the chemistry between KJ and Faith; however, the appreciation of young love was dampened by their current circumstances.

Gabe turned away from the monitors. "There's really no need to sit her and stare at nothing. If the alarm goes off again, we'll catch these guys on camera." He got up and motioned for them to return to the dining area. "Let's finish dinner; my best guess is they are long gone."

"And hopefully they think no one is at the lodge," Chris added. "I can't help but wonder if Mrs. Nicholson has said anything to tip them off." His voice waned as he added in contemplation, "Coincidence they would show up so shortly after her kidnapping?"

The team finished dinner constantly on edge concerned the alarm would activate again. By dinner's end the team had relaxed convinced the men were gone, at least for the time being. Chris said nothing but expected these evil men would soon be returning.

"Let's go," Chris directed KJ and Faith. "Richards is probably waiting for my call."

The three exited the tunnel. The darkness greeted them as the fake rock door closed securely behind them. Flashlights in hand, they walked silently. Cave exploration was Faith's passion, so she felt right at home. KJ took her arm and slipped it through his allowing her to guide him through the darkness. Faith was enjoying this cave journey more than any before. KJ could faintly see the smile on her face in the dim light. This was the moment he had been waiting for. He leaned over and whispered, "You do know I care about you; I just wish circumstances were different."

Faith leaned her head on his shoulder and with a breathless whisper confirmed, "Me, too."

Being in deep contemplation of all that he needed to discuss with Detective Richards, Chris was unaware the two had slowed their pace to allow for a private conversation behind him. As they approached the end of the tunnel, faint light from the moon filtered into the mouth of the cave. Stepping into the crisp fall air they simultaneously took a deep breath, feeling refreshed in both body and soul.

"I can think a lot more clearly out here as long as no drones are flying," Chris stated, looking into the sky to detect any possible drone activity. "And crows don't fly at night, so if we do see one, we'll know."

KJ took the opportunity to be alone with Faith. "I know you need some time for your call, so we'll get out of your way for a few minutes." In the moonlight the two sat down by the rushing creek and for the first time had a brief time to share privately with an open heart.

Even though it had been over an hour, it was much too quick for their liking when Chris called them. "Ready, guys?"

Reluctantly KJ got up and extended his hand to help Faith. He did not release her hand until they were reentering the bunker. Chris still in deep thought paid no attention to the bond that had been solidified between KJ and Faith. However, as soon as they stepped into the presence of the team, it was obvious. Even though they tried to pretend all was normal, it was written all over their faces.

"Well, well," Gabriella teased. "What do we have here?" She went to her best friend and gave her a big hug. "I'm so happy for you."

"Oh, hush, Gabi," Faith replied, smiling ear to ear.

Caleb slapped KJ on the back. "Good for you, my friend. You've got a good one there."

Aaron did not have a romantic bone in his body. He looked from KJ to Faith questioning what everyone was making a big deal about.

KJ did not try to hide his feelings any longer, he put his arm around Faith's shoulders and declared to the entire team, "Okay, I admit it. I've fallen head over heels for this woman."

Sandee laughed out loud. "Well, it's about time you admitted it. We've all seen the signs since the day you arrived." She looked at Aaron, "Well, almost all of us," she joked as the team joined her laughter.

"Are you laughing at me?" Aaron questioned, still oblivious to what they meant.

Caleb spelled it out for him. "KJ and Faith sitting in a tree..., get it?"

Aaron raised his eyebrows, "Huh?"

"Some people are hopeless romantics, and some are just hopeless," Gabriella laughed. "He'll get it eventually."

Gabe pulled the team back to reality. "I hate to put a damper on this love fest, as wonderful as it is, but I'm sure Chris has information from Detective Richards."

The team settled back into their normal circle for group conversation. KJ for the first time pulled his chair next to Faith's and held her hand while Chris relayed the information.

"First, there is still no news on Mrs. Nicholson. Richards is following every rabbit trail that could possibly lead to where they took her. Naturally, the doctor is in a panic and Officer Cohen still has him and the hospital clerk in protective custody. Cohen has his hands full trying to keep those two settled down and safe."

Caleb looked at Gabriella and commented, "I know what it's like to see the woman you love in danger and feel like you could lose her any minute. I'm sure Doc is almost uncontrollable."

"I can't even imagine what that young lady, I believe Leah is her name, what she's going through emotionally," Sandee added. "She was just willing to help and didn't even know who she was helping or anything about our situation. Bless her heart." Her words faded with emotional sympathy. "Go on, Chris, sorry to interrupt, it just breaks my heart, you know."

"I know," he affirmed with compassion. "It's difficult for all of us and in different ways, but I do have some good news, or at least I hope it's good news. Richards will figure out a way to get the microchips. I gave him a brief overview and he too was shocked by the information, so he's going to buddy up to Strozza, pretend he's on their side to see what he can find out. He knows him from some former international cases that involved Israel and hopefully that will give him a door in." Chris got up and starting pacing back and forth in contemplation. "It appears our information is running parallel with Richards. We've both been digging for information from two different directions and coming up with the same results. The recent war has made him question some things on who really controls the various governments, even Israel's and he also believes there is an international Deep State controlling everything. He said we cannot trust what is being reported by the media and the only way to find the truth is to be on the inside where it's happening."

"Like a double agent?" Gabe questioned.

"Exactly, and he's putting everything on the line to do this, literally." The concern in Chris' face was evident as he continued: "But he's willing to do it for the greater good. He's always believed there was a nefarious international control with some government officials in all nations, but never could put his finger on the pulse. With the information we've been giving him, he's connecting dots that he's needed and realized we've all been deceived on many levels. He now believes the Khazarian Mafia could very well be at the center of it all and Strozza could be the key to knowing the truth. He's going to work on a plan tonight on how to get Gabe's information and let me know on our morning call."

"This could be very dangerous," Gabe stated, realizing another person's life was now in danger because of the Luciferian revelations on the microchips in his possession.

— Chapter 19 —

The team had retired for the night, each restless as they lived with the uncertainty of what the next day would bring. Neither Gabriella nor Faith could sleep and talked into the wee hours of the morning about their hopes and dreams of marrying the men they loved and having a family, a future; however, both accepting it most likely would never be. Both longed for children of their own and shared their mental agony of what Gabe had revealed regarding the child satanic rituals.

"No normal human being could do such things," Gabriella muttered, tossing, and turning. "This evil is straight from the pits of hell." Then the truth dawned on her, and she sat straight up in her bed. "Now I understand," she exclaimed.

"What?" Faith sat on the side of her bed facing her "What are you talking about, Gabi?"

"Remember our last exploration in Saudi Arabia? The cave where we found the ancient writing that continued the prophecy on the scroll given to Professor by the mysterious prophet?"

"Of course, I remember, but what are you getting at?"

"Something evil was released when Caleb and Aaron moved that rock exposing the pit and the cave writing. Remember? It was right after that discovery that Arcturus, let me rephrase that to the actual truth, when Abaddon appeared in my dreams and began satanically deceiving me."

In the dim light she could see Faith nod, confirming she remembered it all before Gabriella continued: "We've heard Professor for years discussing the book of Enoch, the second chapter of Peter and from the Book of Jude about the fallen angels being kept in captivity until the time of the end; and then Revelation 9 giving the time frame of their release upon the earth."

"Yes," Faith confirmed, trying to follow her friend's train of thought. "Where are you going with this?"

"There is an explosion of depravity on this earth like never been in human history, and the release of the demons from the abyss would explain it. Wouldn't it, Faith? We know we're in the end days when Satan will release his great wrath knowing his time is running out."

"Hasn't Professor explained this to us already, Gabi?"

Gabriella leaned forward her body language proclaiming her personal epiphany, "Yes, he has, but now all the pieces fit together for me personally, like the puzzle he has talked about for years. Dad's information about the children opened my eyes wide. It's always been about the children, Faith, don't you see? When the fallen angels had children with the daughters of men, the Nephilim, those children were cursed forever, there was no redemption for them. When those hybrid beings died who were the seed of Satan, they became soulless, disembodied spirits searching for someone to inhabit - demons who's desire is to control man until they are cast eternally into a burning hell that awaits them."

"I see where you're going now," Faith exclaimed. "Since Satan's seed is non-redeemable, he is determined to destroy the redeemable seed of Adam, especially the children."

"Exactly! What did the evil Pharaoh do?" Gabriella answered her own question. "He killed the baby boys. What did Herod do? The very same thing. Sacrificing children to Molech, Baal...it's always been about killing the children in an effort to destroy God's creation." She took a deep breath before stating, "Dad's information was the final glue to the pieces. These satanic child abuse rituals are beyond the scope of anything previously known to man."

"Because Satan knows he is running out of time," Faith restated.

Both women plopped their heads back on their pillows in anguish. Before Gabriella drifted off to sleep, she made one last comment: "Jesus told us the final evil days would be like nothing man has ever seen before, nor will ever see again; we're seeing his prophetic words fulfilled in real time."

Gabriella turned to her side and finally was able to sleep, but her sleep was not restful. She flipped from side to side, tossing and turning. *When a deep sleep finally settled in, another night journey began. She was exploring an unknown cave with only a flashlight to guide her way. She could hear the sounds of children crying out for help. The anguished screams echoed through the dark tunnels. Sensing the presence of others behind her, she stepped into a crevice of the cave wall to hide. Soon passing her was a multitude of soldiers carrying weapons she had never seen before. They were dressed in camouflage and totally silent as they advanced forward in the direction of the children's* cries. She was unnoticed as this huge army of men passed by. When the last one passed, she followed behind them for what seemed several miles. None of them uttered a word the entire time.

When they stopped, each man did something with their weapons that appeared to get them ready for firing, but the procedure made no noise at all. She intuitively knew a surprise attack was about to occur and she would be witnessing the entire battle. Her heart was beating fast, and she could barely breathe as the men started advancing forward. Shortly after, she heard weapons firing and voices screaming. They had reached the entry of an underground city where children were held captive.

Gabriella stepped into an underground world she never imagined existed. In the surprise attack, the soldiers had either killed or taken captive the overseers of this satanic place. She was now aware she had once again entered the supernatural and could see everything without being seen. Watching the events play out, the captives who had survived the army's take down were being shackled. The compassionate soldiers were going from cage to cage releasing the children who were petrified even of these men, not knowing their pure intentions; however, as the strong men took the children in their arms and held them close, promising they were now safe, the agonizing cries reduced to whimpers of hope. The tortured children began to respond to their rescuer's solicitude.

Gabriella went from room to room in the underground city of hell seeing the horrendous conditions which were much worse than the journalist had revealed to her father, much worse. She also realized in the supernatural realm she could mentally process her environment, whereas had she been in her natural world she would not have been able to even look upon these things.

She felt immense relief as she watched the soldiers carrying the children out, rescued from a living hell. She followed the men out through the miles of tunnels. She expected to see daylight but instead they came to an intersection where the tunnels became subterranean roads like the ones beneath the Haifa hospitals; there were vehicles waiting for the children to be transported to safety and care. Once loaded they traveled at high speed to their destination. In the supernatural, Gabriella could travel as fast as the vehicles and followed them to an underground hospital where personnel were prepared for the children's arrival. Gabriella knew the children would need both physical and emotional healing.

"Where am I?" she questioned. "Prophet, are you here with me?" She felt a hand touch her head and then smelled the sweet aroma of the anointing oil as it flowed through her hair. She turned to face Elijah.

"Everything I have previously shown you is for this revelation, Daughter of Zebulon. "The Indian girl's healing, the child delivered from demonic possession in the hospital, they were both to give you supernatural compassion for the children in this end of days. Your anointing is for the children who are the heart of The Father."

"Can you tell me where this place is, Prophet?"

"It is not just one place, Daughter. These vile prisons exist in many places all over the earth with tunnels running to and fro. The time has come."

"What time?" She questioned as the scene faded away and a voice was calling her name.

"Wake up, Gabi. The alarm's going off again." Faith was shaking Gabriella from her night vision back to reality.

She jumped from her bed and followed Faith towards the security room. "What's going on, Faith?"

"I don't know yet, but I'm sure it is not good."

Joining the team, Caleb pulled Gabriella to his side as they waited for more information. He ran his fingers through her rumpled hair. "Do you know you have oil in your hair?"

"I had a night vision again. I'll explain later."

KJ and Gabe were at the monitors watching the secured entry gate. A black SUV had stopped and parked with two men exiting the vehicle. Without the code no vehicle could enter the lodge grounds so they parked as close as they could get. The camera zoomed in revealing the return of Russo and Moretti.

"These guys are back again. They must have stayed close by last night and waited for daylight to come back thinking no one is here," Gabe surmised. "But how are they getting on to the grounds?" he questioned. "The chain linked fence surrounds the entire property." The cameras followed the two men along the fence line to a grove of trees where it was difficult to get a clear view. They disappeared completely from the cameras and shortly after they emerged from the grove inside the fenced area and were headed towards the lodge.

Chris was trying to reason for a possible scenario why they would return if, in fact, they really believed no one was at the lodge. As they moved closer to the lodge another camera followed their movement. They circled to the back of the lodge where their movement was picked up by another monitor. The two men were looking in every direction, obviously trying to locate any surveillance equipment or security cameras. Russo was holding up a device waving it in the air.

"What is that?" Dr. Brotman asked, stretching around Gabe to see the monitor.

"That device is supposed to give off a signal if there is a security system activated. They will never get a detection from my security," Gabe chuckled. "The whole system was designed for such a time as this." He reached to his left and switched off the back up security system to the back door alarm, leaving the manual door alarm to activate when someone enters. Chris immediately understood his plan.

"Good move, Gabe," he said patting him on the shoulder.

KJ looked at the two of them questioning, "Why would you turn the alarm off?"

"Off?" Faith gasped at the point of tears. "That makes no sense at all." The team members were looking at each other in total confusion.

"I left the manual system on so these thugs would think they had deactivated the alarm. They will have no idea they are being both seen and recorded. How else are we going to find out what they're up to unless we give them free reign to play it out?" Gabe answered in a voice now tempered with deep concentration.

They all knew silence was expected as the three men at the monitors made sure every movement was being captured. Moretti put down his backpack by the back door and pulled tools to open the lock. Once the lock clicked allowing access, he slowly pushed the door open, and the alarm was activated. Quickly he snipped the wire and the warning sound ceased. He turned and smiled at Russo laughingly declaring, "Mission accomplished."

Gabe sarcastically returned the laughter. "They think they're home free to scout the entire house undetected. Surprise!"

Watching them enter the kitchen area, walking right past the pantry was a bit unnerving to the entire team. "A little close for comfort," Gabe muttered, while the men continued towards the great room captured now by the interior cameras. They moved from room to room on the first level and then up the wooden stairs to the guest bedrooms, searching every drawer and closet.

Chris explained, "I would expect them to do this very thing, looking for any possible clue that might help locate us; something maybe left behind with a phone number, address, anything that could be a possible lead." Each member of the team verified they had left no personal information when they escaped to the bunker.

"If they go to the guesthouse, they'll find my personal belongings, but that's no big deal. They know I'm alive now anyway." Gabe stated. "But they'll have to find me first to find what they're really looking for." He wrapped his hand around the locket hanging from his neck and silently prayed they never would.

Moretti and Russo returned to the great room, commenting once again on how nice the lodge was. The two men sat down in recliners and gazed at all the architectural details. "Strozza would love this place," Russo commented. Looking out the large picture window facing north, he added, especially that view of Mt. Hermon."

"I'm sure he would," Gabriella stated sarcastically.

Chris looked at her, not sure what she meant. She had to keep reminding herself that even though he was with her in the visions, her supernatural journey was not real to him. She explained, "Mt. Hermon was the supernatural portal for entry of the fallen angels who left their first estate, heaven, and chose to become mortal beings of earth. It's the holy place to Luciferians."

"I've lived in Israel all my life, and never heard that," he replied in amazement.

Gabe motioned for silence as he turned up the speakers to hear the two men converse upstairs. "I wish we had something positive to report to Strozza," Moretti commented. "I don't think the old lady was in her right mind."

"They're not here, that's for sure," Russo answered him. "She was a real firecracker; I'll give her that." He reached into his pocket and retrieved a metal device and placed it under the coffee table out of sight. "If anyone shows up, we will know."

"Mrs. Nicholson?" Sandee exclaimed. "Do you think they're talking about Mrs. Nicholson? Did she tell them about the lodge?" A foreboding settled on the team as they continued to watch the two men above them.

As they got up to make their way towards the back door of the lodge, Russo noticed a box containing Dr. Brotman's tins of cherry tobacco. "Hmmm, my favorite. I think I'll take one of these with me."

Once again, they passed directly by the pantry door, having no earthly idea how close they were to those they sought and commenting once again on their way out, "I believe she led us on a wild goose chase. She was a feisty one."

"Was?" Dr. Brotman questioned? "Past tense?" The uncertainty of Mrs. Nicholson cast a somber mood on the team as they returned to the living room. Chris and KJ remained in the security room to continue to monitor and make sure the two men returned to their vehicle and left the property.

Gabriella's prior night's dream, plus questions about the doctor's wife, haunted her. Sensing her distress, Gabe put his arms around his daughter and held her close.

Leaning her head on her father's shoulder, she whispered in his ear, "I saw the children last night in a dream. I saw much more than you told us."

He pulled her back into his bedroom for privacy and motioned for Caleb to follow. "What did you see in your dream?"

She closed her eyes, seeing again the horrible atrocities. "I don't know if I can even speak what I saw, Dad."

"I need to know what you saw, Gabi. Be strong, you can do this," he encouraged her.

Caleb led her to the side of her father's bed and sat her down. He sat on one side of her and Gabe on the other. "You can do this, Gabby Girl," he encouraged her, holding her hand firmly.

She took a deep breath. "I saw rooms where experiments had taken place on these innocent babies, horrible things, Dad." Tears began to flow as she relayed to them the details of the depth of depravity. "Was what I saw real?" she questioned him.

Gabe dropped his head in his hands and nodded yes.

"How in the world could any human do these things?" she questioned her father in despair.

"They are no longer human; they've given themselves over to a reprobate mind and their conscience has been seared. They have no human emotions in their satanic bodies. They are now a hybrid, a human form possessed and controlled by demonic spirits." Gabe once again took his daughter fully in his arms. "I'm so sorry you have to know these things, Princess; but when Yahweh calls us to a mission, He will also anoint us with strength to accomplish it."

Gabe released his daughter to the man she loved knowing she needed a mental break from the horrendous things she had seen. "I will give you two a little private time. I have some things to discuss with KJ and Chris," he gently caressed the top of her head before returning to the security room. "I'm right here if you need me, Gabi." She forced a smile as he closed the door behind him.

"They're gone," Chris informed him as he took a seat. "But I have a feeling they'll be back."

"Me, too," Gabe agreed.

Chris turned to face Gabe. "Did you get the feeling Mrs. Nicholson said something that made them think we were here?"

"Yeah, I did, but apparently the bunker was never mentioned," he answered. "If they used truth serum, she would have told them everything. Right?"

"There are some drugs that an extraordinarily strong person can still manage to lie while under the influence, but what this cabal would use would be infallible. I keep wondering how she kept from telling them the whole truth and my police officer mentality only comes to one conclusion," Chris stated somberly. KJ and Gabe both knew what he meant but did not push any further.

"I'll be going out shortly to call Richards," he continued. "Maybe he'll have some new information for us and an idea on getting your microchips, Gabe."

Once again Gabe wrapped his hand around the locket hanging around his neck. "After twelve years of keeping these in my sole possession, it's going to be tough to let go."

"You know I can download the information to your computer, Gabe," KJ informed him. "All I need to do is put the chips back in a flash drive."

"I know. I just never was willing to take that chance before, even though I believe the IP address cannot be tracked nor my system hacked; but with technology today nothing is one hundred percent safe."

"Let's do this then," KJ offered an alternative. "I'll make a copy of the chips for the detective, and you keep the originals."

"That's what I planned to do, there's no way I'm letting this information leave me." Gabe sighed as he admitted, "Giving a copy to anyone automatically puts their life in danger too. Every person who's seen or known about this has been silenced...but me, and only because they thought I was dead."

Chris assured him, "Richards is totally aware of the chance he's taking, but he's also determined to do whatever he has to do to expose this cabal. He's the one man we can trust."

KJ's breath slightly caught. He and Aaron had just been discussing as they left the hospital to not trust anyone outside of their team. He questioned Chris one more time, "You're absolutely sure the detective cannot be bought off, blackmailed, or something that would comprise him? The cabal has lots of traps."

"Let me put it this way, if we can't trust Richards, we can forget ever finding anyone to help us." Chris felt neither KJ nor Gabe was totally convinced, but there were no other options.

"I've reached the day which I knew would eventually arrive," Gabe resigned himself. "From this point it is in the hands of our Heavenly Father."

"And Detective Richards," KJ added. "We really need to be praying for that man."

Chris looked at his watch and pushed himself from his chair. "Speaking of which I need to get out the tunnel to call him."

"I'd love to go with you," KJ said with regret in his voice, "but I need to get these flash drives ready just in case the detective has a plan, and I've got some more leads to follow on the Khazarians. Lots to get done. On your way out ask Faith to come help me please."

Chris smiled, "Will do." Chris tapped on the door to let Gabriella and Caleb know he was coming through.

They were standing waiting for him to enter the room. "We heard you say you're headed out," Gabriella informed him. "We're going with you. Give me a minute to change and freshen up. I've not even combed my hair this morning." She quickly hurried to dress, reluctantly wiped the oil from her hair and rejoined them.

"KJ needs your help, Faith," Chris winked at her and then motioned for Caleb and Gabriella to follow as he exited through the kitchen into the pantry area anxious to get going and make his call.

"I'll have pancakes ready when you get back," Sandee called to them as she prepared breakfast.

"Precious Sandee," Gabriella commented as they entered in the tunnel. "Always thinking of everyone else but herself. I wonder why she and Professor have never admitted they have deep feelings for each other? It's as obvious as day and night."

Caleb took her hand and laughed. "We don't need any more romance right now in the midst of all the chaos."

Chris was not listening to the conversation as he was deep in thought regarding safely getting the flash drive to Detective Richards. Ideas kept circulating through his mind, but nothing seemed a safe option. He knew the cabal would be watching every move Richards made.

Reaching the end of the tunnel, Chris had barely stepped outside the cave opening before he once again saw the drone circling above the trees. He motioned for the duo behind him to stop. They stayed inside the cave as Chris monitored the movement; he was convinced the crow-looking drone was surveilling the entire area.

"We can't go any further during the daylight hours, not if that drone is circling. Thank God I've enough signal to make calls." Immediately he pulled out his phone and soon had the detective on the other end of the conversation. Caleb and Gabriella could tell from Chris' tone of voice something was wrong but hearing only one side of the conversation kept them waiting in dreaded anticipation.

"Are you sure?" Chris asked the detective. "When?" Chris glanced up at the drone that was still visible. "Yes, it's still circling." He glanced at Caleb and Gabriella and shook his head slightly indicating his concern. "You know they're following your every movement." Silence for a moment before Chris' voice belted out, "That would be crazy!" Again, Chris was silent for several minutes listening to the detective. "Okay, I trust you, Richards. We have a group of people in this bunker who know how to pray, and I'll make sure they are, we all are. Be very careful." With those words, Chris disconnected the call.

"What's going on?" Caleb quickly questioned.

"Let's get back to the bunker so I can fill everyone in at one time," Chris instructed. The tone of his voice was mournful, and his expression spoke volumes. They did not push him for any information during the hurried journey back through the dark cavern. The normal thirty-minute walk was done in half the time. The three were out of breath as they reentered the kitchen.

Sandee had breakfast ready and turned to greet them, stopping suddenly when she realized something was very wrong. In a faint voice, she questioned, "What's happened?"

Chris motioned for her to follow him to address the entire team. They gathered around him to hear the information given by Detective Richards. He spoke with his police officer-controlled voice trying to hide his personal emotions: "The police station was called last night to come to a reported incident in a shopping center parking lot. Richards was working late, as usual, and was informed about the call. He didn't think much of it until he heard the description of the accident, and his intuition told him to go; an employee at the center saw an elderly woman passed out behind the wheel of a car and was unresponsive. He tried to awaken her and when she did not respond he called the police. Richards was on the scene within minutes."

"Oh, no," Sandee cried. "Please don't tell me it was..." Her throat choked and she could not say her name.

"Mrs. Nicholson," Gabe finished Sandee's sentence.

Chris nodded his head, dreading continuing. He knew the team was hoping to hear she was going to be alright and now she was safe.

Chris brought his emotions under control and continued: "They transported her to the closest hospital where she was pronounced dead on arrival."

A shock wave went through each member of the team and exclamations of unbelief echoed through the bunker as Chris continued: "All indications are she had a stroke, but we all know there's a whole lot more to it. We don't know how much information she gave before she passed, but we can assume she didn't tell them about the bunker. If she had, Russo and Moretti would have been on a hell-bent mission looking for the entrance when they were here." He paused before adding, "Richards thinks she may have had the stroke while being questioned because some of the truth serum drugs can have deadly affects, top side affects are a stroke or heart attack, if given too much. She probably died before they asked her if she knew where we are hiding."

"That's the reason those two thugs referred to her in the past tense." Gabe's voice was filled with anger. The team was both in shock and grieving, each member struggling to process that another person's life had been sacrificed.

"Poor Dr. Nicholson," Sandee and Faith commented in unison.

Dr. Brotman was heartbroken for his friend and dealing with the guilt that he was personally responsible. "This is all my fault. Mrs. Nicholson is in a better place, but I don't know how Doc will take this." He looked at Chris and questioned, "Does Doc know yet?"

"No, not yet. Richards is wanting to tell him in person and trying to figure out how to do so."

Chris stood up and began pacing back and forth. "This is no one's fault." His voice took on a tone of resolve: "We are at war, people," he exclaimed. "This is the war of good and evil, unfortunately there are casualties of war.

Yes, it's hard, very hard, but it should give us each the resolve that we must finish this mission...no matter what the cost." He stopped his pacing and faced the group who were intently listening to Chris' every word as if they were waiting for their commands for battle. He spoke words they were not expecting to hear from him: "We must pray and allow the One True God to show us the way."

"And pray we will," Dr. Brotman affirmed in an anguished voice.

Chris sat down and allowed the team time for mental processing, each one struggling with this horrible news in their own way. The sounds of sobs came from the women. The men were trying to control their anger mixed with determination to do whatever it took to help bring these evil people down.

Caleb had taken Gabriella in his arms as she cried on his shoulder. He held her close acutely aware that even though they wanted to take the entire team out, she was one of their main targets.

Gabe was struggling with his personal guilt of Mrs. Nicholson's death and now could be adding Detective Richards to their hit list by getting him involved with the microchips. However, he agreed with Chris, this was war and the only way you can win is to battle. "Does Detective Richards have a plan to get the microchips?"

Chris nodded. "We discussed the microchips and how Richards would get them. He gave this a lot of thought and decided to come to the lodge to get them." Before he could explain the plan, he was interrupted.

"What," Gabe exclaimed. "That's crazy, he's going to lead the cabal directly to us."

"That's what I told him, Gabe, but he's not only going to lead them here, he's going to bring them here."

"He has to be out of his mind," Gabe countered. "What is he thinking?"

"I thought it was an insane idea until I heard his explanation. Listen, he's using the concept of keeping your friends close and your enemies closer. He believes if he brings them here under the precept that he is working with them and has information to help them find us that they will never suspect we are in the very place he brings them to. While he's here he secretly picks up the flash drives, literally right under their noses and they are none the wiser."

"This double agent stuff could backfire really quick, and my information could fall into the hands of the very people I have it hid it from for decades," Gabe argued, extremely concerned.

Chris' voice was determined. "He really believes if we try to arrange a meeting it would be taking a bigger chance than convincing them he's on their side. This way he gets both the microchips and inside information from the cabal. Yep, it's taking a big chance but remember this is war and entering the battle ground is the only way a war can be won."

Gabe was processing through all Chris had said and realized the detective was right. "It seems that this lodge that I spent so much time and money building to protect us all from the enemy is about to become their gathering place and I'm opening the doors for them to come. Lord, help us."

— CHAPTER 20 —

Sandee had prepared breakfast and encouraged the team to try to eat. Gathering around the table, each team member picked at their food, but the grief of Mrs. Nicholson's death was so overwhelming, they had little appetite.

Dr. Brotman was concerned about how his friend, Dr. Nicholson, would handle the news knowing his wife was the anchor of his world. Chris was trying to wrap his mind around Detective Richards, bringing the enemy literally to their doorstep, and trying to decide where he would hide the flash drives for him when he came. Gabe was struggling with deep guilt over the lives that had been lost because of him, and battling the agony of mind that there most likely would be more before it was all over. Sandee and Faith had developed a deep friendship with Mrs. Nicholson during the three days secluded in the bunker and their hearts were overwhelmed with sorrow and what the poor woman endured before her death. Gabriella was heartbroken for Mrs. Nicholson, but she had not spent time with her as the others had, her mind could not escape the children and what she had seen in her dream. KJ, Caleb, and Aaron tried to be strong and emotionally supportive despite their concerns of safety for the entire team. Each team member battled different strongholds of their minds.

Dr. Brotman broke the silence. "Chris, do you know what they will do with her body until Doc can make memorial arrangements for her? They have no children and, as far as I know, no other family at all." The professor sighed, sharing empathic guilt with Gabe that none of this would have happened if they had not pulled all these people into their quest for truth.

"Richards said they would keep her at the morgue for as long as necessary. Of course, we have no idea how long that will be."

"Any word on Doc and the young lady with him?" The professor asked.

"No change, as of now," Chris replied. "They're still with Officer Cohen in safe hiding for as long as it takes. Richards originally thought Dr. Brotman's attempted assassination would be a relatively simple case to solve and

I would only be assigned to your team for a few days. He now realizes he's dealing with an international cabal, multiple murders, and he has no idea who he can trust to discuss the facts with or get information from. He's not even sure he can trust the Haifa Police Chief who's very chummy with members of the Mossad. He says his only choice is to get on the inside and pretend he's working with them to get information, and hopefully find out who he can and cannot trust."

Dr. Brotman shook his head and commented, "Very risky business, very risky."

Chris assured him: "For Richards this is not just another crime to solve anymore, not simply a who dunnit, and then just move on to the next case. He believes this is the most important case of his life and perhaps all of his police and detective training has been for this moment. He's never been a spiritual man, but he already sees this is a battle of a good and evil and he is an incredibly good man."

Gabriella was listening intently to their conversation, realizing the outline of her supernatural vision was forming in real time; however, she had not seen any specific details during her alternate dimension but was convinced the details of her prophetic visions would soon be filled in. One of the last things she saw before her awakening was Detective Richards taking possession of the flash drive which Chris had copied from the security cameras in the lodge, proving the plans of these evil people; and Richards' planning to go undercover with the cabal. Now in real time he is coming to take possession of flash drives while undercover with the same evil men she saw in her visions. This was as far as she had seen and had no idea as to how it would play out. As she was silently questioning in her spirit what her personal assignment in all this evil exposure was, she could hear the voice of The Prophet whispering, "Daughter of Zebulon, The Lamb will lead you."

KJ was filled with frustration not knowing what to do. "The only weapon I have in this war is to be a digital soldier. If there is information anywhere on the web, dark or otherwise, I will find it; and I can expose it as needed." He got up from the table and started toward the security room.

Chris jumped up and quickly joined him. "I see a plan formulating here."

Faith's confusion showed through her grief. "What plan? I have no idea what you're talking about."

"Lots of work to do first," KJ affectionately squeezed her shoulder before leaving the room. "Then you'll understand."

Dr. Brotman grinned as KJ left the room. "I knew I was doing the right thing when I brought that computer genius onto our team, I just didn't know it would be for this reason."

"Yahweh knew," Gabe added. "It's all part of His divine plan and we all should feel honored to be part of it."

"As honored as John the Baptist? You all know what happened to him," Aaron added half-kidding and half-dreading what lay ahead of them.

A grave expression crossed Dr. Brotman's face making it obvious that analogy did not sit well with him.

"I was joking," Aaron explained the quickly added with sincerity, "It's always an honor to be in my Lord's service, especially now."

"We all know what happened to John the Baptist, Aaron." Dr. Brotman's voice was normally kind and soothing. This voice the team did not recognize. "He was beheaded for exposing evil and not bowing down to the wicked king. Solomon wrote what has been, will be again and we see John the Baptist's scenario happen again in Revelation 20:4...*I saw the souls of them that were beheaded for the witness of Jesus, and for the word of God, and which had not worshipped the beast, neither his image, neither had received his mark upon their foreheads, or in their hands...*"

An expression of regret filled Aaron's face. He knew well that many martyrs would be beheaded under the reign of Antichrist. "I'm so sorry, that was really stupid of me to say."

Gabriella offered her observation: "Maybe not, Aaron. Maybe that was a nudge for us all to fully open our eyes to the battle we are in and what the outcome is going to be for many warriors before the victory is complete. Just maybe our Heavenly Father is asking us if we are fully committed to the battle ahead knowing what the outcome could be."

Reality hit each team member in full force. All their years of discussing the end days, searching ancient scriptures, and exploring caves for ancient writings or petroglyphs which could be decoded as end time messages, had not prepared them for this moment when they would look end of days reality dead in the eyes.

Gabriella recalled the words of the prophet instructing her to follow The Lamb. She was determined to do so even knowing The Lamb willingly laid down his life when his mission on earth was complete. Her father sensed the direction her mind had taken and put his arms around her in comfort. She leaned against him and without words affirmed she was not afraid.

Chris reentered the room and brought the attention of the team back to the business at hand. "I've been thinking about where to hide the flash drives for Richards. Remember Russo took one of Professor's cherry tobacco tins? I could wrap the flash drives in plastic and put them in one of the tins for Richards. He could just nonchalantly admire the fragrance and decide to take one with him, commenting that the professor would not be returning to use it."

"I think it might just work," Gabe agreed. "I can't think of any better idea, just got to pray it works." He questioned his decision one more time and announced without reservation, "I'm convinced now's the time."

"That's what the prophet said to me in my dream last night," Gabriella exclaimed. "That it is time and now I know what he meant. It's a confirmation, Dad." All eyes focused on her for clarification. Dreading to relive it once again, she relayed to the team all that she had seen in her night vision, reopening, and cutting further into the emotional wound of all that her father had revealed to them.

"We're taking a chance, no matter how we do this, but I know we all agree it's worth the risk if we can help save the children." Chris' determination was evident in both his words and his countenance. "KJ has the flash drives ready, and I'll take them up today so whenever Richards comes, they're ready to pick up."

"What about that bug device he put under the coffee table, Chris?" Caleb questioned. "Won't they know someone's in the room."

"That device is mainly to hear conversations, but I'll still need to be extremely quiet to make sure no sound is detected."

"Risky business, I tell you," Dr. Brotman interjected his concerns again. He hesitated and reluctantly added, "but I agree it's time."

Chris had the copied flash drives in his pocket and asked Sandee for plastic wrap. Once the discs were safely wrapped, he ascended upstairs to hide them. Slowly he opened the secret pantry door to avoid making any noise. He had only socks on his feet to make sure he could move around quietly. Retrieving one of the cherry tobacco tins, he returned to the kitchen to open it should any sound occur while removing the lid. He placed the flash drives underneath the tobacco out of sight should the tin be opened by someone else. He took a black marker from his pocket and made a faint dot in the upper right-hand corner marking the container. Cautiously he returned the tin to the box and placed it on the top reclosing the lid and silently exited returning to the bunker.

Gabe greeted him at the bottom of the stairs. "We watched you with the sound turned all the way up and we didn't hear a thing. Job well done, Officer Harris," he congratulated him.

Chris let out a long breath of relief. "Phase one complete."

Gabe also felt relieved. "After all these years, finally I can let go. If the cabal does find the flash drives, there's nothing on them they don't already know. They just wanted to make sure their evil stayed hidden. Normal people live their entire lives having no idea of the Luciferian control that stretches across the world and into exceedingly high places. I would have released the information a long time ago if I had only known who could be trusted. I know I'm regressing, but despite what could happen, I feel a sense of peace now that I've let go. Does that sound crazy?"

"Not at all," Chris replied. "I've often seen police cases where the subjects confessed to crimes or when witnesses came forth and they were actually relieved afterwards that the truth was known. Something that weighs heavily on the mind relieves the soul when you've done the right thing."

KJ handed Gabe the locket he had worn throughout the years. "The original microchips are back where they were."

Gabe put the chain around his neck and clasped it together. "For future reference, the entire team now knows where the originals are."

KJ held notes in his hand waiting for the right opportunity to relay his findings. "I've been digging on those seven mountains Professor mentioned as it relates to the Khazarians."

"And?" Dr. Brotman was anxious to hear any additional information.

"We already know the world elitist took over the American economy through the Federal Reserve in 1913, that research led me to information on the Titanic. Are you aware there were three of the wealthiest men on earth on the Titanic when it went down? All three were against the creation of the federal reserve bank, John Astor, Isador Srauss, and Benjamin Guggenheim. They just happened to be personally invited aboard the maiden voyage."

"How odd," Dr. Brotman observed. "Go on."

"Interestingly, J.P. Morgan, who funded the building of the Titanic, mysteriously cancelled his trip just hours before departure. The three rich men who had prevented the creation of the Federal Reserve were all taken out at the same time. They go down with the ship in 1912 and the Federal Reserve is created in 1913." KJ laid his notes in his lap and stated, "As the old saying goes, something is rotten in Denmark. Coincidence, Professor?"

"You know I do not believe in coincidences, KJ." He replied sternly.

"Exactly," KJ confirmed. "Plus, the Titanic broke in half and from everything I've read, only an explosion would cause that, not water coming into the ship from hitting an iceberg. When I do an internet search on this topic, it pops up that the information is false or a conspiracy theory. However, I kept digging and there's a lot to uncover. It's always the top links that pop up first saying false information, but the truth is there if you go deep enough. That's the way the cabal tries to discredit the truth, and sadly most people fall for it. I just want to shake people and scream for them to wake up."

Chris agreed. "Anytime I see Snopes or any other website say the links are false information, that's my cue to dig deeper." He stared into space for a moment thinking through KJ's information before adding, "If your information is true, it makes you wonder how many other tragedies have been executed for their evil purposes and then the truth covered up."

"Sure does, and most just believe whatever the mockingbird media tells them and don't question anything," KJ agreed. "Which brings me to the fact that the term conspiracy theory was made popular by the CIA when President John F. Kennedy was assassinated; it was their way of making anyone who questioned the circumstances of Kennedy's death appear to be a person of questionable intentions or not mentally stable. Instead, the cabal wants you to believe a lone assassin, Lee Harvey Oswald, shoots the president and is caught in just over an hour? Then we are supposed to believe that out of nowhere, with policemen all around, Jack Ruby shoots and kills Oswald at the Dallas Police Headquarters before they can question Oswald? And even crazier the news cameras are rolling when Ruby is shot and killed by the police for the entire world to see. Sure, nothing to question here, just keep swallowing their lies and move on. If you question any part of it, you are labeled a conspiracy theorist, their way to control the minds of the people."

KJ's voice indicated the frustration he felt as he continued: "People are so gullible when it comes to believing what the government feeds them, any government. The truth is President Kennedy had declared openly that he was going to splinter the corrupt CIA into a thousand pieces and within weeks, he was conveniently eliminated. Coincidence? I don't think so and the corrupt CIA is alive and well still today."

"You all know I had my own personal encounters with the CIA, and quickly found I could not trust them. It caused the death of my beautiful wife," Gabe's voice faded in agony. He struggled to regain his composure and added what the entire team was already well aware of, "Anyone who gets in the way of the Luciferian cabal, is targeted to be eliminated by whatever means necessary, anyone."

— CHAPTER 21 —

Chris felt the intensity of their situation quickly escalating. He did not want to alarm the others but needed to confide in Gabe about possible scenarios. Gabe was the only person that knew every detail of the lodge security system and how to respond as it might soon be needed. Some private time would be required for discussing possibilities.

"I need to make a quick run out to call Richards and let him know where I've hidden the flash drives and I'm hoping for a heads up on when and how this will go down." Chris casually invited Gabe as to not alarm the others of his concerns: "Gabe, you want to go with me?"

Gabe immediately discerned Chris' intentions but replied in a normal tone of voice, "Sure, I need the exercise." To eliminate anyone else accompanying them, Gabe quickly added, "I know KJ has a lot of research to do and Dr. Brotman is wanting more discussion, so let's give them some time."

The two men were soon out of the bunker into privacy. "What's up?" Gabe asked. "I've come to read your body language pretty well, Chris."

As they walked the tunnel with flashlights in hand, Chris explained: "I have no idea how Richards bringing the enemy here will all go down, maybe with no problem at all; but we need to know how to respond to several possible situations, just in case it goes south."

"What's your thinking?" Gabe questioned, with ideas already forming in his own mind.

"Apparently Mrs. Nicholson said something that led Russo and Moretti to come to the lodge, whether it be that we were there, had been there, or something else, we just don't know; however, our location is on their radar now. Richards didn't know about the lodge bunker until after the war. Remember, we told him at the hospital?"

"I remember," Gabe confirmed wondering what his point was.

"I don't think we told him where the entry to the bunker was, just there was a bunker underneath the lodge. Right?"

"I do believe you're right, Chris. So, he couldn't tell anyone how to find us even under the control of truth serum."

"That gives us one layer of protection when they show up. You did a heck of a job with that secret entrance. I don't believe I would have ever found it."

"That was the intent," Gabe chuckled. "I sure hope it works...for all of our sake."

"Me, too," Chris agreed. "But let's go one more scenario, in the event worse comes to worse and the entrance to the bunker is discovered, what should we be prepared to do at that point? You know the women would panic, and there wouldn't be enough time for the men to make decisions on the spur of the moment. We need a plan in place so at a moment's notice everyone is prepared for action.

As they arrived at the end of the tunnel Chris could see the expressions on Gabe's face. He was surprised it was one of confidence. "I've thought about that possibility many times, especially when designing the lodge and bunker and I made back-up plans just in case. Money was not a concern, so I poured plenty of it into the future protection of the people I loved." He hesitated and turned to look Chris directly in the eyes. "You're going to have to trust me on some of this, my friend. If you don't know, then no one can get my back-up protection plans from you, should that scenario ever arise. You know what I mean. Right? Some things will have to be on a need-to-know basis. I hope you understand."

"I do understand, and I trust you, Gabe. I will know, if and when I need to know, but I hope that time doesn't come. We do need to have an exit plan for the team, if needed, so no one panics if something happens suddenly."

"I agree fully with that, and we will do it soon. I've got this, Chris." Gabe confirmed.

The afternoon sunlight was shining through the mouth of the cave. "Stay inside, Gabe. I need to check the air space, see if the drone is still circling." Chris stepped just far enough outside of the cave to get a good view. He motioned for Gabe to follow him. "I don't see anything but clear view skies above the trees. The drone could have just been hunters monitoring the wildlife, but we can't take any chances.

"Hopefully, that's the case." Gabe also knew nothing could be assumed and every precaution had to be taken. To clear his mind, he took a deep breath inhaling the crisp fall air. "Geez, the fresh air sure is wonderful, you don't realize how much it refreshes the mind and spirit until you don't have it regularly." I'm going to start the Jeep and let it run for a bit, just to make sure my battery doesn't die for non-use. Never know when it will be needed."

Gabe disappeared through the grove of trees while Chris made his call informing the detective where he had hidden the flash drives. "I put a small black dot on the top right-hand corner of the tobacco tin to make sure you take the right one, it's easy to spot but not obvious. I just hope this works," Chris admitted his concern.

After the two men discussed the details regarding the arrival of Strozza at the lodge, Detective Richards had discouraging news for his officer.

"Oh, no," Chris responded. "Any ideas on what happened?"

Gabe returned just in time to hear Chris' last question and stood silently until the conversation with the detective ended. "What's going on," he questioned, knowing it was not good.

"I need to some time to process what I just heard and will fill you in when we get back to the bunker."

Gabe did not press him but instead informed him of some disturbing news of his own. "The lock on the garage door has been tampered with and there are fresh footprints around the area. Hunters? Maybe, but..."

Chris interrupted him finishing his sentence. "But someone has definitely been here and that is not a good sign. There could be intruders watching us right now from a distance, or even cameras planted in the area recording everything moving. Even if it is just hunters, we still don't want anyone to see us. We better get out of here."

The two men quickly returned to the cave and hurried back to safety with their flashlights guiding their steps. A couple of times they stopped and listened for any sounds echoing through the tunnel which could indicate being followed. Reaching the entry, Gabe asked before they entered, "Do we tell the others?"

"No need to right now and add more fuel to the fire of uncertainty. What I have to tell will be more than anyone wants to hear." Chris responded, opening the camouflaged entry.

Once inside the pantry, Chris closed and securely locked the secret door and pushed the shelving unit back in place to hide it. Dr. Brotman's voice could be heard coming from the gathering area and as Gabe and Chris joined them, the professor was reading aloud from his Bible. He paused, laying it in his lap when he saw the two men returning.

All eyes focused on Chris waiting for updates from the detective. He sat down in the wooden dining chair he pulled from the table area. "Good news and bad news," he told them. "The good news is Richards made contact with the International Intelligence Director, Strozza. What he told him so far was actually the truth, that he was assigned Dr. Brotman's attempted assassination case and after the assignment had taken the professor's research team to a mountain lodge for safety until he could solve the case. He also told Strozza that I had been assigned to stay with you indefinitely for protection and immediately after we arrived at the lodge the war started. He informed Strozza he wasn't in touch with any of us until I notified him that Gabriella was taken to Elisha hospital when the bombing stopped. That was when he had found out that Edward Gabe Russell was still alive; and after doing some research on Gabe, he discovered the International Intelligence Agency had an open case on Gabe, so he was calling to offer any assistance in any way he could."

"Well, that is all true until the last sentence of offering help. What was Strozza's response?" Gabriella quickly questioned, struggling with fears of these evil men once again hunting her father down like a wild animal.

"Richards said he could tell Strozza's voice was guarded, but his need for information pushed the conversation forward. The director didn't give Richards any details, just said Gabe had stolen top secret information from the CIA before his death and the case was never officially closed because the information was never retrieved. He did admit they had recently discovered his death had been faked and actively reopened the case. Richards read between the lines that Strozza has no idea the lodge you all escaped to is owned by Gabe."

Gabe's face was blood red. "I did not steal anything, and they know it!"

"We all know it, Gabe," Chris tried to soothe him. "But they tell what they want people to believe and what justifies their actions. The truth has nothing to do with it."

Gabe slowly calmed down and refocused. "There is no way they will connect my name to ownership of this lodge. I went through all kinds of legal hoops to change my identity and erase all tracks from my past."

"That definitely works in our favor," Chris assured him. "And another positive detail is Richards was never informed on the entry to this bunker. He only knows there is a bunker underneath the lodge, and he said he does not want to know at this point. As the saying goes, you can't get blood out of a turnip. He can't be forced to tell what he does not know. He only knows I have to go outside to call him, but he has no details on how I get outside or where I go, nor does he know there's a secret upstairs entry. The less he knows right now, the better."

"Does he know when Strozza will be coming to the lodge?" Gabe asked the question, and the entire team wanted to know the answer.

"Actually, Strozza brought it up which really played into Richard's plan. Strozza didn't mention the fact he had men already casing the place, but Richards knew Russo and Moretti had already clued him in on the Mt. Hermon location when Strozza said he'd like to see the lodge for himself. Richards told him he had the security code to get on the grounds and a set of keys from when the location was affirmed to be the hide-out location for Dr. Brotman and his team." Chris took a deep breath and added what they were waiting to hear, "Strozza is flying into Tel Aviv from Rome tomorrow and they will be coming here the day after."

"If that's the good news, what's the bad?" Caleb questioned, not sure he really wanted to hear.

Chris began pacing back and forth trying to form the right words to explain what had occurred. Detective Richards had just blurted the information out to him, but he wanted to soften the impact, especially for the women. "The cameras monitoring the cottage where Dr. Nicholson, Leah and Officer Cohen are hiding recorded the same car continually driving by the security gate and slowing down then speeding back up when it passes by. It's been going on for a couple of days now. A zoom in caught the license plate number and when Richards ran the plate, it was registered to a bogus corporation which, of course, is a red flag that something is not right. It's also a dead end for information on who owns the car. He was making plans for Officer Cohen to move them to a new location when the security cameras all went off. He tried to contact Cohen multiple times by phone and got no answer. When I called Richards, he had just arrived at the cottage to personally check on them. The secured gated entrance to the driveway was standing wide open and they were gone."

"Gone," exclaimed Faith. "Gone where?"

Chris shook his head, "He has no idea. The cameras weren't working so there is no video. Cohen's phone cannot be tracked or hacked, so there's no leads there. Richards said it looked like they had left in a hurry, but no signs of a struggle. They left the hospital in such a hurry that they took no personal items with them, so we don't know if they left voluntarily, which would have been noted if their personal items were also gone; or had no choice, like Mrs. Nicholson. Richards did notice a black roll bag with

Gabriella's name tag on it and remembered Cohen told him she had left it at the hospital, and he was taking it with him when he left."

"He found my bag?" Gabriella exclaimed. "Will I get it back?"

Chris nodded his head, "Richards is taking it to the police station for safe keeping."

She was so relieved and anxious to have the turquoise bracelet back in her possession. It was her tangible proof she had visited the supernatural realm; as important as that was to her, her thoughts currently were focused on the people missing. "Does Detective Richards have any leads at all, anything?"

"Since the car that the cameras picked up can't be traced, he's at a stalemate right now. All this just happened on top of finding out Strozza is arriving tomorrow and he's in a tailspin not knowing in which direction to go. He again emphasized he didn't know who to trust for assistance. I sure wish I was there to help him," Chris added regretfully.

Silence gripped the atmosphere. The 'what ifs' were playing out in every team member's mind. Dr. Brotman broke the silence: "Today at sundown begins the Day of Atonement and Torah tells us to fast and pray from sundown to sundown, 24 hours of repentance and seeking Yahweh's guidance and protection. After dinner we will begin our day of convocation." The professor gave no options, the matter was settled. "This is a time for a solemn assembly and that is what we need for strength."

Although Chris was a Jew raised in Israel, he had never gone to synagogue nor been taught from the Torah. So, while Sandee prepared their dinner, Dr. Brotman explained to Chris why they would be observing the commandments for God's holiest day of the year. He turned his Bible to Leviticus 23 and began to explain: "Over 1500 years before Messiah was born, Yahweh gave Moses the instructions on how the children of Israel were to live and how to obtain sacrificial forgiveness of sins. In the instructions of the seven holy convocations given in Leviticus 23, the prophecies of the coming Messiah were given starting from Passover, Yeshua's first coming to earth, to the Feast of Tabernacles which is his second coming to rule and reign on earth eternally. The Holy Convocations in between are prophetic foreshadowing of everything in between the two. This evening starts the sixth of the seven appointed times, Day of Atonement."

Chris was transfixed by the professor's commentary absorbing every word as Dr. Brotman continued: "On the Day of Atonement, which in Hebrew is Yom Kippur, the High Priest would choose two goats. One is sacrificed to Yahweh and the other carries the sins of Israel into the wilderness to die." He quickly turned the Bible pages, holding in place his original text. "In Leviticus 16:21-22, Aaron, the High Priest, is given specific instructions regarding the two goats. It reads: "*Then Aaron shall lay his hands on the head of the live goat and confess over it all the iniquities of the people of Israel, and all their transgressions, all their sins, putting them on the head of the goat, and sending it away into the wilderness by means of someone designated for the task. The goat shall bear on itself all their iniquities to a barren region; and the goat shall be set free in the wilderness*"."

Chris' face reflected confusion as he struggled to process what the scriptures meant. Dr. Brotman laid his Bible in his lap and explained in layman's terms: "The High Priest would confess the sins of Israel on the goat being sent into the wilderness, representing the sins of the nation were gone forever. The Mishnah, the historical writings, says the High Priest would tie a scarlet wool thread around the head of the second goat to be sacrificed to Yahweh. When the scarlet thread miraculously turned white, the priest knew the sins of Israel were forgiven and the goat could now be sacrificed. Isaiah 1:18 refers to this when he writes, "*though your sins be as scarlet, they will be white as snow*"; and the greater meaning is the prophetic foreshadowing of the coming Messiah who would be without sin and would be sacrificed for the sins of the world."

The professor laid his Bible down and continued: "The Day of Atonement is the only day of the entire year the High Priest could go into the Holy of Holies and make atonement for sin. He would take the blood of the goat and sprinkle it on the mercy seat, interceding for God's people. All the nation was commanded to repent, fast, and pray from sundown to the next sundown. On this day Israel started a new year cleansed and holy, a new beginning." His voice reflected his personal resolve to keep this command-ment of observance as he further explained: "Yahweh said it was to be a perpetual convocation to all generations, meaning it never ceased. That is why we still fast and pray on this holiest of days; however, now we do not sacrifice goats because Yeshua, our High Priest, became the final sacrifice needed for forgiveness of sins. The Day of Atonement prophetically signifies Messiah's first coming and his second coming for the final judgment when the King of Kings and Lord of Lords returns to judge the nations."

"Amazing," Chris responded. "How could I have been so blind all these years living here in the very land where the Messiah lived and taught, and know none of this?"

"People only see what they choose to see, but now your eyes are open, Chris." Dr. Brotman's voice was soothing. "A couple more things about this holy day that most people do not realize. The term scapegoat comes from the goat that was sent into the wilderness allowing Israel to escape their sins, that word is used by people all over the world and not even realizing it originates from Torah. The second, and the one that captivates my thoughts because of our Watchers project, comes from Leviticus 16 giving the scapegoat a name, Azazel."

The team members all knew where Dr. Brotman was going with the commentary, but Chris was totally confused until the professor explained: "The scapegoat named Azazel represented sin and all that was evil, and the scapegoat was taken into the wilderness to be destroyed. Azazel was an evil name known by all of Israel as identified in the Book of Enoch. Azazel was the leader of the fallen angels who rebelled against God and entered the earth realm as described in Gensis 6, creating the Nephilim. Many Jewish scholars say Azazel is another name for Lucifer from which all sin derives. When el is added at the end of name, it means god, Azaz'el. Lucifer is the god of this world according to II Corinthians 4:4; however, his days are numbered. Very soon Lucifer will meet face to face with the true God of this earth, our Messiah, and that judgment day will be on the 10th day of the Hebrew month of Tishri, the Day of Atonement. It's already scheduled on God's calendar."

Dr. Brotman ended his commentary bringing the information full circle: "The facet of Azazel and the Day of Atonement represents the very core of our Watchers project, starting with the days of Noah and the fallen angels and ending with Luciferian Azazel's final destruction, Mystery Babylon and the Beast. Do you see how it all ties together? It's a thread woven from Genesis to Revelation."

"Amazing," Chris repeated himself knowing no other words to describe The Word of God.

"Yes, it truly is," Dr. Brotman agreed, laying his Bible back on the side table still opened. "It's so sad that most people have no idea how rich the Word of God is, and how the precious pearls of truth, mercy, wisdom, instructions, and prophecy are strung from the first to the last page."

Gabriella was sitting on the other side of the table where the Bible lay. She glanced down and her breath caught. "Professor, I see you've written pesher by Leviticus 23. Can I ask what that means?" She knew it had special significance because in her visions of the future, she had possession of his Bible and had seen the word noted throughout.

"That's my way of piecing prophetic puzzles together, Gabi. Pesher is an Aramaic word that means explanations through making connections.

When I am studying, I am always connecting the biblical texts with historical writings." He could tell by her expression this was more than a casual observation. "Why do you ask?"

"In my visions I had possession of your Bible. When I escaped from this bunker, I took your Bible and Dad's with me. I wanted to read and learn as much as I could. In your Bible I kept seeing pesher noted throughout the first five books of the Old Testament. I thought it was some kind of mysterious code." She reasoned for a minute and added, "I understand now what the Spirit was showing me."

Dr. Brotman did not look surprised anticipating her answer, "And what is that?"

"How everything is connected to Torah," she answered. "How the entire Bible is built on the first five books, even the New Testament."

The professor nodded in agreement and confirmed her analysis: "The New Testament is really a continuation of the old with the two being separated by The Lamb of God, slain before the foundations of the earth. The Lamb, Yeshua Jesus, came in human form not to abolish the Law but to fulfill it. He was both man and God, human and divine. Most people read right over John 1:14 and have no idea of the meaning: *The Word became flesh and dwelt among us.* Yeshua is The Word, and The Word is the Torah." An expression of sorrow crossed his face as he added, "When people say the Old Testament has been done away with, they do not realize they are actually saying Torah, Jesus, has been done away with."

"I've got so much to learn," Chris admitted, realizing there was very little time left to do it in.

Aaron stated in his dry, yet sincere tone, "Stick around this group very long and you'll learn quickly. It's our main topic of conversation."

Sandee was setting the table for dinner, their last meal before starting the 24 hours of fasting. "It's ready," she called to the team.

Dr. Brotman took his place at the table. The team all bowed their heads as the professor led them in blessing the food with the traditional Hebrew prayer.

Gabe thanked Sandee for all the hard work in the kitchen. "You've done an amazing job with the storage food from the pantry," he complimented her.

"Well, you did an amazing job in planning," she replied. "The selections of freeze-dried foods and seasonings allow me a great amount of flexibility. You've made my job easy, under the conditions."

The team realized they had taken Sandee for granted and would show greater appreciation and offer more help anyway she needed it. Gabriella spoke for the team, "We really do love and appreciate you, Sandee. Just let us know what we can do to help."

Sandee's face slightly flushed. "Oh, honey bunny, you know I love taking care of all of you. You're the children I never had." Her heartfelt emotion touched them all. Seclusion had brought an emotional bond beyond anything the team had experienced during their many years together.

Discussion of the biblical holy convocations continued during dinner with explanations specifically geared for Chris. "These appointed times are often referred to as feast days and non-Jews believe they are only for the Jewish people, but that is not true. Romans Chapter 11 makes it very clear that anyone who has accepted Yeshua as Messiah is grafted in and there is no longer Jew and Gentile but One New Man, the body of Yeshua. Additionally, in Galatians Chapter 3, Paul writes that we are all sons of Father Abraham and heirs to the promises given to him and Torah is part of the promises. See how these pearls all continue to string together, Chris? You cannot take just one scripture and build your theology on it; you must build precept upon precept to understand this spiritual life."

Again, Chris was wondering just how much time he would have to understand and regretted he had waited so long to start. "Being with this team has totally changed my life. For that I will always be grateful, no matter what the future holds."

The professor felt they needed a break from the heavy conversation. He pushed himself from the table and went back to his recliner. "Let's turn on the TV, Channel 2 usually shows the temple mount opening ceremony for the Day of Atonement."

With a click of the remote, Channel 2 News immediately came on. Anchorman Michael Adelson was front and center of the current news. This was all so familiar to Gabriella. Many of her future visions played out on this very TV watching this same man reporting. However, at this moment his reporting was not about world news; he focused on Israel, the aftermath of the war and the holiest day of the year.

The newsroom scene cut to on-sight reporting from the wailing wall, the last standing wall of the ancient Jewish temple which was destroyed in the recent three-day-war.

Gabriella's thoughts quickly became her spoken words: "That was where my visions of the future began. The wailing wall I saw was marking the starting point for the future prophetic visions to begin. If I'm correct, the reporter will soon start showing Orthodox Jews chanting and with signs saying, we will rebuild." She had barely voiced the words when the camera panned the area confirming her vision.

Crowds of religious Jews had gathered to declare to the nation and to the world that the third temple would be rebuilt. The men from the orthodox community surrounded the fallen wall carrying signs declaring "We WILL Rebuild". The sun was setting behind the men dressed in all white linen clothing as instructed by Torah for the Day of Atonement. As the last rays of the sun went down, a multitude of shofars began to sound heralding the day of the great fast had begun. The hypnotic blasts echoed through the air, transforming the temple site into a holy atmosphere and declaring a solemn warning to pray and fast until sundown the next day. As the sun disappeared, the men in white prostrated themselves with their faces to the ground and began to wail in prayer to Yahweh, confessing their sins and the sins of Israel.

The team sat silent, mesmerized by the television broadcast as the cameras panned the entire temple area revealing thousands of men on their faces crying aloud. The holiness of the scene permeated through the television screen and filled the bunker atmosphere. Dr. Brotman followed the lead of the orthodox men at the temple sight and prostrated himself on the bunker floor, with the rest of the men following. The women knelt on their knees and bowed their heads. Their solemn assembly had begun.

— CHAPTER 22 —

During their time of prayer, the mighty Presence of the Holy Spirit permeated the atmosphere. The room was silent as each person felt the heaviness of the anointing unable to move. It was a time of soul searching and repentance; but above all, it was a divine preparation for the days ahead.

The team continued in prayer and reading from the Psalms until after midnight when Sandee suggested they all get some rest. She reminded them, "Remember, Professor is still recuperating, and Dr. Nicholson ordered him to rest as much as possible so he can regain his strength." Just the mention of the doctor ushered in another wave of grave concern.

Dr. Brotman stood up and held his hands out to each side indicating joining him to make a circle of prayer. "Before we retire, we will petition the throne of heaven for the protection of Doc. Our Father knows every detail of their whereabouts and we put Him in control of their lives." They all joined hands as the professor led them in a prayer of protection. Peace flooded the room replacing the spirit of heaviness, and in unison the team thanked Yahweh for hearing their prayers.

Sandee accompanied the professor to his bedroom making sure his steps were steady. "Do you need anything?" She asked before leaving him to settle in for the night.

"Thank you, sweet Sandee, I'm fine. You don't need to worry so about me." He leaned down and kissed the top of her head. "Get some rest," he stated affectionately as she turned to leave. He closed the door behind him wondering why he had never told her how dear she was to him. He admitted to himself that after his wife passed, he buried himself in his research and shut the door to any romantic relationships. Now he had regrets, but it was too late, he could not turn back time. He got in bed and pulled the blanket up around his neck wondering what might have been.

The silence of night settled into the bunker. Everyone was soon asleep, everyone but Gabriella. She was searching through the memories of her visions for any clue to where the trio could have disappeared to. She recalled nothing from her visions of the future that could connect to their mysterious disappearance. "Protect them, Lord," she whispered, as a restless sleep captured her.

She awakened to the sound of slightly familiar voices but could not discern who they were or what they were saying. She sat up in bed and listened to the voices arguing in the next room. The faint nightlight guided her to the door where she slowly pulled it open, not knowing what to expect. Sunlight poured into the room from the big bay window looking out on the Mediterranean Sea. Immediately she recognized where she was...the seaside cottage where she and Chris had hidden. She could hear three voices arguing as the scene morphed from a blur into a clear view. Officer Cohen, Dr. Nicholson, and the clerk from the hospital were in a heated debate.

"Are you sure?" Dr. Nicholson demanded an answer from Officer Cohen. "This does not feel right."

The officer answered in a commanding voice, "I am absolutely sure, and we must leave now."

"Where are we going?" Leah's voice was mixed with fear and uncertainty.

"Leave that to me, I know what I'm doing. Let's go," Officer Cohen demanded emphatically, giving the other two no options.

"I don't like this, not at all," Leah's voice was rising as trepidation consumed her. "We're safe here, I don't want to leave."

Gabriella knew she could not be seen and moved closer to the trio listening to every word spoken. Officer Cohen's phone rang, he glanced briefly at it and stuck it in his pocket without answering. "Let's go...now!" He commanded. He went to the security monitors and turned the system off before ushering the two out the door and into the white Toyota which had been their vehicle to escape from the hospital. The officer jumped behind the wheel and went speeding to the end of the gravel driveway, stopping only long enough to put in the code for the security gate to open. He jumped back behind the wheel and sped onto the highway, not taking time to close the security gate behind them. Gabriella stepped out the front door of the cottage, hoping for a better view, but the car was completely out of sight. Quickly she turned to reenter the cottage hoping to find clues for their quick departure.

When Gabriella opened the cottage door, the bunker living room was on the other side. She was sleep walking and the dream ended. She was now wide awake.

"Are you okay?" Faith asked. "Where are you going?"

Returning to her bed, Gabriella sat down on the side. "I'm sorry I woke you up. I just had the strangest dream or maybe it was a vision, I just don't know."

"Do you want to talk about it?"

"Not now, maybe in the morning. I need a bit of time to think it through." Actually, she wanted to talk to Chris first and get his opinion on Officer Micah Cohen. Could he be completely trusted?

"Okay, I'm here if you need me, Gabi. Wake me up if you want to talk." Faith turned over on her side and was soon asleep.

Gabriella propped her head up, closed her eyes and relived her night vision, questioning why the officer forced Dr. Nicholson and Leah to leave so suddenly. Where did they go? Were they safe? Over and over the dramatic scene played out in her mind and she could make no sense of it.

When she could not sleep, she went into the living room and settled on the couch. She would have enjoyed a cup of her favorite caramel coffee which soothed her emotions and helped her to think more clearly but the holy fast took precedence, she would not eat or drink until sundown. Instead, she would spend time in prayer and seeking discernment for the source of her dream.

The nightlights gave a peaceful glow to the room, and the Holy Presence still lingered in the atmosphere as she questioned aloud, "Was the Spirit showing me what happened or was it simply my human concern for their safety manifesting in my dream?"

"What dream?" Chris asked as he entered the room.

Gabriella sat straight up on the couch and gasped, "I thought I was alone."

"Sorry, I didn't mean to startle you, Gabi. I guess you couldn't sleep either."

"No, I couldn't, I came in here so I wouldn't keep Faith awake with my tossing and turning." She had wanted to talk to Chris alone about the dream and it seemed divine intervention had made that possible. "I'm glad you're here though, I just had the strangest dream, and I want your opinion." She proceeded to verbally relive what she saw in complete detail. "I'm not saying this actually happened, I just don't know. What I do know is I questioned the motives of Officer Cohen as I watched the scene play out in my dream. It was obvious he did not want anyone to know they had left or where they were going."

The light was dim, but she could still see the shock on Chris' face. "That doesn't sound like Cohen at all. He's always been a straight shooter following instructions." Chris thought for several minutes and added, "I'm not sure that dream was one of your supernatural visions, Gabi."

She detected a tinge of uncertainty in his voice and did not comment further regarding the trustworthiness of the officer. She did share her supernatural vision of this similar scene: "I know this sounds incredulous, but before I woke up in the hospital a few days ago, the last vision I had was of the same seaside cottage that I saw in my dream last night. The difference was you and I were there." Before he could state his surprise, she stopped him. "Hear me out before you say anything and let me explain."

Gabriella was cautious with her words as she continued: "You already know you were in my visions of the future. I just haven't given you details and really didn't plan to, but after my dream last night, I really need your opinion. In my last supernatural vision just before I awakened in the hospital, you and I were hiding in that same cottage. We were warned by Detective Richards to leave immediately, that our lives were in danger. We went speeding away just like they did in my dream. You left the security gate open, just like Officer Cohen did. That's as far as I saw in my dream of them last night, when they pulled onto the highway the car was out of my sight."

"I have the feeling your vision went further than your dream?" Chris questioned.

She nodded, continuing: "In my vision of us fleeing, as soon as we pulled onto the highway, we were being followed and it ended in a car chase by Russo and Moretti. When their car sped up, you did also. You tried to lose them, but they managed to stay right with us. At one point their vehicle was side by side with ours, Moretti pulled out a gun and aimed right at us to shoot. You screamed for me to put my head down, the Jeep started spinning and we came to a sudden stop when we hit a tree. Shooting pains went through my head and the next thing I remembered was waking up in the hospital, back to my real life." She knew Chris was already struggling with the details she shared so she stopped at that point. "Do you think that vision could be linked to what's just happened? I'll be honest, Chris, I just don't know what to think."

Chris stared at her, not certain how to respond. His professional opinion was Gabriella was experiencing human concern for Dr. Nicholson and Leah and her emotions wrapped into her dream, causing her to replay the vision she had while in a comatose state. He could not imagine Officer Cohen going rogue under any circumstances; however, he had to admit to himself she had been right about so many things that he could not totally disregard her dream.

"Can you describe the cottage you saw, Gabi?"

She gazed into the air as she relived the vision: "It was a quaint, white cottage nestled in a grove of juniper trees and sitting at the end of a long gravel driveway. We went through a gated entrance when we arrived, and you told me it was one of the locations used when someone was taken into temporary protective custody. When entering the cottage, you immediately are drawn to the large bay window with a breathtaking view of the Mediterranean Sea. To the right there was a small, fully equipped kitchen and a white wooden table with four chairs. The kitchen and living room were one open area. The bedroom I used also had a view of the sea and was decorated in light blue, my favorite color. It had everything I needed as far as toiletries, etc. You told me it stayed fully stocked and ready for a sudden need."

She focused her eyes back on Chris' amazed face. "Does that sound familiar?"

"How could you know all those details? You've perfectly described the location they were at." Now he was questioning his police instincts regarding her dream, there was no way she could know. "I need to discuss this with Richards. He trusts you, Gabi, in what he calls your paranormal visions." He was on the verge of asking about other visions she had of the two of them but choked back the words when Caleb's bedroom door opened.

Caleb entered the room and took a seat next to Gabriella in a possessive manner. "I thought I heard voices," Caleb dryly commented, his voice edged with jealousy.

"We couldn't sleep," Gabriella explained, "and apparently you couldn't either, my love." She took his hand and leaned over kissing his cheek.

He wanted to say, "It's hard to sleep when you hear your fiancé talking to another man in the middle of the night;" but, instead, bit his tongue and just nodded in agreement pulling her closer, waiting for an explanation.

She guarded her words closely not wanting to add to Caleb's jealousy. "I had a very disturbing dream about the others disappearing. I wanted Chris' opinion as a police officer." She proceeded to tell Caleb about the dream, but not about her vision with Chris. "My dream felt so real, but Chris believes Officer Cohen can be totally trusted."

Caleb's voice was tender as he responded giving her emotional support, "Did your dream feel like the visions you had while you were comatose, anything to compare it to?"

She thought for a moment and replied, "The one thing that remained consistent in my visions was when I would have short glimpses into the real world I could see the people around me, but no one could see me or hear me. Several times, I could see all of you and hear your conversations, but to you I was still comatose. That's how I knew my dad was still alive; I could see him, and I heard his explanation to the team regarding his fake death. I would try to open my eyes or move my hand, but my body would not respond. I was comatose to the people in the real world but very much active in the spiritual world, living future events and interacting with the people in my visions making that existence feel more real than reality itself." She rolled her blue eyes and added, "That sounds so crazy when I say it out loud."

Caleb took her in his arms and held her close desperately wishing he could relieve her emotional pain and their lives could be as they were before their Saudi Arabia exploration. "Gabi, there was a couple of times while you were, uh, sleeping or in a coma, whatever it was...that you did open your eyes and you looked straight into mine and whispered to me that you were sorry. My hopes would soar that you would return to me, then you would close your eyes again with no response at all to my touch or words. I cannot describe the agony of thinking you were leaving me forever."

Overwhelming love engulfed her leaving her barely able to verbally respond. She leaned closer and managed to whisper, "I will always love you, Caleb, only you."

Chris felt he should give them some privacy and got up to return to his bedroom. At that same time Aaron and KJ came from their bedrooms unable to sleep. Within an hour everyone had gathered again in the living room in a solemn assembly.

After their morning prayer time, Dr. Brotman retrieved his Bible and turned to the book of Jonah explaining to Chris, "Jonah is read every Yom Kippur, Day of Atonement, in remembrance of Yahweh's mercy and forgiveness, without those we would have no hope."

The professor read verse by verse taking time for individual comments and observations, also allowing the team to ask questions and make comments. Chris hung on every word soaking in the beauty of God's Word and feeling a unity with this group of people like nothing he had every experienced before, knowing it was beyond the natural world. After the reading, the team all prayed together for guidance and protection.

Reluctantly, Chris left the team to make his morning call. "I've got to call Richards, or he'll be worried about us too. That poor man is mentally loaded down with all that's going on...not a good time to be playing both sides of the fence; of course, there's never a good time to be a double agent. I'm really concerned, because if something happens to Richards, we have no connections outside this bunker, none that I would trust."

"Your ox is in the ditch, Chris, go make your call." The professor instructed him.

"Huh?" The team laughed knowing Chris had no idea what the phrase meant.

Dr. Brotman explained, "Yom Kippur is a shabbat, a day we do not work but spend time in prayer and fasting, however, there are some emergency things that must be done even on a day of rest. Yeshua refers to those as the ox in the ditch in Luke 14:5. So, go make your call, Chris, and we will be praying the detective is given supernatural wisdom and protection as he steps into this extremely dangerous position."

No one offered to go with the officer on this trip to the outside world. Their total dedication was to use every moment of this appointed day in the Presence of The Lord. Knowing they were entrenched in spiritual warfare, they prayed for instructions from their Commander in Chief, Jehovah God, dedicated to following His every command.

The rocky path through the tunnel had become familiar to Chris and he was able to move quickly. He stopped short of exiting the cave to stay out of the view of cameras or drones. Making sure he had enough phone signal to make his call, he clicked redial to Detective Richards.

On the first ring, the detective answered. There were no casual comments, he went straight to the business at hand. "Strozza will arrive late this afternoon and we will be at the lodge around noon tomorrow. I believe I've convinced him that I am working with them."

"That's good," Chris commented.

"And you will be able to see and hear us from the bunker?" Detective Richards was reaffirming.

"Yes, we can. The security system Gabe installed is amazing."

"Okay, I think we're all set then. I don't think we will be there exceedingly long. Strozza said he wants to get a feel for the place, whatever that means," the detective said in a questioning tone.

"Dr. Brotman can tell you exactly what he means about getting a feel for the place, and it's not good," Chris informed him. "I guarantee you Strozza will be very interested in the view of Mt. Hermon."

"What are you talking about? That makes no sense at all."

"Let me put it this way, Richards, Mt. Hermon is historically connected to pure evil and a place of worship for these people you are going to be a double agent with. They are not just corrupt leaders; they are evil to the level of demonic. Nothing is too depraved for them."

There was silence on the detective's end for an uncomfortable minute before he commented, "This doesn't sound like you at all Officer Harris, all this stuff about demons. Has being secluded with these people messed with your psyche?"

It was obvious to Chris that his boss was questioning his judgment, which also brings into question his ability to rightly perform his duties. In the all the years he had been a police officer, his reputation was above reproach and he had never been subject to scrutiny. It was an extremely uncomfortable position for him, and he was cautious as he answered.

"You know me well enough to know my job takes precedence over everything else," Chris immediately responded trying to convince both Detective Richards and his self that the words were one hundred percent true.

"That's what I want to hear, Officer. I trust you won't let me down no matter what your job requires. It's not always easy to do the right thing as you know." The detective's voice was more of a command than an observation. "We are all set then? I know where the flash drives are hidden, I will look for the black dot to identify if I have the right tobacco tin, and don't be surprised at anything I say, keeping in mind I will supposedly be working with them. Got it?"

"Yes, Sir," Chris replied, with a foreboding spirit engulfing him. He had every intention of telling the detective about the dream Gabriella had of the cottage, but something inside warned him to stop. Instead, he simply said goodbye and disconnected the phone.

As he returned through the long dark tunnel, he contemplated what his boss would demand as the right thing for him to do in the coming days and would his new spiritual convictions conflict with those 'right things'?

— CHAPTER 23 —

Detective Richards' words replayed over and over in Chris' mind as he journeyed through the dark tunnel back to the bunker. Something was not right, but he could not put his finger on it. His mind played through numerous scenarios of how the following day would play out when Strozza arrived but ultimately, he really had no idea what would happen. He finally resigned himself to the fact that he had no control over anything that would take place in the lodge, he would only be a spectator. He prayed passionately with his words echoing through the tunnel, "Heavenly Father, give me the wisdom and discernment I will need in the days ahead."

As he reached the entry to the bunker, he decided not to mention his concerns. He knew the team was on edge already and nothing else needed to be added to the mix. He reached up and pulled the lever that opened the camouflaged door to the bunker; as it slid to the side, he immediately felt the holy Presence. It was a comfort to his soul which he desperately needed. He no longer struggled with the battle between divine spiritual guidance and his officer training; they had meshed into one giving him greater discernment. He shook his head in disbelief at how his life had been transformed in a matter of days.

Sandee was in the pantry deciding on what their evening meal would be to break the Yom Kippur fast. He anticipated her question before she asked. "Chris, is there any news on Dr. Nicholson, Leah and the officer?"

"Sadly, there is not. Richards is dealing with that situation as well as Strozza arriving tomorrow. I sure wish I could help him."

"I know you do, you're a fine young man, and Yahweh has his hand on you," she stated without reservation.

"Sandee, can I ask you a question?"

"Sure, anytime." she replied. "I'm always available for you kids."

Her love and compassion allowed him to honestly display his confusion.

"How do you know when the Spirit of Yahweh is trying to tell you something or when it's just your human emotions?"

Her face was filled with compassion as she answered: "That's a question every person struggles with, and people discern in different ways. I can tell you how I know. When I am trying to decide I get a gut feeling, kind of like sick to my stomach, if I'm about to make the wrong decision and believe me, I have made plenty of wrong decisions. If I am making the right decision, I feel total peace." She gave Chris a motherly hug and added, "When you ask for wisdom and discernment, the Spirit will guide you. God's word promises if you ask it shall be given, seek and you shall find, knock and the door will be opened."

"Thanks, Sandee. I experience a similar feeling when making police decisions, I know in my gut what to do and I know if someone is lying to me. You've really helped me," he assured her.

"I'm always here if you need me. Gabe wants to talk to you. He told me to let you know as soon as you returned. He's in the security room."

Chris briefly addressed the team in the living room before he joined Gabe. "Everything is set for tomorrow and it should go down around noon if all goes as planned. All we can do at this point is pray and have a plan, just in case it all goes south. We'll address that after while." No one responded verbally, but each team member battled mentally with what to expect.

Joining Gabe and KJ, he gave them the same quick update before asking, "What's up, Gabe?"

"KJ's been researching Sotoreo and the UN connections to the Khazarians."

"Let me guess," Chris retorted sarcastically. "The UN is Khazarian controlled, too?"

"You nailed it," KJ answered. "In 1945 the UN was founded. Their headquarters was built in New York City on property donated by the Rockefeller family. The United Nations has been, since it's very inception, nothing more than a Jesuit-Rothschild-Rockefeller tool of global control; in short, the United Nations acts as a central banking front-organization, designed, and built with the sole purpose of eliminating national sovereignty, by bringing about global governance."

"And now we have Khazarian controlled Sotoreo as their leader who is connected to the Jesuit controlled Vatican," Gabe added. "It's amazing how all the evil roads in the world lead back to the Khazarian Jews, who are not Jews at all. KJ, show him that map at the UN."

KJ pulled up a link showing a giant map of earth that hangs at the UN. "Look at this, Chris, and tell me what you see."

Chris scrutinized the map and looked up at KJ and Gabe raising his eyebrows. "Now that is weird. What is that?" He questioned pointing to the outer edges of the map.

"That's what we're trying to figure out," Gabe stated. "It's been in plain sight since the UN was founded and no one questions what it is? Don't you find that very strange?"

"Strange indeed," Chris agreed bending over KJ's shoulder to get a closer look.

"I've researched further, and it appears we may have been lied to even about our earth." KJ informed Chris.

"Okay, I'm totally lost on this. What are you talking about, KJ?"

KJ made a circle with his finger around the center of the map? "What is this, Chris?"

"That part is easy, that's a map of the earth. It's the rest of it that makes no sense to me."

"It didn't to us either until I started researching ancient maps of the earth which included lands beyond the known earth realm. When you look closely at the UN map section this is our known earth." KJ pointed to the area on the map he was referencing. "You can see an ice wall completely surrounding the part of this map which we know as earth, separating it from what sure looks like more land beyond what we've been taught about geography. Is the UN map revealing this land, not telling us, but showing us?"

"And probably laughing at the world for not seeing what is in plain sight," Chris added with derision in his tone.

"I'd say you're right about that," KJ agreed. "The biggest portion of the lands beyond the ice wall is named Terra Vista on the map which means hidden lands," KJ showed Chris several links on his computer showing ancient maps that also included the unknown land mass and the ice wall surrounding the known earth. "I need to do more research into the ice wall and Antarctica. Something's not adding up. Did you know it is forbidden to visit or even fly over certain regions of Antarctica? That alone makes you wonder what's going on."

"If that is true, what are these demonic controllers of this earth hiding?" Chris questioned in total confusion.

"That question we have no answer to right now, except the same evil players behind the Luciferian United Nations are the same ones controlling all the other things we've researched," Gabe answered. "I keep going back to the fact that everything we believe is from what we have been taught by our educational system, the media and even many corrupt religious systems. We didn't question any of it, just accepted it as facts."

"That's reminds me of something else I wanted to tell you, Chris." KJ added. "Being from America, I researched when and how our educational system became officially organized. I was not surprised to find that in 1902 the Educational Act of the United States was passed and funded by John D. Rockefeller with a total investment of over 180 million dollars. That was a fortune in those days, but he literally bought the right to control the minds of the children. He was even so brazen as to say he did not want a nation of thinkers, but a nation of workers; better said, slaves to the cabal without them even knowing they were slaves. That ties back to the Federal Reserve where all Americans pay their taxes, controlled by the same Khazarian Jews. With unlimited resources Rockefeller's plan was to have people yield themselves with perfect docility into the cabal's molding hand." KJ threw his hands up in the air and exclaimed, "I have been so ignorant! Everything I've been taught was controlled and I had no idea." His voice was filled with anger and his face blood red.

"We are wide awake now and sheep no more," Gabe declared as he recited from Luke 8:17: "*For nothing is secret, that shall not be made manifest; neither anything hid, that shall not be known and come abroad.*"

"We need to get Professor's opinion on this map," KJ suggested. "Maybe he's got some insight."

The three men joined the rest of the team in the living room where they were discussing both Azazel and the names of other fallen angels, referencing additional non-canonical books.

Aaron was speaking when they entered. "Mastema in the tenth chapter of the Book of Jubilees is called the chief of the demonic spirits. This refers to the time after the flood when the demonic spirits once again invaded the earth in the time of Noah's third generation. I've wondered if Mastema is Lucifer himself or is he one of Lucifer's Arc Angels?"

Dr. Brotman looked up from his notes and from the expression on the three men's faces, he knew the subject was about to change. "Hold that thought, Aaron. I think we have some new information incoming."

KJ had printed a copy of the map for each team member. "I want you to all look at this and tell me what you see. Don't say anything yet until everyone has time to think about it." For several minutes, each person looked at the various parts of the map, glanced at each other, then at KJ and focused back on the map again.

Dr. Brotman laid the map down first and broke the silence. "I've seen this map before. In fact, numerous times in my research; however, I had no idea it hung in the United Nations building in New York."

"And what's your opinion, Professor," KJ questioned.

Dr. Brotman looked at the map once again and laid it in his lap. "I have questioned many times the validity of the hidden lands. We all know it went against what science has taught." KJ was ready to make a sarcastic statement about the educational system when the professor bluntly questioned, "Can science be completely trusted? Are we given bits and pieces of the truth or even sometimes has the truth been altered? There are places in God's Word where science does not line up with the holy scriptures."

KJ felt a wave of relief flow through him. Whether he was right or wrong wasn't the point at this juncture, it was the confirmation that Dr. Brotman agreed that even science should be questioned.

Dr. Brotman picked up his pipe and settled back in his recliner, his obvious sign there was much to discuss. The team members turned their notebooks to a new page ready to make notes.

"When I was translating the Dead Sea Scrolls, some of Enoch's writings made no sense to me whatsoever when compared to science as we know it, or better said, what we have been taught to believe. There was a particular section of Enoch's book that I questioned if it was metaphorical, allegorical, or literal. I'm specifically referring to the angelic tour that Enoch is given by Uriel, the holy angel who is over the world and over Tartarus."

"Tartarus?" Chris questioned. "Where is that."

The professor was never upset with interruptions when there were honest questions needing clarification and the team realized this was all new to the police officer. Dr. Brotman patiently answered: "Bible scholars believe this to be the place the fallen angels are held until their release in the end of days." He quoted from II Peter 2:4: *"For God did not spare the angels that sinned, but cast them down to hell, and delivered them into chains of darkness, to be reserved unto judgment."*

He paused for a moment then added, "Enoch told the names and authorities of all the Holy Archangels, and if my memory serves me correctly that is in Chapter 20." The professor lit his pipe and puffed exhaling the cherry tobacco aroma as he pondered his next words. "Truth is, I still have not come to a definitive decision on Enoch's tour. I have no doubt the previous chapters concerning the Watchers are literal, so I have battled with the following segment being otherwise; however, compared to modern science it's hard to mesh the two."

"In what way?" KJ questioned.

"I would have to go back to my notes for all the details, but science teaches us the sun is stationary and the earth revolves around it. Chapter 41 of Enoch says exactly the opposite." Sandee got up to retrieve his copy of The Book of Enoch from the bookshelf. As she handed it to him, he thanked her adding, "You're a real jewel, Sandee. I believe you can read my mind." An endearing smile crossed his face and she slightly blushed. Faith and Gabriella looked at each other and smiled remembering their many speculative conversations on the bond and attraction between Sandee and Professor.

Flipping the pages, the professor found the chapter and began to read. "This is an example of what I'm referring to in Enoch 41:5-6: *And I saw the chambers of the sun and moon, whence they proceed and whither they come again, and their glorious return, and how one is superior to the other, and their stately orbit, and how they do not leave their orbit, and they add nothing to their orbit and they take nothing from it, and they keep faith with each other, in accordance with the oath by which are bound together. And first the sun goes forth and traverses his path according to the commandment of the Lord of Spirits.*"

He looked up from the book and flatly stated, "That contradicts everything we've been taught about the sun. How can it traverse and be stationary? Again, are Enoch's writings literal?"

Aaron supported Dr. Brotman's questioning. "I've read Enoch's writings many times and had the same questions. Many readers just assume it is poetic writing based on what Enoch understood from his contemporary time, but we must consider this is an Archangel directly under the command of Adoni, the creator of the heavens and earth, who is giving Enoch a tour explaining the creative mysteries. There is so much more in Enoch's journey that brings into question his expose as compared to science today. My assumption is if we believe the first chapters about the Watchers and take it as fact because it perfectly aligns with Torah and the Bible as a whole, then we need to have an open mind as to the rest of Enoch's book and go back to God's Word to align those writings also."

"If it doesn't fit with our science," KJ said sarcastically, "we just assume it is metaphorical, or whatever, and don't even question - because the demonic controllers have taught us what to believe. I have no doubt, Professor, that there are a lot of truths that's been hidden from us."

It was obvious to the team that Chris was in total confusion. Dr. Brotman addressed his confusion with understanding: "Chris, you've not been privy to our years of study, commentary and analysis of the extra biblical writings so please feel free to ask any questions."

"You're right, Professor. I am really confused. How do you even know the Book of Enoch is real, any of it?"

"A very fair question but the answer is not a simple one," Dr. Brotman responded. "There are many that believe Enoch's writings are not real or written by someone else. There is no way to say for sure. However, when I had the distinct privilege of translating portions of the Dead Sea Scrolls decades ago that began my search for their validity. These ancient texts had been hidden and preserved in caves for millennia and were discovered in the late 1940's. They were written in several different languages, Hebrew, Aramaic, Greek and Ethiopic. As they were translated, the amazing thing was nothing contradicted the Bible or other non-canonical books. Moreover, it verified what we already knew and filled in gaps that were missing." The professor relit and took another puff from his pipe before adding, "Personally, I believe these translations are part of Daniel's prophecy when he wrote that at the end of days knowledge would be increased."

Aaron jumped in the conversation again, "And I will add the fact that the Book of Enoch is canon in some Bibles, the Ethiopic Bible being one of them. If you trace back to when the King James Bible was compiled and canonized, you find it was the Roman Catholic Church that made those decisions. With what we know now, that opens a whole new Pandora's Box."

The confusion on Chris' face had not disappeared with this onslaught of information. "I guess I need private lessons," he tried to joke, and then added, "But I do completely trust what this team says and believes. You've put the time and research into seeking truth, and I am the beneficiary of the bottom line." A huge smile crossed Dr. Brotman's face. These were words he loved to hear, the fact that his time invested and sacrifices made had not been in vain.

He brought the team back to the original question. "So, what do I believe about this map that KJ gave us? I believe we must question everything, research for ourselves, and do not blindly believe anything we are told. The Word of The Lord tells us to build everything precept upon precept, line upon line, and we are to search out a matter. Humanity has miserably failed by simply accepting what they have been told by the controllers of this earth, Mystery Babylon."

The professor picked up the map again stating, "I do not see anything on this map that contradicts what the Bible tells us or information from the extra-biblical writings such as Enoch, Jasher and Jubilees; but I do see things that contradicts what science tells us."

Gabriella had been silent throughout the discussion. She pondered if some of the statements could connect to her visions of the future. She decided to bypass her visions for now and address the obvious: "It's apparent we have gone full circle from the beginning of our project. We started with the Book of Enoch, and now many things we are discovering lead us right back to where we started. It began with the fallen angels explained in detail by Enoch and the corruption they brought to earth. Now here we are living the end of days with their Luciferian corruptive lies all around us in the form of these demonic controllers. There truly is nothing new under the sun."

"Under the traversing sun?" KJ jested, then added, "Bad joke, I know. But seriously, I joined this team not very long ago as your personal computer geek to help process and glean information. In my education, I was head of the class in being indoctrinated to believe every aspect of computer science which was based around science in general. I see how the world has been blind to it all just like I was. There's so much information I'm struggling with already and now I've added to my list to research Antarctica, the hidden lands, and the traversing sun. Lord, help me," KJ exclaimed throwing his hands up in humorous frustration.

Chris brought their full attention back to the matter at hand. "I realize the work of this team is on-going, but we must keep in mind our safety issues also. Tomorrow when Richards and Strozza arrive it is going to be very telling as to what the future days will hold and we must be prepared for any possible scenarios."

"I totally agree, and trust me on this," Gabriella said, "There's a very good chance we will have more visitors coming to the lodge." All eyes focused on her as she raised her eyebrows and cocked her head to affirm her belief. "If my visions continue to be accurate, we will see not only Strozza, but soon Sotoreo himself accompanied by The Black Pope." She turned her eyes to her father stating, "Dad, it's no coincidence you built this lodge in this exact location for such a time as this."

— CHAPTER 24 —

A beautiful sunset graced the Golan Heights bringing Yom Kippur, the Day of Atonement to a close. In Jerusalem, Orthodox Jews had gathered where the wailing wall had stood prior to the Three-Day War. A solemn assembly had been declared to pray for the rebuilding of their holy temple. There were no shouts, protests, or demands on this day; only a sacred atmosphere of wailing prayer.

In the bunker, Dr. Brotman was leading his team in their final prayer, bringing the scripturally demanded great fast to a close. In prior years, the team would experience an atmosphere of hope and excitement for the coming year as The Day of Atonement ended, but this day felt very different with impending danger literally at their doorstep.

Sandee excused herself and began preparing dinner. "Do you need my help," Gabriella asked with Faith echoing the offer.

"No, honey bunnies, I know you all have much to discuss, but thank you." Sandee responded as she turned on the oven. "I have everything ready to start baking."

Chris took this opportunity to discuss possible scenarios that could develop in the coming days and

their potential responses. "We have no idea how this will play out in real time, and we can't wait until something goes down and then try to develop a plan." He turned to Gabe and commented, "I've seen that arsenal of weapons and ammunition you have in the stock room."

"For such a time as this?" Gabe questioned. "And Gabi and I both know what to do if and when the time comes."

Faith took a deep breath and exclaimed, "Surely not! Shoot someone?"

"If necessary, yes, "Gabe replied without hesitation. "There is no way I would let these evil people come near any of you, not if I can do anything to stop them."

KJ wrapped his arm around Faith's shoulders and pulled her close to his side in protection. "I'm from the mountains of Kentucky where we grow up with guns. My dad started teaching me before I even started school how to safely handle a weapon. It's second nature to me...y'all." KJ intentionally inflected a deeper southern accent to make his point.

"Anyone else know?" Chris questioned, laughing at KJ's humor, yet thankful for his weapons expertise.

Aaron responded, "You know I can since all Israelis have to serve in the military."

Dr. Brotman nodded his head. "I sure know how also, Gabe made sure of it. We both knew the future possibilities and didn't want to be blindsided. I just hoped the time would never come to actually need them."

Caleb weighed in on his knowledge of weapons: "In Germany the gun laws are strict, but it's still legal to own a gun and my father made sure I knew how to use one. He was old school having been taught by my grandfather the details of WWII. I haven't used one except for target practice, but I think it would be like riding a bike, you never forget." His voice turned to one of sorrow being reminded of his dad and expressed what his peers were also feeling, "I know my parents are worried sick about me and wondering why I haven't contacted them after the war."

Faith fought back the tears expressing her fear: "Will we ever see our families again?" KJ tried to soothe her; however, he battled the same concerns.

Chris would not admit he longed to make a call to his parents to let them know he was safe. It would be adding fuel to the anxiety already saturating the room. "Richards took a big chance when he checked on your family's safety. He said he'd love to contact them on your behalf, but he can't risk that right now since he's going to be presumably working with them. If the cabal found out he knew where we were, that would be the end of Richards and our having anyone on the outside helping us to get out of here." He got up from his chair and began pacing in contemplation before commenting, "Speaking of getting out, I just can't make any sense of what Officer Cohen did."

KJ and Aaron looked at each other knowing exactly what the other was thinking and remembering their conversation at Rambam Hospital about trusting no one. Both wondered if Officer Cohen was a double agent also. In fact, that very thought was going through the minds of all the team.

The aroma of baked bread began to fill the air and Sandee attempted to break the dire atmosphere. "Enough talk of guns as we end our fast. Dinner is almost ready if you girls want to set the table for me." Faith and Gabriella jumped to their feet to follow her request, relieved to exit the morbid gun conversation.

Very soon a very hungry group gathered around the table and after blessing the food, broke the Yom Kippur fast, enjoying every bite of Sandee's wonderful cooking. Although the day of holy convocation had ended the Holy Presence remained and a supernatural peace filled the atmosphere despite the soon arrival of Strozza.

KJ was anxious to do more research and immediately after dinner returned to the security room with Gabe following him.

Chris excused himself and went to his bedroom for privacy and a quiet place to allow his police intuition, and the Holy Spirit, to guide him. Seclusion was needed to try to mind map the unexpected twists of the trio disappearing, the arrival of Strozza, and Detective Richards' questioning of his police ethics of doing the right thing. He got down on his knees beside his bed praying, "Lord, please guide me. Give me supernatural wisdom to know what the right thing to do is and when to do it." He stayed on his knees in prayer, seeking understanding, experiencing time alone in the Presence.

The rest of the team lingered around the dining table discussing the various subjects the day had introduced. Dr. Brotman continued to expound on Enoch's heavenly tour, science, and his inability to resolve the two. He finally said aloud what he had thought for many years, "Sometimes I feel like an educated fool."

Sandee reached across the table and took his hand. "Now, now, Professor, we all know that's not true. You are the most intelligent man I've ever known, and the most caring." She glanced around the table adding, "Look at what you've done for this entire team. You helped Gabe to fake his death and escape the cabal, you were like a father to Gabi when she thought her father was dead, you've guided this entire team into greater knowledge as they've loved and assisted you in every way possible with your project. You've created an atmosphere of family for this team." She squeezed his hand gently finishing with, "And you've been my dearest friend for many years."

Again, Gabriella and Faith looked at each other and smiled knowing Professor's and Sandee's feelings were much deeper than they were willing to admit to themselves. Faith leaned over and whispered to Gabriella, "Aren't we lucky to have special men in our lives?"

Gabriella nodded but felt a gut punch, regretting all the years she had wasted doing exactly as Sandee and the Professor had done. She reached out and took Caleb's hand and scooted closer to him. He put his arm around her as she laid her head on his shoulder, again wishing she could turn back time. She briefly closed her eyes reminiscing of the years exploring caves, working together and being the best of friends; however, she would never allow herself to admit her deeper feelings. After losing both her mother and father, the fear of loving and losing consumed her.

"Oh, how I wish I could go back and do things differently," she whispered in Caleb's ear.

Caleb leaned closer to her and whispered back: "I'm not taking our precious time together to regret the past, instead I treasure every moment we have now, Gabby Girl." He brushed her long blonde hair back from her face and kissed her cheek.

Aaron was oblivious to the obvious romantic overtures in the room and attempted to resume the deep Enochial discussion with Dr. Brotman. Faith again smiled, leaning to whisper to Gabriella, "Aaron is hopeless. Not a romantic bone in his body."

Sandee looked at the clock and commented, "Professor, it's getting late, and I don't need to remind you that you're still recuperating. Tomorrow could be a very long and stressful day and you will need your rest."

"Okay, mother hen," he jested. He was ready to push his chair back from the table when KJ and Gabe rejoined them.

"I've found something very interesting that I think ties into the hidden lands." KJ sat down next to Dr. Brotman with notes in hand. "There's still more research to be done, but we're anxious to see what you think on what we've found."

Sandee threw her hands up in the air, knowing there was no way the professor would go to bed now. "Do I need to go get Chris for this?"

Gabe agreed Chris needed to hear the information and waited for him to join the team before he started. "Have you heard of Operation Highjump, Professor?"

Dr. Brotman thought for a moment and responded, "I vaguely remember reading about that. Wasn't it right after WWII, some kind of U.S. Antarctica expedition?"

"It was," KJ responded, having the full attention of everyone in the room. "My research on the UN map of hidden lands linked me to Admiral Richard Byrd who headed Operation Highjump not long after WWII ended. I'm going to give you a quick overview which has many more tentacles requiring additional research.

"To summarize, the 1946 Operation Highjump, according to the official government narrative, was simply an operation to establish a research base in Antarctica for the United States to claim the territory as Little America for future military bases. The official report stated the purpose was to train personnel in frigid conditions and test how instruments would function. It was scheduled to be an eight-month operation with unlimited finances and a mega fleet of ships, artillery, and military personnel. It's obvious, right off the bat, they would not need a military fleet for the expedition purposes stated."

"Like all the other lies the government tells, I gather there is much more to the story," Dr. Brotman commented in a voice edged with sarcasm.

KJ and Gabe said in unison, "Much more."

"And it's really amazing how this could all link back to your project, Professor," Gabe added, motioning for KJ to continue.

"Admiral Byrd had done four previous expeditions to Antarctica starting in 1928 and he had already gained notoriety as the famous polar explorer before the Project Highjump mission, which apparently was very different from his previous assignments. This was his final expedition and when he returned to Washington what he discovered was never released to the public. Byrd was given a huge parade and honored for his work and yet no one knew what he was honored for. The project became top secret. It wasn't until Admiral Byrd died and his son found his journal in 1986 that the truth was revealed." KJ looked at the team members and stated, "Brace yourself, this is some wild stuff."

Looking at his notes, KJ began with Byrd's personal diary: "He kept a military journal of all his flights and this operation was no different. He would enter dates, hours, and a detailed report. Admiral Byrd wrote, I must write this dairy in obscurity and secrecy concerning my arctic flight. There comes a time when the rationality of men must fade into insignificance, and one must face the inevitability of truth. At this writing, I am not at liberty to disclose the following documentation, perhaps it shall never see the light of public scrutiny, but I must do my duty and record here for all to read one day. In a world of greed and exploitation certain mankind, there will come a time when the truth can no longer be suppressed."

KJ paused and looked up. "I would love to know where the documented proof disappeared to. I do have a good idea."

"The cabal, no less," Gabe stated the obvious.

KJ agreed while he flipped his notebook to the next page. "A base for the operation was established at the South Pole before his aerial exploration began. The Admiral's flight entries for his last flight began at 0600 hours on February 19, 1947, with normal information such as destination, preparation, etc. Take off was normal, flight was normal, everything normal until 0910 Hours when the magnetic and gyro compasses began to wobble and controls begin to spin, he could no longer maneuver the direction of the aircraft. His airplane was being controlled by some unknown force, taking him off his path into unknown territory. Twenty-nine minutes later, in the distance, he could see mountains he had never seen before on any of his four previous expeditions. Beyond the mountains was a valley with luscious green trees, beautiful flowers, and cascading rivers, all this in a place that was supposed to be all ice and snow. The light was different on the other side of the mountains and there was no sun in the sky."

Dr. Brotman interrupted KJ, "If this is real, that could explain the hidden lands which brings in a whole new dimension to our project. Very, very interesting. Continue, KJ."

"That's what Gabe and I were thinking too, Professor. Now get this! Byrd's airplane was joined by two flying discs, one on each side. He described his flight as being in a vice grip which he no longer had control over. He had lost all communication with his military base; however, another strange voice came through his radio speaking in English saying, Welcome, Admiral, to our domain. We shall land you in exactly seven minutes. Relax, you are in good hands."

"What in the world," Faith exclaimed. "I've never heard any of this. This is just crazy."

"Oh, it gets crazier," KJ responded. "The plane's engines went off and his aircraft still stayed buoyant for several minutes before beginning a smooth downward descent deep into the earth. He landed in an underground shimmering crystalline city where he and his radioman were met by two hosts waiting to escort them. He goes into a lot of detail describing the city, his experience, and a description of the hosts. They had skin that was extremely fair, blue eyes, faces that illuminated, and blonde hair that glistened like sunlight. Their countenance was gentle, and they told them not to fear. These hosts took him to meet the Master."

"Master? Oh, my!" Gabriella exclaimed. "That is how Arcturus described himself to me. He said he was an Ascended Master; but I was in a supernatural realm when my encounters with Arcturus took place, and it seems

Admiral Byrd was in the natural realm. Do you think these Masters could be connected?"

"I do believe so," her father answered. "As Byrd's story unfolds, there are many possible connections." He motioned once again for KJ to continue.

"Okay, Admiral Byrd was taken to the one called Master. Byrd wrote that the place he was taken to was too beautiful and wondrous to describe with human words so he would not even try. The Admiral was very poetic in his description of where the Master resided. I won't go into all the details of the magnificent city, but as he described the Master, it made you feel like one you could trust. He described him as cordial and gracious with a warm and kind voice, that his appearance was delicate in features and his face gracefully etched with age. The Master tells Byrd they have monitored his previous expeditions and his reputation is a man of noble character on the surface of the earth, and he had been chosen to visit their Inner World of Arianni."

"Chosen?" Gabriella exclaimed again. "That's exactly what Arcturus told me! I was chosen from among the people of earth."

Dr. Brotman interjected, "That's Lucifer's game plan. He makes a person feel special, above everyone else, and then seduces them into his trap. Sorry to interrupt, KJ, but I think we all see a pattern forming here. Go on."

KJ read from his notes: "The Master told him the earth belonged to the Ariannians and even though they lived in the hallows of the earth and allowed humans to dwell on the surface, they were monitoring all activity and watching mankind slowly destroy both themselves and their surface. When atomic bombs were dropped on Japan, humans had gone too far, and intervention was now necessary."

KJ flipped another page and commented: "This part of The Master's words I have written precisely as Byrd entered it into his journal because I wanted to get it exact. It appears to line up with biblical prophecy in some ways: Your earth has reached the point of no return and there are those among you who would destroy the earth rather than relinquish their power. In 1945 we tried to make contact with your race, but we were met with hostility. The military fired upon our aircraft, and they were pursued with malice by your fighter planes. So, I say to you, my son, now there is a great storm gathering, a black fury that will come upon the surface of earth. There will be no answer in your arms, no safety in your science. The dark ages that will come now will gradually cover your earth like a pall, but I believe some of your race will live through the storm. We see in the distance a new world stirring from the ruins of your race, seeking its lost and legendary treasures that we have here, my son, safe in our keeping. When the time arrives, we shall come forward and help revive your race. Perhaps, by then, you will have learned the futility of war and strife…and after that time certain of your culture and your true science will be returned for your race to begin anew. You, my son, are to return to the surface world and take this message. With The Master's closing words, our meeting ended. I stood as if in a dream and then bowed in respect and humility. The two beautiful hosts returned to my side to escort me out. I turned to leave then looked back one more time at the Master. A gentle smile was etched on his delicate and ancient face. Farewell, my son, he spoke and motioned with a slender hand, a motion of peace and our meeting ended. I was taken back to my aircraft and told I must return immediately with The Master's message to be given to the human race."

Dr. Brotman sat in amazement mulling KJ's information. Finally, he spoke: "Very interesting that he referred to true science being returned to humanity, as if truth has been withheld; and like you said, KJ, the words of the so-called Master are very similar to the Book of Revelation prophecies. Man is destroying himself and this earth; and you can feel the storm gathering around us even now. Dark days are ahead and over half of humanity will die. Lest those days be shortened, no man would survive," Professor quoted from Matthew 24. "There is much to decipher here."

"That beautiful place Admiral Byrd described sounds very much like where Arcturus took me when I would astral travel," Gabriella stated in an agonized voice. "It makes me literally sick now to know how badly I was deceived, how Satan appears as an angel of light, so kind and seductive; and I fell for it." Agony had captured her face as she reflected on Arcturus' seduction.

"That's all in the past, gone forever," her father encouraged her. "However, it has taught you to discern good from evil. That's what makes a good warrior in times of battle."

She was not going to be pacified, "I just thought I was smarter than that. I've never been gullible."

Dr. Brotman stepped in with his wisdom, "That is not gullible, Gabi. Satan is the Master at deceiving, even the elect if it were possible. Now that you are part of the elect, he can never deceive you again. Isn't it interesting, though, how he always refers to himself as Master? He still believes he will win in the end…but we know better." The professor refocused on KJ's information. "What happened then? Let's let KJ finish and then we mind map this information."

KJ continued: "I'm paraphrasing on this part to get to the main points, Admiral Byrd wrote in his journal that the two shimmering hosts took him back to his aircraft where his radio operator was waiting anxiously. The Admiral assured him everything was okay, and it was urgent they returned immediately to Washington. Their aircraft was still being controlled by the hosts and they navigated it back out of the underworld and into the sky. None of the plane's controls worked until a message came through that they were turning the aircraft back to their control. At that point, the flying discs disappeared, and Byrd's aircraft was picked back up by his base camp radar. He immediately returned to base and made plans to return to the Pentagon to make a full report. Everything was documented and President Eisenhower was informed. Byrd made an entry in his journal that he was questioned for six hours and thirty-nine minutes. He wrote that the questioning was extremely intense and a real ordeal. He was informed by the Pentagon that his mission is top secret and ordered to remain silent regarding everything he had seen and heard." Gabe picked up the narrative. "There is more to add to the mix. After WWII there were many of the German scientists that were taken to America. There are several different narratives about what actually happened, but a long-standing and pervasive story is that of the Nazi UFO base in Antarctica. The story basically goes like this…Nazis went to Antarctica to look for possible sites for submarine bases just before the outbreak of World War 2. In their search they stumbled across ice caverns that led to a meeting with a race of aliens with advanced technology. They built their own base there combining alien technology with German science. When Germany lost the war, that technology was brought to America via their scientists who were given the option of death or working for the U.S. Government. Soon after is when the whole UFO phenomenon exploded with the Roswell event which resulted in Area 51. Coincidence?" KJ chuckled and looked at Dr. Brotman. "Okay, we all know there are no coincidences and the word coincidence does not exist in the Hebrew language."

"I've taught you well in the short time you've been with us, KJ," the professor replied, smiling. "You have brought us full circle, right back to the reason Gabe and I first met when he was researching ancient aliens and asked for my help in translating cave writings he had discovered. It was Gabe's belief that extraterrestrial life was real and when he found out they were a demonic deception, we ended up working together and the rest is history."

"Best decision I ever made was contacting you, Professor. You literally saved my life." Gabe glanced down at the notes he had made. "Back to Hitler, let me add that it is well known he was an occultist which makes perfect sense as to how he would easily be seduced by this alien race, who I believe are actually deceiving demonic beings."

Chris interrupted with a question. "Can I ask how demons can manifest themselves in the form of a person or some type of other being?"

"Always feel free to ask, Chris." Dr. Brotman assured him. "Many times, as people open themselves to the occult, demons will possess that person and use their body and voice at their command; however, in Enoch 17:1 it gives another explanation which says: when they wished, they appeared as men. The Bible tells us of many instances where angels appeared as men, and that we often entertain angels unaware. Satan imitates with his demonic forces everything Yahweh does. That's why we are to test the spirits to see if they are of the Holy God. Does that answer your question?"

Chris nodded, trying to process the volumes of information hitting him all at once. "I just need some time to think all this through."

"It is a lot to digest," KJ agreed. "And I've got more information to add that brings us full circle in our research on Mystery Babylon. Very interestingly, Byrd named the mountain range he discovered that led to the hidden lands the Rockefeller Mountains. Was that a clue to who really controlled the expedition? One more interesting name is an area of Antarctica called New Schwabenland, named after the expedition, which was financed by Klaus Schwab's father, major players in the Khazarian Mafia. Klaus is head of the World Economic Forum with the main agenda to bring a One World Government."

"Well, well," Dr. Brotman's voice was filled with excitement. "The prophetic pieces are definitely falling into place."

"Let me land this plane, a little play on words there," KJ smiled, flipping his notebook to his last entry. "This is a synopsis of Byrd's final entry in his journal. He wrote that the following years were not kind, but he faithfully kept the Highjump Operation top secret even though it went against his moral beliefs to do so. Before his death he wrote: the dark night was coming and the truth would not die with him, the truth would triumph. After Admiral Byrd's death when his son found his journal, he released the information to a trusted source. Two years afterwards, Byrd's son was found mysteriously dead in a warehouse with no explanation. Nothing more was reported afterwards of the how, who, etc. Information about his death just faded into the night becoming a cold case. There are even some questions about the supposed heart attack Admiral Byrd had which took his life, but that too was swept under the rug."

Gabriella looked at her dad and stated the obvious, "Apparently there are many people who are pursued and even eliminated to silence their discoveries, you weren't a lone wolf." Then she looked around the room and added, "From generation to generation they continue to hunt down and silence anyone who has truth that will reveal the cabal's evil. Now we are all on their list."

"That's a comforting thought," Faith retorted with sarcasm. "But we all know it's the truth...the janitor, Mrs. Nicholson; and now Dr. Nicholson, Leah and Officer Cohen missing. When does it end, or does it end?"

"That's the question we have no answer to," Gabriella reluctantly replied.

— CHAPTER 25 —

It was a restless night for all the team, dreading the arrival of the International Intelligence Director and Detective Richards. Gabriella was replaying in her mind the visions she had of the lodge and the various scenes that played out while she was in the supernatural realm, wondering how close to reality those visions would be. It was a comfort to her having Chris with the team and had no doubt he was in those visions as confirmation he was to be trusted and was divinely appointed to oversee their protection.

The vision which concerned her most was the entrance of the bunker being found. She and Chris had to leave immediately having made no preparations to escape. Was that why he kept saying they had to be prepared for every scenario? Was it a premonition? She tossed back and forth all through the night praying constantly for guidance and discernment in the days ahead. Finally, towards morning, she relaxed enough to sleep; but sleep was only a gateway to another vision.

The familiar hazy mist once again enveloped her. She could hear faint voices in the distance and moved in the direction of the sounds. Sunlight filtered through the blur, illuminating the path before her, leading to a small cabin in the mountains. She moved up the path towards the rustic front porch following the voices that were growing louder. Before she stepped onto the porch, she could see someone inside walking past the window. Her breath caught, realizing who was in the cabin. Quickly she peered inside where Officer Cohen, Dr. Nicholson, and Leah were in a heated discussion. Pressing her ear to the window, she was only able to hear certain phrases, none of which made sense to her. She could discern from the tone of their voices that they were not in agreement with whatever the discussion was regarding.

"There are things I cannot tell you," Officer Cohen said. "Trust me about..." his voice muffled becoming imperceptible. Gabriella pressed her ear harder against the glass aware there was something she needed to know, or she would not have been brought to them.

She heard Dr. Nicholson say, "Can't believe," and the rest of the sentence faded. She turned her face to peer inside the cabin and saw Dr. Nicholson sitting on a wooden chair at a small log table. He was holding his face in his hands and tears were running down his face, body trembling. "No," he kept repeating over and over. Leah pulled a chair beside him and put her arm around his shoulder trying to soothe his grief. Officer Cohen stood by the stone fireplace trying to professionally camouflage the despair he felt for the doctor. Gabriella knew this was the moment Dr. Nicholson was told about his wife's death.

"Why am I seeing this," she questioned with tears of compassion running down her face, feeling the agony of this man's soul.

A voice from within spoke, "You asked for discernment, now discern what you see."

Officer Cohen walked over to the doctor and placed his hand on his shoulder. He said nothing, however the gesture confirmed he was a compassionate man, allowing Gabriella the comfort of knowing the two people in his charge were in safe hands. The hazy mist engulfed her again and the vision faded when she felt the touch of a hand on her arm.

Faith was gently shaking her arm. "Wake up, Gabi, Chris is wanting to talk to all of us before Detective Richards arrives." Faith was already dressed and ready to join the others.

"Okay, I'll be right there," she answered, sitting up on the side of the bed brushing her long curly hair back out of her face. The revelatory dream was fresh in her mind, and she was anxious to share it with the others. Quickly she dressed and joined the team.

Chris and her father had an assortment of handguns lying on the dining table. Boxes of ammunition were placed beside the weapons. Her excitement of sharing her dream quickly faded as a gut punch of dread hit her stomach.

"This is not what I wanted to wake up to," Gabriella muttered.

"None of us want this, Princess," her father said as he crossed the room to give her a big hug. She wrapped her arms around him and remained in his embrace still amazed and so thankful he was with her again. Reluctantly she released him to get back to the business at hand.

Chris turned to face the team who were anxiously waiting for his instructions. "It's better to be safe than sorry, guys. I truly hope none of these weapons are needed, but in the worst-case scenario we need to be prepared. I will let you each choose your own weapon, load it, and we will put them all on the table by the steps for quick access, if and when needed. Also, keep a backpack with your essentials ready to grab if we need to make a quick exit."

To help ease the anxiety of the team, Chris assured them, "This is only a precautionary measure. No one that will be in the lodge today, except Detective Richards, will know we are here; and even he doesn't know how to access this bunker." He paused, realizing his error, "That is not completely true, one other person does know....Dr. Nicholson. He knows where we are and the hidden entrance to the bunker from inside the lodge. The doctor's knowledge is the weak link in our safety chain, and I have no idea why Cohen moved them."

Gabriella now had the right opportunity to share her dream. "I don't think we need to worry about that, at least not now." She proceeded to give a detailed account of her night vision. As she described the scene of Dr. Nicholson finding out about his wife, the entire team had tear-filled eyes for the loss of his precious soulmate. Also, it was a constant reminder that the same fate was planned for each one of them by this evil cabal.

She refocused the team with a positive note: "I do believe Office Cohen took them to a new location to protect them, but from whom? Why would he not let Detective Richards know?"

Chris felt relief they were safe yet felt apprehension due to the secrecy. He did not immediately comment, needing a few minutes to digest the details of her dream. "A cabin in the mountains?" He questioned Gabriella.

"Yes, it was small, totally secluded, and very rustic. It had the appearance of being vacated for a while."

"Hmmm, I may know where that is, but it hasn't been used for years as a protective custody location. If their cottage was compromised and he needed to relocate, why would he not communicate with Richards and go to a currently used location?" He shook his head indicating his confusion. "It just isn't adding up. Gabi, you're sure Cohen wasn't being controlled by nefarious sources?"

She nodded her head, "I believe that was the intent of the dream I had, to let us know they are currently safe, and the officer could be trusted. I just couldn't hear any detail as to why he left like that."

Chris started towards the pantry explaining as he went: "I'm going to make a quick trip out the tunnel and try to call him. Maybe he'll talk to me, we've always had a good working relationship and I've had no reason to ever question his actions or distrust him."

Gabe quickly joined him. "I'll go with you. If the coast is clear, I need to check my garage since it appeared someone had tried to break in it."

As the two men exited Sandee called to them, "I'll have brunch ready when you get back." She turned and faced the others, "Everyone needs to eat before the lodge visitors arrive."

"Okay, Mother Hen," Dr. Brotman attempted to jest, unable to conceal the affection in his voice. "But I wouldn't call them visitors, it's more like intruders." He turned his attention to his team, taking advantage of the time they had before all the focus would be on the lodge above them. "I spent a lot of time thinking through the details KJ shared with us yesterday on Project Highjump.

"The Book of Enoch tells us about the hollow chambers of the earth and what dwells there. I believe this Ariannian race that Byrd encountered deep underneath Antarctica are demonic beings appearing as angels of light. The Master told Byrd that all the earth belongs to their race, which Satan is the god of this world to those who do not believe in Yeshua. Satan deceived Byrd into believing they wanted to help humankind. Everything Byrd wrote is a perfect description of Satan's deceptions; and we know the evil one can appear as light and would deceive the very elect if it were possible."

"I just had a thought," Gabriella mused. "According to Admiral Byrd's journal, The Master told him he wanted a meeting with the president of the U.S. There is a vast amount of information that Eisenhower actually had meetings with aliens at Edwards Air Force Base in 1954 and signed an agreement with them. I read one time they had white hair, blue eyes, and very fair skin, exactly as Byrd described them. A major technique to distract people when you don't want them to know the truth is to get them focused in one direction while something really big is happening in the opposite direction, look here not there. NASA began in 1958 under the presidency of Eisenhower. Could it be that NASA was developed with the main intention of getting mankind focused on what is above and not beneath?"

"Wow! That is a really interesting observation, Gabi, and could directly connect to the strong delusion prophesied." The professor reached for his bible and turned the pages to read II Thessalonians 2:9-11: *"Even him, whose coming is after the working of Satan with all power and signs and lying wonders, and with all deceivableness of unrighteousness in them that perish; because they received not the love of the truth, that they might be saved. And for this cause God shall send them strong delusion, that they should believe a lie."*

He closed his Bible and looked at his team saying, "Satan will come in the form of a man as the great savior of the world which is on the brink of destruction. According to Revelation 17, this man who will be the beast or better known as the Antichrist, will destroy Mystery Babylon, causing humanity to believe he is actually saving the world from evil. He will usher in a time of peace and great prosperity for all the earth, and it will appear that humanity has entered the Age of Aquarius, the Golden Age; but, in fact, what has happened is the man of deception, Lucifer himself, has set his trap to control the earth; and the Master who Byrd wrote about could play a major role in that strong delusion."

Aaron reflected on many prior conversations regarding this topic. "Professor, as long as I have known you, you've believed that UFOs and alien beings will be used as part of the end time delusion. You told us that President Reagan made a speech to the UN in 1987, saying an alien invasion would be the only thing that could unite all of humanity. I wonder if he was actually telling the world what would eventually happen? If Eisenhower met with the Master at the request of Admiral Byrd, it would be a matter of record for all following Presidents. At just the right time the Master could bring his flying discs and land on the White House lawn just in time to save humanity and the whole world would be watching in one accord. If the leader of the free world agrees to join with this demonic being, who appears as an angel of light to save the earth from destruction, I do believe all other world leaders would follow. This Master could even appear as the Second Coming. Yeshua said he would return the same way he went away, into the sky."

Dr. Brotman's voice expressed his conviction that Aaron's narrative was a distinct possibility. "I do believe it could happen something like that. Possibly even happens when Mystery Babylon falls in one day, the world is in total chaos and a savior appears. However, it comes to fruition, it's amazing to me how we really have come full circle now, having the major pieces to our prophetic puzzle in place. Just to recap: Gabe's UFO research, resulting in all the information stored on his microchips; our Watcher's project regarding the return of the Nephilim and end of days' timelines; just in the last few days identifying the Khazarian Jewish Mafia, the Royals and the Vatican as the Synagogue of Satan having worldwide control; and yesterday Admiral Byrd's diary bringing us full circle back to UFOs. As we put these pieces together one picture emerges, Mystery Babylon. Only the Lord of Lords could have revealed this to us."

"And if we have correctly identified Mystery Babylon then her destruction is imminent," Aaron added. "The Book of Revelation infers that Mystery Babylon would remain a mystery until the end time at which point the beast will hate her and destroy her. Her destruction marks the arrival of the Antichrist. My friends, if we are correct, we are not only living in the end time but living the final days."

Their discussion continued until the return of Chris and Gabe. When the two men walked into the room, a portentous atmosphere arrived with them. The team's discussion immediately ceased, and they waited with bated breath fully focused on Chris.

"I called Cohen, and he did answer," Chris informed them. "However, he was very evasive and gave me no factual information. I asked if they were okay, and he replied he was doing what he had to do to protect them. He did confirm they were at the location I suspected and told me under no circumstances to tell Richards and never to mention we communicated. Then he disconnected the call before I could ask any further questions." Frustration and confusion were written all over Chris' face. "I am sure he wanted me to know they were safe, which means he does trust me; but I don't know what to think about that last comment about Richards."

"That's very strange," Caleb said out loud what the entire team felt. "I wonder if Dr. Nicholson has told the officer about the lodge, and staying here in the bunker during the war, maybe even where the secret door is. The doctor is the only person on the outside of this bunker that knows how to come from the lodge down where we are."

Gabe quickly replied, "We were discussing that very thing on the way back in. I don't know if Doc even realizes he is the key to our staying safe here. We even wonder if Officer Cohen took them totally off the grid, not even letting Richards know, for that very reason. Nothing else makes sense. That way he's not only protecting the doctor and Leah, but he is protecting all of us. He's personally seen how vicious these people are."

"He's a very smart officer, I know that for sure," Chris interjected. "A quick thinker with great instincts. He served ten years in the Israeli military as a member of the Shayetet 13 team with the highest security clearance you can achieve. Men like that don't cross authority without a very good reason. Another positive thing, is his military training taught him to survive under almost any circumstance, so Dr. Nicholson and Leah are in good hands."

Some relief was felt by the team knowing the doctor and hospital clerk were now safe for the time being. KJ and Aaron looked at each other, both remembering their discussion of trusting no one. They had all fully trusted Detective Richards and now were questioning that trust.

"Dad, what about your garage?" Gabriella questioned. "Is anything missing?"

"I wasn't able to get to it. There are currently several obvious drones circling around the lodge area. We think it's surveillance before the arrival of

Strozza. I couldn't take the chance to go outside the cave, but I'll try again after they leave the lodge."

Sandee had brunch ready for the team. It was obvious appetites were minimum as each team member wrestled with so many uncertainties, especially the men soon to arrive.

Gabe debated on asking a question that was consuming his very being. He could no longer hold back, needing to know before Detective Richards and Strozza arrived. "Chris, are you absolutely sure we can trust Detective Richards with the information? No doubts at all?"

Just a few days prior, Chris would not have hesitated. The very fact he did hesitate sent red flags up to the entire team. Racing through his mind were the recent questionable conversations with his boss, Officer Cohen's request to say nothing, and above all his prayer for discernment in every decision he made.

Before he could form an answer based on recent developments, Gabe answered for him. "I knew it. You're not sure now, are you? There are many lives at stake outside this bunker with the information on those flash drives, especially concerning the children."

"I'm sorry, Gabe, when I hid them for Richards to pick up, I would have sworn on my life he could be trusted; but after praying for discernment something just does not feel right. What do you want to do?" Chris asked with an agonizing voice.

"Do we have time to get them back?" Gabe questioned looking at the clock. "It's fifteen minutes till twelve now."

"We can sure try. Richards wasn't positive exactly what time they would get here, possibly around noon. You monitor the security cameras for their arrival, and I will retrieve them now." Chris headed for the stairs.

Gabe hurried to the monitors and quickly focused on the entry gate to the grounds. Just as Chris arrived at the secret door to enter the lodge through the pantry, the security gates entering the lodge grounds swung open, and a fleet of black SUVs started up the driveway.

"Holy molly!" Gabe exclaimed. "Who are all these people?" He rushed to his bedroom door and yelled to Chris to hurry they were on the grounds." Quickly returning to the monitors, Gabe was followed by the entire team crowding into the small security room or standing in the doorway straining to see the monitors. They simultaneously watched the outside arrival of the enemy on one monitor and Chris in the great room of the lodge on another monitor as he was rushing against time. The vehicles pulled up to the front entrance, just as Chris was struggling to be extremely quiet knowing the bugging devices Moretti and Russo left in the lodge would pick up any sound. He silently retrieved the tobacco tin containing the flash drives just as the men stepped to the door. He heard the beeps of the security system being deactivated as he quietly maneuvered back through the kitchen. He was closing the secret bunker door, locking it into place just as their unwanted guests entered the lodge.

Sighs of relief were exhaled from all the team members as they moved out of the way for him to join Gabe and KJ at the security monitors. "That was too close for comfort," Gabe admitted, slapping Chris on the back. "I know we made a split-second decision and I hope we made the right one."

Chris wasn't sure either way. "It's 50/50 in my mind, Gabe. But! If there is the possibility your information wouldn't be used for the good of humanity and the cabal just wants to destroy the evidence, it's worth the chance of making a wrong decision." He focused on the men entering upstairs commenting as he sat down, "I just forfeited my job and any hope of a future in police service. I'm here now not as an officer on assignment, but as an ex-officer offering my protective services...and I have no regrets."

His declaration solidified for Gabriella that her visions of Chris as a God ordained protector were true. However, now she questioned just how that protection would be needed in the coming days.

— CHAPTER 26 —

Chris, Gabe and KJ sat at the computer monitors adjusting them to watch and record every move both outside and inside of the lodge. The first men to enter were obviously bodyguards who quickly went from room to room making sure the coast was clear. Detective Richards, Director Strozza, and several additional men remained at the front door until they were given the clearance to enter. Among those men were Russo and Moretti.

"I just can't get away from those evil men, they're in my visions of the future and in my reality," Gabriella muttered. Chris gave her a quick piercing look as though he knew what she meant then quickly refocused on the monitors.

Caleb detected something personal in the quick exchange between the two and felt another jab of jealousy. He put his arm around Gabriella's waist and pulled her closer swearing to himself no one would ever come between them again.

She was totally oblivious to Caleb's emotions, being absorbed in the events above them. "Geez, this is way too familiar," she said with a slight quiver in her voice. "Strozza is going to walk over to the picture window with the panoramic view of Mt. Hermon. He will comment that UN Director Sotoreo would love the view."

The team was amazed when just as Gabriella predicted, Strozza was drawn to the majestic view and quietly stood for several minutes gazing at the sacred mountain where the fallen angels entered earth's realm. Mesmerized, he commented precisely as Gabriella had foreseen: "Sotoreo would love this view." He suddenly turned to face Detective Richards, "Perhaps this would be the perfect place for a private meeting with him."

Chris noticed the change in the detective's expression and mentioned his observation to the team: "That comment made Richards very uncomfortable as though he does not want that to happen." He mentally calculated the detective's body language before continuing, "He knows we're watching - seeing and hearing everything. If Sotoreo comes here, he knows we will be privy to top secret plans. Is Richards concerned we'll see and hear more than he wants us to know if more meetings are held in the lodge or is he wanting to protect us?"

Gabe answered with conviction, "The case against trusting Detective Richards is building." His next comment was more to himself than the team, "I do believe we made the right decisions on the flash drives."

Extreme disappointment saturated Chris' voice. "I never thought I would see a time I would question the motives of my boss, or should I say, soon to be former boss. When he can't find that tobacco tin, I'm done on the Haifa Police Force."

"You've got a much greater mission, Chris," Gabriella stated with certainty. "And mark my words, there will be more meetings held in the lodge."

Chris turned around to face her and forced a smile, "I hope you're right on that greater mission, Gabi." He noticed Caleb pulled her closer in a possessive gesture, so he quickly refocused on the monitors trying to avoid any jealousy issues. Strozza had reluctantly left the panoramic view and settled into Dr. Brotman's recliner. "This is going to be very interesting," Chris commented.

"To say the least," Gabriella added, still unaware of Caleb's jealousy.

"I wonder who the other men are? The ones that followed them in after the security check," KJ questioned.

Chris raised his eyebrows indicating he had no idea. He glanced back at Gabriella with questioning eyes. She affirmed she knew. "In my visions, they were referred to as the 33rds. They are technological geniuses working for the Illuminati Cabal and those are not normal computers. I saw some very strange things that they were capable of doing."

KJ zoomed in on the computers and gasped: "You're right, Gabi, those look like quantum laptops. I have been reading about their development but had no idea they were available. If I were a betting man, I would wager all those laptops are connected to a quantum motherboard assimilating all the information to one source. The potential for their capability would be almost limitless."

Chris muttered, "I wonder what the cabal is planning for Strozza to need these guys traveling with him. I'm sure it's not good." He noticed Detective Richards looking at the end table next to the recliner, locating the basket with the tobacco tins. "Richards has located the basket and is going to be very upset when he filters through those tins and doesn't find one with the black mark on the corner. I told him it would be on the top." He took a deep breath, and added, "He is not a pleasant man when things do not go his way."

"If he is in bed with the cabal in any way at all, he is not concerned with things going his way, he's concerned about crossing his controllers...and the consequences." Gabe knew this fact all too well.

"I'm still 50/50 on what to believe," Chris commented again. "Richards told me to not be surprised by anything I hear him say while he's meeting with Strozza. He indicated it was because he would be a double agent pretending to be on their side, but will he really be pretending?" He ran his hand through his thick black hair in confusion, "I just don't know what to believe at this point," He reinforced his position while silently praying for discernment from the Highest Power, acknowledging his own human limitations.

Strozza had made himself at home in the lodge, comfortable in the recliner next to the stone fireplace and gazing around the wide-open space of the great room. "Gabe Russell sure has good taste, I will give him that," he commented. "That man is a bit too stubborn for his own good though. You would think he would've joined us long ago and stopped fighting the inevitable."

Chris immediately focused on Richard's body language in response to the director's comment. He was obviously uncomfortable, but that would be normal playing both sides of the fence; and he still was giving no indication of which side he aligned with.

"Hell would freeze over, before I would ever join these evil people," Gabe stated with venom in his voice. "And Strozza knows that to be a fact. This cabal murders my beautiful wife and mother of my child, then wants me to join them? No way!"

Chris knew the cabal's tactics and stated: "They come across very few people they cannot control with the promise of power and wealth. If that doesn't work, then threatening their family or blackmail usually does. If they can't control them with any of those, well we know the rest."

"All too well we know," Dr. Brotman answered, again feeling the pain of guilt for the lives that had been lost trying to help him. Sandee silently patted him on the shoulder in comfort. He put his arm around her in a gesture of affection and she leaned her head on his shoulder. Normally Faith and Gabriella would have noticed the moment of intimacy and exchanged smiles, but they were too absorbed in the nefarious events.

All eyes in the bunker were focused on the lodge activity. Detective Richards sat down on the opposite side of the fireplace facing Strozza, waiting for him to open the discussion. The men Gabriella identified as the 33rds pulled chairs around them creating a circle. Each of the 33rds had small computers on their laps ready to make notes or research information as needed. Moretti, Russo and Strozza's security men stood behind them protecting both the front and back doors of entry.

Strozza picked up a tin of tobacco and opened the lid holding it to his nose. "Dr. Brotman's taste in tobacco is exquisite." It was obvious Detective Richards was uncomfortable. Strozza replaced the lid and placed the tin back in the basket stating, "I'm not a smoker myself, but I do enjoy some of the fragrances."

Detective Richard's sigh of relief would not be obvious to the common eye, but Chris knew his body language well. The detective managed to casually comment, "I do enjoy a good smoke now and again. Would you mind passing that basket to me? I'm sure the professor wouldn't mind gifting me one," he smirked as he reached for the basket offered by Strozza. The basket contained four tins of tobacco and he looked at each one searching for the black mark which obviously was not there.

Strozza was closely watching him with questioning eyes. "Looks like they're all the same flavor," Detective Richards commented in an effort to camouflage why he was gazing so intently at each box. "Oh, heck, I might as well take the whole basket, it's not like Dr. Brotman will be returning here any time soon." He set the basket on the table next to him and focused full attention on Strozza. "Let's get down to business."

Chris knew what the detective was doing. "He thinks the flash drives are in one of the tins so he's going to take all of them. Then you know what will really hit the fan when he has time to search each tin and realizes I've double crossed him. Wrong or right, the decision has changed the entire direction of our plan."

Gabe motioned for them to be silent and focus on the monitors. He turned the volume up so everyone could hear clearly the conversation between the two men.

Director Strozza opened the dialogue. "When Chief Hoffman contacted me about your having information on Gabe Russell, Moretti suggested this would be the perfect place for us to meet in privacy," he glanced towards the picture window framing the majestic view of Mt. Hermon. "I totally agree, it is absolutely perfect. I certainly did not want to meet at the police station; it's imperative our conversation goes no further, understand?"

"Of course," Detective Richards responded without hesitation.

"I'm aware you are working on Dr. Brotman's case. Attempted murder is suspected?" Strozza's sarcastic smile made it obvious he knew exactly what had happened. "I'm also aware Gabe Russell has returned from the dead, and I do give him credit for coming up with that escape plan. We really thought he was silent for good. Gabe's a smart one with way too much information for his own well-being and he's lucked out so far in getting away from us," the director's voice changed with a threatening tone as he added, "but his luck is running out. The top-secret information he has possession of is of international importance and we cannot allow that information to be shared with the wrong sources. In your line of work, I know you understand what I mean, Richards." He leaned back in the recliner and turned the conversation over to the detective. "So, you have information for me?"

Detective Richards leaned forward looking Strozza directly in the eyes. "I do," he confirmed.

"Richards went to the police chief first?" Chris exclaimed, very surprised. "He didn't tell me that. It makes sense, that he wouldn't make a move like this without telling him, but why did he not mention that fact to me?"

"Maybe the Police Chief is compromised?" Gabe questioned.

Before Chris and Gabe could discuss further, Detective Richards took out his notes from his pocket and began his dialogue of information. "I'm going to start at the beginning so you can understand where I am now with this case. A few weeks ago, Chief Hoffman assigned me to Dr. Brotman's accident to determine exactly what happened. It was suspected foul play and since the professor is very high profile with his notoriety of working on the Dead Sea Scrolls, Chief personally wanted all the details." The detective looked Strozza in the eyes waiting for any questions. Strozza made no response and motioned for him to continue.

"He's fishing right now," Chris commented to the team. "Seeing what kind of response Strozza will give to the information he already has. This is all pretty much police protocol so far."

The detective continued: "Dr. Brotman's car had run off a mountain highway on the Golan Heights, luckily being stopped by a guardrail. The front of his vehicle showed evidence someone had swerved into him, probably causing him to lose control. Since the person did not stop to help, I assumed it was intentional. A few yards earlier and the professor would have gone off a cliff and all evidence that someone hit his vehicle would have gone with him. Brotman was taken to the hospital and his research team came immediately to be with him, and I interrogated each one with nothing suspicious. Not until Gabriella Russell, one of the team members and Gabe's daughter, told me she had very recently received a mysterious box with her father's research in it. The return address on the box was the funeral home her father had been taken to when he supposedly passed away. She said her father had been dead for over twelve years and just recently the box mysteriously showed up. I began a background check into her father's death, the people he knew, etc., to see if there were any connections."

"And what did you find?" Strozza asked, leaning forward.

"Almost nothing, the funeral director who supposedly sent her the box had passed away many years prior and his son had taken over. His son was in college when Gabe died and had no knowledge of the mysterious box and knew no one else to discuss the matter with. Gabriella allowed me to see the contents and it was about UFOs and stuff that made no sense to me, but due to the fact the professor had a questionable accident right after the mysterious box arrived, I had to investigate if there was a connection. The team mentioned they used this lodge for R&R when I was questioning them, and I thought it might be a good place for them to be off the radar while I was investigating further, just to be on the safe side. So, I talked to Chief Hoffman about placing the team in protective custody here until we got things sorted out. I assigned one of my best officers, Chris Harris, to stay with them."

"And where is all this going, Richards?" Strozza was obviously wanting something he didn't already know.

In the bunker Chris quickly commented, "Richards made no reference to the microchip information

in Gabe's documents. That's interesting." He commented no further to make sure he did not miss any conversations in the lodge.

The detective flipped his notepad and briefly summarized the events leading up to the escape from Elisha hospital. The team in the bunker was holding their breath waiting for what information Detective Richards would give regarding how they escaped and where they went. When he got to that point, he threw everyone a curve by completely changing the subject.

"Director Strozza, are you familiar with Dr. Nicholson and his connection to the professor?" Detective Richards laid his notepad in his lap and waited for an answer.

"Not really, what's he got to do with Gabe Russell? He's the one I'm interested in." Strozza looked at Russo and Moretti for any information they could add in reference to the doctor.

Russo stepped closer joining the conversation, hesitant to admit their failure. "We suspected the doctor of helping them all escape when we had them cornered in Gabriella's hospital room. The doctor's wife is the only other person directly connected to these people that wasn't at the hospital to escape with them. We were able to abduct her for questioning despite the patrol car watching her house," he smiled, indicating they had done something right.

Strozza ignored Russo's bragging and cut through the chase, "Did she cooperate?" His eyes were piercing as he questioned him.

"Yeah, with a stroke," he answered with no remorse. "We gave her a little serum, not much, to find out what she knew, and the old lady died before we could get any information."

Director Strozza gazed out the window for several minutes before stating, "Sounds like someone or ones blew their opportunity." The tone of his voice obviously reflected his dissatisfaction with Russo and Moretti's job performance.

Russo tried to redeem their failure by adding, "We know for a fact Dr. Nicholson did not leave with the professor and the rest of the team." He rolled his eyes toward Detective Richards implying that he would know where he was.

Detective Richards quickly confirmed, "I do know where Dr. Nicholson was taken by one of my officers, but Officer Cohen went rogue and moved him without my permission. I went to their assigned location, and they were already gone; and even though I've tried multiple times to reach him he has not communicated with me. He's never done anything like this before and we can assume one of two things has happened: the doctor offered my officer big bucks to help him escape or they were taken out against their will. Our security cameras had picked up the same car slowly driving back and forth in front of their location on the day they disappeared. I suspected someone was surveilling their hideout. The cameras were intentionally deactivated indicating one or the other has occurred." The detective rolled his eyes back at Russo, indicating perhaps Russo was involved.

Strozza glared at Russo and then Moretti. "Well?"

They both threw up their hands declaring simultaneously, "Not us."

Chris immediately noted several things, "Richards is trying to cast doubt with Strozza regarding Russo and Moretti's trust. Also, Richards never mentioned Leah and he deflected from talking about his involvement with the hospital escape. Makes me wonder...," his voice trailed off as the conversation above them continued.

Strozza demanded to know, "Does Dr. Nicholson know the hiding location of Gabe and Brotman's team? Do you know, Richards?"

The team in the bunker held their breath, waiting for the detective's reply. Chris was thinking ahead and already knew Detective Richards had to tell the truth. A little truth serum is all they needed if they had any reason to doubt him.

"Dr. Nicholson and I both know," Detective Richards answered honestly. "And that is the reason I wanted to meet with you. Chief Hoffman told me to give you all the information I have and help you anyway I could and..."

"Then why do we need the doctor if you know," Strozza interrupted him. "Where are they?" He demanded.

The detective obviously chose his words very carefully: "I know for a fact Gabe built an underground bunker somewhere in these mountains planning a place to escape if anyone discovered he was still alive. I just don't know where. Only Dr. Nicholson knows."

Russo's face was flaming red. "I bet that old woman knew too," he exclaimed. "We were so close to finally finding Gabe Russell." His voice spewed contempt, blaming Mrs. Nicholson for his failure.

"Well, he did tell the truth," Chris commented, "and he did it without telling them anything that would put us in immediate danger. Even if they gave him truth serum, he still couldn't tell them anymore about our location than he just did, except for the little detail that it's located directly under their feet."

"Little detail?" Gabriella questioned sarcastically.

"You know what I mean, Gabi; and the fact Richards did not mention the microchip information, Leah, or that little detail keeps me second guessing which side he is on; but then that is precisely how a double agent performs." Chris again ran his hand through his hair pondering their decision to retrieve the flash drives.

The intelligence director got up and went directly to the picture window gazing at Mt. Hermon, replaying their conversation in his mind and questioning if the detective was being totally honest with him. Richards nonchalantly filtered through his notes pretending not to be aware of Strozza having any concern about trusting him.

Strozza turned away from the window looking directly at the detective. With an ominous voice he addressed him: "I'm sure you understand the significance of this meeting and the necessity for you to tell me everything you know, and I do mean everything, Detective. Sotoreo gets very upset if he is, let's say, misled in any way. You do know what I mean, right?" The intelligence director stared at him for a full minute before ending his verbal threat. "I'm sure you want to make sure you have a good future in law enforcement and those you love are safe."

The director crossed the room to the rear of the lodge and looked out the window towards the guesthouse. His voice changed from menacing to cordial as he stated: "Let's have a tour of the grounds so I can personally report to our UN Director what a magnificent place this is." He instructed the young men to continue their work as he and the detective exited the room.

The bunker team watched as Strozza and his security men followed the detective towards the back door. Before exiting Strozza turned to look Detective Richards directly in the eye. His voice morphed into a threatening tone as he stated: "You will find Dr. Nicholson...soon. Understand?"

Chris took a deep breath and slumped back in his chair while Gabe and KJ continued to monitor Strozza's entourage.

Chris knew the team was waiting for his personal assessment of the meeting and a judgment on trusting Detective Richards. "It appears to me the whole meeting was played like a chess game by Richards. He would make a move and wait until Strozza made his countermove deciding, move by move, how to play the game. His reaction to Director Strozza's threats showed no signs which tilt my trust one way or another. We know well if someone does not cooperate or crosses the cabal, these evil people have no qualms about eliminating them or worse yet, eliminating the people they love. I just need to know without a doubt which side Richards is on. Even if his original intentions were pure, threatening your loved ones, can control your ultimate decisions. Lord, help me discern," Chris prayed. "Help us all."

— CHAPTER 27 —

Gabe, Chris, and KJ continued to monitor the security cameras while Detective Richards led Strozza on a tour of the lodge grounds. He obviously was enjoying every minute with the view of majestic Mt. Hermon constantly in view. Strozza's security men stayed outside the cottage as he and the detective entered the guesthouse where the video and audio picked up crystal clear.

"I can't help but question why Gabe Russell chose this location to seclude himself in," Strozza commented as he moved from room to room in the quaint cottage. "He certainly has good taste in everything he creates."

Gabriella looked at her father choking back a laugh answering Strozza's question, "Yes, my dad does have good taste and he chose that cottage because I was created there." She chuckled as she stepped a little closer to the chair her father was sitting in and put her hand on his shoulder as she explained to the team her amusement. "That cottage is where I was conceived when my parents were doing cave explorations in Israel and the very reason Dad bought this property to escape to."

Dr. Brotman had been part of the elaborate plan to relocate Gabe after he faked his death and already knew why the lodge property was chosen. He added to the explanation, "Everything Gabe did from the day he supposedly died was for Gabriella. He wanted his necessary separation from her to be in a place of wonderful memories. He built the lodge for our retreats where he could watch her from a distance; and, of course, for our place of escape if ever needed."

"And here we are watching our enemies invade Dad's place of solace as we hide in the bunker he prepared for our safety," Gabriella added. "It's just too surreal."

After the tour, the men returned to the lodge to rejoin the 33rds who were now sitting around the massive cedar dining table, diligently working on their quantum computers and chattering back and forth with details that made no coherent sense to the bunker team. The disjointed sentences and unfamiliar terminology gave no cogent explanation as to what they were working.

Strozza took the seat at the head of the table to question their progress. "The Pindar will want an update before he arrives in Haifa tomorrow. What can I tell him?"

A man who looked to be in his mid-thirties, sitting at the far end of the table spoke up. He obviously was the lead person for this tech group. "I am happy to report all aspects of the Great Commission are now jelling. Each one of us has focused on a different element of the whole of the project. I have a synopsis of the final steps we are working on. Of course, all information has been downloaded to the motherboard."

He pulled his computer open and began: "To bring humanity into submission, the World Health Organization will declare a worldwide pandemic shutting down society and locking them in their homes. This will be a test run as to how well these stupid humans, especially Christians, will comply with government control. The virus has been developed in a lab in the United States and will be released when the time is right from a lab in China to shift the blame to the CCP. The pseudo-cure for the pandemic has been developed and people will line up to get it believing life will then return to normal, having no idea their normal will never exist again. When the mRNA is injected, it will contain lipid nanoparticles, containing microscopic robots, which will allow control of every person who takes the vaccine. They can be controlled through frequency and vibration technology - and the formation of the third strand of DNA begins."

Gabriella exclaimed, "The third strand! Dad, that's the information you've had for decades."

"Exactly the reason they wanted me silenced, that's been their plan all along," her father replied, then pointed back to the monitors indicating he did not want to miss any of the synopsis being given.

The young man continued: "At that point we will trigger world chaos on several different fronts, setting the stage for The Appearing of The One to save humanity. Amid our extreme weather manipulations, created wars, and fears of another pandemic, the financial devastation caused by the first pandemic will be like dominoes falling, resulting in a worldwide financial crash. The stage will be set for The One to appear and save mankind from complete destruction. He will have all the answers to bring peace out of chaos and the entire world will experience a great reset with The One – our Master, Lucifer - ruling over the entire earth. Our Master will introduce a debt jubilee, wiping out all debt world-wide and will introduce a new economic system with a one-world digital currency. Digital money will be the only way to buy and sell and will be monitored by a microchip planted under the skin. The monetary system is only the beginning of how humanity will be controlled with the chip and through the third strand of the DNA."

Strozza interrupted his synopsis, laughing out loud: "People will be willing to take the mark just to get all their debts eliminated. It was the plan from the beginning to get them enslaved to the debt system, a setup for our Master to liberate them and bring them into total submission; and they never realized they were being manipulated every step of the way to the Final Phase." His countenance morphed from humor to seriousness: "And you're ready to implement the plan to entice all peoples to want this chip, not make it feel like it is being forced upon them?"

"Absolutely, Director. Society has been fed exactly what we want them to believe by our mockingbird media and they fall for it - hook, line and sinker. Also, we've continually created soft disclosure of everything we have planned through all aspects of entertainment, to the point many people worship Hollywood and our controlled entertainment stars and want to be like them."

Strozza interrupted again with a controlled laugh, "Our people have done a heck of a job in that aspect. "We promise them fame and fortune and they are willing to sell their souls and become part of our controlled industry. That plan has worked perfectly." He motioned for the 33rd to continue.

"The more we can connect our Final Phase to that seduction, the easier it will be. When the Final Phase is completed, there will be an international celebration of The New World Order. An anointing ceremony will be held in Jerusalem, which will be The One's capital. World leaders will be present to hand over their power to The One. He will announce the arrival of the Golden Age...peace on earth for all mankind, all debts forgiven, free energy, medical miracles for all diseases, and so much more as humanity lives in harmony on earth. It will be live streamed throughout the world with free access to view the anointing ceremony. At that time, The One will declare to all citizens of this new world that all of these wonderful blessings are available to everyone. The only thing they must do is worship him for the miracles he has done in bringing peace on earth and goodwill for all humanity; then step into the Golden Age by willingly receiving a microchip under the skin which will be their new identity to access the blessings. Most humanity will worship him having no idea they have sold their souls to Lucifer. The end of the ceremony will be a concert of our controlled entertainers who will lead the world in praise and worship of The One, the new Master, who will take his rightful place as God."

Strozza's voice took on a threatening dynamic. "Even with the wonderful life The One will offer, we still actually expect some religious rebels. We will allow no one to stand in the way of the greater good." He glanced towards the panoramic window where Mt. Hermon majestically stood. "And we have already planned for that scenario also, if you know what I mean."

"Yes, we have," the 33rd agreed. "Agenda 2030 is on schedule."

Strozza leaned back smiling and applauded the information. "Well, done, 33rds. Well done. Sotoreo should be very pleased. You didn't mention CERN, I assume that aspect is ready also?"

The 33rd immediately replied: "CERN has been repeatedly tested. The collider is ready to activate and open the portal for our divine leader to enter our realm. The Appearing will mesmerize the entire earth." They began chanting with incoherent words which obviously declared their commitment to Lucifer. The very sound of their voices riddled with satanic worship.

Strozza walked back to the window displaying the panoramic view of his sacred mountain. "Only Israel stands in our way now; but not for long. The Russian bear and his cohorts plan to take care of Israel and then he thinks he can wipe us out, too. Well, he has another think coming." Strozza paused to laugh at his own humor before pronouncing judgement upon the Russian President. "He and his cohorts are traitors to the New World Order and will be stopped. Agenda 2030 will prevail and The One will usher in the Golden Age, nothing can stop what is coming."

Gabe broke the silence in the security room. "Finally, I hear the plan on why the microchip was so important to them and how it will be used. They have planned this for decades, putting it together piece by piece, and had to make sure their plan was not interrupted."

Dr. Brotman added his revelation gleaned from the lodge conversation: "We have witnessed the steps of Mystery Babylon planning The One World Government, but the two cannot be one. The destruction of Mystery Babylon was not included in their Final Phase that was just presented. We will discuss that prophecy when they leave. If Strozza thinks prophecies are silly, he's about to be blindsided."

Gabriella questioned: "Did you catch the fact they are referring to Antichrist as Master, the same term which Admiral Byrd used for the entity in Antarctica? That cannot be a coincidence."

Chris ran his hand through his thick, black hair attempting to process the information he had just heard. He turned from the monitors to face the team, specifically Gabriella. "Do you know anything about the other information, Gabi? All these plans they're making?"

Gabriella tried to no avail to measure her response and just blurted out, "We heard all this, Chris, I mean I heard and saw all of it in my visions. The Pindar is the UN Director, Sotoreo, and I guarantee you he will be visiting here soon. He is one evil man." She stopped short of telling them what she had seen when the UN Director came to the lodge. She hoped and prayed it would not end as it did in her vision.

The activity in the lodge drew all attention back to the monitors, all except Caleb who had picked up on the 'we' in Gabriella's answer, again feeling the knife of jealousy pierce his soul. He knew she loved him, but there was an apparent supernatural bond she had with Chris that could not be denied. There was nothing he could do to change it or control it, having taken place in an alternate dimension where he had no access. It was very similar to her travels with Arcturus when he felt helpless, knowing that all his physical strength meant nothing in a supernatural battle. He bit his lip and managed to keep his thoughts to himself, but the churning in his stomach would not stop. What cut him even more deeply was the fact she was oblivious to his feelings, as she was caught in a maze of destiny between two worlds of reality. He choked down his emotions and tried to focus on the monitors with the rest of the team as the entourage upstairs prepared to leave.

"It's been a very good meeting," Strozza confirmed as he motioned for his security team to check the outside before exiting.

Detective Richards picked up the basket of tobacco tins before following the director out, locking the door behind him and resetting the alarm.

"I would love to be a fly on the wall when he opens those tins and finds nothing," Gabe commented.

Chris agreed, "Me, too. The language that will come out of Richard's mouth when he finds out the flash drives are not there as promised will not be what any person in this room would want to hear." He paused imaging what the scene would look like and could already hear in his mind all the vile words his boss would be calling him. "I sure hope we've made the right decision, but there's no turning back now."

The caravan of vehicles exited the lodge grounds. The monitors followed them until the security gates closed and locked. Once out of sight the entire team breathed an air of relief and returned to the living room. Caleb made sure Gabriella was by his side every step of the way with his arm around her shoulders. Gabriella did not notice his possessive gesture, but Chris did. His ability to read expressions and body language told him volumes without Caleb uttering a word.

"At least no guns needed today," Faith attempted to lighten the atmosphere as Sandee went to the kitchen to prepare lunch. "Do you need any help, Sandee?"

"I'm good, honey bunny, I'm sure Professor has much to discuss with you all." Sandee made sure she was in listening distance of whatever would be the topic.

Gabriella opened the conversation pressuring Dr. Brotman for an explanation of the Revelation prophecy he referred to. "What prophecy do you think was left out of the synopsis?"

The professor settled in his recliner and reached for his Bible, flipping the pages back to Revelation 17. "What they refer to as the Final Phase describes the end time events' biblical description leading up to the arrival of Antichrist, which they refer to as The One. How all the details would actually come to fruition was always up for interpretation; but the synopsis we heard today was very probable. What comes into question is Revelation 17:16-17: *And the ten horns which thou saw upon the beast, these shall hate the whore, and shall make her desolate and naked, and shall eat her flesh, and burn her with fire. For God hath put in their hearts to fulfill his will, and to agree, and give their kingdom unto the beast, until the words of God shall be fulfilled.*"

He laid his Bible in his lap to give his personal interpretation: "I do believe Mystery Babylon is in fact the international Luciferian Deep State Cabal, with the Khazarian Jews being the fulfillment of Revelation 3:9. If I am correct, this cabal who are currently the most powerful people in the world, are going to be hated by the beast, Antichrist, and destroyed by his newly formed coalition of ten nations that will align with him. Lucifer will not share his glory with Mystery Babylon who has ruled for thousands of years. He used them to set up his coming kingdom, and they were pawns in his plan, just as humanity was pawns in theirs. It was all part of Lucifer's master plan. When Antichrist takes his throne, he will demand all worship to be given to himself, Lucifer incarnate. Verse 8 in that chapter tells us he will ascend from the bottomless pit and the world will wonder after him."

"Dr. Brotman cleared his throat and continued: "Revelation 9:11 reveals who comes from that pit. *And they had a king over them, which is the angel of the bottomless pit, whose name in the Hebrew tongue is Abaddon, but in the*

Greek tongue hath his name Apollyon. That transfer of power from Mystery Babylon to the Antichrist was nowhere in the synopsis given to Director Strozza. Apparently, they believe they will be aligning with The One to bring in the Golden Age and that cannot be true based on these scriptures."

"And we know why CERN is so vital," Gabriella reminded the team elaborating on the technical aspects she had learned. "CERN is built on the ancient temple of the god Apollo or Apollyon; it's a hyper technical sorcery using mechanical, electronic, and magnetic means with the intention of opening the bottomless pit to release Satan himself, releasing him into our natural realm. Just like Nimrod was trying to build a tower into the heavens to penetrate the firmament and create a portal, this time it's the Tower of Babel upside down."

Dr. Brotman quickly agreed once again flipping the pages of his Bible. "I do believe CERN is the cipher key to the bottomless pit. Revelation 9:1-2 says, *Then the fifth angel sounded: And I saw a star fallen from heaven to the earth. To him was given the key to the bottomless pit. And he opened the bottomless pit, and smoke arose out of the pit like the smoke of a great furnace.*" He looked up somberly stating, "If what we've just heard from Strozza's men is true, CERN will soon open that portal and the time of The Great Tribulation will be released upon the earth with Mystery Babylon being destroyed and Satan ascending his earthly throne to be worshipped."

Aaron interjected a question, "Professor, if the way I am understanding this is correct, Mystery Babylon who is controlled by Satan falls so Satan alone can rise to power to get all the glory sharing it with no one, right? Satan controls both?"

"Exactly, Aaron. He is the evil mirror image of everything our Holy Yahweh is, and Yahweh shares His glory with no one, and neither will Satan. Our Heavenly Father is our Holy Creator and deserves all worship creating mankind for that purpose. It's been the mission of Lucifer from the time of his fall from heaven to harness all that worship for himself. He has ruled through the pagan gods of Mystery Babylon since the Tower of Babel. In fact, even back to the Garden of Eden when Adam and Eve chose to defy Yahweh. That one act of rebellion gave the lease to this planet to Lucifer making him god of this earth. He uses his power, fame and riches as his god to worship. His ultimate plan was to rule the earth eternally and now the stage is being set for his appearance. When he comes the world at large will see him as the deliverer from Mystery Babylon who had held humanity as slaves. He will be the false Messiah appearing as the savior from Mystery

Babylon and be worshipped as the anointed one. But! Lucifer's lease and dominion are about to expire."

Chris was shaking his head in confusion. "Do you guys know how crazy all of this sounds? I'm not saying I don't believe you, but you must admit that it sounds insane. Who's going to believe a portal to an alternate universe opens and Satan walks into our reality and takes over in a physical form?"

Dr. Brotman laughed, "Oh, it won't be that simple, Chris. That's the short version, he will ascend to his throne because of the signs and wonders performed by the False Prophet who heralds his arrival. People follow miracles whether they be of our Holy God or not. Most of humanity does not know we are in a battle between good and evil spirits, nor how to test the spirits even if they do know."

"What do you mean, Professor?" Chris questioned even more confused.

"Yeshua told us that false Messiahs would arise working signs and wonders and would lead astray the very elect if it was possible, and warn us not to be deceived by miracles. Deuteronomy 13 tells us how we are to test the prophets, and it is not by the miracles a person can work no matter how convincing they are; but our test is if they keep Torah, the Laws of Yahweh. We are not to believe them if they are not keepers of God's Holy Word."

"And how many people even know God's Word?" Aaron questioned with conviction. "Most of mankind will be deceived having no idea what they're doing."

"Unfortunately," Dr. Brotman agreed. "However, we are promised the gospel will be preached to the whole world before the end comes. Every living man will have to make his choice as to whom he will serve."

Chris sat silently pondering the wisdom and knowledge of Dr. Brotman. He vaguely heard the discussion which continued among the team as he evaluated his own life, silently praying he would not be deceived by anyone. He re-played in his mind the information given by Strozza's tech team, admitting it was not shocking to him, and it all sounded familiar. He too had caught Gabriella's comment to him of 'we' and wanted desperately to ask her what she meant, but that would stir even more jealousy in Caleb, and he was determined not to create any negativity.

Sandee announced lunch was ready and the group gathered around the table. After the blessing, the discussion continued, not missing a beat. Dr. Brotman again emphasized how their project had come full circle and all pieces were in place, estimating the timetables based on the massive research they had done over the years.

"We are all aware we cannot know the day nor the hour of the return of our Messiah; however, the season will be known to us by the prophetic signs." The professor laid his fork on the table and leaned forward announcing, "Everything we heard today has confirmed we are very close to the final prophetic events being fulfilled and now we have a birds eye view of how they might play out." He noticed Chris was very quiet and addressed his concern. "Are you okay, Chris? Is this all too much to process?"

"It's not that," he answered. "As interesting and overwhelming as the prophecies are, I have to concentrate on practical matters. Do I call Richards for his reaction; and how do I explain the microchips not being in the tobacco tins? If I don't call him, I will have put his targets on our backs also, plus being considered a turncoat by the department. I must warn Officer Cohen that Richards has been given orders to find Dr. Nicholson...or else. I have to admit this is overwhelming, I have never been in the position of defying orders or not trusting my superior." Chris' normal countenance of being totally in control had morphed into uncertainty and the team was surprised when he admitted his weakness.

The wise words of Dr. Brotman helped sooth his soul. "It's in our weakness that we experience the strength of our Lord; and we realize that without Him we are nothing. Yahweh wants you to be led by His wisdom and not your own understanding." A warm smile crossed the Professor's face as he observed the officer's demeanor. "Chris, you have allowed yourself to admit you cannot do this alone. That humble attitude is when the power of the Holy Spirit can step in and guide you in every step you take and every word you speak, no matter how the storm of life rages around you."

Chris dropped his head hiding the tears glimmering in his eyes. He needed some private time and left the table headed back to the security room informing the team he was going to re-watch the video recording of the lodge conversations. "Maybe I can interpret some body language I didn't notice live. I was focused more on what they were saying."

Gabe motioned for everyone to stay seated and not follow him. "He needs some time alone. I'm sure being entombed in this bunker with all of us can be a bit overwhelming."

"A bit?" Aaron sarcastically questioned. "This team has been together for over a decade and it's overwhelming for us to be locked up like this."

"I do love you all, but how I long for my condo overlooking the sea. I don't even know if it survived the war," Gabriella admitted. "I would love for you to see it, Dad. The view was amazing."

"I may have not seen it from within, but many times I stood on the marina and looked up to your balcony longing to let you know the truth and hold you in my arms. I thought it was just too dangerous and, apparently, I was right. I came back into your life and now not only you, but all the team is in danger." Gabe paused, reflecting momentarily on all the events of the past few weeks. "Now that I think about it, seems odd to me that Detective Richards was assigned to investigate Professor's car accident and then almost immediately the entire team was to be in protective custody until Richards solved the case. He knows now who was behind the attempted murder and why, but we are no closer to getting out of protective custody. Does that make sense to you all?" He paused again as Chris stepped back into the room.

"I wasn't eavesdropping, I forgot my notepad and came back to get it when I overheard what you're saying, Gabe. I know where you're going with this train of thought and I had never considered that possibility. Did Chief Hoffman know who caused the accident, even was in on the plan, and used Richards and me as the guinea pigs to get information for him without us even suspecting the chief was working with the cabal? I'm sure he knew if I was with you all, day in and day out, I would find out plenty on Gabe to report back to Richards. It's very possible the war threw everything into helter skelter for their plan."

Gabriella was seeing a totally unexpected picture starting to form and anger began to fester. "Maybe even Detective Richards is in on it, Chris, knowing you could be trusted to do exactly what he told you and glean all the information you could feed them without you even knowing what they were planning. Maybe, just maybe, you are the real guinea pig in all of this."

— CHAPTER 28 —

The normal evening time for Chris to check in with Detective Richards was approaching. Chris was not a man given to confusion and doubt; and had prided himself in the fact of having abnormal intuition, especially in police matters. This situation of doubting Detective Richards had taken him into a mental confusion he never experienced.

"I'm going outside and spend some time praying about my next move. I'm not sure yet if I'll call Richards, I'll decide after I get there." It was obvious Chris wanted no company on this trip to the outside world and no one offered to join him.

"Can we pray for you before you go?" Dr. Brotman asked.

Chris simply nodded his head and stopped in his tracks. The team circled him, laying hands upon his back and shoulders as the professor led them in prayer: "Heavenly Father, we come to your throne of mercy and grace through the blood of Yeshua our Messiah, petitioning for our brother to have divine wisdom and guidance in every word and thought. You, our Lord, know the hearts and intentions of Detective Richards, and can impart that discernment to Chris. Your Holy Spirit dwells within Chris and will guide him and protect him from deception. We agree together and decree it to be according to Your promises."

"Amen" the team all said in unison as the Presence once again saturated the bunker atmosphere. Chris unashamedly wiped the tears from his eyes. His mouth was quivering so he did not try to speak, he simply nodded his head once more and left. The team stood silent until the pantry door closed behind him. Still silent they took their normal seats in the living room and continued to intercede for their police officer protector whom Yahweh had sent them.

Slowly Chris walked through the darkness of the familiar tunnel with the flashlight illuminating his steps. Mentally he was comparing his black cave environment to the turmoil of his soul. "Lord, help me to step from this darkness of confusion into Your light of truth."

As he reached the end of the tunnel, the evening shadows were closing in. He cautiously stepped outside surveying the skies for any sign of drone activity. All was eerily quiet as the mountains were slowly fading into the darkness of night. He sat down on a rock by the mountain stream and listened to the mountain stream cascading by him, allowing the tranquility of God's nature to flow through his soul. He knew the time was right to call Detective Richards and walked back to the mouth of the cave to avoid any sound interference from the mountain streams.

After only one ring, the detective answered. His tone was light and pleasant, "Hello, I appreciate you checking in on time, Officer." Chris was confused by his boss's greeting until he added his name in his next comment: "Nathan, is everything going as planned?"

Chris knew immediately that Strozza was still with Detective Richards. Nathan was the code name used whenever he needed to disguise Chris' identity on calls involving other people. Knowing it was possible Strozza could hear every word he spoke, he prayed for wisdom on how to proceed. Supernaturally, the words came.

"I've hit a few unexpected obstacles, boss. I've been tailing this guy since you gave me this assignment and he's been meeting with some questionable characters. It's really hard to tell which side he's on, good or bad."

"Roger that," Detective Richards replied, confirming he knew the message Chris was attempting to convey without revealing his assignment or identity to Strozza. "From our intel, Nathan, he's following orders. Just stay on his tail a few more days and check back in with me as scheduled. Keep using that police intuition, you're always right on. Talk later," he said abruptly ending their conversation.

Before Richards disconnected the call and without Strozza being aware the phone line was still open, he made a comment he obviously wanted Chris to overhear. "Hey, Moretti, I hope you're enjoying going through the professor's tins of tobacco."

The brief conversation told Chris all he needed to know. Against his will, his boss was under the control of these evil men; but he was still doing all he could to protect the bunker team. Chris was convinced had Detective Richards got possession of the flash drives, Moretti would have found them, and the microchips would already be in the hands of Strozza with the incriminating information being destroyed - and not by Detective Richard's choice. There was no doubt, the last-minute decision to retrieve the flash drives was the right decision; however, now there was no direction on what to do next with Gabe's microchips. With his boss being controlled, Chris questioned how he would know when Detective Richards' words, actions and instructions were to the cabal's benefit or to help the bunker captives.

As he retraced his steps back to seclusion, he prayed continually for God's direction. He paused before opening the secret door to the bunker. "Lord, how will I know the right thing to do, what and who to trust?"

A still small voice from within whispered, "I will lead the way, my son." Peace settled in the police officer's soul, which was reflected in his countenance as he rejoined the team.

An air of relief was felt by everyone when Chris entered the room. Obviously, his call had gone well, and they anxiously awaited his information which he immediately gave: "You might say it was a sweet and sour conversation with Richards." He told the team, word for word, the conversation between he and his boss, adding, "I guess maybe I am still on the police force, at least for now. Richards made it clear in camouflaged wording that it was the right decision not to leave the flash drives for him. The conversation was not what I expected at all, and with Strozza listening, every word Richards said was guarded with hidden messages."

Gabe sighed in relief, "Thank God we did make the right decision, but with Detective Richards in the cabal's control, even though it is against his will, where does that leave us? Now what do we do with this information, especially about the children and the proof of the world elitist being not only involved, but willing doing these horrible atrocities? Every day that I live, I am fighting the anger of what is being done to these innocent ones and pray for some way to help them. The cabal has managed to keep me silent about the microchip technology which I've had since before Gabi was even born; and apparently that technology will soon be used in some form by the Antichrist to introduce his pseudo–Golden Age that's on the horizon. But the children...I just can't sit on this information like I did the chip." Gabe was consumed with agony knowing everyday more children were kidnapped into child sex slavery, and worse.

Chris stood up and began pacing back and forth. "There's got to be a way - the right person to get this information to that can be trusted. I do believe now Richards would have helped if Strozza had not threatened his family, his career and even his life. None of us know what we would do if the people we love were in danger and we had to make decisions that would protect them, good or bad. Richards apparently made his decision and is now controlled by the very people who control the international trafficking ring. He's off the list of being any help at all."

KJ had hoped, as the others did, that Detective Richards would have the answer to communicate the information to the right authorities; however, he also questioned what authorities could be trusted knowing there was corruption even to the highest levels of all governments, including Israel. As much as he hated to admit it, his own country America was the deep state ringleader for this worldwide evil and finding a trusted source there would be few and far between. Even if one could be found they would be eliminated immediately, one way or another. He had been mulling the possibility of anonymously disseminating Gabe's information but had not felt the time was right to share his thoughts, until now.

He leaned forward in his chair and cleared his throat. All eyes turned to KJ as he explained: "This is just an idea but hear me out before you jump to a decision. There are internet sites which are not accessible through a random search referred to as off-site IRC channels. One I am specifically familiar with is called 4-chan which is an anonymous channel where IP addresses cannot be accessed. I know Gabe set this computer up so the IP address cannot be traced so that would give us another layer of protection with any information shared."

Chris was already catching KJ's direction. "I had never considered that possibility."

"What possibility, what are you talking about?" Gabe questioned in confusion.

"Let me explain it this way," KJ continued. "4-chan has what's called boards where you post information for anyone to read but no one knows who is posting or from where, and no way to find out. Viewers of posts can anonymously share the information on their boards with the potential of reaching their followers, all of whom could also share the information. There is no limit to how many people can be reached from one original post. What if we downloaded the flash drive onto a 4-chan board? We are talking about multi-millions of people who could see the child trafficking information and start researching for themselves. I bet you, most people have no idea this exists and there could be a worldwide awakening, an army of digital soldiers to fight for the children, creating a revolution to save the children." KJ tempered his enthusiasm by stating, "What's the worst-case scenario from posting? Maybe there's not many hits? But any at all is better than none."

Gabe saw the potential in what KJ shared and admitted, "This could be the very best solution of taking my information directly to the people. I really doubt the true and complete information would have ever been released publicly if given to any one person, Detective Richards or anyone else."

Chris was nodding his head in agreement as he paced back and forth, "I also believe this could work. We already know if Richards had taken the information the cabal would already have it and destroyed it. Even if we could get it to a trusted source, it doesn't mean public awareness would be the result."

"That's what I have always wanted, mass exposure without putting anyone in danger...again," Gabe interjected. "These evil people have covered their debauchery way too long and it's time there is an awakening of humanity."

"Exactly," KJ agreed. "And with a click of a computer mouse, your information is accessible worldwide and no one can know where or who it came from."

"Brilliant and yet so simple," Dr. Brotman added. "Yahweh's timing is always perfect, and we will be a step ahead of what these Luciferians are planning." A smile crossed his face as an unexpected thought crossed his mind, "Wouldn't it be wonderful if we could play a part in destroying Mystery Babylon? I believe her filthy iniquities and vile fornications have reached unto heaven as John the Revelator prophesied. What is filthier and viler than what is being done to the children? The destruction of the Great Whore could be in our sight."

"Dear, God, I hope and pray so," Gabriella exclaimed. "I can't unsee the images of the children and it haunts me day and night. I believe that most humanity would unite in a war to end crimes against children; and the ones that would not are part of the horrendous evil and need to be exposed. Showing the people of our earth the truth can turn the tide, I truly believe that. KJ's plan sounds to me like an answer to prayer."

"I believe that, also, Gabi," Chris replied. "I have seen the vilest of men in prisons unite against pedophiles. We would have to put them in solitary confinement to protect them; and honestly, the police officers would have preferred just to let the prisoners take care of them, if you catch my drift. We hated protecting them."

Sandee had been listening with a grieving heart and reminded them from Luke 17:2: "Yeshua's judgment will be upon every last one of them. He sealed his verdict on people who hurt children when He declared it was better a millstone be tied around their necks and they be cast into the sea than to harm one of his little ones. I believe there is a deeper, more tormenting place in hell for these monsters." Her normally kind voice was consumed with anger as she spoke. "At least I hope so."

"Well, what are we waiting for? Let's do this, KJ." Gabe instructed, jumping to his feet and heading for the security room with KJ and Chris following him.

KJ took his place at the computer and soon had the 4-chan board displayed on the monitor ready for download. He inserted the flash drive and looked at Gabe for final approval before clicking the mouse to send. Gabe heart and mind filled with peace knowing they were making the right decision when he nodded his head. One click, and within moments the monitor displayed the download was complete.

"It's done," KJ confirmed, leaning back in the computer chair. "Now we wait and see what happens. We can follow the number of people who click on the board, share it, and read comments. We just will not know who they are, nor will they know who we are."

"I'm sure members of the cabal will see it, too," Chris acknowledged.

"Yeah, they can see it," KJ confirmed. "But there is not one thing they can do to take it down. I'm sure we will see negative comments on the board attempting to convince people this is all a lie, etc. However, after the initial shock of our viewers, that could just help feed their determination to know the truth and research for themselves."

"That's what we'll pray for," Gabe said, thankful a heavy burden had been lifted from his shoulders. "It's all in your hands now, Father," he prayed out loud.

"Amen", KJ added to Gabe's prayer with his eyes still focused on the computer. "I'm going to set the 4-chan board to give a signal anytime there's a view. It will ding so we'll know another person has seen the truth."

When the settings were complete, the three men rejoined the team confirming the download. There was an obvious air of relief as the flash drive's contents had finally been released to open the eyes of a deceived world.

As they anxiously awaited notification that the board had been seen, Gabe shared another fact on the atrocities of child trafficking: "Sex trafficking of children has become the number one money maker business in the world, more than drugs or any other illicit business. Our precious children are a commodity that is abused, tortured and ultimately murdered all for profit – often selling their organs on the black market for an additional source of income when they're not considered 'fresh' any longer."

The momentary relief quickly morphed into agony of soul. Faith dropped her head and sobbed out loud. The others desperately tried to control their emotions, but the grief and anger obviously consumed each one of them.

Dr. Brotman attempted to reign in the emotional agony with a positive observation. "Think of the good this information will do, and the children that could be saved as people open their eyes to the world around them. I would think parents and caretakers would be more aware of their surroundings, more protective of their little ones, reporting anything that is suspicious, and be prepared to take whatever measures necessary if their children are in danger of being abducted. Yes, I know there has always been some information circulating on child abductions, but nothing to the degree of what Gabe discovered."

Gabe's voice was broken as he added, "What people do not understand, and we must make them aware of too, is it's so much more than the horrible kidnapping from a park or public location. They disappear into sex slavery though the social services systems, adoptions, even supposedly being rescued from natural disasters and never seen again, there are so many ways these children end up in this horrible slavery. Every 40 seconds a child goes missing in the U.S. alone, millions worldwide every year. If we can save just one child, it will be worth all I've sacrificed through the last decade." He reached for his daughter's hand, "Even separation from the person I love most in this world."

"I do believe it will be much more than that," KJ encouraged him. "Much, much more." He had no more than got the words out of his mouth when a ding was heard coming from the security room. Then another and another continuing with consistent notifications that the board was quickly going viral. KJ rushed to the computer and opened the notifications. He ran his hands across his bald head and leaned back laughing and praising God. "This is unbelievable," he exclaimed loud enough for the team to hear in the other room. They all jumped from their chairs and bolted through Gabe's bedroom to the security room.

KJ turned to announce, "Almost every person who is viewing our board is sharing it to theirs. We've had hundreds of hits already and it's been less than half an hour. We're getting lots of comments too with people posting they had never heard this before and questioning if it could really be true and they plan to dig deeper. Others are verifying they knew some but nowhere near the information we posted." He held up his hand indicating he needed a minute to focus before anyone made a comment. "Now this is very interesting."

"What?" Gabriella could not suppress her curiosity.

"There is a board that has shared our post that is relatively new but already has a multitude of followers. The tag signature is the Gospel of Q,

The Source. Scrolling through their previous posts, whoever is posting has already been giving some information very similar to ours, and that gives instant credibility to followers of The Source to trust our board." KJ paused to read further. "I'm going to need some time to go through all these posts, but whoever this is sure seems to have access to information from the highest levels; and is constantly referring to Bible scriptures, especially Ephesians, stating the world is in a spiritual battle to save humanity."

The computer was dinging so repeatedly that KJ turned the signal off as he continued to monitor the hits on the board. "Many people are posting links for additional information, statistics, etc. to verify our post. It sure appears a digital army is arising to fight for the children. Someone just posted a link to an article revealing private islands used for the sole purpose of vacations for the rich and famous with children being provided. There is a link to follow about Epstein Island. Another posted to dig deep into the Standard Hotel in Hollywood. Another, The Vatican's Ninth Circle and red shoes. Many are posting about the tunnels all around the world through which they traffic children."

Gabriella caught her breath remembering her dream about the tunnel leading to the underground captivity of children. "Dad, your proof will verify for many who are questioning and open the eyes of a multitude who have no idea whatsoever. I feel a tsunami of truth coming across this world and I'm expecting an outpouring, a great awakening, of the Holy Spirit before Antichrist takes control. The children just might be the catalyst."

Dr. Brotman repeated the promise of Yahweh from Joel 2:28: "*In the last days, I will pour out my Spirit upon all flesh; and your sons and your daughters shall prophesy, your old men shall dream dreams, your young men shall see visions.*" We know this outpouring is coming soon, and perhaps you are correct, Gabi."

Throughout the evening, KJ gave updates to the team on the board posts and the number of shares. "I'm following some of the links to see the response on other 4-chan boards and there has been relatively few counter posts saying it's a farce; overwhelmingly the responses have been a mixture of shock and confirmations. I've never seen information move so quickly on the web."

"Divine direction," Dr. Brotman flatly stated. "When Yahweh's hand is upon a matter there is no stopping it."

— CHAPTER 29 —

Late into the night, Gabe, Chris and KJ surrounded the computer monitor following links that had been left on the 4-chan board. Gabe, especially, was overwhelmed with the information already circulating on back channels exposing atrocities done to children.

"I had no idea that through the past decade while I was hiding the information about the children, that the truth was leaking out little by little from sources all over the world. I've always heard the truth has a way of rising like butter to the top and I'm so thankful the world is waking up, and yet I feel guilty that I've waited so long."

KJ brought a silver lining in the events taking place. "Gabe, your information has a solid rock foundation with undeniable truth which will help verify what these other people are posting. They are labeled as conspiracy theorists because they cannot prove the information they are finding. You have the proof and it's for all the world to see now."

Chris added, "When it's just posts on some random internet board, most people do not take the information seriously and they are largely ignored by the cabal; but when you have proof, like you do, Gabe, it's a whole different threat to these evil people and why they never give up on shutting them up until that threat is completely silenced. There's no doubt in my mind that many people have had proof and when they tried to reveal it, they were quickly silenced, just as you would have been if they had known you were still alive. You've been able to keep your proof protected until a safe way was found to release it. God's timing is perfect."

"And Mystery Babylon is going down," KJ's voice was half jesting and half determined.

The encouraging words erased the regret in Gabe's soul, and it was replaced with a spiritual excitement as they continued to watch the hits on the board. Many of the comments were linking child trafficking to specific names, big names that any person in the free world would know immediately.

One comment lead them back to The Source board where pictures of very famous people involved in nefarious children activity were posted.

"I am captivated by this board," KJ admitted. He opened another screen and did a quick internet search on 'Gospel of Q' finding the name was associated with an ancient book referred to as The Source of Truth. "How interesting," he observed. "Especially when the current information coming from The Source must be comms from high level intelligence sources."

Chris quickly agreed. "The way they're disseminating the information indicates it's coming from a military source. It appears whoever created this board was bypassing the mainstream media, which we know reports only what the cabal tells them to. Through 4-chan The Source communicates what is really happening in this cabal-controlled world. Just skimming through the posts tells me they are upsetting every political apple cart in the world because these details are phenomenal. I bet you, this board will be quickly labeled a psyop by the deep state."

Gabe looked at the time and even though he could watch the board all night, he knew the wisdom of rest. "It's really late and we need to get some rest, guys. I'm sure everyone else is already in bed. I'm not as young as used to be."

KJ shut down the computer and gave the monitor a pat as he got up. "You've served us well, my computer friend."

Gabe smiled, thanking the good Lord he had the foresight to design the security room and computer system for such a time as this. Had he not...he did not even want to think of the alternative possibilities.

As if KJ read his thoughts, he said, "God knew this time would come and what would be needed to accomplish our mission."

Gabe nodded and gave him a fatherly hug. "Your computer brilliance sure has been a blessing, KJ. It's a gift from Yahweh. Sleep well, son, there's still much to do."

The bunker was silent as the team rested for the night.

Gabriella was deep in sleep when a loud noise awakened her. She jumped from her bed and ran into the living room where Chris was standing over a cup of coffee he had dropped.

"I'm sorry, Gabi, I'm a bit clumsy this morning."

"You're up early," she commented, stretching. "I'm surprised my dad isn't up yet. He's usually the first one out of bed."

"*What are you talking about?*" Chris questioned with confusion.

"*I said my dad is usually the first one out of bed,*" she repeated.

She wondered why he still looked confused. "*Are you okay?*"

"*Yeah, I am,*" he answered. "*Are you?*"

Gabriella ran her fingers through her long blonde hair trying to straighten it from tossing and turning in her sleep. She looked around the room and gasped. There were no signs of anyone else being in the bunker. She ran to the bedrooms the team used and they were empty. She rushed to the kitchen area and there were no signs of Sandee having used the kitchen. "*Oh, no!*" she cried.

Chris crossed the room and embraced her with a brotherly hug. "*Tell me what's going on, please.*"

She shook her head in disbelief. "*My father, Professor, the team they were all here when I went to bed.*"

He held her close to comfort her. "*Now, now, apparently, you've had another dream, Gabi. Remember, it's just you and me.*"

She pushed him away and plopped on the couch. "*No, this is not real, that world is real.*" She sat silently acclimating to her alternate reality, realizing there had to be a purpose, a divine reason she had returned. "*Lord, help me understand,*" she inwardly prayed.

"*Can I get you anything?*" Chris' voice was filled with heartfelt concern.

The bond of trust and friendship created in her alternate existence was pouring through her again. "*Just give me a minute to process what's happening.*" She dropped her head in her hands and waited for directions. In her confusion, she asked, "*What day is this?*"

Chris sat down beside her answering, "*This is the day Sotoreo will arrive.*"

The cloud of confusion lifted, and she sat straight up facing him, looking him directly in the eyes. "*Listen to me closely, Chris, embed this in your memory and do not forget. Sotoreo will find us. He is divinely led by Lucifer himself and will supernaturally follow his spirit guide through the kitchen, into the pantry and to the hidden doorway to this bunker. We must make plans now on what we will do before he arrives.*"

"*I don't understand, Gabi, did you see this in one of your visions?*"

"*It's too hard to explain, just trust me on this. Remember my words, Chris, it's a matter of life and death for all of us.*"

"*You mean for both of us?*" He questioned, still confused.

"No, I mean for all of us, and I can't explain that either. Just please trust me and promise me you will remember."

"Okay," he patronized her. "How can I forget when you're here constantly to remind me?"

She gave him a big hug and whispered, "If I had a brother, I would want him to be just like you."

She closed her eyes to momentarily cherish their supernatural bond. When she reopened them, she was still in her bunker bed with Faith fast asleep in the bed beside her.

She quickly showered and dressed, anxious to start the day and wished for a moment alone with Chris, which was never possible. Her father was making coffee when she entered the kitchen area.

"You're up early," he greeted her with a big hug. He noticed she clung to him longer than normal, like she did when he first returned. "Something wrong, Princess?"

She released him and sat down on a bar stool to watch him finish his morning routine, attempting to find the right explanation for her dream vision. "I know I can tell you anything, Dad, and I am so thankful for that. But let's not say anything to anyone else just yet about what I'm going to tell you."

Gabe poured them both a cup of coffee and sat down next to her. "Whatever you say," he agreed. "Now what's wrong?"

"First, I'm going to tell you what I saw regarding Sotoreo in my vision before I awoke from the coma. I've already told you that Chris and I were in this bunker alone during my vision. I've also told you that in my vision the UN President Sotoreo and The Black Pope came to the lodge. What I did not tell anyone is when they came Sotoreo used his black magic to find the secret door leading down to the bunker. Chris and I were totally unprepared and only by the grace of God did we escape." She shared with him her previous night's dream ending with, "I believe my dream is warning us to be ready."

"I've got some backup plans if that becomes necessary, plans I have shared with no one, except Professor and that was in the event anything happened to me." His voice was reassuring there would be a way of escaping.

"Is one of those ways some type of chemical that can be released that immobilizes everyone in the lodge?" Gabriella questioned.

"How did you know that?" he asked, shocked. Then adding, "Of course, you saw it in your vision. Right?"

"I did," she confirmed. "Chris discovered it and how to activate it which allowed us time to escape out through the tunnel. What we did not know was if the people in the lodge were just sedated or..."

He knew exactly what she wanted to know. "It would depend on the amount of chemicals that are released. There is a control mechanism. They can be temporarily sedated or permanently eliminated."

"Maybe it's time to share your emergency plans with Chris, just to be on the safe side, so he can put a plan together for the entire team. Then he can let everyone know what to do if and when Sotoreo actually comes to the lodge."

"You're right, it is time. I had prayed through the years this day would never come, but I was going to be ready to the best of my ability to protect you if it did."

The smell of morning coffee filled the air and bedroom doors began to open with the team filtering into the gathering area. With each passing day, hope to escape soon seemed less likely; and each team member was struggling to keep a positive attitude, despite the uncertainty that consumed them, but also thankful for a safe haven.

When Chris joined the team, he noticed Gabriella staring at him and then quickly looking away. He felt an intuition she needed to talk; however, Caleb had sat down beside her at the bar, also noticing the prolonged gaze. Chris avoided eye contact with her and sat down across the room.

Dr. Brotman sensed the unsettled atmosphere of all his team and encouraged them: "It's a good thing we have this time in seclusion, both to keep us safe and to have had the time to discover all we have. I know we are all getting a bit stir crazy and I'm praying for divine intervention." He paused, and added, "And you have to admit, we have made a lot of headway in our secluded time here."

Gabe interjected, saying, "Last night we discovered even more. Fill them in, KJ."

After relaying information on The Source, KJ added, "There is a huge amount of information available on these alternative internet channels for anyone who starts researching. The problem is most people have no idea of the real world we live in and question nothing, especially to the extent of trying to dig out the facts; however, what I see on these boards are many beginning to wake up from the cabal coma they've been in and the only way the cabal can stop the factual information circling the earth is to completely shut down the internet."

"Don't be surprised if they do just that," Gabe interjected. "They will do whatever necessary to protect their lies and deception. Even to the point of a fake UFO invasion, like we discussed a couple of days ago. President Reagan has already set the stage for that scenario.

"Speaking of that," Chris questioned. "Please explain to me in simple terms what this team believes about UFOs. It's really been hard for me to follow you sometimes. Real? Not real? Demons? I really am confused."

All eyes turned to Dr. Brotman to answer, which he did in a manner anyone could understand. "Chris, this whole world has been programmed since the mid-twentieth century to believe there are extraterrestrial beings who have visited us; some Ufologist saying these aliens are simply watching over us, some say we are planted here by aliens, and some saying they're planning an invasion. Yet others believe alien beings of non-human origin already dwell among us. The UFO phenomenon has continued to be assimilated throughout the decades slowly building towards an international disclosure when the cabal will present their evidence of proof to deceive the world into believing a lie."

Caleb who had been silent, simmering in his jealousy, finally joined the conversation. "During our cave explorations we often found ancient petroglyphs of UFOs and beings that were non-human which we believe were drawings of Nephilim, not aliens."

Gabriella squeezed his hand agreeing with him, "Yes, and we also believe ancient societies painted those cave wall scenes for future generations, a form of historical writings."

"Another proof we are being programmed for disclosure, "Aaron added, "is The Vatican announcing to the world that the pope says it is okay to believe in God and aliens and he would baptize our extraterrestrial brothers if they asked. What concerned me most was his statement that they could bring us an international unified belief in God."

The professor nodded his head, "All of this is true, and adds to the confusion of knowing what the truth really is. He paused to take a sip of coffee deciding the best way to answer the officer's question biblically without too much confusion. "I do not believe the Bible supports extraterrestrial life in the form of beings from another planet, galaxy, universe or anywhere outside our firmament. What I do believe is God's Word does support that demonic spirits are inter-dimensional and can appear and disappear in many different forms within our earthly realm. Psalms 68 says God has thousands upon thousands of chariots. Ezekiel went up in one of those chariots. Remember, Satan is the evil mirror of our Holy God."

"Are you saying that every UFO sighting is demonic?" Chris questioned.

"No, but I do believe many are and that is what confuses the overall answer to your question. Other sightings are advanced military aircraft, or simple things that can be explained such as weather balloons, photo shopping, CGI etc. An additional possibility which I think could really deceive mankind is holograms. Those can be used to display anything you want the world to see, using the sky as the screen for the cabal's projector, and that plays into Project Blue Beam. As we've repeated over and over the mainstream is controlled by the deep state cabal and will report whatever they are instructed to. This is where we must use discernment in every report we hear, especially when the MSM reports one day soon that the government is finally releasing classified documents proving they have known about alien life for decades and even secretly interacted with them. Those entities are demonic." He took one more sip of coffee and summed up the UFO phenomenon in one sentence. "It's all part of end time plan, including the return of The Watchers - as it was in the days of Noah."

Chris was nodding his head indicating he now understood. "That makes sense and with the cabal being exposed by internet truthers, it would be the perfect time to get everyone looking up for an alien arrival instead of looking at all the facts around us being revealed."

"I do believe that is their plan. One thing I find very interesting is more and more people, literally millions, believe we've been lied to even about the earth itself and that NASA was created by the cabal for that purpose. Many believe the earth is flat and enclosed in the firmament which Yahweh created in the beginning of the Book of Genesis. So, an extraterrestrial scenario will not be believable to them, and the cabal knows it. So, they must have an answer that will appease everyone. Recently, they have started using UAP instead of UFO."

"UAP, I've never heard that before," Chris stated.

"It stands for Unidentified Aerial Phenomenon. That takes outer space completely out of the equation for flat earthers because the UAPs can come from anywhere. Just think about what Admiral Byrd described...beings living inside the earth with flying saucers. There's a multitude of reports regarding aircraft that seamlessly come out of water and fly away into the sky and vice versa."

Aaron entered the conversation, adding, "And we've already discussed the fallen angels and demonic beings held in the hollows of the earth which would seem to tie this possibility all together."

"Yes, Aaron," Professor agreed. "We've often discussed if the appearing of Antichrist will be in some form of alien arrival. Strozza referred to The Appearing yesterday, so apparently, they already have a plan on how he will dramatically arrive for the world to see."

Gabriella remembered conversations with the professor when he would share some of his deep thoughts concerning the end days. "I remember you telling us, Professor, since Satan imitates everything that Yeshua does and when Satan sets his kingdom up on earth, he will follow the pattern of Yeshua Jesus - even appearing in the heavens to come to earth in the same way Jesus ascended to His Father. Yeshua said he would return in the same manner as they saw him leave."

Dr. Brotman confirmed, quoting from Acts 1:11: *"Men of Galilee, why do you stand gazing up into heaven? This same Jesus, who was taken up from you into heaven, will so come in like manner as you saw Him go into heaven.* It only makes sense Satan would make a grand appearance proclaiming to be The Messiah, since that is the way in which Yeshua said he would return. It will be an appearance that would deceive the very elect, if it were possible."

"It does makes sense," Chris agreed. "Finally, this is all jelling for me."

"I'm so glad, Chris," Gabriella said, in an intimate voice which Caleb mistook as too personal. He shifted in his seat and possessively took her hand, looking straight in the eyes of Chris.

To avoid any confrontation, nonchalantly Chris got up and announced he was going out to make his morning call to Detective Richards. Gabriella looked at her father saying without audible words to go with him.

He took her direction. "If it's okay, I'll venture out with you, Chris. I need to try to check my garage if the coast is clear."

Chris motioned for Gabe to join him and the two quickly disappeared. To make it appear normal and raise no questions, Gabriella suggested, "If Chris says it's safe, I think we should all go out later for some exercise and fresh air. If you don't use those muscles, you're going to lose them. Hopefully, we still have cave explorations in the future, and we need to keep our strength built up." She attempted to create hope that there was life after their bunker captivity; however, her true motive was to make sure everyone was strong enough to escape, if necessary, knowing that a couple of weeks of no mobility causes the muscles to go into atrophy. Her greatest concern was for Professor who was still regaining his strength after the car wreck.

"Just the thought of getting out into fresh air lifts my spirits," Sandee admitted.

"Me, too," Faith agreed looking at KJ and hoping the two of them could find a few minutes to themselves, longing for a private conversation the bunker would not allow. KJ smiled, reading her mind.

As they made their way towards daylight, Chris and Gabe chatted about the information flow on 4-chan. Gabe had decided to wait until after Chris made the call to his boss to talk about a plan of action to escape the bunker.

As the exit from the cave appeared, they slowed their pace and approached with caution, listening for any unusual sounds or activity. The distant sound of rushing mountain streams, along with birds singing their morning praises to God, was all that could be heard. Chris cautiously surveyed the skies above the trees for any drone activity before stepping into the open. He sighed in relief, informing Gabe all was clear and he could exit the cave.

"I'll check the garage, while you make your call." Gabe said, and soon disappeared under the thicket of trees.

Chris pushed redial on his phone, anxiously awaiting the sound of his boss on the other end. The phone rang over and over with no answer. He disconnected the call and tried again with the same results. A foreboding captured him, with his intuition telling him something was very wrong. He paced back and forth playing out in his mind the possible scenarios that could have occurred and how he would respond if any proved to be true.

He attempted one more call just before Gabe returned. Still nothing.

Gabe read Chris' demeanor very quickly. "Something wrong?"

"Richards is not answering. He told me to be sure and call him this morning, and he's never missed my calls."

"Let's sit by the creek for a few minutes. I need to talk to you. You can try again before we go back in, maybe something unexpected came up."

"That's what I'm concerned about," Chris answered, obviously meaning something nefarious.

The two men sat on the bank and normally would have enjoyed the beauty of God's nature; however, that was the last thing on either of their minds.

Gabe shared the conversation he had with his daughter that morning. "And Gabi is right, I need to tell you every back up plan that's in place so we can plan accordingly. Through the years while separated from my daughter, I was always thinking of her safety from the evil men who had haunted us through all her years of growing up. After they murdered her mother, I swore they would never touch my daughter no matter what sacrifices I had to make. I tried to imagine every situation that might put her in danger and then create a way of escape. Professor often told me I was going overboard, and my imagination was out of control. Sometimes I thought he was right, but, like I said, I had way too much time. Plus, I had made a fortune on early investments in technology and had nothing better to do with my money."

Chris' curiosity was at a peak wondering what extents Gabe had gone to. "I understand where you're coming from. I'm sure if I had a child, I would do the same." An expression of regret crossed his face, "I always thought I had time for a relationship and family later. Maybe not," he whispered with regret.

Gabe patted him on the shoulder in comfort. "Nothing is playing out the way any of us wanted it, but I am so thankful I went safety crazy for my princess. Let me explain." Gabe revealed his secrets and the two men spent until lunch time making plans A, B, C and D, not knowing what to really expect but to prepare for whatever could potentially occur. When they felt they had solid plans, they started back to the cave.

"I'm going to try one more time to call Richards." Chris was still hopeful he would answer.

This time the call was received, and an unfamiliar voice on the other end said, "Hello, Officer Chris Harris, or should I say Nathan?"

"Who is this?" Chris demanded, putting the phone on speaker so Gabe could hear both sides of the conversation.

"That really doesn't matter. What does matter is we paid a friendly visit to your parents, and they swear they don't know where you are and hadn't heard from you since you went on your last assignment before the war. I know they're telling the truth, because they are worried sick about you. No harm done...this time, but we may need to pay them another visit, if you know what I mean. Think about it and call me back at 6:00 this evening with Gabe Russell's location. All you must do is cooperate and that second visit won't be necessary."

"Don't you dare touch my family! Where's Richards?" he demanded to know, but the only answer was the phone disconnecting.

— CHAPTER 30 —

The mixture of Chris' military and police training kicked into high gear with the threat against his parents. He immediately placed a phone call to his parents' home. He knew their phone would be tapped by the cabal and was thankful he had the foresight to have a family emergency plan should such a situation ever arise.

The phone rang several times with no answer. Panic began to set in when finally, the voice of his beloved mother answered in her sweet tone. "Harris residence."

He disguised his voice with a British accent and calmly said, "So sorry, wrong number." Immediately he disconnected the phone. He longed desperately to keep the call open and tell her how much he loved them and assure her he was okay, but that was impossible on a landline call. The first thing the cabal would have already done was tap their phone.

"What was that all about?" Gabe questioned, confused.

Chris sat down on the bank next to the cave entrance, obviously struggling with fear for his parents. He regained his composure explaining, "When I was in special operations for the Israeli military, we trained for all possible scenarios, especially survival. When I joined the police force to do undercover work, I knew if I was exposed there would be the potential of having my family threatened to control my actions. My father, mother and I had a long conversation on what to do if that situation ever arose. The wrong number call I just made with a British accent would be their warning to activate the plan.

"You do know the cabal will have someone watching their every move." Gabe warned.

"I know," he agreed. "We planned for that as well. Like most Israelis, my parents' home has a bomb shelter beneath it. The difference with theirs is their shelter connects to an ancient Knights Templar tunnel that leads to the city center of Tel Aviv. My top clearance military training allowed me information most Israelis do not have especially regarding underground

Israel. The tunnel is big enough to drive a golf cart through and there's been a cart there since I first joined the force. Occasionally my parents will have a dinner date in the city and bypass the heavy traffic by using the tunnel, and to ensure the cart stays in good running condition. Also, during war times it gives them a route of escape if their home is hit."

"I'm not at all surprised you have a plan in place. You're a lot like me, Chris, trying to prepare for what might be in the future." He patted him on the shoulder encouraging him, "Now we pray your plan works, and they safely escape. I'm sure you've also planned for where they will go when they get to the city center."

"Absolutely. Undercover agents in the police force are always using fake IDs, so I got them for my parents along with a passport to use if they ever needed to secretly leave the country. Between the constant threat of war in Israel and the threats of my job, a backup plan was essential. They have bank accounts under those fake IDs that will give them the finances they need to relocate. We moved to Tel Aviv from England when I was young, and they will return there and seclude themselves until I contact them. Part of the plan was to always have a bag packed with what they would need to leave at a moment's notice and keep hidden in that bag a cell phone like mine, which can't be hacked or tracked. They know only to charge it for use if they have to leave. When they're safely out of the country, they'll call my phone to let me know they're safe." Chris took a deep breath and slowly exhaled. "I've done all I can humanly do; the rest is in God's hands."

"Guess that's where we all are right now. I've done all I can do to prepare for my daughter's protection, and she's also in God's hands, we all are." Gabe stared into the forest wondering which of his backup plans would soon be necessary.

Chris was estimating how much time his parents had to escape. "Since I was instructed to call back at 6:00 with your whereabouts, I'm confident they'll do nothing but surveil my parents' home until then to make sure they don't leave. That will give mom and dad all day to get to safety. What the cabal response will be when they find out they've been outwitted is anyone's guess."

Gabe was thinking ahead knowing decisions had to be made soon. "How do you plan to handle the 6 o'clock call demand; and what about Detective Richards?"

"About the call, I should know by then if my parents are out of the country, and we will discuss with the team our next steps. Bunker Plan A may be on the horizon. About Richards, there is nothing we can do to help him, but he's a very smart man and I'm sure he's had back up plans as well. He's been divorced for years but kept a good relationship with his ex-wife and his stepchildren. He once told me he was married to his job, and it destroyed his real marriage. He tried to hide his regret and seldom spoke of his family, but it was obvious he still loved his former wife and her children. Seeing what happened to him was one of the reasons I avoided a relationship. I didn't want to repeat his mistakes." Chris' comment was laced with a bit of relief, adding, "At least I don't have a wife and children of my own to have threatened. I can't imagine what you've lived through all these decades worrying about Gabi constantly being on the cabal's radar."

"There is no way to describe that agony and the very reason I kept pouring more money into ways of escape for her if they found out I was still alive."

It was Chris' turn to pat Gabe on the shoulder. "I would have done exactly the same thing, Gabe."

The sound of a helicopter could be heard in the distance and the two men quickly went into the mouth of the cave out of view. The whirling sound kept coming closer and closer, until it was hovering very near their location.

"If that bird is low enough, they will see our SUV under the tree thicket, Gabe; and if they are scouting for us, it's going to be obvious we're somewhere nearby. Richards told them we were hidden in these mountains, and the radius around the lodge would be their first look." Chris attempted to give a bit of hope adding, "Of course, that bird may not even be looking for us."

"Do you really believe that?"

"No," Chris answered gravely.

The two men continued to listen to the whirling blades of the helicopter until finally the ominous sound began to move away and the mountain silence returned.

Chris was thinking ahead as he said, "There very well could be boots on the ground here soon, which would cut off our way of escape. We need to get back to the bunker and let the team know what's going on, but I need to call Officer Cohen first."

Within a minute, the two officers were conversing with Chris quickly updating the other. "Do not trust Richards, he's become a controlled asset for the very people you're hiding from. Not his choice."

Officer Cohen responded, "I suspected this could happen and the very reason I fled with the two I was put in charge of protecting. After the hospital janitor was murdered, I was very antsy, but then after the doctor's wife, I wasn't taking any chances. I'm having a difficult time keeping these two cooped up here, especially with Dr. Nicholson losing his wife. He took that really hard, naturally, and it sent Leah into a panic followed by deep depression. I need to get them moved, but I don't trust anyone on the inside of the force now for instructions."

"I totally understand. I can feel this team I'm protecting starting to get stir crazy; but be assured you can trust me, Micah, and I'm going to fill you in on what we've recently discovered." Chris proceeded to inform his fellow officer regarding the international cabal much of which the officer knew, but having no idea they were their pursuers. "We both are in the same boat, protecting people we were put in charge of by Richards and now he's under enemy control. We are on our own, buddy. The cabal is closing in on our location and I'm not sure what we will have to do, but I will keep you informed, and you do the same. I'm sure you've considered the fact that the cabin you're in is still on the protective custody list even though it's not been used in years. If they strongly interrogate Richards, and you know what I mean, he might be forced to tell them all locations the department uses both present and past. They will stop at nothing to get Dr. Nicholson, he's the only person who knows how to get to us."

"I'm mulling possibilities and do realize the trouble I'm in with the department, but now I know for sure, I made the right decision." Officer Cohen was filled with a mixture of relief in making the right decision and uncertainty about what he should do next.

Chris confirmed his peer's conviction: "You definitely made the right move and once this is over, they will both thank you for it." Chris in no way indicated his concern of how either of their assignments could end, knowing a positive attitude and faith in The Almighty were essential to stay focused. "I have no phone signal inside the bunker, but I'll be checking messages at least twice a day." Before he hung up, he gave Officer Cohen a bit of advice, "If you're not a praying man, I suggest you start...now. We will talk soon." Chris hung up and turned to Gabe. "Let's go."

Hurriedly they retraced their steps back through the dark tunnel. "After all these trips in and out, I believe I could walk this blindfolded," Chris commented.

"I know I could," Gabe replied. "I've been in and out a multitude of times through my long years of isolation; and by the way, I didn't get a chance to mention someone broke into my garage. It didn't look like anything was missing, which makes no sense. Why would someone break in and just look around? Unless..." Chris knew the rest of the sentence without Gabe elaborating. Neither man attempted further conversation, concentrating on getting back to the team as soon as possible.

Once inside the pantry, Gabe made sure the camouflaged door was securely locked from the inside. Then he set the alarm to sound if the door moved. Chris had already rejoined the team who were sitting around the dining table.

"Pancakes are ready," Sandee announced, carrying a platter to the table as Gabe walked in.

The chatter around the table immediately stopped when Dr. Brotman held up his hand indicating silence. "Gabe, I know that look. What is it?"

Chris and Gabe looked at each other and Gabe nodded for Chris to be the one to explain, which he did giving a detailed account of events ending with the threat to his parents and their plan of escape.

"Do you think they know where we are?" Faith questioned with fear in her voice.

Chris assured her, "No, not exactly where, but if that was in fact a cabal helicopter, the pilot was low enough to have seen the SUV and a search would be initiated from that location and work outwards in all directions."

"Someone has been in my garage, too. There were fresh footprints around the garage and 4-wheeler tracks leading from there to the mountain path." Gabe added. "Didn't take a thing but had broken the lock to get in."

"We are being closed in on," Gabriella's voice was certain but indicated no fear.

"What do we do?" Caleb was ready for action. "I will do whatever is necessary to protect Gabi, just tell me." He looked Chris directly in the eyes with a tone to his voice making it obvious she was more important to him than life itself and no one would come between them.

"I know you will, Son," Gabe answered him so Chris would not have to. "And we've got a plan, in fact several potential plans. We just won't know what we need to do for sure, until we see what their next move is."

"Do we just sit here and wait?" Caleb questioned. "Don't we need to be proactive instead of waiting until they find us?" He put his arm around Gabriella in a gesture of protection.

She warmed Caleb's heart when she snuggled closer to him, finally realizing he needed confirmation of her love and trust in him. No words were necessary, just her touch said everything he needed to know.

"Normally I would say yes, Caleb" Chris agreed. "But we're not in a normal situation. We are safer to sit tight for now."

Dr. Brotman took command of the conversation: "The first and the most important thing we will do is pray. Yahweh is not surprised by the turn of events and His plan is always perfect." The team gathered into a circle of prayer led by the professor and prayed for guidance and protection including prayer for Detective Richards and Chris' parents. They continued to pray until The Presence once again saturated the bunker and peace settled in their midst.

"Our Father is in control," Dr. Brotman confirmed. "We will trust Him to guide us."

KJ had been waiting for the right opportunity to offer a suggestion: "Gabe, what would you think of downloading your microchip information to the 4-chan board? People need to know about that too, what's being planned and not be deceived."

"I've been thinking that same thing. I always thought getting the truth to a news source or high government official that could be trusted would be the answer; however, now I see there is no source that can be trusted to do the right thing."

"KJ and I have been saying that very thing," Aaron agreed. "And not just the mainstream news but people in general. There's no way of knowing who is being controlled by these evil people."

KJ nodded. "That's why these internet back channels have become so popular. Regular everyday people are now citizen journalists with no agenda but to expose the truth. A person can post what they are seeing in real time, take a picture with their cell phones and have it on the internet for the world to see in literally minutes. Sure, there are some scammers, but all in all, it's changing the tide of the cabal-controlled media."

"Do you think people will even believe my information?" Gabe wondered. "You have to admit the UFO information, altering the human DNA, and controlling humanity with a microchip the size of a grain of rice sounds like a science fiction story."

KJ laughed, "You do realize science fiction is becoming an everyday reality now, right? And that it was planned that way for programming people to accept it when it did come? This tech savvy generation is way ahead of the curve and they are truth seekers. They're waking up to the lies and want to know only the facts."

"I can give them some truth, that's for sure," Gabe answered. "What they'll do with it is another story."

"I think you'll be very surprised," KJ grinned, motioning for Gabe to follow him. "Let's go get some work done."

"How about my pancakes?" Sandee called to them as they left the room.

"Save us some," Gabe shouted back.

Chris, needing a break from concern for his parents, also joined Gabe and KJ. "Save me some too, Sandee." He gave her a quick hug on his way out.

The trio took their seats around the computer with KJ in control. In short order he had the 4-chan board up ready to post. Without hesitating, Gabe handed him the flash drive containing his years of research. "This has been my purpose all along, to know that if anything happens to me, the truth I've discovered will live on and there is nothing anyone can do to stop it."

KJ inserted the flash drive and prepared for downloading. He looked at Gabe one more time for final approval. Gabe nodded, and decades of research which the Luciferian cabal had tried to stop was downloaded on the worldwide web in less than a minute.

"Done," KJ confirmed. "With the people who are already following our board, this information will explode like wildfire."

Gabe felt the weight he had carried for years lifted from his shoulders. "I don't know if people will really understand, but my prayer is they will search for themselves; and as UFO disclosure and a microchip under the skin becomes mainstream news, they will question everything they hear and see and not just believe a lie."

KJ assured him, "You'll have the ability to explain your information when questions are asked on the 4-chan board. Other visitors to our site can read both the questions and the answers, like an on-line classroom teaching what you've learned in over a half century of research. I'll have to watch the channel closely; I know there'll be web bots that try to destroy us. Every truther is experiencing these kinds of on-line attacks."

Chris had been silent so not to interrupt the download and waited for the right opportunity to enter the conversation. "While we were in the bunker during the war, your UFO research was referred to a few times as the reason for The Omega Watchers Project, but you were too worried about Gabi to focus on anything else then and I didn't want to ask for an explanation. The way the team has referred to your microchip is intriguing, but I'm not totally clear on the details or why the chip you have is so important to the cabal."

Gabe turned his chair slightly to face Chris with the answer. "This really hasn't been fair to you, because everyone else in the bunker understands most of my research and I've been so consumed with all the new information, I've failed to fill you in on what brought us here. You've heard bits and pieces of a very long story, but I'll put it in a nutshell to try to make the pieces cohesive, ending with the most important element which only Professor and I know."

KJ briefly interrupted: "What? I'm trying to watch the board and you drop this, Gabe? We're already getting lots of views, comments and questions in the chat. Y'all go ahead and talk and let me know when you get to that part."

Gabe continued his quick walk down memory lane and reluctantly mentally revisited some places he never wanted to go back to. "I was born after WWII about the time all the UFO phenomena began. When I was in grade school, they showed the entire school the movie 'The Day the Earth Stood Still', and it instantly captivated me with an obsession to find out all I could about extraterrestrial life. It became my life mission, which eventually became a living nightmare. I do believe showing those UFO movies to grade school children in the 1950s was the beginning of programming minds to believe the lie which would eventually lead to world control. The cabal knows that whatever parents believe is passed to their children and on down. As we've said before, these Luciferians have set the stage for centuries preparing the way for The One, the Light Bearer, the Morning Star, all names for Antichrist who will at the given time rule and reign on earth. They believe he is the brother of Jesus and the battle between the two sons of God is for the throne of earth."

"That definitely explains spiritual warfare between good and evil," Chris replied. "And why the Bible says choose whom you will serve."

"Yes, it does, and there are only two sides, no neutral territory. I found out that fact years after I was deep into believing ETs were real. Angelina, Gabi's mother, paid the ultimate price in the battle when we found out too much. My daughter was only five when her mother was murdered, and it was obvious they planned to take me and Gabi out also, but their plan failed. As a result, we spent all of Gabi's growing up years on the run and hiding from those who I thought were CIA operatives, but now I understand those operatives were part of the international cabal. You already know I faked my death and the years that followed."

Chris nodded his head indicating he understood the back story and waiting for the microchip explanation.

"The research Angelina and I did was massive, interviewing people from many nations who had UFO experiences, or what they thought to be extra-terrestrial encounters. At the time, we thought so too. The one interview that changed everything was a man who had been abducted while he was sleeping. He thought he was dreaming when he was taken into a UFO craft where they examined his body and did various tests on him including the insertion of a small object under his knee. He realized it was not a dream when years later he was having an x-ray done on a broken leg and the doctor discovered a piece of metal just beneath his knee. Further tests on the man showed his DNA was changing. It was then he knew it was not a dream and wanted the doctor to remove whatever it was. You can probably guess the result."

"A microchip?" Chris answered.

"Yes, and even though he allowed the doctor to test it, confirming it was nothing that could be explained in known medical terms, the man demanded to have it returned to him. It had a short play on some news channels but soon the story disappeared. He agreed to tell us his story because he wanted the truth known before something happened to him, convinced he was being followed and someone wanted that chip back and him eliminated."

"What happened to the chip?" Chris asked, intrigued by the information.

"He gave the chip to Angelina and me to put it in safe keeping as proof of what the aliens were doing to humans. At the time we believed it was ETs responsible too. Shortly after that he mysteriously died and must have been forced to tell who he gave the chip to before he was taken out."

"That was the reason for your wife's murder." Chris deduced.

Gabe nodded, momentarily too overwhelmed with emotion to speak as he relived that horrible day and the emotional distress he and his daughter had lived through. He regained his composure enough to continue: "Angelina and I suspected we were treading on forbidden ground after the first few interviews which made us even more determined to find the truth. It was too late when we realized we had entered the domain of very dangerous people who would make sure their evil plans would not be discovered. Her murder caused me to start questioning who exactly was behind the UFO phenomenon, it certainly was not ETs blowing up our car attempting to kill my entire family. Everything pointed to an on-earth, not off-earth threat."

Gabe took a moment to get better control and focus on the vital infor-mation and not the consequences he had experienced. "While Gabi and I were constantly fleeing for our lives, I kept researching. First, I thought our government was working with extraterrestrial entities, then by the grace of

God, I met Dr. Brotman and finally after decades of confusion I understood... it's all demonic based. There is no such thing as visitors from outer space, just as Professor said. These supernatural entities are inter-dimensional demonic beings controlled by Lucifer and Lucifer's minions. And I agree with Professor that this will be the platform used to introduce the fake Messiah who will appear to save humanity before we destroy ourselves."

Chris was seeing the picture coming together and agreed, "I can definitely see that possibility, but why is the chip you were given so vital to all of this?"

Before he answered, he announced to KJ, "This is the part you do not know."

KJ swerved his chair around with full attention as Gabe continued: "Professor and I believe that microchip is the major key to bring this all together. For over a decade he and his team have worked on the biblical timelines for the end of days, searching through ancient scriptures. Gabi's archaeological team explored ancient caves and ruins putting together pieces that confirm we're living in the end of time as man knows it. When we combined his information with my UFO and technological research, we have a pretty good hypothesis of how the Bible prophecies could conclude. Any prophecy student is familiar with Revelation 13 and the Mark of the Beast; and that has been a subject of debate since John wrote the book. When you combine the infamous mark with the prophecy of Yeshua concerning the signs of his coming, you have two elements that merge as one - the return of Nephilim and the mark."

Gabe took a deep breath and leaned forward in his chair. "I know it sounds crazy, but before you jump to any conclusions, hear me out. We've already heard Strozza admit they are planning some big event to introduce The One through signs and wonders deceiving people to believe he is the Messiah and worship him. He also said a microchip insert will be required to receive his marvelous benefits and blessings. Now consider this possibility: what if that chip contains the actual DNA of Lucifer and alters the human DNA to create a satanic hybrid being, part man and part fallen angel; but not just any fallen angel, but Lucifer himself. He would have forever stolen God's creation and altered them into his own race of beings replacing his DNA with that of our Heavenly Father satanically mirroring the creation of Adam and Eve. These implanted humans would not just be demon possessed, which demons can be cast out, but they would literally be half fallen angel and half man, aka Nephilim, with no hope of deliverance - the seed of Satan."

For a moment both KJ and Chris were speechless. KJ broke the silence.

"That explains Revelation 9:6: "Men will long to die, but death will flee from them. A normal man could willingly end his life, but once they take the mark, they cannot escape, not in this life or the life to come.""

Gabe leaned back in his chair stating with conviction, "I do believe the microchip I have in my possession is proof that is exactly what they've been planning."

"I knew there was much more to that chip." Chris exclaimed. "No wonder they are desperate to find you, and I'm supposed to call them back at 6:00 to rat you out. Well, that will never happen."

Gabe felt relieved that finally the entire team, especially his daughter, would understand why the decisions he had made through the years were essential. He concluded his nutshell synopsis: "Now you all will know why The Omega Watchers Project is so important and why these Luciferians will stop at nothing to eliminate everyone involved."

"Professor and I have kept that part of the project secret not knowing if we were correct. Some things are better not known; but we've reached the time when there can be no more information withheld. We wanted to protect the younger team as long as possible. With the conversation Strozza had with Richards, I believe we have our confirmation now."

KJ remembered what Dr. Brotman said a couple of days prior about Nephilim. "Professor was questioning if the Khazarian Jews, Black Nobility and anyone who has joined their satanic cult have had DNA altering, making them Nephilim. Do you think they've already taken the mark?"

"I do. Just as Nephilim did in the days before the flood, drinking blood and being cannibalistic, these evil people do the same as part of their Luciferian sacrifices, mostly of children. What normal person would do that? Yes, I do believe they have taken the DNA of Lucifer becoming unredeemable no longer being in the image of their Creator. Yahweh prohibited the drinking of blood and cannibalism in the Torah for a reason, his Creation was to have only His DNA. I've even wondered if that is what will separate the sheep from the goats."

"And I always thought Nephilim would return by a new incursion of fallen angels," KJ said. "However, this makes so much sense."

"Here it is in a nutshell," Gabe reviewed. "Our Heavenly Father created man in his own image, a being to worship and reflect the beauty of The Creator on earth. As we've said many times, Satan wants everything that belongs to God. Since the fall of Eve, he has wanted a race of beings that belong to him. He cannot create life, but he can corrupt what God has created to be his followers. That's what Satan did before the flood creating the need for God had to cleanse the earth. Only Noah was not corrupted by Nephilim DNA."

"Genesis 6 told us that Nephilim would return again after the flood," KJ added. "And Yeshua told us when."

"And obviously the when is now," Chris stated with gravity, finally seeing the entire picture.

— CHAPTER 31 —

Gabe, KJ and Chris monitored the 4-chan board, amazed at the immediate response to the last flash drive download. KJ set up an anonymous chat room to allow Gabe to personally respond to questions.

Gabe's astonishment was reflected in his voice: "I could be here all day answering these questions and I will answer them; but, first, let's have some of those pancakes Sandee made. I'll fill the rest of the team in on the microchip details while we're eating."

"The pancakes are cold," Sandee jested when the three men returned to the dining table. "Seriously, I'm making you some fresh ones. "There's none left from the first batch." She returned to the kitchen and while she was cooking was also listening intently to Gabe's revelation. By the time the pancakes were ready, Gabe had explained the secrets of the microchip and why he and Dr. Brotman had shared the information with no one.

The young team sat wordlessly, processing what this revelation meant, especially as to why the cabal would silence anyone who knew. Finally, Gabriella spoke: "I knew whatever it was you would not tell me had to be big, Dad, but I had no idea how big."

Dr. Brotman admitted, "You have no idea how many times I wanted to tell you all, but Gabe and I agreed it would only add to the danger you were already in."

"Danger that we didn't even know existed, until your attempted murder," Faith answered, with a quivering voice.

Guilt once again flowed through the professor. "I cannot tell you the depth of regret I have for putting this team in harm's way, and for..." He could not finish his sentence; however, they knew he felt a heavy burden of guilt for the deaths of Mrs. Nicholson and the hospital janitor.

Caleb reminded the team: "We are in a war and as hard as it is to accept, there are casualties of war. We either fight with all means possible, or we surrender to the enemy. There are no other choices." He took Gabriella's hand adding, "We fight for the people we love."

"This is a battle for all of humanity," Aaron added, then turned to face Gabe. "Lucifer's DNA in the mark of the beast to create the end days Nephilim – wow, I just never considered that possibility; and once they willingly take his mark, they become unredeemable, doomed for eternity just as the fallen angels are? It's been the missing piece to this prophetic puzzle, and you've had that piece all along and not told us." He looked at Gabe with an expression of unbelief.

Gabe's countenance reflected no regret as he answered: "Because I wasn't positive, Aaron. I suspected, but not until we heard Strozza's plans was it confirmed for me. From the time God created Adam and Eve as perfect beings in His own image, Satan has been determined to corrupt mankind and create his own Luciferian race. This is Satan's last Hail Mary, and mine also. Anonymously releasing my research through the web is like throwing for that last touchdown, it's your last hope and determines if you win or lose."

"You may be anonymous to your followers, but the cabal will suspect the original source and be more determined to find you...all of us," Aaron replied.

Gabe nodded in agreement. "True, but it's already too late; and even if they find us the truth has already been revealed. Speaking of that," Gabe continued, getting up from the table, "I'm going to start replying to the message board. I've never been a soldier in man's army but looks like I'm going to be a digital solider in Yahweh's."

Gabe and KJ returned to the computer ready to expose the enemy. Had it not been for the Presence of the Holy Spirit, Gabe's information would have created a new level of concern for the team; however, they had reached a unified spiritual resolve knowing their steps were ordered by The Lord of Lords and they would trust in Him for each decision. Fear was no longer a factor.

Dr. Brotman asked the question that all the team wanted to know the answer to. "Chris, what are you going to do about the 6:00 PM call?"

Chris got up from the table, and momentarily paced back and forth. They all now understood this was his way of focusing on the matter at hand and no one interrupted his concentration. Shortly, he turned to face them stating, "First, I make sure my parents are safely out of the country. Once that's confirmed, I will place the call to Richards just to test the waters, so to speak, to see if they unwittingly give any clues to what they're planning. It can't hurt to try and, at least, they'll know we're not caving to their demands."

"You may be stirring up a hornet's nest," Dr. Brotman observed, but knew there really were no other options at this point.

"Chris, what if they threaten my parents, too?" Faith asked. "And KJ's, Caleb's, and Aaron's. There's no escape plan for them."

"I've been thinking about that, Faith, and I really don't see that happening as of now. I'm sure they've been surveilling your families and probably tapped their phones; they know you've had no communication with them since the war and your families have no idea where you are. The only way their control works is to be able to communicate to you their threat and as of now - no communication, no threat. If you contacted your parents now, that would be stirring up a hornet's nest."

"So, we have no idea when we can talk to them. I know my parents are sick with worry," Faith replied.

"The phrase 'war is hell' is so true," Chris replied, empathizing with Faith.

Chris started pacing again and changed the subject to get the focus back on the immediate plans. "Since Richards cannot inform us when they plan to revisit the lodge, we will have to stay at the ready and it's time to discuss our plan of action." Chris called for KJ to rejoin them, and they spent the entire afternoon going into full detail about the various plans he and Gabe had discussed, making sure each team member knew exactly what to do in any given situation. Once all questions were answered and optional plans were exhausted, Chris assured them, "Being ready is half the battle."

Dr. Brotman gave spiritual encouragement quoting from Ephesians 6:16: "*In all circumstances take up the shield of faith, with which you can extinguish all the flaming darts of the evil one.*" Our faith will be our guiding force and protection in the midst of the battle."

Chris looked at his watch. "It's go-time. I have a half hour to get out to make the call."

"I had hoped we could all go and get some exercise, but I guess that's not possible now until you know more about that helicopter?" Gabriella already knew the answer to her question.

"It wouldn't be wise, Gabi, not until we know for sure," Chris confirmed.

"How about Caleb and I go with you then. I think we would all feel better if you weren't alone," Gabriella countered.

"That's fine," Chris reluctantly agreed, "but we need to get going now. Grab your flashlights and hurry." He was already going through the pantry door when Caleb and Gabriella grabbed their backpacks which contained their flashlights and rushed to catch up with him.

Chris was moving at a faster pace through the now familiar tunnel ahead of the couple. Caleb intentionally slowed his pace giving some distance between them and Chris. "We'll catch up in a few minutes," he called out.

"Okay," Chris yelled back.

Caleb pulled Gabriella to a full stop and took her in his arms. She willingly rested her head on his shoulder and savored the stolen moment in time. Chris whispered although he knew no one was in hearing distance, pouring out his heart: "Every moment has been like a whirlwind ever since we arrived back at the bunker, and I totally understand this entire situation is out of anyone's control; but that doesn't change our love, does it, Gabi, our commitment to each other?"

"Nothing can change that," she passionately affirmed, lingering in his arms. "If there was any way possible, I would marry you right now, today. There is no circumstance that could ever stop my loving you, Caleb."

"That's all I needed to hear, Gabi." Although he longed to spend more time alone, he knew they needed to catch up with Chris. "We better hurry." He reluctantly released her, and they rushed through the cave arriving at the exit shortly behind Chris who motioned for them to stay inside.

"Is something wrong?" Gabriella asked.

Chris held up his finger to his mouth indicating silence. Neither of them moved a muscle waiting for Chris' directions. Shortly, he obviously relaxed and motioned for them to come on out. "I thought I heard voices coming from the other side of the tree thicket over there," motioning in the direction of the hidden SUV. It must have been the wind blowing through the trees. No sounds now, but it looks like a storm is brewing."

"In more ways than one," Gabriella responded as she and Caleb sat down on the rock beside the cave entrance watching the storm clouds ominously move over Mt. Hermon in their direction. They waited for Chris to make his calls, keeping their eyes on both the dark clouds and the trees camouflaging their vehicle.

Chris first called his parents and soon had them on the speaker phone where everyone could hear the conversation. "Mom, Dad, are you okay?" Chris asked anxiously.

"We are fine, Son," his father replied. "We followed the plan and drove to

Cairo, completely out of Israel. We will be leaving this evening on a flight to London."

"That's wonderful news. Now just stick with the plan and lay low until you hear from me. I'm fine and don't worry," Chris assured them.

"How can a mother not worry?" Her sweet voice questioned.

For a split-second Gabriella desperately longed for her own mother, but she immediately pushed the desire from her mind. She accepted as a young girl that the need for her mother would never go away neither would it ever be fulfilled in this life; longing for her would only make the pain deepen. Caleb reached for her hand, sensing her sorrow. She wrapped her fingers around his strong hand clinging to his strength. Both remained silent until the short conversation ended.

A glimmer of tears was in the strong police officer's eyes as he prepared for his next phone call. "Well, this will be interesting," he commented as he regained his composure and placed the call. To his surprise it was Detective Richards who answered immediately, not Director Strozza again.

"Hello, Officer Harris," the cold, impersonal voice said. "I'm sure you're ready to cooperate with the information, you don't want another visit to your parents, do you?"

Chris looked at Gabriella and Caleb, shaking his head in confusion as he responded to his boss: "I told those thugs to leave my parents alone, Richards."

Chris could hear a cold, smirking laugh in the background instructing Detective Richards: "Ask your officer what he thinks he's going to do to stop us. We have their house surrounded as we speak and if he doesn't cooperate, we're only one step away from making him very sorry."

Richards controlled voice resumed. "Officer Harris, I suggest you follow their instructions and cooperate. They do mean business."

Chris' voice left no room for interpretation as to his anger, blurting out, "Detective Richards, you tell them that I said they only think they're one step away from my parents, but I'm a mile ahead of their game." Chris could hear the flurry of background chatter asking what Chris meant as he disconnected the call.

He turned to face his two companions smiling as he confirmed, "I just threw a monkey-wrench into that plan." His smile of victory quickly was replaced with consternation. "We've won a battle, but the war is still raging." He put his phone back in his pocket and asked, "Did you notice Richards called me Officer Harris?"

"Is that significant?" Gabriella asked.

"Very, it's one of our conversational codes. If he initiates a conversation by addressing me formally, then I know he's in a situation where he cannot speak openly and honestly. If I reply in a formal manner, he knows I understand. He's being controlled for sure, no doubt about it," Chris deduced.

Gabriella was about to respond when Chris once again held up his finger for silence and motioned for them to go back inside the cave. The three silently navigated out of sight and waited. Voices could be heard in the distance with the sound intensifying as they moved closer. Chris motioned for the three of them to move further into the cave. As quietly as possible they backed into the cave, just far enough where they could not be seen but still could see the mouth of the cave illuminated by the fading evening light. The entrance darkened as the outline of several men stepped up to the entrance and looked inside.

The voice of a man asked, "Anyone have a flashlight on them?"

"I'll go grab some from the four-wheeler," another voice answered.

Chris slightly pushed Gabriella and Caleb further into the cave tunnel signaling to keep going. He whispered to them to put their flashlights in their backpacks and follow his lead. Having made enough trips in and out, he could maneuver without the need of a flashlight. He put his left hand on the cave wall allowing it to guide them through the dark and with his right-hand grabbed Gabriella's hand to lead her; she in turn held Caleb's hand and the three slowly and quietly retraced their steps though the darkness and back towards the bunker entrance. They paused and looked back to determine if they were being followed. Distant flashlights could be seen slowly maneuvering through the tunnel. The slow pace made it obvious these were not seasoned cave explorers.

Chris picked up the pace to get inside the safety of the bunker without being detected. As they moved faster, Gabriella tripped and before Chris and Caleb could stop her fall, she hit the side of her head on a jagged rock in the cave wall. Falling to the rock floor, she felt blood running through her hair. She heard the voices of both men momentarily hovering over her in the darkness before complete silence captured her.

Temporarily she lost consciousness. When she awakened something felt different. She whispered into the darkness, not wanting the unknown men approaching to hear her: "Caleb, Chris, where are you?" No one answered. She felt her head and there was no blood in her hair, not even a pump knot on her head. The flashlights following them had disappeared, there was nothing but a dark world engulfing her. She reached over her shoulder for her backpack which contained her flashlight and there was no backpack there. Pushing herself to a sitting position, she prayed for guidance while waiting for someone to come for her. Surely, Chris and Caleb would not have gone far, but she was confused as to why they would both leave her alone, especially with unknown pursuers in the cave.

She was trying to get a bearing as to which direction led to the bunker when a dim light appeared on the cave wall opposite her. She peered through the darkness attempting to focus while the light grew until it illuminated the entire cave wall. Then she realized - this was the place The Prophet appeared to her with visions of the future. Her gaze was fixed on the cave wall as she watched the scene play out like a movie in a giant screen theatre.

Seated around a huge conference table were ten men. Another man of supreme authority stood at the head of the table. His hair was white and glistening, his skin looked almost translucent, and his eyes were piercing as though he could see inside you and know your every thought and intention. When he spoke, his voice mesmerized the ten and they were entranced by his words: "The time has come. The harlot believes herself to be queen of all and her evils will never be exposed. She is convinced she will never be cast down from her throne; however, the exposure of her fornications are already being revealed and in one day we will once and for all destroy her. She believes her vile kingdom will announce my coming and she will reign with me over the world; but I have no need for her and will share my glory with no one. I will reveal to the entire world her deception, her thirst for blood and the manipulative control she has had over all nations; and the nations also will hate her iniquities and worship The One who has destroyed her. If you align with me, you will be kings, ruling and reigning under me, over the entire earth replacing Mystery Babylon. Together we will bring The Golden Age for all humanity; ending wars, giving a jubilee forgiveness of all debts, releasing medical breakthroughs that have been held back by the harlot system and making available technologies only known to the great harlot. We will have peace on earth and good will for all men. The whole earth will then be mine, divided into ten kingdoms of which you will rule and reign over."

The ten men stood up and bowed to The One, pledging their allegiance. Their supreme leader had ten crowns on the table. He picked them up one by one and circled the table placing royal crowns on the heads of the men, announcing which of the ten kingdoms they would rule. Each man bowed to their master as they were coronated.

The One returned to the head of the table where a massive crown, adorned *with many jewels, awaited. He picked up the crown and placed it upon his head, coronating himself. A jeweled scepter lay on the table in front of him. With royal ceremony, he wrapped his hand around the handle and held it high, announcing, "The earth now belongs to me." The light began to fade until darkness once again engulfed her.*

"Gabi, are you okay?" Caleb was shining a flashlight into her face, looking into her eyes. "Your head is bleeding." He reached into his backpack and retrieved a knife, cutting a sleeve from his shirt to wrap around her head to stop the bleeding.

She reached up and felt the blood trickling down through her hair. "I think I'm okay," she replied, as he tenderly ministered to her wound. "My head does hurt. Shouldn't you turn that light off" she whispered, remembering the men following them in the tunnel.

"Don't worry about those men, they've turned around and headed back out. We did hear them say they'd come back later with better lights."

"Oh great, that's all we need," she replied. "Now they know where our way of escape is."

Chris was kneeling beside Gabi, ready to do whatever was needed to help. "Our advantage for safety is the rock wall dead end when they get to the bunker entrance, they'll have no idea where we disappeared to; but you're right, Gabi, now they know how we exit and be waiting for us." He pushed himself up from the cave floor. "What we need to worry about right now though, is getting you into the bunker and check that wound out."

Caleb helped her to her feet and wrapped his arm around her for support. "Do you feel dizzy?" he questioned.

"A little, but I think I can make it." She leaned against him to keep her balance. She took one last look at the wall where her vision displayed before turning to follow Chris. "I have something to tell you when we get back to the bunker."

Chris was curious as to what she meant but would wait until she felt like talking. His flashlight was focused on the tunnel path as he led the way back to safety.

As soon as they entered the bunker, Gabe came running to his daughter. "What happened, Gabi? Are you okay?" Caleb released her into the arms of her father who led her to the couch. "Sit down, Gabi, tell me what happened."

Feeling weak and nauseous, she looked at Caleb to explain. While he recounted the events leading up to her fall, Sandee retrieved a first aid kit and attended to her wound.

Dr. Brotman questioned, "Chris, do you think these men are Strozza's men or just curious game hunters?"

"I have no idea, but with the helicopter circling yesterday and these guys showing up today, my guess would be they are Strozza's men, and we can't take the chance of thinking otherwise."

"How about your parents and did you place that 6:00 o'clock call?" Professor was anxious to know all the details.

Chris recounted the details of both calls to the team, giving the specifics of the conversations with his parents and Detective Richards. "It was right after the calls we heard voices and immediately returned to the cave," he ended.

"I'm glad to know your parents are well," Dr. Brotman replied. "And relieved to know Detective Richards is sending you coded messages that he is not acting in his own will. I am very concerned for him though."

"Me, too," Chris admitted. "I can't help but believe, he also made plans for his family if he ever became captive. I don't know for sure, just a hunch, knowing he was so meticulous in everything he did."

Gabriella waited until her head stopped pounding and the dizziness passed before entering the conversation. "Professor, I need your expert opinion on this. When I hit my head, I must have momentarily passed out, and while I was, I had another vision." After she shared what she had seen detail by detail, she added, "I believe this vision was given to me as an explanation to what you were questioning."

"I was thinking the same thing, Gabi, as I was listening to the details," Dr. Brotman agreed. "The Luciferian Cabal, Mystery Babylon, believes they will introduce Antichrist to the world, and they will rule with him; however, we know from Revelation 17:16 that is not going to be how eschatology is fulfilled." He quoted from John's prophecy: "*The ten horns which you saw on the beast, these will hate the harlot, make her desolate and naked, eat her flesh and burn her with fire. For God has put it into their hearts to fulfill His purpose, to be of one mind, and to give their kingdom to the beast, until the words of God are fulfilled.*"

"I remember the verse before that which identifies exactly who the ten horns are?" Gabriella said and quoted from Revelation 17:12-13: "*The ten horns which you saw are ten kings who have received no kingdom as yet, but they receive authority for one hour as kings with the beast. These are of one mind, and they will give their power and authority to the beast."*

"Yes," he confirmed. "The ten kings who join with the Antichrist to destroy Mystery Babylon are not yet known to the world as kings. I do believe they may be world leaders who are already in power, but not under one supreme authority. This will be a completely new world alliance for the final seven years of time. We've discussed that the first three and one-half years will be a time of deceiving the world into trusting the new world leader and the earth will be wonderful, no one wanting for anything; but then, as God's Word says, when everyone is saying we are living in peace and safety, sudden destruction will come. In the middle of that seven years is when the man you saw in your vision, Gabi, will declare himself as The One and only God. With the miracles he has performed and humanity living what they believe is the Golden Age, most have been deceived into believing his lies and will worship him. Only the elect will not be deceived."

"I can't help but wonder just how Mystery Babylon will be destroyed, how all the evil will be revealed," Gabriella mused.

KJ had begun to put some thoughts together based on the 4-chan board activity. "I've been watching the boards and how quickly news spreads. People around the world have already been questioning many of the things we've been discussing, discovering the cabal's lies and deceptions that have been taking place for generations. The Source, is for the purpose of revealing truth about the Khazarian Mafia, The Black Nobility, The Vatican, The Royals, and so much more, especially regarding some of the information Gabe had about the children. The Source says everything being done to stop the evil started with the crimes against our children; and they sure are revealing a lot of facts and advising people to not take their word for it but do their own research and then share the truths they find. They have millions of followers and it's still growing by leaps and bounds. I see an international uprising starting to form."

"Ahhh, isn't that interesting," Dr. Brotman muttered, seeing a clear picture form. "An unknown source releases the facts, allowing the world to see the Luciferian Cabal that controls them, getting them ready to fight for good, especially for the children, and when a savior steps in and destroys that unspeakable evil, liberating humanity from centuries of oppression, the stage is set for that savior, The One, to be worshipped."

"I see what you mean, Professor. He will not have to force anyone to worship him," KJ added. "And only the elect will understand this is the fulfillment of prophecy and will know The One also biblically named as the Man of Perdition - Antichrist -the Great Deceiver – the Lawless One has arrived to take his throne."

Gabriella continued to question, "I see how that could happen just that way, but there must be a trigger point that causes everything to suddenly collapse destroying that worldwide control held."

Dr. Brotman, as usual, had a hypothesis. "The entire eighteenth chapter of Revelation is about riches, merchants and commerce; it's all about the wealth with which Mystery Babylon has controlled everything and everyone. The trigger point will be a worldwide collapse of the monetary system taking the power from the harlot Babylonian system with a new economy to replace it – the Antichrist economy. Aren't we already hearing about a digital currency replacing the fiat worthless dollar? Find out who will control the new money, and you have a sign pointing directly to the new one world government that will take over when the harlot is destroyed."

"That new monetary system is being planned right now by the cabal," KJ answered. "That information is on the web, and it's called The Great Reset which is part of bringing in The New World Order. The Source says there is an international alliance planning to destroy The Great Reset and replace it with The Great Awakening which is for the good of humanity. Could it be...?"

Dr. Brotman nodded. "It appears they already have the Antichrist Monetary System ready to step into place on the day Mystery Babylon falls. And probably already know how they plan to derail the cabal's roll out of their digital money. I'm sure it will be done in such a way that will expose the Luciferian evil and bring in The One who will save the world. Amid a world financial collapse and post chaos, The One will have the answers."

KJ suppressed a laugh, commenting, "It appears to be Lucifer bringing down Lucifer."

"That's exactly what it is, KJ," Dr. Brotman firmly stated. "And that's part of his plan. How does Lucifer deceive the world? He exposes his evil, wicked followers, aka Mystery Babylon, for who they really are and what they've done to humanity, and then The One, Lucifer incarnate, appears as an angel of light to save the world – as the Bible says, he is the great deceiver."

Chris had been intently listening to every word, but still had questions. "I can see this scenario; in fact, we've seen this new world order forming for decades. What confuses me is how all the UFO stuff fits in. The two don't seem to mesh very well."

Dr. Brotman motioned for Gabe to explain, which he did. "We know the Antichrist will have the DNA of Satan, and I believe could even be born of a woman, just as Yeshua was born of a woman with the DNA of Yahweh. As we've often said, Satan mirrors everything Yeshua does. However, can you imagine anyone willingly accepting the DNA of Satan? I don't think so; but, if the world was deceived into believing The One who destroys Mystery Babylon was actually part human and part extraterrestrial, having supernatural powers, they would be all about accepting that person. Humanity has been programmed with movies like Superman who came from another planet with superpowers. Just think of all the entertainment - movies, TV shows, cartoons, video games and on and on - that portray extraterrestrials as super beings. Kids and even adults dress up as them and want to be just like those characters. It would be a dream come true for many people to have superhuman abilities, not realizing when they worship the beast and take his mark, they become unredeemable Nephilim, a human being with the DNA of a fallen angel – as in the days of Noah.

"Wow, that's a lot to process" Chris replied.

"It is," Gabe agreed. "The entire UFO phenomenon, which is controlled by the cabal, has conditioned society to accept extraterrestrial life through programming minds with entertainment, which is also controlled by the cabal. The two have worked together to seduce the world into their alien web."

"Enter, stage right, The One," Dr. Brotman added. "And I still believe somehow, the pseudo savior of the world will make his appearance in the clouds, mirroring how Yeshua said He will return. Strozza called it The Appearing and planning a big production, not realizing he won't have any part in it." A smile crossed the professor's face as he thought of Mystery Babylon being destroyed, but it was quickly replaced with consternation knowing what would immediately follow.

"Chris, you have just been given an outline of The Omega Watchers project," Gabriella summarized. "The final objective of the entire project was to expose Satan's plan to rule the earth - when and how, and the picture is now complete."

— Chapter 32 —

"Gabi, you really should lay down and rest. That was a hard hit to your head," Sandee instructed in her motherly tone.

"My head is pretty sore," she admitted, looking at the clock. "It's still early, but I'm exhausted. With no instructions coming from Detective Richards, we have no idea what tomorrow will bring; and then being followed through the cave, by God only knows who, I need to be rested and ready for...whatever."

Caleb jumped up and helped her from the couch. "If you need anything at all, Gabby Girl," he spoke with an endearing voice, "I'm only one door away." He kissed her cheek and made sure she was steady on her feet before releasing her.

Gabriella's heart fluttered as it did every time Caleb called her by his nickname for her. He only used Gabby Girl when he was playfully teasing or deeply concerned for her, and her response was the same either way – a rush of love flowing through every fiber of her being. Her endearing smile for him spoke volumes to everyone in the room. As Chris watched the display of true love, for a brief moment he longed to experience such a relationship, but quickly suppressed the thought focusing on their immediate danger.

When Gabriella's bedroom door closed, the team resumed their conversation discussing the what ifs that faced them and their concerns of having their path of escape cut off. While they were deep in discussion, Gabriella struggled to get comfortable in her bed, carefully placing her head on the pillow to not put pressure on the wound. She could hear the voices of the team's chatter as she slipped into a deep sleep and visions of the future returned.

She opened her eyes to an unfamiliar location. Two men were sitting at a computer monitor speaking in angry voices. She moved closer to listen to their conversation. Both turned to look in her direction as if they knew someone had joined them. She then recognized it was Director Strozza and Sotoreo, The UN President. When they turned back to the monitor, she was aware they could not see her, so she moved closer to hear their conversation.

"Is there any way to find out where this originated from?" Sotoreo asked.

"I've had my best men trying, and they've come up with nothing, some of these back channels are set to be anonymous, and almost impossible to hack through." Strozza responded. "My men have traced the IP address from the original post, and they keep hitting a dead end." Sotoreo's anger was obvious and Strozza tried to soothe him, "but they are still working on it."

Sotoreo's voice spewed pure rage, stating, "Almost impossible and impossible are two very different things and I expect results, Strozza. There is no doubt who is behind it, and I want him found." The UN President looked directly at Strozza leaving no room for doubt in his words: "And I mean the sooner the better. Am I clear?"

Strozza nodded his head, "Yes, Sir. There is someone, and probably the only person, who knows exactly where he is."

Gabriella knew they were talking about her father, and Dr. Nicholson being the only person who knew his location. She could almost taste the venom in the vile words Sotoreo said: "Let me guess, Strozza, you don't know where that only person is. Right?"

"Detective Richards has one of his officers holding the doctor in protective custody, so Richards will be getting that information for us very soon." Strozza was obviously trying to buy some time and pass the buck. "It might be a good idea for us to make a trip up to that lodge of Gabe's. Richards says Gabe, Dr. Brotman, and his whole team are hiding out somewhere in that area, for sure."

"For your sake, and that beautiful family of yours, Strozza, I sure hope you're right."

The look on Strozza's face was priceless to Gabriella. He was the very one threatening Detective Richards with almost the same exact words; and the very person responsible for the deaths of Mrs. Nicholson and that sweet janitor, Joshua, for which Strozza obviously felt no remorse. "So how does it feel, tough guy, when it's your family being threatened?" she questioned out loud, moving closer, knowing she could not be heard.

Sotoreo stood up and looked directly towards Gabriella, and asked Strozza, "Did you hear that?"

Strozza turned and listened. "I don't hear a thing. What did it sound like?"

"It was a woman's voice." Sotoreo didn't move a muscle for a full minute listening for any further sound. "I sense another presence with us, a hostile spirit." He sat down on a nearby chair and closed his eyes, muttering some *type of chant. Gabriella listened closely to his voice, which kept going up in frequency until he hit a pitch which connected him with the spirit world.*

She began to back away from the two men, praying for protection, realizing she was treading on the enemy's territory. She was looking around the room for an exit when Sotoreo suddenly stopped chanting and stood up. His eyes were narrow and piercing when he started walking directly towards her, however there was no eye contact; he still could not see her but felt an intruding presence. She was staring directly at him, but he was gazing past her – Gabriella was concealed by the Holy Spirit.

"I know you are here, unwelcome spirit, who are you?" Sotoreo questioned with extreme animosity. His eyes darted all around her trying to make contact. He again began to chant at a high frequency, calling up the demons within him to light the spirit world and give him eyes to see. A mist began to form before him and in it stood Gabriella. The spirit world had opened, and his evil eyes locked with hers. They were standing face to face.

Gabriella was transfixed calling upon the Spirit of The Holy God to protect her. While the spiritual encounter took place, Director Strozza stood motionless in the background as if frozen in time.

She spoke with supernatural authority declaring to the demon within the UN President, "By the Blood of the Lamb, Yeshua the Messiah, you cannot touch me!"

Suddenly Sotoreo let out a blood curdling scream when a pillar of fire appeared blocking access to Gabriella. "NO!" His voice screamed defeat; he knew his Luciferian powers could not match the power of the Lord of all Spirits.

Gabriella's eyes flew open expecting to see the flaming fire, but she was confronted only by the darkness of the bedroom. The demonic image of Sotoreo was branded in her mind while she replayed, over and over, the conversation she had been privy to.

Hearing voices in the living room, she looked at the clock noticing Faith still had not come to bed and it was after midnight. She reached up and felt her head, which was sore to the touch, but no longer pounding. She decided to join the others where she found only the younger members of the team were still awake.

Caleb immediately came to her, asking, "Are you alright, do you need anything? How's your head?"

She gave him a quick hug assuring him she would be fine and needed nothing. "Why are you all up so late?"

KJ answered, "There's something strange going on with the 4-chan board. It's obvious that hackers are trying to get in and shut us down."

"And trying to find out where the original posts are coming from?" Gabriella asked.

KJ looked at her confused. "How did you know that?"

"A few days ago, I would have said you won't believe me, but now I know you do. I heard a conversation in a dream vision I just had," she answered. After relaying the details, she added, "I knew Strozza and Sotoreo were discussing my dad's information being released to the world. So far, they've not been able to hack in, but he said the best of the best in the tech industry was working on it, and they would not give up."

"They can try," KJ retorted, "but the way Gabe had this IP address set up, the hacking will bounce all around the world before they could get to the original source and even then, it won't be right. They won't find us by finding this computer, I can guarantee you that."

"But they will find this bunker, eventually." Faith glumly said.

"Not necessarily," Chris encouraged her, and we've made some pretty good escape plans if they do.

Gabriella stated the facts: "Sotoreo has satanic supernatural powers, you know; and any situation can turn on a dime when he enters the spirit realm. There is a chant he does and a certain frequency in his voice which releases demonic forces." She did not say out loud what was going through her mind - Arcturus had told her she was chosen because of her vibrational frequencies being so high. She had no idea what he meant but his seductive words convinced her she was highly favored in the spirit realm. She pushed his deceptions out of her mind and revealed instead, "There seems to be a connection to sound frequencies and opening the spirit realm."

KJ nodded in agreement. "I saw a post on one of the boards about that, but not had time to delve into it, but I certainly will."

"Thanks, KJ, I'm convinced it's something we really need to understand," she replied before getting back to the immediate threat. "Listen, guys, if Sotoreo comes to this lodge, and it is almost definite he will, his spirit guide will lead him to the pantry door upstairs and reveal the secret door. Besides that, these people following us in the tunnel could be closing in and we will be cornered." She looked at Chris for answers. "The multiple plans we made about where to go and what to do if we had to leave in a hurry were based on getting out the same way we came in, through the tunnel. Now what?"

Faith's eyes were growing wider by the minute. "Are we literally going to have to shoot our way out of here?"

Gabriella wanted to assure her they would all be okay, but she could not. Fighting in the natural world was very different from the battles in the spirit realm and she was fully aware there are casualties of war. She tried to comfort Faith with the promises from Psalms 91 and assured her, "The battle is the Lord's, Faith, and He is with us every step of the way. Yeshua told us we are not to fear what man can do to the body and He promises the evil ones cannot kill our soul."

"I know, but I've never experienced spiritual warfare like this," Faith admitted. "This is the book of Ephesians on steroids."

Gabriella reached across the table and took her hand. "We are living the Book of Revelation...but we know how this war ends. That's our blessed hope."

Faith squeezed Gabriella's hand and released it, leaning back on the couch and resting her head on KJ's shoulder. "I just always thought I would live a normal life, get married, have children and die of old age. Even with all our research and conversations about the end days, the reality of it all just never really hit me until we came to the lodge to hide."

Aaron had been intently listening but stayed silent until he stated in his usual blunt manner: "Some generation has to be the last one, and it looks like it's going to be ours."

A loud sob escaped Faith's mouth before she could control it. KJ wrapped his arms around her in comfort as the room went silent and the blatant truth settled in. One by one they departed for the seclusion of their bedrooms without saying a word, needing time alone for spiritual preparation.

The next morning KJ was early out of bed. Gabe had coffee made and was reading his Bible when KJ joined him. "I heard you all last night, KJ. You were up late."

KJ struggled for the words to adequately describe the previous night's conversation. "For weeks we have all danced around the truth of what we're facing. We all knew, and we've discussed possibilities for escape and all that, but when it hits you in the face that you have no future, none of us, no matter if we escape or not...well, it's like a ton of bricks falling on your shoulders. Life as we know it is about to end and nothing can stop what's coming. Professor has told us that over and over, but the full weight hit us all last night."

Gabe knew eventually this conversation would happen and had rehearsed how he would respond, especially to his daughter who wanted desperately to marry Caleb and have a family, a future. There were just no adequate words to lift the heavy atmosphere when it hit the entire team simultaneously. The promise of a new world coming fell short of encouragement considering what it was going to take to get there.

Gabe took a deep breath and gave it his best shot: "KJ, no warrior looks forward to the battle, they look beyond the intense warfare and keep their eyes on the victory. The fact we are fighting a war that is very different from armies engaged on a physical battleground makes it even more difficult. Psychological war is the worst because you can't just fire a gun and make the enemy go away; and that is the war the cabal has created, the war to control the people through controlling their minds and what they believe to be true."

"*Casting down imaginations, and every high thing that exalts itself against the knowledge of God and bringing into captivity every thought to the obedience of Christ,*" KJ quoted from II Corinthians 10:5. "My mother quoted that scripture to me all through my growing up years, but it now takes on a whole new meaning. We can't let our minds dwell on what might happen but stay focused on being obedient."

"I know that's easier said than done," Gabe replied. "However, if that becomes your clarion call, the battle becomes The Lord's, not yours."

"Thanks, Gabe, that really helps," KJ replied. "I'm going to take my coffee and go do some research. Gabi mentioned something last night that I'm anxious to delve into. She can fill you in when she gets up."

Gabe refilled KJ's coffee cup and motioned him towards the security room. After the door closed behind KJ, Gabe dropped his head in his hands praying for wisdom and discernment, feeling the spiritual darkness closing in on the bunker. Shortly, Sandee and Dr. Brotman had joined him at the dining table. He shared his conversation with KJ and together the elders of the group prayed fervently for the young team. The prayer continued as one by one the bedrooms emptied and everyone was gathered around the table interceding for the direction of the Holy Spirit as the final days ahead unfolded.

Gabriella sat close to Caleb clinging to his hand, wishing for more time, but accepting time was running out. Chris focused fully on protecting this team at whatever personal cost was demanded. Each was lost in their individual thoughts when KJ came bursting into the room.

"Really? Really!" He repeated in anger. "You won't believe what I just found." He plopped down in the dining chair and pounded his notes on the table. "About the time I thought we had uncovered all the cabal's nefarious doings, I find this. I don't believe there is an end to everything they've changed, satanically distorted and lied about."

In unison, the team all questioned him. "What?"

He leaned forward and pointed to his notes made from the morning's research. "This is what Gabi was talking about last night, frequencies. It's something you can't see, or touch, and your ears can't distinguish the difference, but the body responds to...is frequencies; and the cabal has manipulated even that." Anger saturated every word KJ spoke.

"You're not making any sense, KJ," Gabriella responded. "Details, please."

"I'm getting there and it's complicated. I don't completely understand it myself, but I've narrowed it down to a simple overview that hopefully will make sense." KJ picked up his notes and summarized: "Light and sound are generated and measured mathematically, according to frequencies. Everything God created has a frequency and the frequencies balance nature bringing the earth into perfect harmony. Lucifer has used the cabal to change God's frequencies in several ways, one being a major change in music."

"How's that possible?" Gabriella questioned, engrossed in KJ's every word.

He attempted to explain the scientific process. "Since ancient times musical instruments were created using 432 Hz, the A note which is referred to as the God note. It soothes the body, spirit and soul and creates healing harmony with God's creation. The birds sing at 432 Hz and when they sing in the morning it is a wake-up call for the pores of plants and flowers to open and absorb the morning dew to nourish them for growth. God's beautiful earth was created in perfect frequency balance for peace, love and harmony with the Creator, which Lucifer hates. He especially despises the universal God note, which would have been Lucifer's music frequency before he was cast out of heaven. Lucifer was literally music personified before he rebelled against God. Through his Luciferian minions he has corrupted healing music by totally changing the frequencies."

Gabe retorted, "Music? They've controlled people through music too?"

The shock on the team's face told KJ no one had heard this information before. "Yes, music," he exclaimed. "Listen to this, between World Wars I and II there were scientific studies in frequencies and how they affected the human body. Hitler's scientists discovered the 440 Hz frequency of music - the music frequency best suited for arousing emotions conducive to war-making and violent behavior. I give you one guess who funded it?"

"You've got to be kidding," Gabriella exclaimed in total amazement. "Really?"

"Yep, the Khazarian Jews. It was funded by the Rothschild-Rockefeller alliance, represented by the Rockefeller Foundation and working with the U.S. Navy. The 440 hertz causes aggression, psycho social agitation and emotional distress predisposing people to a war mentality. By listening to music, any music, at the altered frequency people's entire mentality began to change which has become very evident with the change in society as a whole since WWII." KJ paused, "I'm not really surprised those Khazarian names are connected but what makes me so angry is the Deep State operating within the United States Government was in on it, the government that was supposed to be for We the People."

"The Deep State truly does run deep," Dr. Brotman sighed. "Mystery Babylon is integrated into literally every aspect of our lives and most people have no idea."

"I sure had no idea," KJ agreed. "The cabal changed the arc of civilization from ascent, belief in God which is focused on love, joy, purity and selflessness to descent which is focused on power, wealth and physical gratification. It was the dawning of The Enlightenment, when the Illuminated Ones took over and believed themselves to be the keepers of the light, that a worldwide moral decline into darkness began, slowly boiling the frog into complete deceptive oblivion."

Gabriella summed up KJ's discovery in one sentence: "Big money is made through monopolizing the music industry with altered frequencies and at the same time keeping people distressed, divided and hating one another."

"Good summation," KJ agreed, "but, thankfully, millions of people are waking up now to the truth. The media can say it's just conspiracy theories, but those theories are proving to be reality very quickly, resulting in a tsunami of digital soldiers to rise, exposing the enemy through social media."

"I didn't mean to interrupt you train of thought, KJ, did you find anything else?" Gabriella pushed for every detail.

"There's so much information, I had to pick and choose what to browse first. Like I said, everything God created has a frequency. Tesla discovered the earth's frequency of 8 Hz in 1899 but like all the other miraculous discoveries he made, it was suppressed; and his earth's frequency information took fifty years before a physicist, Winfred Schumann, proved Tesla's discovery was right. It is known now as the 7.8 Hz Schumann Resonance. It's been proven if you stand barefoot on the ground 20 to 30 minutes every day, God's earth frequencies will rise through the over 8000 nerve endings in your feet, up through your body bringing natural healing of the body, mind, soul and spirit."

"Amazing," Gabriella responded. "Is that why the ocean waves, gentle rain, a walk through the forest, those kinds of things, bring such peace and tranquility? It's from earth's frequencies tuning with the human body?"

"You got it, Gabi. Exactly, right. What is destroying us is all the new technology that gives adverse frequencies, things we use or are affected by every day: cell phones, cell towers, internet WiFi, microwave ovens, iPads, Bluetooth, radio and television transmissions and countless other devices. They keep us endlessly bathed in a scrambled energy soup that disconnects us from our natural frequencies."

Dr. Brotman made a brilliant scientific analysis stating, "We are engaged in a conspiracy reality in which ultimate power and control is waged bio-energetically and bio-spiritually through frequency modulations, affecting all consciousness and impacting biology, physiology and human behavior."

"That's the bottom line," KJ agreed.

"Oh my," Sandee muttered. "I had no idea."

"Like most everyone else, Sandee." KJ affirmed that most of humanity had been deceived. "But we do know now; and I did a bit of research on 432 Hz music and there's a lot available to listen to. Many musicians have begun recording only in God's frequency as people are awakening to the truth."

Dr. Brotman reminded his team of the story from I Samuel 16: "Remember when King Saul was troubled by an evil spirit, and he called for a musician that could play the harp and drive the evil spirit away, healing his body with music? These scriptures can be so much better understood with information like KJ has given us. It makes God's Word come alive."

"There's a lot more frequencies the cabal has manipulated than just the music and nature's resonance," KJ continued. "From what I found, for decades they have had the cure for many diseases, but those cures don't make them the big bucks. The cabal owns BlackRock and Vanguard which are the two investment companies that control all major corporations on earth, including big pharmacy who intentionally is keeping people on chemical drugs not allowing natural cures. As we know, many of these drugs have side effects that create other physical problems which then requires more drugs with more side effects; and they're not cures, they just treat the symptoms and people end up living their lives on medications. It's a vicious cycle. One that has made billions on top of billions for the Khazarians."

"I've heard rumors for years about this," Gabe interjected. "They have a cure for cancer, while they let millions suffer horrendously and slowly die."

"I saw an article on that, too, on how frequencies can be used in healing cancer." KJ answered. "It took years of trying combinations of frequencies, but finally they found one which kills cancer cells and blocks them from recreating. Many diseases apparently can be cured in what they call Med Beds where frequency healing is used. They have it and keep it for themselves only, while getting rich on the diseases of the common man."

"The more I hear, the angrier I get," Dr. Brotman exclaimed in a voice abnormal of his usual softer tone. "The sooner Mystery Babylon falls, the better."

"But then we know what comes on the heels of her destruction," Gabriella added. "The rise of the Antichrist and The Great Tribulation."

"Lord Jesus, come quickly," Sandee whispered with a room full of amens echoing her prayer.

A somber mood had settled on the team with each person struggling in their own way to process the satanic cabal information that continued to be discovered. Chris had said nothing the entire morning, finding it difficult to believe just how deep the evil goes; however, he did not question the validity. As amazing as all the information was, he knew he had to keep focused on his assignment.

"I need to try to contact Officer Cohen. Thank God we still have one person outside this underground world who I can communicate with...if I can get to the outside." Chris pushed himself from the table, went to the cabinet where the weapons were stored and retrieved his pistol.

"I'm going with you," Caleb announced. "No one needs to be alone outside this bunker not knowing who those men following us are."

"No," Gabriella cried out. "Don't go, Caleb."

Aaron jumped from his seat and grabbed his revolver. "I'm going too. One thing I learned in the Israeli Military is you don't hide from your enemy; you face them head on."

"Dear, Lord, help us." Faith mumbled.

Chris tried to assure them one more time, "We don't know for sure the men that followed us into the cave are cabal operatives. They could just be curious hunters." His words were not convincing but did leave a little window of hope. "We can't just hide in this bunker indefinitely; we need to know what we're dealing with and there's only one way to find out."

While the three men prepared to exit, Gabe met them in the storage pantry. "Wait, guys," he instructed. He went to the section of the pantry that had guns and ammunition stored. He pulled three bullet proof vests from a storage container. "You can't be too careful, put these on."

Chris agreed it was a good idea, once again amazed at the details of Gabe's planning. "Follow Gabe's orders," he instructed Caleb and Aaron as he took his shirt off to put the vest underneath.

Gabriella had followed them into the pantry. Seeing Caleb putting on a bullet proof vest sent chills down her spine. Forcing herself to be strong, she straightened her back and stood firm declaring Yahweh's protection over them.

Caleb hugged her close assuring her he would be fine. "It's just precautionary, Gabby Girl. Nothing to worry about."

She struggled to smile as the secret pantry door closed behind them. Her father caught her as her knees weakened and she started to collapse. Clinging to him, she sobbed, "Dad, I can't lose him. We've come through too much for me to lose him now."

Gabe stroked the top of his daughter's head in a soothing gesture. "That's exactly the way Caleb felt when he thought he was losing you; but Yahweh brought you back to him and He will bring Caleb back to you. I'm sure of it, Princess."

"I pray you're right, Dad." She rested in his arms until the sobbing came under control, forever thankful her father was again in her life.

The tunnel was silent as the three men stepped into the dark. There were no flickers of light ahead of them nor voices echoing through the cave, no indication anyone was nearby. "It should be safe to turn our flashlights on," Chris advised.

The tunnel ahead was now illuminated and the trio, led by Chris, silently began their exit. When daylight appeared, Chris put his finger to his mouth signaling to Aaron and Caleb not to say a word until the coast was clear. He stopped just outside the mouth of the cave and held his hand up for the other two men to stay inside until further instructions. Chris took a deep fresh breath of mountain air and gazed momentarily at the fall foliage saturated with morning dew. The sun reflecting off the moisture laden leaves transformed the landscape into a tranquil paradise. He longed to have time just to bask in the morning sun and replenish his soul with the beauty of nature, but that time was not now. He quickly turned his attention to his immediate surroundings, searching for any movement in the air or on the ground. So far, so good and he motioned for Caleb and Aaron to join him.

He pulled his phone from his pocket and quickly called Officer Cohen. After a couple of rings, he answered, "Hello."

"Hey, Micah, how's it going?"

"Not so good," Officer Cohen answered. "Definitely not the conveniences we had at the seaside cottage. There was some survival food stored in the pantry when we arrived that's held us over, but that's almost gone. This place hasn't been used for years and we're going to be forced to change locations soon. This young lady in my charge has tried to be a real trooper but she's showing signs of extreme anxiety. The doctor just sits and mourns for his wife, and I'm concerned he might do something to himself. The only thing he says is there is no reason for him to live." The officer took a deep breath adding, "I'm sorry to dump so much on you, but I've really got my hands full here."

"That's a tough situation you're in, my friend. Any idea where you could go? With Richards under cabal control, they will be checking every protective custody location the police department has, past and present, including where you are now. You know, Dr. Nicholson is at the top of their most wanted list, being the only person who knows our location. The cabal will stop at nothing to find him."

"I've been racking my brain on what to do, and just haven't come up with a solution," the officer admitted. "Leah says she has a safe place to go if I can get her back to Haifa. Since she was simply caught in the middle and has absolutely no information about anything going on, she might be safer there than with the doctor who knows everything."

"Sometimes the simplest answer is the right one," Chris agreed. "Like I said yesterday, if you're not a praying man, you better start. It looks like that's the only hope we have in this mess. I'm pretty sure the cabal's men are closing in on us; and after I talked to you yesterday, some men followed us into the tunnel. Could be hunters, but I seriously doubt it. I'm trying to stay vigilant, eyes wide open, you know."

"That's your only way to escape, right?" Office Cohen questioned.

"That or through the lodge which is being constantly surveilled. Gabe told me he has a Hail Mary plan and he's going to clue me in tonight, but it would be a last resort. I have no idea what he has planned and so far, he's given no clues. I'll check in with you this evening. If you don't hear from me, you'll know our access to the outside has been cut off."

"Take care, my friend," Officer Cohen replied. "I'm not sure how to pray but I'm going to give it a try. It sure can't hurt."

Caleb and Aaron were keeping watch in all directions when Chris disconnected the call and rejoined them. "This entire situation gets more intense every day, especially for Micah. He's literally on his own trying to decide what to do, at least we have the moral support of each other and plenty of supplies. I have no idea what I would do if I were in his position."

"Pray," Aaron answered in one word.

Chris smiled, "I told him that very thing, but I wonder if he took me seriously. He knew me well before I took this assignment, and I wasn't a good example of a praying man. He has no idea how much I've changed."

"We will keep praying for him," Aaron added. "To any problem, Yahweh always has an answer; He can reach into the most desolate situation and make a way of escape." He slapped Caleb on the back who had been silently listening. "Right, brother? You saw that with Gabi's paranormal deception."

Caleb nodded with a glimmer of tears saturating his deep blue eyes. "There was nothing I could do to help her. But God..."

Chris interrupted, when he noticed a device anchored to a small juniper tree close to the entry of the cave. Had the sun not been reflecting off the metal, it would have gone totally undetected. "Oh, no."

Aaron and Caleb turned their focus towards the tree and with the light's reflection, immediately saw what Chris was referring to. The three men hurried towards the cave. Before entering, Caleb, being the taller of the three and physically strongest, reached up and grabbed the solar camera, breaking off a three-foot section of the tree limb with it. They didn't slow their pace until they were back safely through the tunnel and in the bunker pantry.

The trio were breathing deeply, catching their breath as they removed the bullet proof vests. Gabriella came running in followed by the rest of the team. It was obvious the three men had rushed back. "What is it? What happened?" She demanded to know.

Caleb held up the tree branch with the camera still attached. "This," he answered.

Chris instructed everyone to return to the dining area where he could sit down and check the camera. He detached the device from the tree limb and laid it on the table inspecting it detail by detail. "This is no hunter's camera," he confirmed as he took it apart. "This is above the grade of even the police force, I've never seen one like this."

"How long do you think it's been there?" Gabe questioned.

"There's no way to know." Chris inspected further, commenting, "It's solar charged, both recording and monitoring movements in real time. Without a doubt, there's someone somewhere planning to watch who goes in and out of the tunnel. If I had to guess, it was put there yesterday after we were followed into the cave to try to capture video of who's inside. It's amazing the sun reflected perfectly on the metal to catch our attention."

"No coincidence," Dr. Brotman stated emphatically, as he always did when he believed there was a divine intervention.

"True, Professor." Caleb added, "I'm sure they already have seen us and know we have their camera, but at least we have a heads up, we weren't taken off guard. No doubt, they'll be back with proper cave lights and follow the tunnel to the dead end. When they come to the dead end, they'll know there must be a secret exit out of the tunnel somewhere, we didn't just magically disappear."

"The tunnel is half mile long and finding that exit will be a major challenge. I had that secret entrance specifically designed to look and feel like real rock for this very reason." Gabe said, encouraging the team they still had some time.

"We are completely cut off from the outside world," Faith spoke out loud what the team was thinking. "This bunker is beginning to feel more like a grave."

Gabe's voice cut through the doom and gloom atmosphere. "I still have a backup plan."

"What plans, Dad?" Gabriella pushed for more information. "There's only one other way out which is through the lodge, and we all know how dangerous that would be."

Gabe put his arms around his daughter and held her close. "Trust me, Princess."

— Chapter 33 —

Gabriella accepted the fact that her father was not going to reveal his plan to escape, not yet. Gabe completely changed the subject, focusing on the immediate situation asking Chris, "How's Officer Cohen?"

"Not good, he's pressed to make some tough decisions very soon. Micah said the doctor is in deep depression, which I think we can all understand. He's concerned he might be suicidal."

Dr. Brotman knew his longtime friend well and gave his personal observation: "His wife was his reason to live and losing her the way he did probably has pushed him to the edge. I'm sure he can't imagine living without her, but ending his own life? He has too much faith in his Heavenly Father to do that."

"You'd be surprised what a person will do when they're pushed to the edge," Chris countered. "Believe me, I've seen it."

Gabe's face was solemn as he added, "Believe me, I've lived it. When Gabi was growing up, I could never have imagined, under any circumstances, making the choice to willingly exit her life. Desperate situations require desperate decisions."

No one could argue with Gabe's analysis knowing the sacrifice he had made. Gabriella tried to turn the conversation to a positive note: "If you hadn't made the sacrifice, Dad, most likely you and I would not even be alive today; nonetheless, our team having worked with Professor all these years, the amazing things we've discovered along the way, and the wonderful relationships we've been blessed with." She looked at Caleb and winked.

KJ quickly added, "And all the things we've discovered just these past few days about the Khazarian Jews and their international control."

Dr. Brotman had retrieved a book before sitting down and turned the pages to read. "This morning while praying, I was reminded of a prophecy in 2 Esdras from the Apocrypha which I had never understood until the

Khazarian Conspiracy was revealed to us; and it further substantiates what we've been researching regarding the final kingdoms from Revelation 18."

Chris quickly questioned: "I've heard you refer to the Apocrypha. What exactly is that?"

The professor patiently explained, thankful the police officer truly wanted to understand the inspired writings: "The Apocrypha is a selection of books, which for many centuries were considered inspired scriptures and were part of the original King James Bible published in 1611 A.D. These apocryphal books were positioned between the Old and New Testament for 274 years until being removed in 1885 A.D."

"Removed? Why?" Chris questioned further.

"That's a very good question with no solid answer, Chris. Originally, the argument was there were no Hebrew manuscripts which could be found to verify their authenticity. However, when I was part of the team translating the Dead Sea Scrolls, there were many fragments found from the apocryphal books, but they've not been re-added to the Holy Scriptures. Since these books further verify and do not contradict the 66 books we have now in our Bibles, I certainly believe we should give them consideration."

"Makes sense to me," Chris replied.

Dr. Brotman picked up the book and explained: "This writing is attributed to Ezra, the great Jewish leader and scribe who was instrumental in the rebuilding of the temple after the Babylonian destruction. The prophecy setting is the end of days, and if what I'm now thinking is correct, then 2 Esdras 11:1-2 could be referring to America: *Then I saw a dream, and behold, there came up from the sea an eagle, which had twelve feathered wings, and three heads. And I saw, and behold, she spread her wings over all the earth.*"

He paused from the reading to explain, "We know in prophecy the sea or waters mean the nations, so the eagle, which is the emblem for America, was to arise from many nations with the twelve feathered wings being a combination of nations to become the most powerful on earth. The three heads of the eagle nation, I now believe, are the three Khazarian controlled cities from Revelation 17 which we have identified as The City in London, Washington, D.C., and Vatican City – the monetary, military and religious capitols for Mystery Babylon. That chapter goes into many details, and when you go to Chapter 12 there's an explanation of what Chapter 11 means aligning further with Revelation 17 and 18. Verse eleven states the eagle was the same eagle Daniel saw but was not expounded upon in the Book of Daniel prophecies. Additionally, in 2 Esdras 12:23-24 it gives further explanation saying the three cities are three kingdoms, the heads of the eagle, that will rise in the last days and rule the earth with great oppression."

The team was intently listening in amazement to every word as the professor continued: "Chapter 12 continues to interpret that the eagle will be feared above all the kingdoms of earth and gives details of the nation's control. Verse 18 says great strivings will arise and the eagle shall stand in peril of failing." Dr. Brotman looked up and questioned, "Is that not what we see now? America is on the brink of collapse?"

"Without a doubt," Gabe quickly agreed. "It's just like Revelation 18:2 says, *She has become a dwelling for demons and a haunt for every impure spirit.*"

"That's one of the many Book of Revelation connections I'm referring to, Gabe. It's really amazing how these two prophecies align. Now here is the extremely interesting part of verse 18, referring to the eagle: *but shall be restored again to his beginning.*"

Gabe quickly countered, "America will *not* be destroyed, Professor?"

"That's what is written, at least not at that time. It indicates the eagle nation will come very close to total destruction but then will be restored as in the beginning, which would seem to mean back to the original religious foundation. Could it be when Mystery Babylon is destroyed and all the wickedness and evil deception is exposed that people will repent and the last outpouring of the Holy Spirit, a great revival, will take place? In God's mercy humanity is given one more opportunity before the Beast arises?" Dr. Brotman questioned, seeing it as the most probable translation.

"I've often wondered how the prophecy of the last outpouring could happen in my country and that makes so much sense," KJ spoke with a voice filled with hope. "A great revival could reach around the world when the Mystery Babylon is destroyed, because every nation has been controlled by the cabal's evil deceptions."

"I definitely agree," Dr. Brotman said. "As Chapter 12 continues, the prophecies begin to align with the prophecies of the beast nations in Revelation 17:7 both stating the kingdoms that arise at the end will only rule for a short time. In the final verses of 2 Esdras 12, just like in Revelation, the Most High God will bring the final judgment."

Dr. Brotman laid his book to the side and encouraged Gabe: "Now going back to the original conversation, I agree with KJ and Gabi, if you had not made the decision to fake your death, I question being able to have finally put all the prophetic pieces together about the Watchers, Mystery Babylon, and the Beast system. My work on the Dead Sea Scrolls translations and their connection to prophetic mysteries had become my life's passion. You made that possible, my friend."

Sandee attempted to lighten the atmosphere jesting, "And I couldn't be making these wonderful meals for all of you if you hadn't stocked the pantry with such precise planning." Her voice turned solemn adding, "The list really is endless, Gabe, as to the many blessings you've been."

Gabe was humbled by the recounting of the positive decisions he had made; however, he couldn't escape the heaviness of the greatest decision that was yet to play out, his Hail Mary. It was looking more and more to be the only option as the cabal was closing in.

Sandee looked at the clock. "Speaking of food, it looks like it will be brunch today, instead of breakfast," she announced, headed for the kitchen. "No one had an appetite while you three were outside, worrying so about you." She paused and looked back over her shoulder, "Thank God, you're all okay." She turned back towards the kitchen and prayed under her breath, "Father, continue to keep them safe in the days ahead."

"Do you need help, Sandee?" Gabriella asked.

"No thanks, I'm good."

"If you do just come let me know, I think I'll lay down for a few minutes, my head's aching again." Caleb got up and walked with Gabriella to the bedroom, his facial expression reflecting his concern. "I'm okay, Caleb, really, no need to worry about me. I was just so worried about you that the stress triggered a headache. A little rest and I'll be fine, my love." She reached for his hand and gave him an assuring squeeze.

"I'll sit with you, just in case you need anything." His voice was firm, and she knew no argument would change his mind. He pulled a chair next to her bed and held her hand until she fell asleep. Gently releasing her hand, he stroked the top of her head, careful not to touch the wound. He ran his fingers down her cheek, gazing at her beautiful face framed by the curls of her long blonde hair, longing for the day she would be his wife and battling the fear it would never be. After her days in a coma, he fought the nagging fear every time she went to sleep that she would not wake up and their life together would end. He took a deep breath and slowly exhaled whispering his reality, "One way or another our life together will end...soon. Nothing can stop the end of days."

Gabriella was in a deep sleep when she entered another vision. Again, she was at the mountain cabin where Officer Cohen had taken Dr. Nicholson and Leah. Two men emerged from the dense woods next to a tree thicket where

Officer Cohen's white car was parked, the same car the three had escaped in from the seaside cottage. This would verify for the two men that the trio they pursued were in the cabin. Silently and cautiously, they approached the entrance; Gabriella could see they both had guns in hand ready to fire. She ran towards them screaming for them to stop, but her voice was unheard. Carried in the Spirit, she was immediately inside the cabin as the intruders drew closer. The three inside were totally unaware of the danger approaching.

Gabriella screamed in a voice of panic. Although they could not hear her, the spirit of the officer was alerted. Quickly he moved to the window, slowly and cautiously pulling the corner of the curtain back just enough to peer outside. The two men were stepping onto the wooden front porch nearing the locked door.

"Come with me," he whispered, motioning for the doctor and Leah to follow him. He grabbed the keys to the car and pushed them towards the small storage room at the back of the cabin with only a window for possible exit. Gabriella watched as the three entered and the officer locked the door pushing a storage cabinet against it and placing a second one behind the first for added security.

The cabal's men attempted to kick the front door open to no avail, soon followed by gun shots to blow the lock off. Officer Cohen knew time was running out and pushed the closet window up for them to climb through. Leah went first, followed by the officer who wanted to be on the outside to help Dr. Nicholson safely come through.

The doctor made no attempt to climb out. He motioned and spoke low enough so not to be heard by the men approaching. "You two go, now!"

"I'm not leaving you," Officer Cohen exclaimed.

It only took a couple of minutes for the men, once inside the small cabin, to narrow down exactly where the three had hidden. The escapees could hear their evil voices as the two men pushed the closet door and then kicked to break through the lock. The storage cabinets blocking the door slowed their entry, still leaving time for the doctor to climb through.

Officer Cohen reached inside the window pleading with him, "Come now. We're out of time."

Dr. Nicholson shook his head no. He grabbed his chest; his face was turning white and then purple as he collapsed on the floor with his body now completely blocking the men from pushing the door open to gain entry.

The officer turned away from the window and grabbed Leah's hand pulling her towards the thicket of trees.

"We can't leave him," she cried trying to slow their pace.

Instead, he sped up knowing there was nothing he could do to help the doctor. He explained as they ran to the car: "He's home now, Leah. He won't grieve anymore."

Dr. Nicholson's body was the extra blockage needed to give time for Leah and Office Cohen to get to their car and escape. Once the intruders gained entry to the storage closet, the white car was already out of sight. The only person who knew where Gabe Russell was hiding had left this world. The truth serum the intruders planned to use was worthless now.

Gabriella had a supernatural view of Dr. Nicholson's departure from life. She felt the peace radiating from his spirit as it transcended space and time entering his eternal existence. She watched him crossing the river of life entering the resplendent field filled with singing flowers of vibrating colors where he was welcomed into the arms of Yeshua and Mrs. Nicholson who awaited him. It was the same reposeful river which separated Gabriella and The Lamb when she was at the brink of death. She had not been allowed to cross; her existence in time was not yet over.

The paradisaical vision was consumed by a brilliant burst of light and disappeared. Gabriella smiled in her sleep, consumed by a peace that passes all understanding. Caleb had watched her the entire time as she went from a restless sleep, to agonizing moans, and ending with a tranquil smile.

Opening her eyes, she looked directly into Caleb's questioning face and announced, "Dr. Nicholson has gone home."

"What? What do you mean, Gabi?" He reached for her hand pulling her to a sitting position on the side of her bed.

"I saw it, I saw him leave this earthly existence, Caleb. It was agonizing on this side of life, but immediately became eternally peaceful." A radiant smile captured Gabriella's face, remembering the celestial scene. "Let's rejoin the others and I'll explain."

He pulled her to her feet and took her in his arms, momentarily holding her before reluctantly letting go. "I love you, Gabi," he whispered.

"Ditto," she whispered in his ear, giving him a quick kiss on the cheek then leading him back to join the team who were deep in conversation. They all immediately hushed when they noticed Gabriella's countenance had completely transformed from prior to her nap.

"What's happened, Princess?" her father questioned now recognizing a supernatural glow which radiated from his daughter when she emerged from a vision.

Sitting down next to her father, she took his hand for moral support verbally replaying, step by step, all she had seen.

Shock radiated throughout the room, but no one questioned the validity. Chris wanted desperately to run to the end of the tunnel and call Officer Cohen to verify her vision and give his fellow officer moral support. However, that was no longer an option. "I need to talk to Micah."

"You know you can't," Gabe responded. "That would be too dangerous... for all of us."

Chis nodded his head in agreement. "All telephone communication with the outside world has been cut off. At least Leah is in good hands. Micah will do his best to get her to a safe place."

Dr. Brotman sat silently, emotionally dealing with the loss of his dear friend and wondering who would be next. Sandee pulled her chair next to his recliner and took hold of his right hand in comfort. He in return put his left hand on top of hers and pulled her closer, feeling her love and compassion as she closed her fingers around his.

"Professor, I wish you could have seen the peace and joy on his face as he crossed the river of life," Gabriella comforted him. "There are just no words to describe the glorious essence that radiated from his heavenly body when he went into the arms of Jesus."

"I am beginning to long for that day myself," Dr. Brotman replied. He looked deep into the eyes of each team member, one by one, and affirmed, "That is what we're all working towards and living our lives for - that day when we also will be in the arms of our Lord and Savior." A big smile captured his face erasing the sorrow. "It is our blessed hope, and we will rejoice in the fact our friend has entered in." His tone of voice reflected the peace Dr. Nicholson would now be experiencing after days of anguish in mind and soul.

Sandee quoted one of her favorite scriptures from I Corinthians, Chapter 15:53-54: "*When this corruptible body shall have put on incorruption, and this mortal body shall have put on immortality, then shall be brought to pass the saying that is written, Death is swallowed up in victory. O death, where is thy sting?*"

The familiar Presence of the Holy Spirit filtered through the room and into the hearts and minds of each team member, replacing all sorrow felt for those that had passed into their eternal lives and eliminating all fears for when that time would come for them individually.

Faith took KJ's hand and openly declared, "I'm not afraid anymore, whatever happens, I know my Heavenly Father is in control."

"Gabi, I truly believe Yahweh allowed you to see this for several reasons," Dr. Brotman verified. "We know the enemy is closing in; however, our God has shown you how he can protect us in the time of trouble, how he can make a way of escape if it not yet our time, and why we are not to not fear when our time is up. He's in control of every detail."

"Spiritual preparation for days ahead," Aaron acknowledged. "I think we all needed this, Gabi."

Dr. Brotman gave a quick recap of their project's prophetic timeline. "We all are aware time, as we know it, is ending soon and the fact the Spirit of Yahweh has allowed us to unveil Mystery Babylon and the depth of her deceptive evil, verifies her demise is at hand which places us near the very end. The Khazarian Jews and all they've controlled for centuries with their riches will fall in one hour, opening the door to the beast system to enter and take control. The end of days' deception begins at that point with The One, the Antichrist, restoring order in a world of chaos, bringing an illusion of world peace and prosperity for all; and now it appears it will begin with the rebirth of America and a worldwide revival; but soon after the One World Government led by Satan himself forms and Revelation 13 is fulfilled."

Dr. Brotman took a deep breath and slowly exhaled. "With everything that KJ has found on the internet and all these digital soldiers, as they are referred to, warring with undeniable truth, soon we will reach the time when God's judgment is rendered, and He will put in the heart of the beast to fulfill His purpose and destroy Mystery Babylon." He looked at Gabe and addressed him directly: "Your years of research and documented proof added greatly to the already building mountain of evidence exposing the great harlot. We're now on the precipice with a bird's eye view of her imminent collapse."

Gabriella confirmed the professor's analysis adding, "The Spirit has shown me a glimpse of what will happen during The Great Tribulation, when the Evil One is ruling the earth." She hesitated, pondering if she should share all that she had seen that would take place during the final three and half years of time. She decided to go in a different direction and simply summarized, "Dr. Nicholson, his wife, and the kind janitor were given the easy way out."

She had barely completed the comment when the alarm went off alerting them to something or someone triggering the security system alarm at the front gate. Chris, Gabe and KJ rushed to their posts to check the source, with the rest of the team crowding behind them.

"Well, well," Chris soon commented. "Looks like we have visitors again."

"Who?" An echo of voices chimed behind him before Chris could explain.

"It looks to me like it's the same fleet of vehicles that was here a couple of days ago. I would guess it's Detective Richards joined by Strozza with his entourage."

The feeling of déjà vu seized Gabriella when the gate opened, and the caravan of SUVs proceeded to the front entrance of the lodge. She knew UN Director Sotoreo would be joining them soon and their time of escape from the bunker would be necessary. "Dad, you better get that Hail Mary ready, I think we're going to need it," she announced.

Not a sound could be heard in the bunker as they anxiously watched the black Suburbans park, and the men exit their vehicles. Unlike the first visit, two of the men went to the back of the SUVs and began to pull out roll bags to transport into the lodge.

"That answers one of my questions," Gabe stated. "This will not be another quick come and go visit."

Gabriella added, "I betcha, Sotoreo will be arriving tomorrow and that means time's running out for us."

Chris gave a quick questioning look at Gabe which the entire team understood. They all wanted to know what Gabe's plan of escape was. Gabe responded, "We'll talk after we see what their plans are. I'm still trying to figure out a few details."

After the lodge had been cleared for entry by Strozza's security men, he and Detective Richards entered the lodge, instructing the men where to take their bags.

"Can you zoom in on that luggage by the door, Chris?" Gabriella hurriedly questioned. "That looks like my roll bag I left at the hospital. Could it be...?" With a quick zoom she immediately identified it. "That is my bag!"

"Richards told me he'd retrieved it from the cottage after Micah left. Remember, Gabi?"

"Of course, I remember, Chris. I never thought I'd see it again though. It's so close and yet so far away." With all the supernatural twists and turns of her interdimensional existence, she wondered if the Indian turquoise bracelet would still be on top where she had placed it before zipping the bag the final time. No one understood the importance to her of getting that bracelet back and now was not the time to explain...survival was the mode they were all moving into as they watched every move the men above them made.

Strozza was giving instructions to his men on where to take their bags. "Take mine to the master bedroom downstairs. Richards can choose any bedroom upstairs and we'll decide the rest later." Strozza plopped down in the professor's recliner next to the fireplace. "It's going to be cold in the mountains tonight, I think a fire will be just what we need for evening conversation, Detective." One glance at Russo was obvious that he expected him to take care of it.

"Yes, Sir," Russo quickly replied exiting to the back where the firewood was stacked.

Detective Richards showed no emotion whatsoever as he commented: "I'll go up and choose a room so your men will know where to put my belongings. Be back shortly." He followed the two bags he brought with him up the steps and chose the first door on the left, the bedroom that Gabriella had always used. It was obvious to the team watching, the detective did not want anyone going through his bags when he quickly took possession of them and told the carrier he could leave. After the man exited the bedroom, he pushed them into the closet and closed the door.

Gabriella suppressed a laugh. "They would definitely question why one of his bags was filled with lady's personal items."

"That would be an interesting explanation to hear," Chris laughingly agreed, refocusing the cameras to the main floor where the detective rejoined Strozza.

"Sit," Strozza commanded Detective Richards as one would command their dog.

Obediently he took the chair opposite the Intelligence Director.

"I've just received a very disturbing call, Richards. Two of my men had been going to the various locations you gave us that are used for protective custody. I have good news and bad news. The good news is they found your officer and the two people in his charge, Dr. Nicholson, who knows everything, and some hospital clerk that knows absolutely nothing. They were hiding in one of the mountain cabins on the list we were given of possible locations."

Strozza tried to read the detective's reaction but there was none. Detective

Richards managed to control his facial expressions hiding immediate concern for their safety. He guarded his words and controlled his voice; with a poker face asked, "So they got the doctor, huh? I guess you're relieved."

The director had no indication from Detective Richards' controlled response that, in fact, the detective battled extreme turmoil churning in his gut as he awaited Strozza's bad news. "The bad news is Dr. Nicholson is dead, the only person who knew where Gabe and his crew are hiding. Apparently, the old man had a heart attack, just like his wife; and, just like his wife, before they could get any information."

"That creates a real problem with Sotoreo, no doubt." Still the detective showed no emotional attachment to the situation whatsoever.

"More than you know, Richards. Sotoreo was depending on you to get the information through your officer. Now what do we tell him?"

Detective Richards wanted to laugh out loud at the we part of that question. "Maybe you should tell him the truth? As the saying goes, you can't get blood from a turnip."

Strozza's eyes were piercing as he vehemently replied, "This is no joking matter." The intelligence director was not going to admit that he was now being controlled by Sotoreo, too, with a threat to his own family. "Do you know anything, anything at all that could be a clue to their location, Richards?"

"All Officer Harris told me was Gabe had a hideout in the mountains they were going to. I probably could have found out if you hadn't interrupted our phone call with your threats. A little too late now."

"You're awfully flippant for a man whose feet are going to be held to the fire," Strozza retorted. "You have no idea how far the U.N. President will go to get what he wants, there are literally no limits."

"I think I know pretty well, but I have no answers I can give him. Nothing."

The team had been closely listening to their conversation when Chris echoed the detective's answer. "He really doesn't know and a lot more lives are about to enter harm's way, including ours."

"Hopefully, we won't be here that much longer," Gabe acknowledged. "If Gabi's right and Sotoreo's spirit guide leads him to us, we will be ready to head out."

"How, where?" Gabriella demanded to know.

"You'll see, Princess. Trust me."

The entire team moaned in frustration wanting to know the plan. Chris had kept up the facade of not knowing Gabe's Hail Mary so no one would push him for information, especially Gabriella; however, Gabe knew there needed to be someone that could take control in a worst-case scenario, so he had revealed the entire escape plan to the officer.

Their attention refocused on the two men's lodge conversation. Strozza's piercing eyes had returned to normal, even showing a hint of compassion, but he was obviously very tense. "I'm going to confide in you Richards. I do believe you are a man of integrity and I admire that; there aren't many men I can say that about, not many I would trust."

Detective Richards leaned forward with body language indicating to the director that he had his full attention and was correct in his assumption.

Russo returned with firewood and soon had a warm comforting fire built. Strozza directed him to leave and for his security team to decide on their sleeping arrangements for the night, allowing for a private conversation between himself and Detective Richards.

When the room had emptied, Strozza turned to face the detective: "I have never shared this with anyone, but I need to get this off my chest. You might say it's sort of a deathbed confession of things that haunt me day and night."

The detective was shocked that he would be the recipient of such a confession from the International Intelligence Director, but assured him, "Anything you share with me goes no farther."

"There's no further to go," Strozza was pensive as he replied. "I don't think you realize, Richards, neither of us have time left to share anything. Since we can't produce Gabe Russell and his entourage, as promised, Sotoreo's wrath will fall on us both." Agony filled his face adding, "I am more concerned about my family than I am myself. I was promised this day would never come, if I followed their rules. I should have known I was just another pawn in their international chess game, and easily dispensable."

"They control you, don't they, everything you do?" The detective brazenly questioned.

"They control everyone, one way or another. Most people just don't realize it. Even Sotoreo is controlled, but I can't tell you by whom exactly, they never reveal the powers that be who control secret societies, governments, royalty, even The Vatican. Sure, I know the thirteen family names that are common knowledge, but I also know there is one family that controls even those elites. The name is never spoken, and I have always done as told and never questioned."

"Am I pushing too far to ask how that happened?"

"A couple of days ago, we would never have had this conversation, but now there is no question off the table, time is running out for me." Strozza leaned back in the recliner momentarily closed his eyes, listening to the crackling fire and recalling his climb to international success as the most powerful man among the world's intelligence agencies. "I was very ambitious as a young man, as most are, but I was willing to play ball however they asked me. I started out in the European Intelligence Agency, working out of the Belgium office. In my first few years I was given several assignments with, you might say, questionable ethics; I didn't ask questions, just followed orders."

"Your first mistake, I gather," Richards surmised.

"You are correct, but when you are promised immense monetary gain, a life of luxury for your family, and international clout...well, as a man seeking success for himself and his family, it was a dream come true. It was the beginning of a slippery slope that led to assignments I cringe to even think about. In fact, I struggle every day to not think about the things I've been involved in. I still have a conscience despite my actions, especially when it comes to the children. I'm not one of their operatives that have sold their souls, and I've sure seen plenty of those people."

"I assume Sotoreo is one of those people?"

"Completely," Strozza answered. "There is no turning back for that wicked man."

"What do you mean by the children?"

Strozza continued to focus his eyes on the flames of the fire unable to look the detective in the face. "You must know what I mean. As a high-ranking police officer, I'm sure you've seen and heard it all, just as I have. The things they do to children and babies are unspeakable. The political stuff didn't bother me so much, that was just business, but the children was a whole different ballgame."

Detective Richards nodded his head indicating he understood the details the director did not want to discuss and simply stated, "I couldn't agree more."

In the bunker, Gabe gasped. "I knew the child atrocities were controlled from the very top! The most important intelligence director on earth has just verbally verified the information we downloaded." He immediately hushed, allowing their attention to return to the conversation above them.

Strozza continued his horrendous walk down memory lane: "We have the capability of watching, hearing, knowing everything, literally everything, through electronic devices. The very things people must have for their daily existence were designed to watch and control them. Television tells them what to believe, computers give them the information the controllers want them to have, and the cameras built into both – that's another story. Cell phones track every movement people make and every word they say. There is no privacy left on this planet and my agency uses all this technology to bring down anyone who gets in the way of the plan."

"The plan?"

"The New World Order, Richards. A one world government with international control of everything and everyone." He looked deep into the detective's eyes. "How have you escaped? You know your Police Chief is controlled, right?"

"I suspected as much," he admitted. "But I refused to compromise on principles and Chief never pushed me, I guess to cover which side he was truly on; but he did use my abilities to further his own cause."

"There are few men like you, and those that are will be the first ones eliminated under the new government, people like Gabe Russell who knows too much. They're a threat to the controllers, the threat of waking people up to the truth resulting in an international rebellion. There are already indications of uprisings in numerous countries threatening the plan." Strozza turned his attention back to the detective. "Have you heard of The Source?"

Detective Richards shook his head. "No, I don't believe I have."

"It's an internet dark web channel where millions of people are now going to The Source to read posts presented to be the truth about the satanic controllers, and you know what, Richards? It is the truth." His voice slightly cracked as he acknowledged a major threat to the deep state scheme. "We think it's a small group of powerful military and high political powers who have secretly united to expose the controller's centuries of deceptions engulfing the entire planet. The thing is there is no way to hack the channel to find out who it is; and it's gaining momentum so fast that it's forcing quick counteractions that are not playing out well for the controllers. In fact, some drastic measures are being planned."

"I'm surprised you're telling me all this," Detective Richards admitted.

"It's not like you can do anything with the information. It's just you and me, no one else can hear us, and I don't expect either of us to leave this lodge. You're the sounding board I needed to help relieve my conscience before I exit this world."

Detective Richards fully suspected the entire conversation was being viewed and recorded by Officer Harris from the hidden bunker, so he continued with leading questions to give as much information as possible to his officer. "I've known some good people who went to work for the Mossad and quickly became controlled operatives. As far as I know, they didn't get big fame or fortune out of it. Why would they be so willing to go to the dark side?"

"Simple, Richards, blackmail. They find a weakness in those people, or create one, and set them up with a false narrative that becomes their reality. Then they threaten to expose and destroy them if they do not follow orders. The innocent become victims."

"Just as I expected. Everything has become so diluted that it's impossible to tell what is real and what is manufactured, who is innocent and who is guilty. It's really been a battle as a detective, and this explains why. These controllers, as you call them, can make truly innocent people be convicted of crimes they never committed, just to silence or eliminate them." Detective Richards paused, "Like Gabe Russell and anyone connected to him."

"Exactly, and I've been part of their evil web, thinking I was safe from their wrath."

For over an hour the intelligence director shared cabal secrets verifying the information KJ had found on 4-chan. There was no doubt The Source was to be trusted.

Strozza ended his guilt-trip confession and stared at the fire, listening to the crackle of the logs. "I've probably said way too much, but you need to know where we are in this spider web of deceit. No one is safe, no one that gets in their way; and now that's me. If I can't deliver Gabe Russell, it's over for me." He stared directly into the detective's eyes. "And you."

– CHAPTER 34 –

Strozza had barely voiced his foreboding when his cell phone rang with the UN President calling. Detective Richards could only hear one side of the conversation, but it was obvious Sotoreo would soon be arriving.

"Sotoreo and his spiritual companion will be arriving tomorrow afternoon," Director Strozza formally announced. Seeing the confusion on the detective's face, Strozza explained who his companion would be. "The Black Pope and he expects perfection in everything, all the pomp and circumstance, you might say; and he's not a nice guy...not at all. Don't get me wrong, he has a very charismatic charm that sucks people into his web immediately, but I don't trust him, not for a minute. He's a spiritual guide to Sotoreo, and the UN President makes no big decisions without the Pope's spiritual direction."

In the bunker, Gabriella gasped and confirmed to the team, "This is what I've been telling you, Sotoreo and the Black Pope would be coming to the lodge. Tomorrow is D-Day and we better be ready." She looked at her father speaking without words.

Gabe nodded his head. "I know, Princess."

Chris motioned for them to listen as the conversation above them continued with Strozza warning Detective Richards, "The Black Pope is in on every evil thing the controllers have done, are doing, and plan to do. Do not trust anything he says. I'm telling you; this man is pure evil."

"Are you saying this supposedly spiritual man, who all of Catholicism trusts, is part of what's been happening to the children, too? Politics, I can understand, but the abuse of children?"

"Richards, you have no idea how deep this evil goes and the more you know the more danger you are in. I've looked for ways to get out; and I even thought of faking my own death one time or ending my life, but I stayed to try to protect my family. I kept doing things to protect them, things I deeply regret. I soon realized I was digging my own grave one act at a time; and now time's up. I can't protect them and only hope that my death will release them from potential harm. They know nothing about the things I've been involved in, totally innocent; but that means nothing to the controllers. They want to reduce the population, so a few more that might know something or used for blackmail, are easily dispensed with." Strozza's emotions had taken control and his voice was breaking.

Detective Richards was carefully watching Strozza's body language. He gave no signs of lying and his regret seemed sincere, but the detective was not totally convinced and closely guarded what he would believe. "Couldn't you leave tonight? Get your family and hide somewhere? At least try to escape?"

He shook his head no. "You still don't get it, Richards. There is no place to hide from these evil people. They literally have eyes and ears everywhere, both human and electronic. Trying to escape would be certain death for my family. At least this way, there is a chance of mercy for them; a small chance, but a chance." He paused for moment and added, "I'm surprised Gabe has escaped them as long as he has. That will end soon too, I guarantee it."

Gabe listening from the bunker retorted with escape plans taking on a new possibility that was totally unexpected, "There are no guarantees, Strozza." He glanced back at the team and expressed, "I could actually feel sorry for this man if I knew this wasn't an act to suck the detective into the deep state web; but, either way, it does make me wonder how many good people are caught in the deep state's control."

"Slowly but surely, they suck you in until you're totally under their control, willingly or not." Chris agreed.

"Just like Arcturus did with me," Gabriella muttered. She looked around the small room into the faces of the people she loved and thanked God for each one. "Had it not been for your prayers, I would never have escaped." Caleb put his arms around her and held her close. No words were necessary.

Their attention focused back on the lodge conversation when Detective Richards leaned towards Strozza and whispered, "Can the controllers not hear us right now? I would think this lodge would have ears."

"Every word is being recorded, but it goes to my people, not Sotoreo's; and information is not released to anyone, until I say so. No one will hear our conversation until after we are dealt with for not delivering Gabe to the powers that be. It's a matter of principle for them now, they will not be outsmarted. Gabe's information cannot be retracted but making him pay the consequences is the endgame."

"Let's take a walk and get some evening air. It will be good for both of us," Detective Richards requested.

Chris leaned back in his computer chair as the two men upstairs exited the back door. "He's up to something," he commented. "I know that look and that tone of voice. I just wish I knew what he was planning, maybe we could help."

"What are you thinking?" Caleb questioned, ready to help.

"I'm not really thinking of a specific plan," Chris admitted. "I just wish I could help Richards and if Strozza is sincere, he could be an asset for our side."

Gabe could see the wheels churning in Chris' mind. The two men looked at each other knowing what the other was thinking. Chris raised his eyebrows questioning; Gabe lifted his shoulders and cocked his head, silently answering maybe.

With no activity in the lodge, the team returned to the living room. "I'll stay and monitor their outside movements," Chris announced. "I won't be able to hear them but I'm pretty good at reading lips, if I can get the right camera focus."

"I'll stay with you," Gabe offered. "Two sets of eyes are better than one." The rest of the team were ready to exit the cramped area and get off their feet; they were totally unaware the two men left in the security room were now revising the original escape plans.

Chris grabbed a notebook and handed it to Gabe. "I'll try to lip read and you write down everything I tell you. Afterwards we'll try to make sense of it."

Gabe nodded he was ready. Every word Chris could make out he repeated for Gabe to write. For almost an hour Detective Richards and Strozza stood outside in the cool, autumn air conversing, sometimes turning their faces in directions where the cameras could not pick up a facial view. When the two men finally went back inside, Chris' tense body relaxed.

"I don't know if any of this makes sense. What do you think, Chris?" Gabe questioned, handing him the notebook.

Chris read the choppy words over and over trying to put together coherent phrases. "I'm usually pretty good at this, but the way they kept turning away from the security cameras, I only got bits and pieces. I'm pretty sure Strozza was pushing Richards for any even remote possibility of information that could locate us; and if so, it would save both their hides."

Gabe's expression was quizzical. "Do you think Strozza is playing Detective Richards? Pretending to be guilt ridden and wanting to do the right thing to get the detective to trust him?"

"That thought has crossed my mind," Chris admitted. "The only thing that grounds me to the fact Strozza is being honest is Gabi's dream of the director and his family being threatened by Sotoreo."

"Maybe that's the reason the Spirit allowed her to see that encounter, so we would know who to trust," Gabe reasoned. "These evil people are so deceptive, only spiritual discernment can lead us in the decisions we need to make."

Chris turned to face Gabe with the question they both were pondering, "Do we try to save them?"

The human part of Gabe did not want to put the team in anymore danger, but the spirit man in him knew they had to do what was right, knowing life trumps everything else. "We've got to try, don't we?"

Chris turned the page on the notebook and began to draw out a diagram which could work with their existing escape plan, mapping it out step by step. He looked up and questioned: "But how do we get Strozza and Richards separated from everyone else in the lodge to bring them to the bunker?"

Gabe took the notebook and began to note additional steps that would be needed to help minimize the potential danger. "I don't know what the rest of the team is going to think about this."

"It's to our advantage they don't know anything yet, so adding some details won't throw them off, Gabe."

"I know Gabi has been so upset with me for not telling them how we will get out, but I believe not telling her could potentially be protecting her. I had to keep one emergency plan that no one knew, so no one could tell even if truth serum was used, we've seen the cabal doesn't hesitate to force truth out any way needed. I always question if I've done the best for my daughter." The expression on Gabe's face was saturated with doubt. "Have I done the right thing?"

"Yes, you have," Chris assured him. "We all want to believe things will work out the way we plan, but a backup plan is always essential, just in case. No one in this bunker would ever willingly tell any secrets, but there's always the remote possibility they would have no choice."

The two men refocused on the security monitor when Detective Richards and Director Strozza reentered the lodge. The director turned towards his bedroom. "I'm calling it a night; I need some time alone to think things through." With his short explanation for departure, Strozza disappeared down the hallway.

Detective Richards proceeded to his bedroom, also needing some private time. Once inside, he closed and locked the door behind him, knowing the lock would make no difference if someone decided to enter. He immediately went to the closet and checked his and Gabriella's roll bag to make sure neither had not been tampered with. Nothing appeared questionable. He took his personal bag and put it in the bathroom, leaving Gabriella's in the closet.

Sitting down on the side of the bed he whispered a prayer, "Jehovah God, you know I'm not a praying man, but I do believe you are real, and I need some help. I don't ask for myself, but for the protection of the people I love. I've done all I can in preparing for a time like this, but to escape these evil people some supernatural intervention is really needed. Please keep my family safe."

He went to the bedside chair and sat looking out the window into the darkness of night. The autumn moon cast a faint glow across the mountaintops with Mt. Hermon looming in the middle of his view. He was lost in his thoughts reliving his life, feeling so many regrets, and accepted this could be his last day on earth.

In the bunker the team was meeting with Gabe and Chris finally going over their plan of escape. Exclamations of amazement were expressed as they knew how it just might be possible to get out alive. The only mystery that remained was exactly how they would exit the bunker. That would be revealed when the escape time arrived.

"Dad, I can't believe you planned all this...for me," Gabriella exclaimed.

"It's all I had to do for twelve years, try to make sure the daughter I left behind was taken care of in any possible scenario. With each passing year, I saw special people come into your life," he paused and looked at the team surrounding them before continuing, "and I knew the danger they were in just because they were in your life. If they ever found out I was alive anyone connected to me in anyway would be added to their hit list. Your friends had no idea any of this threat existed until just a few weeks ago, but I have been planning for years how they would be protected too, if that day came. So, I thought of more danger possibilities and how to deal with them, just in case; but as we know, man's best laid plans can still go awry. Even with my best efforts, Yahweh must be with us to make the plans work."

"You're amazing, Dad, and I know our Heavenly Father is with us, no matter what happens."

Gabe pulled his daughter into his arms and whispered, "You're the most important thing in this world to me, Princess. I would give my life for you...again."

"Don't even go there, Dad," she demanded, snuggling in his arms of safety. "I refuse to think about it."

He held his daughter close, silently praying for divine wisdom in executing his plans. "I think we all need to try and get some rest. I have no idea what tomorrow holds."

"But I know who holds tomorrow," Sandee finished his sentence. With her words of comfort, the familiar Presence surrounded them. Fear had no place.

As Gabriella settled in her bed, she closed her eyes and immediately reopened them to the sound of a car engine starting. She was in a limousine in the back seat facing UN President Sotoreo and the Black Pope. The window between the driver and the two men was closed for conversational privacy.

She prayed for the blood of The Lamb to protect her and Sotoreo would not discern her presence knowing there was divine purpose for her to be with these two men. There was no indication Sotoreo felt an intruding spirit as he began his conversation with the Black Pope, believing no one could hear their words.

Sotoreo began with casual conversation: "From what I've heard this lodge has a magnificent view of Mt. Hermon, our mountain of worship. Very convenient, huh?"

The Pope smiled and nodded. "And exactly why are we making a trip to this particular lodge?"

"I have some unfinished business to take care of. Strozza is supposed to have the location of Gabe Russell. I do hope, for his sake, he does. I'm not sure I totally trust Strozza. He's not been willing to be spiritually cooperative, you know what I mean. He's got the job done, and never questioned his commands, but not made the total commitment which affects my trusting him. We've reached a point of all in or you're out. Trust can no longer be a question."

"I totally agree, but why did you want me to come with you?" *The Pope questioned.*

"I needed to talk to you privately with no chance of being overheard." *He pulled out a metal box and put his phone in it and asked his companion to do the same.* "Even those phones have ears," *he stated closing the box tightly.* "This box will close those ears so we can talk."

He shifted in his seat to face the Pope. "There's been some developments that are very concerning for The Master, in fact, for all of us. It's been building for several years, and we are losing our control of humanity – people who are waking up to the truth, mainly through the internet and social media, *led by a mysterious entity known as The Source. Needless to say, The Master blames the controllers for not stopping this breach into the ultimate plan for the New World Order."*

The Pope listened intently to Sotoreo's concerns while battling concerns of his own. "We've also had major cracks develop in our responsibility," he admitted. "These Truthers, as they are called, are digging deep and finding many connections The Vatican has to the plan for world control. It's being exposed on levels we can't continue to deny. All the internet exposure of our priests being involved in crimes against children, the money laundering, and adverse political involvements have made even our parishioners begin to question our leadership. The Gray Pope had a meeting recently with the Black Nobility and it wasn't a good one. They believe the time has arrived for the final solution. As you know, we've been laying the groundwork for decades for the perfect solution to unite humanity...an alien disclosure. It will bring the world together for a common cause."

Sotoreo immediately agreed. "For decades the controllers have been preparing for this time. People have been slowly seduced into believing there are non-human entities existing on some far away planet who have been monitoring the earth. When nuclear war starts and millions are dying, these intergalactic beings will come to save earth from self-destruction. They will be welcomed with open arms. Little will earthlings know, these non-humans are the spiritual offspring of the fallen angels, controlled by The Master."

"The return of the Nephilim," Gabriella spiritually discerned the plan and spoke out loud to ears who could not hear her. She finished the prophetic declaration by adding, "As it was in the Days of Noah."

The evil pope laughed out loud to the UN President's comment, declaring, "The White Pope has already declared he is willing to baptize these beings and welcome them into the faith." The laugh subsided as he added, "It's always amazed me how gullible humanity is. Just let the news media say something over and over, and it doesn't matter if there is any truth at all to it, people will believe it." His voice completely changed addressing the soon to be initiated plan: "The Tic Tac sighting by that American Navy Commander really set the stage for UAP encounters. That was a brilliant move by the controllers resulting in official hearings in halls of governments, where they are now revealing the long-hidden secrets of aliens who have visited our planets for decades."

Sotoreo smiled with self-satisfaction that the many moving parts of world domination were coming together, but knew time was not on their side for completion. "The government's acceptance of the testimonies from military whistleblowers will be covered heavily by all news sources setting the stage for The One's arrival. It will be the beginning of The Golden Age, all that we have worked for, if we move right away. Any delays could derail our entire plan with this mass awakening of humanity.

Gabriella listened as the two men expressed the time gravity of the situation and what it meant for the cabal's ultimate plan. Their conversation confirmed all the things KJ had discovered on the internet back channels.

The UN President continued by explaining the plan for control of nations. "Russia was to be our final piece of the puzzle. We have for decades vilified them to the world, making every nation and their citizens believe the Bear was bad with an evil leader that planned to take over the world and rule with an iron fist. We've been able to keep the rogue nation under control for centuries through international politics, but the current President cannot be controlled. The fact Russia refuses to join NATO throws a big wrench into our control of nations. He separated from the ruling countries – countries where we have been able to program the minds of their citizens to believe NATO and the UN could be trusted. We've recently discovered Russia is working with The Source and is in the process of exposing our operations in Ukraine which is our major hub of operation. Next, it will be the controlled politicians in all nations, our bio-labs, our ways of moving money, The Royals, and even our businesses, all the businesses and you know what I mean."

Gabriella knew exactly what he meant. The business of selling children. She wanted to reach across the seat and choke the life out of this evil man who had no remorse for the horrible crimes against innocent children he was involved in. She was certain he felt her righteous anger when he paused and momentarily closed his eyes. Again, she prayed she would not be detected, needing to know exactly what these evil men were planning.

Sotoreo opened his eyes and slightly shook his head indicating he must be imagining an intruding spirit. He looked at the pope and rolled his eyes, "I'm a bit off today. So much on my mind and there are so many decisions to make. Anyway, Russia has added another layer of threat to our plan, the worst of all, their new financial system."

"I assume you are referring to BRICS? That is a major concern for The Vatican, as well. Do you have a plan to bring the Bear down?" The Pope inquired.

"We do. We've been saving the final solution until all other moving parts settled into place, but we may have to move forward immediately. The Source and Russia, along with the nations that have aligned with them in this new monetary system, must be stopped before we lose all control. They plan to take control of the stock market and when the time is right, collapse the entire market which would destroy the economy worldwide."

The Pope looked shocked, "If they pull that off, we will lose control of everything! In one hour, the markets across the earth would fall like dominoes and our world government plan destroyed. You know well, money and power are our control factors and the fact they both could be gone in just one day; our positions would be useless at that point, we would be dispensable." His voice betrayed the fear he felt for what this could mean. "Centuries of planning... gone. Ruling humanity...gone. Everything thing we have done, every compromise we have made, every deception we've been involved in...it would all be for nothing." He looked at Sotoreo with pleading eyes "Please tell me your solution will stop them."

"We do believe the solution will shift the monetary power back to us. We've had the media reporting for years that World War III was on the horizon as we aligned nations against each other. Israel is our biggest challenge, and the world would be shocked to know the truth." He suppressed a laugh adding, "Foolish people have been so blinded they can't see the controllers have managed both sides of war for hundreds of years. They determine who wins and who loses and, in the meantime, make trillions of dollars. It's their major way of controlling the world economy. Let me put it this way, they control the world's chess game and innocent humans are the pawns."

"In that chess game, I'm certainty glad I'm a knight and not a pawn," The Pope expressed.

Sotoreo looked directly at him, sternly warning, "Knights are sacrificed too, you know."

"I do know," he admitted, with a quivering voice, "but I have a covenant with them, they vowed I would always be protected as long as I followed their demands."

Sotoreo laughed sarcastically, "Yeah, protected as long as you're needed. I've watched some really big players, who also had covenants, go down recently. You must stay viable to the plan to survive now, and rumor is there's compromise within The Vatican."

"Any specifics on who, what?" The Pope pushed for more information.

"I can't verify the information yet, but I've heard The Source knows about the gold stored in the catacombs beneath The Vatican and making plans to confiscate it. No one outside of The Black Nobility is supposed to know. That gold becomes essential should the BRICS nations implement their gold backed currency. Which brings me back to WWIII; there will be a nuclear attack against the United States and Israel, which will be blamed on Russia. WWIII will be declared, pulling in all the NATO nations to align with the

U.S. and Israel against the Bear. The United Nations will expel Russia, and the news reports will all be how NATO has saved the nations from an evil tyrant seeking world dominion - when in fact we have saved our own hides and the implementation of The New World Order."

After processing the consequences of a nuclear war, the Pope added, "That will take care of another objective at the same time, reducing the world population."

"Yes, bringing it to a more controllable amount of people." The UN President agreed. "Still more weeding to be done, but that will be the first round; and the essential move to bring world dominion to our master, The One. It is imperative the controllers hold the timing of the stock market crash and keep it in our control. Our crashing the market will be our shift to the new digital cashless currency, eliminating the fiat dollar as the world standard. Whoever controls the money, controls the world, to quote one of our fearless leaders."

The Black Pope knew precisely the rest of the plan. "And The One will control the remaining humanity with a microchip willingly taken under the skin, so they can continue - what they believe are - normal lives, buying and selling only with their mark. They will worship him for bringing peace out of chaos and saving the planet from extinction."

Gabriella gasped at the plan of nuclear war and the horrendous aftermath. Her extreme spiritual reaction was felt by Sotoreo and he turned to look her directly in the eyes. Their eyes locked just as someone was shaking her.

"Gabi, wake up. Your dad is wanting to go over the plan again before Sotoreo arrives." Faith's voice returned her to reality. "Are you okay?" Faith noticed Gabriella's strange expression as she was pulled from her supernatural encounter.

Sitting up in bed, Gabriella tried to refocus on her surroundings; however, her mind kept replaying the conversation she had just been privy to. She jumped from her bed exclaiming, "I've got to tell the team." She quickly dressed and joined them to relay the cabal's plans, restating all she had heard during the spiritual encounter.

For Dr. Brotman it confirmed what he already believed to be the truth: "The Pope has exactly described the fall of Mystery Babylon. In one day, her destruction will come and just as we speculated, an international monetary collapse will be her final downfall shifting the power to the beast system. When it will happen is the question now."

Gabriella answered, "According to Sotoreo they are running out of time, and something has to be done soon or it will be too late."

"Definitely time is running out," Gabe agreed. "If our plan works, we could become major chess players in this war game they're talking about. Sotoreo and the Black Pope will be here soon so let's run through the details one more time. This won't be easy, but we can do it. Are we ready?"

"Ready," the team chimed in unison.

– CHAPTER 35 –

"Get your bags ready and take only what you must have for backpacking," Chris instructed as the team prepared to leave the bunker. Each person got the gun they had chosen for their personal weapons while Gabe went to the stock room for holsters.

When Gabe returned, he handed each member one and instructed them to put them on. Then he opened another box he had retrieved from the pantry. These contained gas masks. He handed one to Caleb, KJ and Chris. "Are we ready to get Strozza and Richards?"

"Ready as we'll ever be," the three men answered.

"First, I need KJ to send a detailed message on 4-Chan, and then I have to make sure all the security men are inside the lodge. Get your gas masks ready to put on, guys. I sure hope we're making the right decision on this," Gabe stated.

Gabriella pulled Caleb to the side, requesting, "If you get a chance, please get my roll bag. Just if you can, do *not* put yourself in any further danger."

"You know I will, Gabi," he assured her, leaning over to kiss the top of her head.

Gabe went to the security room where KJ sent the message precisely as he was instructed, a private message to The Source. After the message was sent, Gabe activated an emergency alarm inside the lodge which continued blaring as all the security men rushed in to investigate. When they were all inside, going from room to room checking for a breach, Gabe pushed a button releasing a mixture of odorless chemicals into the air of the lodge. Within minutes everyone inside was dropping like flies, incapacitated and unable to move.

"Let's go," he exclaimed. "We've only a small window of time to get Richards and Strozza.

The four men rushed up the steps and through the secret passageway into the kitchen. They stepped over Russo's body, who had been making coffee before inhaling the chemicals. They hurried into the great room where Director Strozza and Detective Richards had passed out in the chairs by the fireplace. Immediately they put gas masks on them and allowed a few minutes for them to breathe normally and regain consciousness. Caleb ran upstairs and grabbed Gabriella's bag from the closet in the interim, quickly taking it back to the top of the bunker stairs where Gabriella was ready to take possession.

When the detective and director opened their eyes and tried to move, KJ and Caleb got on either side of Detective Richards while Gabe and Chris were on either side of Director Strozza. Chris grabbed both men's cell phones lying on the tables next to them, stuck them in his pocket and helped them to their feet guiding them back through the kitchen, again stepping over Russo who was still on the floor, and leading the two men down to the bunker.

Director Strozza wanted to ask if Russo was dead but kept his silence suspecting he was being taken hostage.

The pantry secret door stood open awaiting the men's return. After they had passed through to safety, Gabe closed the opening, concealing their location once again. No one would ever know how the detective and director had left the lodge.

Once in the bunker, the two rescued collapsed onto the sofa. Chris removed their masks allowing them to breathe deeply.

He was preparing to explain what just happened to the very shocked men when Detective Richards breathlessly exclaimed, "I knew you were watching, Officer Harris. I knew I could count on you." He laid his head back on the sofa, taking deep breaths to clear his lungs and mind.

Director Strozza's eyes were questioning and filled with apprehension as he looked around the room filled with unfamiliar faces. Chris decided to let him remain in uncertainty until all their demands were met.

"Are the others dead?" Detective Richards questioned.

"Not dead," Gabe answered, "but they'll be out for a while, even after Sotoreo and the Black Pope arrive, and very disoriented when they do come to. They'll have no idea how to explain what's happened to the two men they were responsible to protect. We'll let Sotoreo deal with that. We'll be gone when they arrive."

Strozza interrupted, "You can't go out that tunnel where you parked your SUV. We've got men waiting if you do. They were able to locate your vehicle with a drone and have video of you coming in and out but couldn't find where you disappeared to when you went back in the tunnel; they've been instructed to keep surveillance until I give them further orders." He took a breath adding, "You've saved my life, warning you is the least I can do."

"We suspected as much," Chris replied. "And we have no intentions of going out that way."

"You're not going back through the lodge, are you? Sotoreo will be arriving anytime." Richards quickly warned.

Chris just shook his head. "No, and we're aware he'll be here soon. Are you strong enough to walk?" He asked the two men giving no further information.

Both men wondered how Chris could possibly know of Sotoreo arriving but dared not to ask. They simply nodded and pushed themselves from the couch ready to follow Chris' lead. The team members grabbed their bags and put their pistols securely in their holsters. They already had put on their bulletproof ready for departure. Detective Richards and Director Strozza watched, not knowing what to expect from this makeshift army.

Gabriella quickly unzipped the bag Caleb had retrieved for her from the lodge and held her breath as she opened the top section. A sigh of relief escaped her mouth when she saw the turquoise bracelet on the top where she had last placed it. She wrapped it around her wrist and left the roll bag and its other contents on her bed rushing to join the team anxious to finally know exactly how they were exiting the bunker to initiate the escape plan. That was the one detail which continued to be kept secret by her father until the moment of their escape.

Gabe was standing in his bedroom motioning for the team to come in. On his bed lay a pile of flashlights designed for cave exploration. "Grab one and follow me." He was holding a remote control the team had never seen before when he opened the door to his closet. Pushing to the side the few clothes he had stored there a solid cedar wall was exposed. Gabe pointed the remote at the wall, and it slid to the side exposing another cave entrance.

"When you said you had an alternate plan for escape, I never imagined this," Gabriella blurted out.

Exclamations of shock and surprise echoed through the bedroom, causing him to take a quick moment to explain before entering their way of escape: "I had this bunker built directly in the middle of this cave, cutting off the tunnel passageway. It gave me an exit on both sides, but I told no one about this second exit, not even Professor. I wanted one totally secret way out, trying to prepare for any possible circumstance. I do believe I was inspired to do so - *for such a time as this*," he quoted from the Book of Esther, reminding them of Yahweh's protection. "Follow me," Gabe instructed them as he entered the dark tunnel with his cave flashlight guiding the way.

"So, this is why my men could not find you," Strozza surmised in amazement as he followed their lead.

KJ was ready to shut down the security system and follow the team out when the alarm went off. He glanced at the monitor before unplugging. He retrieved Gabe's flash drives from a drawer and securely placed them in his pocket, then joined the team being the last one to exit the bunker. "Sotoreo's entourage is coming through the gates now," he confirmed. "I sure wish I could stay and watch their reaction."

"If we stayed in that bunker, Sotoreo's spirit guide would lead him right to us," Gabriella stated emphatically. "Let's get out of here before he gets in the lodge."

Gabe added, encouraging them to move quickly, "Getting out now, I doubt anyone will ever find the bunker, it will become the unknown tomb where we survived the evil ones." He looked back at his safe haven one last time, knowing he would never return. He caught a glimpse of his black leather box next to his bed, filled with his many years of research, realizing it would be forever entombed in this place designed for seclusion and protection. "You've served me well, bunker," he whispered under his breath. "You've done your job."

Gabe was the last one to exit. He pointed the remote at the opening, clicked, and the cedar wall returned to its original location. On the exterior of the cedar wall, where they now stood inside the cave, was the same pseudo cave rock as the bunker's exterior pantry exit. No explorer would ever suspect the truth.

Gabe put the remote in his backpack and turned to face the team which now included Haifa Police Department's top Detective and the infamous Director of the International Intelligence Agency, the most powerful man in world intelligence. Director Strozza had no idea of the plans Gabe and Chris had made concerning him. Gabe silently prayed their plan would work and God's hand would be on them all as they began their journey to safety.

He advised the team as they left, "This is not going to be easy, it's a much longer tunnel than the way we came in. There are some rough spots to pass through, but we can stop and rest, take our time as necessary. In this situation, time is on our side. We're in no hurry. He instructed the younger members of the team to stay close to Dr. Brotman and Sandee to make sure they were okay and let him know when they needed to rest. He and Chris would assist Detective Richards and Director Strozza, who had no experience whatsoever in cave travel.

For over an hour they journeyed through the dark tunnel with only flashlights illuminating the path before them. Often the rocks would narrow, and single file became necessary to pass through. They came to two places where they had to get on hands and knees to crawl through. The rock floor was uneven and conducive to tripping and falling. It was a very tense journey, especially for Dr. Brotman in his weakened condition.

When they reached a large cavern with rocks suitable for sitting to rest, the team took a break. Gabe questioned Dr. Brotman and Sandee, "Are you two okay?" Dr. Brotman took a deep breath and slowly exhaled.

"I'm fine," Sandee replied, "but I do worry so about Professor. He's still not built his strength back from the accident."

"Don't fuss over me, I'll be fine," he assured her, reaching out to take her hand and give an affectionate squeeze. Even in the dim light the look of love exchanged between the two of them was evident.

Faith and Gabriella locked eyes smiling, silently acknowledging what they had known for a very long time. Both women took the hands of the men they loved and leaned closer to them, cherishing every moment together.

"So much love and so little time," Gabriella thought to herself.

While the couples were all enjoying a moment together, Strozza took the opportunity to question his position. "Am I a hostage? Bargaining power for you to try to escape? You know you'll never get away with it, there is literally no place to hide from the controllers."

"Really?" Gabe countered. "I think I've done a pretty good job of it for over a decade." He was not ready yet to answer the hostage question.

"True," Strozza acknowledged, "but it didn't last. They kept surveillance on your daughter all those years which eventually blew your cover. They always win in the end."

"Not this time," Gabe disagreed. "They still have no idea where I am, where any of us are."

"You have to come out of this underground tomb eventually and, when you do, they'll be waiting." Strozza caught a glimpse of the sarcastic smile on Gabe's face and wondered what this Houdini had connived this time.

Gabe stood up indicating the conversation was over. "Everyone ready?"

Caleb helped Sandee and Dr. Brotman to their feet and made sure they were steady before releasing them. Dr. Brotman slightly swayed and Sandee immediately locked her arm in his to assist him in balance. Slowly they moved forward keeping their lights focused on the rocky terrain under their feet. Gabriella and Caleb protectively walked behind the duo.

"This sure makes me miss the other tunnel escape," Gabriella remarked, breaking the silence. "I had that path down pat, I could have walked it even in a coma." She giggled, adding, "In fact, I think I did, several times."

"I'm just thankful we have a way out," Faith expressed. "I've not seen the light of day in almost a week, and it sure works on a person's frame of mind."

"I agree with that," Sandee confirmed. "I want to feel the sun shining on my face and breathe the mountain air."

"And hear the birds singing in 432 Hz?" The team laughed at KJ's question.

Sandee quickly added, "No, I'm serious. I want to listen to the birds sing in perfect harmony, stand barefoot on God's good earth and experience His healing frequencies. We've been robbed of so much and now that we know the truth, I want to experience everything I can. At my age I have no time to waste."

Director Strozza stopped and turned to face Sandee, speaking with a voice that sounded like true regret. "You have no idea just how much you have been robbed of...Lady."

Sandee faced him head on. Even in the dim light her normally gentle countenance was obviously transformed into confrontation. "I think we all have a pretty good idea, *Sir*, but I have no doubt there is more to be revealed, much more."

Gabe recognized the opportunity to question Director Strozza. "It's obvious you have regrets."

"Regrets don't even scratch the surface of what I feel," the director admitted.

"Well, when we reach our destination, you can start to redeem those regrets, if you're serious."

"I'm very serious," he assured Gabe. "But I have no idea how I can prove it."

"You will soon." Gabe informed him.

After another half hour of their journey to the surface of the earth, Gabe suggested another rest break. Dr. Brotman quickly agreed with an exhausted voice and sat on the first available rock. Chris detected something was not normal and knelt beside the professor shining his flashlight directly into his face. Immediately he noticed his facial color was abnormal and eyes dilated.

"Are you experiencing any discomfort, Professor?" Chris questioned.

"A little trouble breathing, but I'm sure it's just the stress of so much walking."

"Any pain at all?" Chris pushed for more details, sensing he was not being forthcoming. "I need to know any details."

"Well, maybe a little pain between my shoulder blades, but nothing too bad. I can keep going."

"You rest now, Professor, don't push too hard," Sandee spoke with an extremely concerned tone.

Gabe assured him, "We're almost to the end, but again, we don't have to hurry. Once we get outside the tunnels, we will encounter the first obstacle which I didn't know how we would handle short of shooting our way out," he looked at Strozza and added, "until last night."

"Me?" Strozza questioned. "What does this have to do with me?"

"Last night when we listened to your conversation with Detective Richards, my answer became crystal clear." An expression of certainty crossed Gabe's face. "You're our scapegoat." All the team understood what Gabe meant, but the expression of confusion on Strozza's face was priceless.

"I don't understand," Strozza looked from Chris to Gabe wanting an answer.

"You will when the time is right. First, we must get off this mountain."

Dr. Brotman felt he was holding up progress and forced himself to continue. "I'm fine, let's keep going."

"I'm not sure that's a good idea," Sandee replied encouraging him to stay seated.

"We're almost at the end, right Gabe?" Dr. Brotman asked. "I can make it a little farther."

"I've got a better idea," Gabe suggested, crossing the cave floor to face his friend in the dim light. "Sandee, Faith and Aaron can stay with you and let you rest about fifteen more minutes. That will give us time to clear the way once we get above ground. We should be ready to pull out by the time you join us."

Sandee quickly agreed: "Great idea, Gabe." She looked at the man she loved and reminded him, "You know Aaron and Faith are expert cavers, we'll be fine for a few more minutes of rest."

He reluctantly agreed, not wanting to be a hinder to their escape. "I suppose you're right."

Gabe patted him on the shoulder. "While you're resting, be praying our Hail Mary comes together as planned. It's our only hope."

Dr. Brotman glanced at Strozza. "I'm sure it will. We've been given a blessing, we didn't expect."

"What do you all mean?" Strozza pushed for an answer. "I'm warning you; the controllers won't let you go because you have me as a hostage. I was already on their elimination list, and they will do anything possible to get their vengeance on you, Gabe. They will follow you until the day you die."

'You mean, until I die again?" Gabe chuckled. "I think you'll be very surprised at what we have planned and now is as good of time as any to clue you in on the next step." He looked into the eyes of the director and detective and declared, unwavering, "You two will be our ticket to safety. When we get off this mountain, we are returning to Haifa, to the police department."

"Are you crazy?" Detective Richards blurted out.

Gabe looked at Chris. "You take it from here."

Chris took over, explaining the plan: "I know it sounds crazy but if you're willing to cooperate, I believe it will work, saving you and your family, Strozza. When we arrive, the three of us, you, me and Richards, will have Gabe Russell and all his accomplices in custody. Strozza, you'll inform Sotoreo the mission is accomplished, putting both you and Richards back in the good graces of the UN President where you will be trusted again. Richards will tell our Police Chief that I was working with him the entire time and had not gone rogue, it was an undercover assignment." The team all knew the plan and was praying the two captives would be willing to cooperate.

"That makes no sense," Strozza countered. "How do you all escape actually being arrested?"

"A detail yet to be revealed, my Hail Mary. Are you willing?" Gabe pressed for an answer.

Director Strozza raised his eyebrows questioning, "What do you think, Richards?"

Gabe, half joking and half serious, interrupted before the detective answered: "It's either that or be left in these tunnels to find your own way out. The choice is yours."

Richards readily agreed, "You rescued us, then we rescue you, at least to the police station; but I have no idea how you can escape from there."

"One bridge at a time," Gabe refused to elaborate past the information given. "Now that we're all in agreement for the next phase of our escape, let's roll." He gave Dr. Brotman one more pat on the shoulder and turned to take the lead.

Picking up their backpacks, the rest of the team was ready to finish their journey back to the earth's surface and prepare to leave The Golan Heights. In less than fifteen minutes they reached a turning point in the tunnel curving to the left. To the right side was a pile of steppingstones going nowhere.

"That's odd," Gabriella commented. Then she smiled, realizing they had reached their destination. "This is it. Right, Dad?"

"Yes, Princess," he answered removing his backpack and opening the zipped compartment to retrieve the remote control he had used earlier. He pointed it above the rocks and clicked. Immediately an opening began to appear large enough to climb through.

"I'll take it from here," Caleb announced, having gone over the plan of escape in detail. Being the experienced rock climber he was, a few rocks less than seven feet tall was no challenge. Once inside the opening, he followed Gabe's instructions.

"The ladder's hanging on the wall behind you, Caleb. Drop it down to me."

"Got it," he replied as he lowered it into the cavern below. He reached down to help Detective Richards come through the opening, followed by Strozza, Chris and Gabriella. Gabe was last to climb up.

"Where are we?" Detective Richards asked looking around the interior of a garage. A Jeep was parked in the middle with shelves on one side filled with boxes, hanging on the other side were various tools. On the floor at the rear were several gas cans, apparently filled to be used as needed.

Gabriella answered him, "This is where you and Strozza become our scapegoat." She was truly enjoying the confusion Director Strozza was experiencing; confusion edged with the fear of uncertainty not knowing what to expect next. He was getting a taste of the bitter medicine he had dished out for decades. However, her satisfaction was tempered by the fact he did appear to be remorseful, but the jury was still out on her final judgment. She whispered to Chris, "Keep a short rein on that one until we know more."

"Absolutely," he whispered back. Turning back to face the others he put his fingers to his lips. "We need to keep our voices down just in case any of Strozza's men are nearby."

"What? My men? Where are we?" Strozza echoed the detective's question in a demanding voice. Remembering he was not in control, his attitude abruptly changed. "Will you tell us where we are?"

Gabe explained: "We are in the garage near the cave entrance your men are surveilling. The tunnel circled back which gave me two ways to exit the bunker and get back to this garage. That's the reason I came out every day to make sure no one had discovered my entrance down to the cave. The tunnel we just took was the longest and most challenging, so I never used it. It was in case of an emergency, like today."

"But my men are still surveilling this area, how are you going to get past them? They've been instructed to take out anyone coming out of that cave, if the suspects try to escape."

Gabe smiled from ear to ear. "That's where you can start redeeming yourself, Strozza. You're going to place a call to your surveillance team's supervisor, informing him you have us captive in the lodge and they need to come immediately. By the time they get there and discover it was a hoax, we'll be headed off this mountain." He looked at his watch. "The others will be here soon. Then it will be go time."

"We have a problem," Strozza informed him. "I don't have my phone. It was on the table next to me when I passed out."

Caleb reached into his pocket and pulled out both the director's and the detective's phones. "Problem solved."

Strozza thanked him, reaching for his phone. "I'm sure glad to have this back. On my command, my men will leave immediately."

"That's what I'm counting on. Once we get back to Haifa, you'll see the next chess move we make and you're going to be essential to that one, too. If everything works out the way we think, you'll seal the deal for us; plus, save your family and your own hide in the meantime."

"I have no idea how that's possible," Strozza muttered. "But I'm willing to give it a try, whatever it is, I sure have nothing to lose at this point. Sotoreo is done with me."

As convincing as Strozza sounded and his willingness to cooperate, there was still something not sitting quite right with Chris and Gabe. They exchanged looks silently saying not to trust him until it was all said and done.

Coming through the hole in the floor, faint voices could be heard in the distance as their final team members approached. Caleb went back down the ladder to assist Sandee in the climb up. When she reached the top, Chris and Detective Richards took her hands and assisted her through, followed by Dr. Brotman. KJ and Aaron at the bottom supported his weight as he slowly climbed the rungs, with the men at the top pulling him up. He was breathing hard, and face flushed when he safely exited the cave.

Once all team members were out of the cave, Gabe clicked the remote and the floor closed back together, leaving no sign of an entryway. He returned the remote to his backpack explaining: "This is the only device that will open the tunnel doors and it stays with me. Now, let's go over how we will divide up for departure. We can't all go in the Suburban, eight would have been tight but now we have ten so both vehicles will be necessary. I'll drive the Jeep. Gabi, Caleb and Detective Richards will ride with me. Chris will drive the SUV and the rest of you go with him."

Gabe turned to Strozza and with a commanding voice stated, "Make that call and make sure it sounds convincing."

"Oh, I can be very convincing, I've had lots of experience."

That was one of Gabe's grave concerns. Was Strozza trying to convince them now that he was on the good side? Was it an act? He did not voice his thoughts but instead demanded as he placed the call, "And one more thing, put it on speaker, I want to hear both sides of this conversation."

Director Strozza quickly found the number and placed the call with the speaker turned on for the entire team to hear. A deep masculine voice on the receiving end answered, simply saying, "Yes, Sir?"

Strozza's voice was firm and did not waiver as he gave his command: "Code X, Mission aborted; we've captured Gabe Russell. We need you all at the lodge, now."

"Loud and clear," the voice responded, disconnecting the call.

"Code X?" Chris questioned; suspicious it could be a warning code.

"It's double confirmation the mission has ended," Strozza explained, not to Chris' satisfaction.

"We'll give them a few minutes to clear out," Chris instructed, carefully watching Strozza's eye movements and body language, still questioning the motives of this man who had been well trained his entire career on how to deceive people.

Within minutes, Strozza's men could be heard running past the garage where the team remained silent. Soon the sound of four-wheelers speeding away gave Chris the all-clear signal.

"Let's go," Gabe instructed, unlocking the garage door and swinging it wide open. For the first time in a week, the bunker dwellers freely stepped into the sunshine and breathed in the crisp fall air. The autumn colors welcomed them back to the surface of the earth as relief flowed through them to now have a way of escape.

"You know this is dangerous, Chris, really risky," Detective Richards warned. "I'm still your boss, you know," he added, trying to sound in control but could not totally camouflage his uncertainty of who was really calling the shots at this point.

Strozza once again warned them, "There is no place for you to hide. The controllers will not stop until you are all silenced permanently, and you've added kidnapping me to their reasons to do so."

"We can certainly try, Strozza. We first thought it would be with Richard's help, but miraculously you have appeared which makes the plan even better, almost guaranteed." He stared the IIA Director directly in the eyes. "You're either all in or we give you back to Sotoreo, the choice is yours."

Chris continued to watch the director's body language as Strozza complied seeing no other choice, "I'm in."

– CHAPTER 36 –

"Keep your bullet proof vests on," Chris instructed not trusting Strozza's alliance with their plan. "Better to be safe than sorry; and pray, we're about to face the most crucial part of our escape. We need every detail to sync."

They followed his directions, also keeping their guns at hands reach just in case the plan for escape went south.

Gabriella, Caleb and Detective Richards waited outside the garage for Gabe to back the Jeep out while the others followed Chris to the SUV.

"Are you okay, Professor?" Sandee questioned, noticing his breathing still was not normal. "I'm really worried about you."

He took her hand and assured her he would be fine. "I can rest while we travel. Let's finish this." Sandee kept a watchful eye as they crossed the deer path to the Juniper tree thicket where the Suburban was hidden.

Aaron, Faith and KJ got in the rear seat, allowing Professor and Sandee the middle seats with more room to get comfortable. Chris wanted Strozza in the front next to him where he could continually monitor his questionable new ally.

Gabe pulled the Jeep out of the garage, allowing plenty of room for Caleb to close the door and bolt the lock. Richards sat in the front passenger seat next to Gabe, while Caleb and Gabriella settled in the rear seats. Gabe took one last look at the garage, saying goodbye to another place that had served him well in his years of living a false identity.

Momentarily, Gabriella re-lived her dream when she and Chris had escaped from the bunker using this very Jeep to do so. She pondered on the many aspects of her dreams and visions which had since become reality. She snapped her mind back to the present, put on her seatbelt and prepared for the bumpy deer's path ahead, their only way of departure.

Before pulling out, Chris questioned Director Strozza, "No doubt Sotoreo is having a meltdown finding your security men lying all over the lodge. Has he tried to call you?"

Director Strozza had already noticed missed calls on his phone which he had silenced. "Yes, several times. It's gone to voice mail. Do you want to listen?"

"Yes, we need to know our present position." he replied.

"I'll put it on speaker phone." The director went to his voice mail and all the occupants of the SUV heard the UN President's panicked voice. Sotoreo's message came through loud and clear demanding Strozza call him immediately with an explanation. He disconnected the phone and turned to Chris acknowledging, "I suppose this is where my total cooperation begins."

"You will call him when we get back to Haifa." Chris informed him.

"If he doesn't hear from me soon, he'll have surveillance all over this mountain looking for me. He doesn't waste a minute."

"I'm well aware of how this works," Chris answered. "The fact you immediately dismissed the men guarding the tunnel will throw up a red flag to Sotoreo. I'm hoping we can get off this mountain before he can get that kind of surveillance initiated. Within three hours, we should be safe."

They had only gone a quarter mile when Chris noticed a four-wheeler following them. It was staying far behind as if not wanting to be detected. He drove up close to the bumper of Gabe's Jeep, put his hand out the window waving forward, hoping Gabe would understand to move as fast as possible. Immediately, Gabe sped up and the two vehicles went bouncing over tree limbs and rough terrain.

"Hold on tight," both drivers admonished their riders as they swerved around the mountain path.

Chris kept glancing into his rear-view mirror, watching the distant vehicle which was still at a reasonable distance. "When we get to the main road, four-wheelers are not allowed, we should be home free then," Chris assured his passengers, praying nothing nefarious would happen before that time.

Before the junction of the main road appeared, the four-wheeler following them began to speed up. Caleb in the front vehicle noticed two more closing in from either side. He warned Gabe who immediately put on his emergency flashers signaling for Chris to beware.

While Gabe concentrated on keeping the vehicle moving swiftly and safely on the path, Detective Richards took out his pistol and told Caleb to do the same. "Be ready on the count of three to shoot for their tires to disable the vehicles." They lowered their windows and prepared to aim and shoot. The four-wheeler drivers to the sides of their Jeep saw the guns pointed at them and hit their brakes to grab weapons of their own. "One, two three... shoot!" Richards yelled, before their pursuers could prepare to respond.

Chris had also seen the additional vehicles closing in from each side, joining the one behind them and knew exactly what Detective Richards' police response would be; immediately he instructed KJ and Aaron in the back seat of their SUV to prepare to shoot out the tires of the four-wheeler pursuing them when he lowered the back window and gave the signal.

Dr. Brotman and Sandee put their heads down for protection as, simultaneously, all three four-wheelers were disabled. They had managed to stop their pursuit and get out of harm's way.

"Looks like Sotoreo decided to take matters into his own hands when I wouldn't answer his call," Director Strozza concluded. "His second call after me would have been to the leader of the surveillance team finding out I'd cancelled their assignment. He's overrode me telling them to stay in position under his command."

"Hopefully, we have enough time to get away," Chris countered. Just as he spoke the words, Gabe's Jeep came to a screeching halt. Obviously, there was something very wrong. Chris jumped out of the SUV to see two black Jeeps parked directly in front of Gabe's, blocking the path. Three men were holding guns pointed directly at their vehicles.

"Everyone, out of your vehicles, now!" They commanded. "Put your weapons on the ground and hands in the air." The three men on the disabled four-wheelers surrounding them came running, circling behind the SUV cutting off any way of escape.

With guns pointing from every direction, Chris instructed his passengers: "Stay calm and do as they say.

Strozza jumped out and went running for safety to the three men who held the others at gunpoint. He signaled for Detective Richards to follow him as he ran past the Jeep. Strozza was breathing deeply in a panic mode when he approached them. "Thank God, you've saved us." He pointed at Gabe and declared, "That's the man we've been after this entire time. Sotoreo is going to be ecstatic you've captured him and rescued me."

Detective Richards had followed close behind Strozza joining the captors. He pointed at Chris and betrayed him, "That's one of my officers who went rogue working with Gabe Russell and his international spy ring. Arrest them all! We'll take them back to the Haifa Police Department until Sotoreo can decide what to do with them."

All the team was looking at each other in total confusion and silently praying for God's protection in this confusing matrix. They had truly believed Detective Richards and Director Strozza were trying to find an escape from the evil Sotoreo, that was the premise they had built their escape on; and now the two they rescued were going to turn all of them over to that evil man? No one said a word as each personally questioned how their discernment could have been so wrong.

Two of the men were retrieving handcuffs from one of their Jeeps while the other men kept guns pointed at their captives. A hunter's distant gunshot momentarily distracted their captors; Aaron made the split-second decision to run for safety - like lightning he was running towards the woods and almost out of range when a single gunshot hit his back and took him down.

"No!" Gabriella screamed.

Director Strozza and Detective Richards quickly jumped in one of the Jeeps blocking the path of escape, fleeing harm's way. An echo of Gabriella's scream came from those held captive as Gabriella started to run to Aaron. Chris caught her and held her back knowing she would also be shot.

Chris released her to Caleb who was chasing after her. He pulled her back away from Aaron's direction assuring her, "He'll be okay, Gabi. The vest stopped the bullet. It'll take a few minutes for him to get back on his feet and he'll be sore, but the vest saved his life."

Strozza put the Jeep window down and yelled out, "Handcuff them all, take no chances."

The man who fired the shot went to Aaron and pulled his hands together with the cuffs, pulling him up from the ground. It was obvious Aaron was in pain, but the man pushed him back towards the vehicles while the rest of the team was handcuffed and returned to their vehicles. Within minutes they had become prisoners instead of escapees. The three that captured them took control of all vehicles to transport them back to the Haifa Police Department. The remaining three took the second Jeep and followed behind them until they arrived at Hwy. 98 where they turned north back to the lodge and to the command of Sotoreo.

When they arrived at the main highway, Director Strozza placed a call to the UN President informing him, "Detective Richards had the location for Gabe Russell. We now have him in custody, along with Gabe's daughter and all accomplices. We're in transit now taking them to Haifa Headquarters."

Sotoreo's extremely pleased voice informed the IIA Director, "You're back in my good graces and I'm sure you know what that means. You know what to do." He left no room for any discussion as to the captive's fate.

Strozza looked at Detective Richards and the two men smiled. Their plan had worked.

The drive back to Haifa was somber. Aaron was obviously still in pain but appeared to be fine otherwise. "I'd probably be better off if I didn't have the vest on," he said with a defeated spirit. "At least this nightmare would have ended."

Sandee wanted desperately to comfort him and was about to give words of encouragement when the voice of the driver demanded, "Quiet back there. No talking."

The captives all complied by being silent but communicated with their facial expressions. Sandee constantly raised her eyebrows asking Professor if he was okay. He would nod to affirm yes, but his color was pale and his breathing labored. He kept squeezing her hand, assuring her he was fine, his physical appearance said otherwise. She held his hand in comfort the entire time back to the city.

Chris was also concerned about Dr. Brotman. He kept glancing at him watching for any signs of distress. As he kept watch over him, he was also soul searching, trying to determine how he could have been so wrong about Detective Richards. Director Strozza he never fully trusted but being double crossed by his boss had thrown him for a mental loop, wondering where he had missed the body language signs that he was lying.

He went through every detail over and over in his mind, every word and every scene, and his reasoning kept coming back to the time Strozza and Richards were outside the lodge the previous night where the security monitors could not pick up their words and Chris was unable to read their lips. Was his boss using him, knowing Chris would try to rescue him? Were the two men making plans as to how they would play it out if they were rescued, pretending to be on the side of their captors until the table could be turned? Nothing else made sense based on their current situation. There was still one last hope, and he was clinging to it with every breath and prayer left in him.

It was almost evening when they pulled into the underground parking lot designed for bringing in prisoners whose identities were to be kept private. Many times, Chris had brought captives into the station this very same way, now he was being brought in by his own boss. He managed to catch Gabe's eye, silently questioning the plan. Gabe's facial expression did not change, and Chris realized they had to maintain full poker face mode.

The three vehicles came to a stop. The drivers exited and opened the doors for the handcuffed team to exit. Strozza's men followed behind their captives while Detective Richards led the way up a flight of stairs into a holding room at the top where they were told to be seated.

Detective Richards gave directions to their guards: "Take their handcuffs off and stay with them. I'll be back shortly." Director Strozza was obviously questioning the detective's decision to uncuff them as the two of them exited the detention room.

One by one, they were released from the chains binding their hands. Each one was shaking their arms to get the blood flowing normally again. Chris stood up to stretch and was immediately told to sit back down and stay still. The team looked at each other trying to read expressions and discern what the others were thinking. When they looked at Gabriella, she shook her head indicating she had no divine vision which would give hope for escape.

Gabe was sitting on one side of his daughter with Caleb on the other. He spoke out loud unashamedly, addressing the entire team, "I'm so sorry. This is all my fault."

Gabriella leaned her head on his shoulder and in a voice absent of all fear replied, "Where there's life, there's hope. It's not over yet, Dad."

Their three guards made no comment, but smirked at her words, silently indicating there was no way to escape.

The color began to drain from Dr. Brotman's face, and he grabbed his chest. "He needs medical help, now," Chris exclaimed, hurrying to his side.

One of the guards began to bang on the door. Detective Richards quickly returned and demanded, "Call an ambulance. Now!"

Sandee grabbed the professor's arm and began to pray. The entire team surrounded him on their knees. Detective Richards waited at the front entrance of the police station to immediately guide the ambulance crew back to the holding room where Dr. Brotman was now lying on the floor struggling to breathe.

While one EMT checked the professor's vitals, the other was preparing the stretcher for his transport. After starting oxygen treatment, they carefully placed him on the bed and quickly rolled him to their emergency vehicle waiting at the front door.

Gabriella and Faith had been sitting with Sandee comforting her while they waited for the technicians to evaluate the situation. When they started moving him, Sandee jumped up and demanded, "I'm going with him; he can't be alone."

Detective Richards nodded to the ambulance driver that it was okay, calling for one of his officers to follow the ambulance and guard Dr. Brotman and Sandee at all times.

"Glad to see you still have a little heart left, Richards," Chris commented sarcastically.

Detective Richards wanted to reply to Chris, but instead addressed Strozza's men: "We're going to move them to separate rooms for questioning. I will be back shortly to take over." He turned to face Chris, "Office Harris, follow me."

The three guards smirked again, sure that the rogue officer was about to meet his retribution.

Despite their deep faith and trust that their Heavenly Father was still in control, concern for Dr. Brotman, Chris and the uncertainty of what they individually were facing was taking an emotional toll on them all while they waited for separation into interrogation rooms, wondering if they would ever be together again once divided.

It had only been a few minutes, but it seemed hours to the team, when Detective Richards returned to move them. "Gabe, Gabriella, Caleb, follow me." He led them into a small room with only a wooden table and chairs and a large, dark mirror which they all knew was for private viewing from the opposite side. "Have a seat and I'll be back shortly."

He then returned to move KJ and Faith into a separate room. Lastly, Aaron was taken to a room isolated from the others. Confusion took on a whole new level as to why they were being separated as they were; and they were not allowed to ask any questions having been told to remain silent until spoken to.

He informed the three guards they would be given instructions by Director Strozza as to their next assignment. "I'm taking charge from here."

Detective Richards returned to the first interrogation room where Gabe, Gabriella and Caleb awaited. He pulled a chair out and sat down facing the three waiting with his back to the two-way mirror. He rolled his eyes towards the mirror, indicating to them they were being watched. They suspected Strozza was listening to every word and could see them, but the detective's face was turned away where Strozza could not see Richards' expressions.

"I am going to help you," he silently mouthed. "Trust me." Then he spoke out loud for Strozza to hear, "Gabe, you've been a tough case to crack, so Strozza tells me. If they hadn't had someone surveilling your lovely daughter, they may never have discovered you were still alive."

Gabriella was praying for discernment to not be caught in a good cop, bad cop scenario. She remembered her vision of her and Chris hiding at the seaside cottage and Detective Richards being on the side of good, wanting to protect them from the evil Sotoreo; even willing to put his own life in danger. "Was that vision to show me to trust him?" she questioned in her mind, uncertain how to respond to him.

"You know it's too late, Detective," Gabe retorted. "Every piece of information I had has been released on 4-chan for the world to see." He looked deep into the detective's eyes trying to read his motives, before continuing: "After over a decade of hiding, thinking I had information which had been concealed from humanity, I find out The Source already has it all and has been releasing it bit by bit on internet back channels for years. I sit before you now with nothing left to give you. Do what you want with me, I've accomplished my mission; but I beg you to let my daughter and Caleb go. They had nothing to do with my possession of classified information. Their only crime was trying to protect me."

"I believe you went over twelve years without contacting your daughter, letting her believe you were dead, right?" Detective Richards asked. "Your sole purpose of faking your death was to protect her?"

"That's right," Gabe answered. "Again, she knew nothing until the last few weeks. She's been caught in the crossfire of all this, Dr. Brotman's entire team has been also."

The detective leaned back in the wooden chair and gazed at Gabe. "I'm curious, did you plan to ever let her know you were still alive or play it out until you really were dead?"

Gabriella looked at her father waiting for an answer, one she was not sure of herself. She had never asked him that question.

He reached over and took her hand. "I wanted to tell her every single day that we were apart, but I knew the danger. I had hoped a time would come when this nightmare would end, and we could live a normal life for whatever time we had left. Since she was five years old, her life has been anything but normal, always hiding, always on the run. She had a semi-normal life after the cabal thought I was dead, but that only lasted until I was, you might say, resurrected." He waived his hand around the interrogation room, "And this is proof of the danger she was in."

The detective ignored Gabe's last comment and questioned Caleb: "How do you feel about being caught in this international espionage? Best I can determine you've had nothing to do with Gabe prior to meeting his daughter."

"True, but when I found out the truth, I was willing to do anything to protect Gabi." The look in his eyes and the love in his voice told the detective all he needed to know.

The door opened and Director Strozza made a grand entrance, standing for a minute staring at the three being questioned before he sat down next to Detective Richards. It was apparent he wanted them to fear his supreme presence. All three looked him directly in the eyes, no fear, awaiting his judgment.

"You know Sotoreo is determined to get revenge on you, Gabe Russell," Strozza declared, and anyone connected to you. You outsmarted him for years and this is his get even time. It's not about the information anymore, it became a personal vendetta for him; and being able to include your daughter, plus everyone else remotely connected to your research is an added bonus for Sotoreo."

Gabe made no comment, refusing to say anything that would add to the UN President's personal satisfaction.

Strozza stood back up and loomed over the table. "I've been with the International Intelligence Agency since I graduated from college, and I've had the elite position of IIA Director for over two more decades - there's little that goes on, or has gone on, in the secret intelligence world that I don't know about. The classified information I have access to could collapse nations, expose the corruption of world leaders and destroy the cabal."

"I have no doubt of your vast importance," Gabe acknowledged with a patronizing voice. "Someday, Strozza, someday..."

The door to the interrogation room swung wide open and Gabe, Gabriella, and Caleb gasped in unbelief. A second Director Strozza walked in and stood beside the first. The first turned in shock, "Who is that? What's happening?" he commanded to know.

"Will the real IIA Director please say so," Detective Richards said with sarcasm as two Israeli Military men came in and handcuffed the IIA Director. They were followed by an Israeli General who told them to take Director Strozza downstairs and wait in the detention room.

Detective Richards was filled with relief when he could finally let the team know the truth. "You are the first to meet the official body double for the International Intelligence Agency Director."

The three being questioned looked from one to the other with unbelief. The body double was a carbon copy of the real Strozza.

Detective Richards explained: "If we can fool you three when you are looking at him directly in the face, then any camera coverage, TV or otherwise, sure won't know the truth."

"The rescue was a set-up?" Gabe questioned, in complete shock with the turn of the events.

"It was all a set-up for us to escape, because everything he said about Sotoreo was true. I had no idea how to get to you; but I knew you were watching and listening, and Officer Harris would do anything he could to get me out. Had I not produced you, Sotoreo would have eliminated me and Strozza after making us watch our family members taken out one by one, leaving all of you to be found by Sotoreo's cabal and meet the fate we would have. The only way I could rescue you was for you to rescue me."

Chris admitted, "Strozza almost had us convinced he was willing to change sides, regretting his nefarious actions. Did you believe him?"

"Not for a minute. When we were in transit to the lodge, I told him I had a plan that could draw you out of hiding and lead us to Gabe. I knew you all were decent, caring people and would feel sorry for Strozza if he pretended to regret his nefarious deeds. I had him convinced that once we were out of the lodge to safety and had your full trust, we could turn the tables and take you all captive. I had to pretend I was working with him to rescue all of you."

Chris was beginning to understand. "You didn't expect his men to close in on us on when we left the garage, did you?"

"Totally unexpected on my behalf. His little Code X apparently told them to do exactly the opposite of what he was telling them. I had to keep pretending to be on his side, or we would all be dead right now. I kept praying for guidance in how I would take control when we got to the station. You can imagine my shock when we arrived. I had no idea I was setting Strozza up to be arrested and replaced with a body double until I was told by my secretary an Israeli Military General was waiting in my office." The detective allowed the general to explain the rest.

He reached across the table and shook hands with Gabe, Gabriella and Caleb. "I'm General Levin, very pleased to meet you."

They willingly shook his hand in shock at the turn of events. "I don't understand." Gabe expressed. Suddenly a brilliant smile captured his face. "Oh, yes, I do understand! My Hail Mary worked," Gabe exclaimed to Gabriella and Caleb.

Gabriella looked at her father in complete confusion. "I thought your plan was to rescue Director Strozza, then he would help us escape as a reward."

"True, at first; but my plan kept being readjusted with each turn of events. I added some insurance at the last minute just in case Strozza couldn't be trusted and something went wrong, back up plans. Right before we left the bunker, I had KJ send a message to The Source informing them I believed the IIA Director could be persuaded to turn evidence on the cabal, with a quick explanation as to why; and we would be bringing him to the Haifa Police Department this afternoon where he could be interrogated."

The General added, "We already had a body double for Strozza, as we do for all world leaders. We are gradually either eliminating the deep state controllers completely or replacing them with, you might say, actors who look like them who work for The Alliance. Gabe gave us the perfect circumstance to replace Strozza. These body doubles must be capable of imitating their voices, their facial expressions, basically become that person. You would be shocked to know how many of the elitists have already been replaced, even to the highest positions. Some cooperate willingly and remain in their positions as controlled operatives; some do not cooperate, and they are replaced, like Strozza is today. We will still get the information we need from him, one way or another."

"The Alliance? What's that," Gabe asked.

General Levin took a seat across the table and explained: "The World Alliance was formed many years ago, consisting of leaders of nations who wanted to be free of cabal control. Within their military were trusted men and women who swore a secret oath to covertly and systematically preempt these evil people preparing for The Great Reset bringing in their The One World Order."

"The World Alliance is part of The Great Awakening," Gabriella concluded. "That's exactly what KJ explained to us from the back-channel information he found." She looked at the general and raised her eyebrows, "It's all true?"

"It is," he confirmed, "and we are very close to achieving our goals. Gabe's timing couldn't have been better for delivering Strozza to us, he's a major player in the final phase. Since I live in Haifa and work with The Alliance, I was contacted this morning to be at the police station when you all arrived and arrange for your safety."

"What better place to pull this off?" Gabe laughed. "Let the black hats believe they have caught us while the white hats arrange our escape."

"My head is spinning trying to reason all of this out," Gabriella confessed. "Even if we escape, they'll still be looking for us and we're right back where we've been all of our lives, always running, always hiding."

"Not if you're dead," the General inserted. "Once you're dead, they move on to the next person in their way."

"What?" She exclaimed.

Caleb put his arm around her. "I'm sure he doesn't mean literally, Gabi."

"Of course, not literally, but the cabal must be convinced. The body doubles work sometimes, and sometimes it's necessary to eliminate the person completely, or make it appear so. If a person knows too much and they're in danger of being taken out by the cabal, we simply help them fake their death. Sometimes suicide, sometimes unexpected heart attacks, car accidents...we have a multitude of ways to help them disappear. A good press release giving details of their demise, the mainstream news takes over from there. We put the icing on the cake with death certificates and no one even questions the validity."

"Where do they go when they're supposedly dead? How are they not recognized by someone if they're so high profile, like you say?"

"That's a very good question, Caleb. If people really think a person is dead, they don't recognize them if they do see them; and with a few small adjustments like hair style change and color, tinted contacts, etc., no one suspects. They just become someone who looks like the person who died. The really hard part for these people is no one can know the truth. It's a whole new identity with no attachment to a former life."

"I have lived that life," Gabe reminded them. "Only two other people knew the truth. I know it can work but it sure is a hard existence."

"That's the only way it will work," General Levin agreed. "All of you that have been hiding together cannot be relocated to the same place, not even the same country; you cannot know where the others have been taken. Officer Harris has informed me of the best way to break this group up. You three will be remain together, the two in the room next door will be together, and the young man in the room alone we've already made plans for. He has agreed to work with us. I'm sorry I can't tell you the details."

Gabriella had managed to hold back her emotions until now. "Our team won't ever be together again?"

A look of compassion replaced the military countenance of the general. "Normally, I would say never, these are usually lifetime commitments; however, after The Great Awakening is complete and the cabal is destroyed, all those who are thought dead, living new identities for safety from these Luciferians, will be able to again step into the light and hide no more. The world will be shocked at how many people they thought were dead, are actually still alive; and how many they thought were alive, are in reality dead. On top of that, how many people they thought were bad were really good and vice versa. Right now, what the world believes is true is far, far from it."

"Will we be able to say good-bye to the others?" Gabriella's voice was quivering thinking of losing her dearest friends, the only family she had known and no guarantee they would ever be together again. "What about Professor and Sandee?"

"For those of you here, you will be able to say your goodbyes. For the professor, a press release will go out tomorrow that the famous Dr. Manny Brotman who worked on the Dead Sea Scrolls passed away with a heart attack. He will be moved to a secure military hospital for his recovery. When he is physically able, he and Sandee will take on new identities and disappear into the sunset. You won't see them again; the risk would be too great."

Tears of emotional agony were running down Gabriella's face. Gabe's heart was breaking to think he would never see his dearest friend again, the man who had opened his eyes to the alien deception and Biblical truths. He could never have survived his years of living a pseudo life without the Professor.

Caleb, too, struggled with the loss of his dear friends, but rejoiced in the fact they were all safe. As long as Gabriella was with him, he could face whatever the days ahead brought.

The General felt their remorse, he had seen it over and over when these protective custody cases were necessary. He encouraged them in the fact they had been a part of a major take-down of one of the most evil men on the planet. "Once The Great Awakening is complete, you will see what a major contribution you have made on many levels. Gabe, you discovered decades ago the microchip that would change the world. The cabal did everything possible to make sure you never let that information reach past their resistance. Then the information on the children you were given; well, that's when a death warrant was put on you. You would never have survived if you hadn't faked your death."

"I see exactly what you mean. It's all come full circle now, hasn't it, General? I'm about to fake my death...again." Gabe leaned back and smiled, amazed at the how God had been one step ahead, protecting them the entire time.

General Levin assured him, "You all will be safe. The Deep State Cabal will believe Director Strozza and Detective Richards followed their assignments in capturing you. Richards will continue as a double agent working with The Alliance and be promoted to Haifa Chief of Police, replacing the current crooked Chief. Strozza's body double will replace the IIA Director funneling information to us until our mission is complete. If everything goes as planned, The Great Awakening will be triggered by a worldwide economic collapse, destroying the money supply for the cabal which also destroys them; but until the kill shot is made all precautious must be made."

"I wonder if The Great Awakening is connected to the fall of Mystery Babylon?" Gabriella speculated.

"What did you say?" General Levin immediately questioned.

"Just thinking out loud."

"What did you say about Babylon?" He pressed her for an answer.

Gabriella shifted in her seat to look the general full in the eyes. "Everything you've described sounds like a playbook right out of the Book of Revelation, the prophecy of Mystery Babylon," she explained. "Dr. Brotman has researched this for decades, from all different biblical translations and believes the Luciferian Deep State Cabal, headed by the Khazarian Jews, is the fulfillment of that ancient prophecy - Jews who are not really Jews at all just as the Revelation 3:9 prophecy says."

General Levin paused before answering, trying to decide how much to tell them since they were not on the inside of The Alliance's plan to destroy the cabal.

Before he replied, Gabriella continued with her explanation: "We've spent days entombed in a bunker; KJ spent the entire time researching and reporting to us how the thirteen richest families, the Khazarian Jews, have taken over the world's economy, governments, education, religion, media, entertainment, even the frequency of music, all for the purpose of ruling humanity with their riches. One discovery KJ found would lead to another and to another until it was obvious that everything we've believed, all our lives, had been built on lies."

"Who *did* rule humanity." General Levin corrected her. "But what I find intriguing is our code name for the cabal is Babylon. What a coincidence."

Gabe, Gabriella and Caleb looked at each other and laughed. Gabriella explained to the general: "Dr. Brotman taught us there is no word in the Hebrew language for coincidence. With God there are no coincidences."

General Levin did not know how to respond to her, but the comment made a profound impression upon him as he continued: "Coincidence or not, they've already lost, and they know it. The low hanging pawns are scattering like rats, jumping ship and turning on each other telling everything they know hoping for a plea deal. This entire plan has been like a chess game with master players, good versus bad. There were many boards going at the same time with moves, counter moves, pawns and knights being taken out until the time one side realizes they have been defeated. No matter what move they make there is no way to win. That's exactly where we have them. There are still the final moves that must be made to the final checkmate but already the winner is known." He leaned back in the chair assuring them again, "We've already won."

"What about Chris?" Gabriella just realized he had not been mentioned in the plans made for their safety. "Detective Richards, if you're Chief of Police now you'll make that decision. You know he was only doing what he was told by you to do, to protect us."

"That decision has already been made," he assured her. "Officer Harris will take my job as Chief Detective and I know he will be a good one, never compromising, even though we are going to let Sotoreo believe he is a double agent with me."

"That's really dangerous for him," Gabe solemnly stated, deeply concerned for his new friend who had come to feel like a son.

"We both knew when we took jobs as police officers the high risk we were taking; and this risk is well worth it, for the good of humanity." He added with a confused expression, "Chris said something odd, something like maybe he was given that position for such a time as this. It sounds profound, but I have no idea what he means."

Gabriella felt an inner spiritual glow, knowing the time they had spent with the officer had impacted his life eternally.

"Did I hear my name spoken by the new Haifa Police Chief?" Chris asked, entering the room smiling.

"You sure did, Chief Detective," he replied, motioning for him to join them. "Any update on Dr. Brotman?"

"I just got off the phone with the officer guarding them. He said Dr. Brotman is stable and out of danger. All plans are in place for the press release of his death; after his complete recovery, he and Sandee will be escorted to their new nation of residence, to begin their new lives."

"Good, that's good." Richards nodded. "Take a seat while we finalize some details on how all of our captives here at the station are going to, uh, depart this world."

"I think what we discussed would work," Chris answered, nodding toward General Levin. "I've discussed it with the general and he's in agreement."

General Levin returned the nod. "The only person we must convince that they're all dead is Sotoreo. We will cover all the technical details, and with Strozza's body double confirming what happened to them, Sotoreo will have no reason to doubt. The UN President will have no idea his controlled Strozza has been taken out of the picture completely and replaced with a psyop."

"Let's have it then," Gabe requested. "How do we meet our demise and where are we going?"

"Strozza is going to suggest to Sotoreo that you all be moved from the police station to a more secluded location where the matter can be dealt with discreetly. In transport, on a curvy mountain road, there will be a rebellion in the vehicle and one of you will manage to get free from your restraints and try to take control of the steering wheel, causing the vehicle to swerve from side to side, plummet over a mountain cliff and explode on impact, with no one surviving."

Gabriella gasped at the very thought.

"Remember this is only the narrative told to Sotoreo, nothing is real," General Levin reminded them. "Of course, we will have to simulate such an accident and have it reported on the news for confirmation to the cabal."

"Sounds like a plan," the new Police Chief agreed. "And with that determined, the quicker we initiate it the better."

"There will be transport vehicles arriving after dark," General Levin assured him. "Destinations have been decided, and tomorrow new lives begin for everyone. For most of you it will be a relief." He looked at the new Police Chief Richards and the new Chief Detective Harris, "But for you two, the days ahead are going to be extremely challenging, playing both sides of the fence. For all our sake, I hope and pray the final chess moves come quickly.

– Chapter 37 –

General Levin instructed Gabe, Gabriella, and Caleb to follow him, leaving the interrogation room.

"What about Faith and KJ? Do they know what's happening?" Gabriella questioned the general. "Can we see them now?"

"They have been informed and you'll have time together before we go down to the garage. Your transport vehicles will be here as soon as it's dark." He looked at his watch and informed them, "Should be within the hour."

They were led to the holding room where they were taken when they first arrived. Faith and Gabriella ran to each other embracing and crying. Faith exclaimed, "This can't be happening, Gabi. I'm losing my best friend forever. They told us we can't communicate in anyway; won't even know what nations we are being separated to."

"It's for all of our safety, Faith," Gabriella tried to soothe her despite her own agony of their circumstances. "It's better than losing each other the way we thought it would be, isn't it? We're still alive and where there's life, there's hope." She motioned for KJ to join their circle of embrace. "For whatever time we have left, you two can be together and live a normal life."

Caleb joined their circle and added, "And so can Gabi and I, finally. I can hardly believe it's just been a few weeks since we returned from our exploration in Saudi Arabia when we were living normal lives: before Gabi's paranormal deception, Gabe's black box arrival, Professor's attempted assassination by the cabal, Gabe returning from the dead, and having almost lost Gabi." The very thought of losing her brought an emotional rush of determination to enjoy every minute they could for as long as they could.

"We believed we were living normal lives," Gabriella interjected. "We had no idea before Dad's black box appeared that this world was being ruled by the Luciferian Khazarian Jews and how long they had been in control; and we learned from personal experience, they will gladly take out anyone who gets in their way to keep their world dominion."

The team all nodded their heads in agreement. For a moment no one spoke, reflecting on all they had come through together in such a short time, and they thanked their Heavenly Father that He had brought them safely through; however, tears filled their eyes knowing they were being scattered across the face of the earth to unknown new lives.

"How can so much happen in such a short time?" Faith questioned, sharing into KJ's eyes with love permeating her entire being. "KJ joined our team and that's when my life first turned topsy turvy. He's been my rock through it all. My heart was breaking to think I had finally found the love of my life only to find out there was a very good chance there would be no life ahead of us."

Gabe and Aaron made their circle complete as the team hugged and said their final goodbyes. Tears were flowing from every eye.

"One last prayer together," Gabe requested. Chris joined the team as they circled once again holding hands with Gabe leading their prayer "Father, we thank you for your protection and guidance as we enter the unknown path awaiting us. We thank you for your hand of healing and safety that is on Professor and Sandee. We thank you for all the time this team has had together to learn, to love and to comfort one another in times of distress. You know our hearts, our commitment to you and our desire to continue in service to your earthly kingdom until the day we take our last breath and meet you face to face. Saturate us with your presence as our new journey in life begins. Amen."

"Amen," the group repeated. No one wanted to let go of the hands they were holding knowing it was time for their separation to begin.

"It's time," General Levin instructed.

The circle reluctantly was broken as clasped hands released. The backpacks which were in their escape vehicles were sitting by the door waiting for them. It was all they had left of their former lives. One by one they followed the general down the stairs into the garage where three SUVs awaited. Each vehicle was driven by Israeli Military.

To their surprise, Officer Cohen was also waiting for them. Detective Richards slapped him on the back. "Good to have you back, Officer Cohen, job well done."

"Thank you, Chief, good to be back."

Chris gave his fellow officer a firm handshake and warmly jested, "I knew you would want to say goodbye to this group of renegades, Micah. Seriously, this has been the toughest assignment either of us have had. It's over now and this is as far as we can go with them. The military will take it from here."

Gabriella gave Officer Cohen a warm hug and said, "Thank you for not leaving my bag at the hospital. There was something in that bag I never want to lose." She looked at the turquoise bracelet on her wrist, her tangible reminder that all she had seen, heard and experienced in the spiritual realm was of divine origin.

She turned and gave Chris a loving, sisterly hug. "God has great plans for you, my friend. We will be praying for you every day. Who knows, our paths may join again somewhere down the road."

Detective Richards' voice slightly quivered as he bid them farewell. "Godspeed."

KJ pulled Gabe to the side for a moment of privacy. Reaching into his pocket he retrieved the two flash drives containing a copy of all Gabe's research and documents that were stored in the black box left behind in the bunker. "You may need these." With a warm smile and a quick hug, KJ turned to rejoin Faith.

The military drivers opened the vehicle doors. General Levin gave the instructions: "Gabe, Gabriella, and Caleb in the first SUV please. KJ and Faith in the second. Aaron, you will be with me in the last one."

The members of the team had been informed Aaron would be working with The Alliance, but wondered exactly what his position would be, and would it be dangerous? They were all going to safety, leaving him, amid the battle.

Gabriella ran to Aaron also giving him a hug even though she knew he was not one given to public displays of emotion. "I love you, Aaron. No matter where you are and what you're doing, know you are loved."

As instructed, they picked up their backpacks and entered their transit as instructed, feeling they were safe but heartbroken their team was all going in different directions.

Gabriella waved to Faith and KJ as they entered their transport. She blew them both a kiss and climbed into their SUV to buckle in her seat.

As they pulled out, she commented: "I didn't see any way we could ever have any sort of normal life again, even for a short time." Gabriella's voice reflected a measure of hope for the future. "The bunker was our place of safety, but it became a prison with Strozza's men closing in and I could see no way out. You always believed, Dad, and God made a way of escape."

"It wasn't exactly the way I planned, but Yahweh had a better one." He took his daughter's hand and comforted her, "We don't understand why we are all going in different directions, but God does. We just have to trust Him and remember Romans 8:28: *and we know that all things work together for good to them that love God and are called according to his purpose.*"

She looked from her father to Caleb. "I'm thankful to be with the two men I love." She leaned her head on Caleb's shoulder thinking out loud, "Perhaps there can be a wedding after all."

Caleb turned in his seat and took her into his arms. He was overcome with emotion and unable to speak.

Gabe's heart rejoiced. "Our Father promised He would give us the desires of our heart and I will willingly give you away; just not too far away," he laughed.

The driver pulled out of the garage into the streets of Haifa. The Feast of Tabernacles had begun at sundown, beginning seven days of celebration throughout the nation. Sukkots were festively lit on rooftops and the sound of rejoicing with singing and dancing echoed throughout Haifa.

"Only Yahweh could arrange for us to be free on this day of all the days in the year." Gabe expressed amazement how the details of their release from captivity had aligned with God's Holy Days. "This is Yahweh our God's appointed time for His people to rejoice, remembering their ancestors being released from the captivity of Egypt and how Yahweh protected them forty years while they were in the wilderness. Today is our day of release from the cabal, who rules the earth just as Egypt did when God delivered them."

"It's our day of release from captivity and we are definitely going into what I would call a wilderness," Gabriella echoed. "We have no idea where we are going just as the Children of Israel didn't know; but we do have the promise our Heavenly Father is going before us preparing the way." Her eyes narrowed and tears formed as she added, "It's so hard to celebrate when we are being separated from the people we love, maybe forever."

"We still have life, Princess, and where there's life there's hope. Maybe we will be reunited again." Her father reached across the seat and took her hand, encouraging here, "I have a feeling in my spirit man, there is still work for us to do, all of us. As Jews all over the world are remembering the miracles of their deliverance, they are also looking forward to the future time Messiah comes to rule the earth in righteousness when they will sing and dance in his Kingdom for eternity."

Gabriella smiled. "I can only imagine what that celebration will be like.

After living through the rule of the Antichrist, Lucifer himself for 1260 days, it will be a time of celebration like never before seen when their final deliverance comes." She continued to stare out the window at the festivities until they left the city area. "I can only imagine," she repeated.

The driver had said nothing until they were on Hwy 2 going south towards Tel Aviv. "We will have a couple of hours drive back to the base. If you need anything, let me know." He kept his attention on the road and drove in silence. He had made it obvious conversation with him would not be part of their commute and asking any questions would be a waste of time.

The day had been long and exhausting with twists and turns the team never expected. Gabe admitted that even he did not know what to expect. "I had no idea if The Source would send anyone, that message KJ sent was a long shot. I told them we could deliver Strozza to them if they could get us all to safety, a fair trade, I thought. I sure didn't know we would all be separated and given new identities."

"Apparently they thought so too, moving that quickly; and being able to replace Strozza with a body double, apparently was high on the list of their priorities," Caleb surmised.

Gabriella closed her eyes and listened to Caleb and her father discuss how the final escape had drastically changed from the original plan, but there could not have been a better solution and they knew only God could work out those kinds of details. As they speculated on where they would be going and what their future might be, Gabriella fell asleep.

"Gabriella, come with me," a familiar voice called to her. She opened her eyes to the Prophet Elijah standing before her. "Come, I will show you what will soon be." He held out his hand and she placed hers into his, immediately being transported to a high mountain overlooking the great city. The form of a man appeared in the heavens with a crown upon his head. His countenance was mighty and great as he spread his arms above the city. The people were standing in the streets and on their rooftops reaching up to him crying out for help. A cloud of agony and despair covered the land."

"Where is this, Prophet? Who is this man?" Gabriella asked with her eyes fixed on the vision.

"This is the great city that reigns over the kings of the earth, Mystery Babylon. The kings of the earth committed vile fornications and lived lasciviously with her and by her sorceries all the nations were deceived. She has been made rich by the merchants of the earth and believes she is the Queen of Heaven and will reign forever. She says, I am queen and will see no sorrow. But alas,

alas, in one hour her judgment will come. For in her was found the blood of prophets and saints, and of all who were slain on the earth."

"And the blood of the innocent children," Gabriella expounded. "Who is the man the people are reaching up to for escape from the evil harlot?" She questioned further.

"He is the world leader that was and was not. Those who dwell on the earth whose names are not written in the Book of Life will marvel after him when he is yet again. When he destroys the harlot system ruling the earth, this self-proclaimed king will become their false savior."

Gabriella could feel the spiritual winds whipping around her as she stood on the mountain pinnacle watching the scene unfold. Ten kings arose from the waters in the distance and joined the image of the man in the sky. Storm clouds gathered, the thunder roared, and lightning bolts were thrown down upon every part of the city by the ten kings burning it to the ground.

The cries of weeping, wailing and torment echoed throughout the nations as the fortunes of merchants around the world were destroyed in just one hour.

A voice cried from the heavens: "Babylon the great is fallen, is fallen, and has become a dwelling place of demons, a prison for every foul spirit, and a cage for every unclean and hated bird!"

The Prophet Elijah raised his hands in the air and proclaimed, "Mystery Babylon, the mother of the abominations of the earth, has fallen! Rejoice, Oh Heavens."

Gabriella eyes stayed fixed on the smoldering ashes. She expected the scene to end, when suddenly out of the midst of the ashes rose the image of the self-appointed king, bringing peace and prosperity to all mankind. Performing signs and wonders, he mesmerized the nations pulling humanity into his web of deceit. Only the elect was not deceived.

"He is The One, isn't he Prophet?"

"Yes, Daughter of Zebulon, and his coming is at hand." Elijah laid his hands on Gabriella's head to anoint her one last time before her ministry began. His hands oozed with oil which ran through her hair, saturating her hair with the sweet aroma of the heavenly anointing.

He stepped into the midst forming on the mountain and raised his hands and blessed her affirming, "Daughter, you have been chosen for such a time as this." His words echoed through the darkness as he faded into the fog.

"Wake up, Gabi, we're here," Caleb spoke softly, not wanting to startle her.

She refocused to reality and asked, "Where are we?"

"We are at a military air base outside Tel Aviv," he answered.

She looked out the vehicle window into the darkness of night and saw a small military jet parked near them on the tarmac, engines running and ready for departure. "It's almost midnight and your chariot awaits, Princess." Caleb was trying to keep the atmosphere light as they prepared to depart into the unknown.

Gabriella was remembering when she and Caleb sat on the balcony of her condo in Old Town Jerusalem overlooking the Mediterranean Sea after returning from the Saudi exploration; it was when the Hasidic Jew had come into her life changing her life forever. She had no earthly idea it was her father in disguise. "Caleb, remember when we looked out on the sea and talked about getting into one of those boats on the marina and sailing away into the sunset never to return?"

He put his arm around her pulling her close, "Of course, I remember. I would have done it in heartbeat if you had been serious."

"I know," she whispered. "But I couldn't leave the other people we loved, the family I never had. Isn't it strange this twist of events? Instead of sailing off into a beautiful sunset, we are flying off into the darkness of night – still without our precious friends." She looked at her father and then back to Caleb. "At least I have the two most important people in this world with me. I can face anything ahead of us."

Their driver announced, "It's time to board." He got out and opened the doors for them to exit the SUV.

Caleb helped Gabriella out and retrieved their backpacks from the vehicle. Gabe led the way across the tarmac where the airplane door was open, and steps ascended. The pilot welcomed them aboard as one by one they entered and took their seats. The humming of the engines and blinking lights on the exterior of the plane signaled they were about to leave Israel. They buckled in and sat silently waiting. The interior lights were turned off when the craft began its taxi to the runway where they were given clearance for takeoff. The three passengers looked out the windows saying goodbye to the country that had been their home for twelve years and having no idea what country their home would now be.

The military craft taxied to the runway. The engines began to roar as the propulsion began. Their craft went faster and faster until the wheels left the ground and Gabriella felt the familiar butterflies in her stomach when airplanes began their ascension into the clouds. The lights on the ground slowly disappeared, and the midnight darkness surrounded them. All that could be seen now were the full moon and the heavenly backdrop of twinkling stars.

Gabriella closed her eyes and relived her vision, the precipice view of Mystery Babylon's destruction and the appearing of Antichrist. The Prophet had confirmed in her final vision that she was chosen for such a time as this.

She opened her eyes and through the dim light gazed at the turquoise bracelet wrapped around her wrist, her physical reminder of her ministry to still be fulfilled. Running her fingers through her hair she felt the oil, a fresh reminder of her anointing given by the Prophet Elijah. Gazing out the window, she saw with spiritual eyes The Lamb guiding their aircraft. All were confirmation she was a Chosen One.

Gabriella closed her eyes and vowed to her Heavenly Father, "I will follow The Lamb wherever He leads me."